THE WOLF & THE WITCH

CLAIRE DELACROIX

DEBORAH A. COOKE

The Wolf & the Witch
By Claire Delacroix

MORE BOOKS BY CLAIRE DELACROIX

THE ROSE RED BRIDE

THE SNOW WHITE BRIDE

The Ballad of Rosamunde

The True Love Brides

THE RENEGADE'S HEART

THE HIGHLANDER'S CURSE

THE FROST MAIDEN'S KISS

THE WARRIOR'S PRIZE

The Brides of Inverfyre

THE MERCENARY'S BRIDE

THE RUNAWAY BRIDE

The Champions of St. Euphemia

THE CRUSADER'S BRIDE

THE CRUSADER'S HEART

THE CRUSADER'S KISS

THE CRUSADER'S VOW

THE CRUSADER'S HANDFAST

The Brides of North Barrows

Something Wicked This Way Comes

A Duke By Any Other Name

Blood Brothers

The Wolf & the Witch

Short Stories and Novellas

BEGUILED

An Elegy for Melusine

~

BLOOD BROTHERS

A MEDIEVAL SCOTTISH ROMANCE SERIES

The three sons of a notorious mercenary should never have met...but now that they are sworn allies, the Scottish Borders will never be the same...

1. **The Wolf & the Witch**
(Maximilian and Alys)

2. **The Hunter & the Heiress**
(Amaury and Elizabeth)

3. **The Dragon & the Damsel**
(Rafael and Ceara)

4. **The Scot & the Sorceress**
(Murdoch and Nyssa)

~

THE WOLF & THE WITCH

PROLOGUE

Château de Vries in Normandy—August 27, 1375

The keep was finer than Murdoch anticipated, but then, it was said to have been the prize Jean le Beau esteemed above all others. It only made sense that the old villain had seen it lavishly maintained after seizing it, even if he seldom crossed its moat himself. Murdoch would never have guessed that the holding was funded by the spoils of war, for all was gracious and elegant, even the châtelain who betrayed neither surprise nor relief that his lord and master arrived in a rough sack, tossed on a cart driven by a lone Scotsman.

As Murdoch had intended, his burden gained him access not only to the keep but a welcome befitting an honored guest. He stood in the chapel, a mere day after his arrival, marveling against his will at the richness surrounding him. He wanted to despise this place, just as he had despised Jean le Beau. That mercenary had stolen all from Murdoch and Murdoch had finally exacted his price. This holding, though, was magnificent.

Jean's widow, Mathilde de Vries, had to have seen fifty summers, but she was as slender as a maiden, her face as pale as alabaster, her golden hair barely touched with strands of silver. She might have been wrought of ice, this noblewoman, her eyes the palest hue of silver blue that Murdoch had ever seen. He tried to suppress his urge to shiver each time her gaze landed upon him.

Perhaps the noblewoman and the mercenary had shared some qualities, after all.

The lady's brother, Gaston de Vries, a lord in his own right, stood beside her at the altar before the stone sarcophagus where her dead husband now reposed. Gaston was accompanied by his oldest son, Amaury de Vries. Father and son were richly dressed, the son's manner revealing that he was much indulged. Gaston shared the fair silvery coloring of his sister, but his son had dark blond hair and eyes of deeper blue. Each of them could have been carved of stone for all the emotion they betrayed.

But then, who would mourn a villain like Jean le Beau? Surely his kinfolk knew his measure better than any others. Surely they were relieved to be rid of him.

The priest raised his hands to begin the service and the company dropped to their knees. The chapel was not full, for it was of generous proportions, but there were a goodly number of servants and villeins gathered behind the lady. Murdoch had a moment to wonder if he was to be disappointed in his goal of meeting the Silver Wolf himself, then the wooden door was thrown open and a man strode down the aisle, clearly indifferent to the fact that he was late.

The Silver Wolf. Known in some territories as the Loup Argent, the oldest son of Jean le Beau was his father's heir in every way—and Murdoch's next intended victim.

The Silver Wolf bent over his mother's hand but Mathilde's expression did not thaw. When the latest arrival and son of the house glanced his way, Murdoch again strove to hide a shiver. This man's eyes were blue but as cold as those of any ruthless predator. His hair was dark blond and his face was tanned; his armor was of excellent quality but without embellishment; his gloves and boots were as black as his tabard, and his black cloak was lined with thick silver fur. A silver wolf rampant graced his tabard, leaving no mystery as to his identity.

This was the fiend Murdoch would kill next, though he strove to hide the truth of it from his expression. He was merely a messenger, so far as all assembled knew, not a man embittered by his losses at the hand of a relentless mercenary, not a man who had taken justice into his own hands—and certainly not a man who burned for vengeance against anyone associated with the wretch who had been his father.

Murdoch anticipated the moment that the Silver realized the truth, and would ensure it was followed by that man's final breath.

Then and only then would his vengeance be complete.

HIS FATHER'S funeral was the first event of merit Maximilian de Vries had ever witnessed in a church. In his years as a mercenary, he had seen churches pillaged, robbed and burned; he had seen them used as brothels and as taverns; he had seen them pressed into service as prisons then set afire, filled with the unfortunate. He knew only their role in war for battle was all he understood.

His father's demise, however, was cause to celebrate. Maximilian's sole regret was that he had not been the one to carve out the old cur's heart himself.

He had left his small remaining company in the forest and took only Rafael and a pair of squires with him to the gates. It suited Maximilian to be underestimated when he was uncertain of his reception—and he thought it fitting for Rafael to attend the rites, given Jean le Beau's revelation that Maximilian's second-in-command was also Jean's bastard son. There was a reason Maximilian and Rafael understood each other so well, for they were blood brothers, though neither had known as much until the previous spring.

Château de Vries was as splendid as Maximilian recalled, and he was aware of Rafael taking inventory as they strode down wide halls to the chapel. Maximilian could have listed all the riches and fripperies of his mother's family home, but he would count his wealth after the seal to the château was in his hand.

He was impatient for that moment.

Indeed, he had been so for years.

The chapel doors were closed, the smell from the censers slipping under the pair of heavy doors to reveal that the service had begun. Maximilian could hear the priest singing and the shuffle of the mourners, likely commanded into attendance for there could be no grief at Jean's death. He flung open the doors, not caring whether he interrupted the proceedings. When they crashed against the walls, the priest fell silent and stared. The mourners jumped as one and turned to study him in obvious fear.

It was the greeting Maximilian expected when he returned home.

He marched down the aisle toward the altar and the large stone sarcophagus before it. He itched to look inside, to verify that Jean le Beau was truly dead—and to spit in the old man's eye as farewell. Instead, he halted beside his mother, awaiting her acknowledgement.

Rafael kept pace with Maximilian, one pace behind and one to his left. The squires remained at the doors, barricading the exit. Maximilian knew he was not the only one with a hand on the hilt of his blade.

His mother turned slowly, her gaze as icy cold and pale as ever. This too was a typical greeting. Mathilde stood perfectly straight, her chin high, and her eyes dry. She was unlikely to mourn the passing of the man she had been compelled to wed, a man whose deeds had seen her own father die of grief, but neither would she reveal her satisfaction with the situation before the household.

"You are late," was the sum of her welcome but even that was more than Maximilian had expected. She seldom addressed him and he did not reply.

Mathilde was still tall and slender, her fair hair possibly touched with more silver than Maximilian recalled. Her dress was the palest hue of blue imaginable, heavily adorned with pearls. Another woman might have appeared ethereal in such garb, or softly feminine, but his mother resembled naught more than a weapon forged of cold steel. Maximilian inclined his head in deference to her, but did not drop to one knee.

His mother inclined her head slightly at the arrival of her only child, her eyes narrowing ever so slightly when she surveyed Rafael. He, of course, gave an elaborate bow, turning his best smile upon her. Maximilian did not even have to look back to know it. His half-brother was as predictable in his compulsion to charm women as night was in following day.

4

His mother did not thaw, much less acknowledge Rafael's tribute. Her nature was as frigid as her appearance, so that had not changed. She smoothly turned her back upon them and made an impatient gesture to the priest.

Perhaps Mathilde also wanted Jean buried as soon as possible.

On Mathilde's right stood her brother, Gaston de Vries, and to Gaston's right, his oldest son, Amaury. Gaston shared Mathilde's coloring but there was an unexpected avidity about him this day. Doubtless he was glad to put the man he had despised to rest, and Maximilian found it curious to have any sentiment in common with his fastidious, rich uncle. On this day, father and son were grim, but perhaps they had disagreed over a trifle both coveted. They certainly did not shed tears for Jean le Beau.

Perhaps Amaury had possessed other plans than attending a funeral. That was the trouble with living out of a father's purse—one's choices were not one's own.

Amaury was not quite a year younger than Maximilian and also a knight, but the cousins could not have been more different. Amaury had been raised in privilege and battled only in tournaments and other pageants of the rich and idle. Doubtless, he would make a rich match and continue in his father's stead at Château Pouissance, living in comfort all the days of his life in the holding of his mother's forebears.

In contrast, there was blood on Maximilian's sword, along with a count on his scabbard of the lives he had claimed. A mercenary killed or was killed, and Maximilian had made his choice early. He owned naught that he had not earned himself—even though much of what he had captured had been claimed by his father. He could easily have despised his cousin, simply for being born to better fortune than his own, but on this day, Maximilian chose to put the past aside.

His father was dead. He could not be denied his due any longer.

On his arrival at the stables, the ostler, Henri, had confided that Jean le Beau's corpse had been delivered to the gates by a rough Scotsman. Maximilian thought it likely to be the one who stood on the opposite side of the chapel from Amaury, his head bowed in prayer. Maximilian could smell his filth from half a dozen paces away and could not begin to imagine what vermin lived in his dirty garb. What he lacked in personal habits, however, this Murdoch Campbell possessed in audacity. Not many men would take it upon themselves to deliver a dead stranger home, and Maximilian could only wonder why this one had done as much.

Perhaps the Scotsman expected a reward.

He supposed that would be his first obligation, when his long-awaited legacy finally fell into his open hands. He spotted then his mother's châtelain, Yves, in the back corner of the chapel, his expression impassive and his composure complete. Perhaps Yves would remain in his own service. He had always been fond of the older man, and indeed, there had been years when the châtelain had been his sole friend at de Vries.

Gaston's lips tightened as his gaze swept over the two arrivals, then he took a slight step away. Aye, he should fear the repercussions of Maximilian gaining his inheritance. He had earned his moniker, the Silver Wolf, and was known the width and breadth of the continent for his merciless assaults. The wise feared even the sight of his banner and so they should.

Maximilian remained at his mother's left. Rafael chose a strategic position, behind Maximilian and to his left, where he could watch the family. The squires, Reynaud and Mallory, stood at the back of the chapel, behind the household mourners, defending the doors. The mourners were wary, accustomed to the uncertainty that Jean le Beau always brought with him. Evidently they expected naught different even though he was dead.

This would be a day of reckoning, one way or the other. Anticipation rose hot within Maximilian and his heart pounded as if he embarked on a battle.

His moment had finally come.

AMAURY HAD no notion of why his father had insisted upon his accompaniment to Château de Vries. What difference to him if Jean le Beau was finally dead? It had been his intention to ride to Paris, to assess the charms of both a promising young stallion and a maiden of noble birth, but here he stood, at the funeral of a scoundrel, instead. He was disgruntled, as he often was when his father meddled in his plans.

'Twas only natural that Amaury imagined the day he attended his own father's funeral, when his days and nights would be his own, when all the wealth of Château Pouissance was his to spend as he saw fit.

It was the first time he had ever envied his cousin, the Silver Wolf.

The presence of Maximilian's companion, clearly another mercenary, was unsettling. Amaury could not keep himself from studying the man, who was swarthy and dark of hair, like a man from the south, but with startling blue eyes.

That mercenary watched Amaury openly, smirking, and Amaury strove to ignore him.

He failed.

When the priest intoned the final 'amen', Mathilde cleared her throat. Amaury itched to depart immediately, hoping he might at least ride to hunt before the day was lost. He had his destrier, his hawk and his hounds, though his squire had remained at home. He could request some beaters from de Vries and perhaps take a boar in the forest here.

That scheme was not to be.

"You will leave," his aunt informed the priest, who was visibly startled. He obeyed her, all the same. She pivoted then and dismissed the other members of the household who had gathered for the service. "As will all of you." She nodded at her châtelain. "Yves, please see that the alms are distributed."

Alms? To members of her own household?

Amaury might have questioned this but his father glared at him, reducing him to silence. He was keenly aware of the Scotsman who had brought the corpse to the gates, and that man's curiosity. Did he speak Norman French sufficiently well to understand them? As usual, Amaury could not read the thoughts of his cousin, Maximilian, though he sensed the tension within that man.

Did something go awry?

When the doors closed again, a ray of sunlight pierced the smoky air of the chapel, like a finger of the divine stretching down to illuminate the lid of the coffin. Aye, if any matter went to ruin, it would be Jean le Beau's fault.

Only when the chapel was cold and silent, like a tomb, did Mathilde speak.

"It is a day for the truth," she said crisply. There was a ripple of agitation through the small company that remained and Amaury knew he was not the sole one whose curiosity had been stirred.

Mathilde held up the ring that had graced Jean le Beau's hand. "This is the ring of my ancestors, the signet ring of de Vries." She stared at it for a moment, choosing her words. "When Jean le Beau assaulted my father's holding and broke down the gates, he demanded the surrender of both me, to be his bride, and this ring, as well as all it represented. My father declined to see me, his sole daughter, surrendered to a rough mercenary. They fought." She straightened. "And in the end, I was seized, surrounded by his men and held down as he took what was not his to claim, while my father was compelled to watch. Jean le Beau cut this ring from my father's hand, and put it on his own finger, with my father's blood in the seal. 'Twas the last moment of my father's life." She turned to Maximilian. "'Twas the sole time Jean le Beau knew me, for I armed myself and locked my door against him, but you were the result." Her lip curled with disdain as she considered her only son. "Wrought in violence and hatred, 'tis no wonder you excel at the trade he taught you."

Maximilian did not flinch, but then he never did.

He put out his hand for the ring, palm up, his expectation clear.

Mathilde closed her hand around it instead. "I have wondered over the years whether any man of Jean le Beau's lineage deserved to possess my beloved home, but in the end, the choice is not mine to make. As my younger brother has reminded me, it is the way of de Vries for this holding to pass to the oldest son of the blood."

Amaury watched in astonishment as Mathilde surrendered the ring to Gaston, who pushed it immediately onto his own finger. Maximilian's gaze burned so hot that Amaury wondered whether he would repeat his father's deed and slice the ring free.

Then the Silver Wolf blinked and averted his gaze, his throat working just once, as he composed himself anew. "Then I am to have no legacy at all?" he asked, a thrum of fury beneath his words.

Amaury took a step back, fearful of his cousin's wrath.

Gaston sniffed with disdain. "You are to have the truth as your legacy, no more and no less."

Maximilian's eyes narrowed. "Mother..."

Mathilde raised a hand, silencing him with a gesture. "You are not the sole one to confront change this day, Maximilian. My brother has tolerated my administration of our family home, but will do so no longer. I am to depart, this very day, with whatsoever I can carry and one maid only, and retire to the convent of Ste. Radegunde for the rest of my days. The remainder of the household have been dismissed."

Maximilian inhaled sharply. Amaury saw his father smile thinly and knew he enjoyed the situation. "I will administer de Vries with my own hand, while my son will become Lord de Pouissance," Gaston said, unable to hide his pleasure. "Of course, there are those loyal to me deserving of reward."

Lord de Pouissance! And this before his father's demise! Amaury was grateful indeed for this good fortune. "I thank you, Father," he began, but Gaston silenced him with a curt gesture.

"Tell him," he instructed Mathilde, whose lips tightened with hostility.

"It might not have been entirely due to my diligence that Jean le Beau only knew me only the once," she admitted. "He liked to be first through the gates, as he oft said himself. When my time came, Gaston's betrothed, Florine, came to be of assistance to me. She was a lovely maiden and so pretty..." Mathilde shook her head as Amaury's dread rose. Naught good could come of this mention of his mother. "Of course, Jean le Beau took what he deemed to be his due, and she rounded with child soon after Maximilian gave his first wail." Mathilde met his gaze coldly. "You are that child, Amaury."

He was stunned. "But that cannot be!"

"It is," Gaston informed him coolly. "I wedded Florine for Château Puissance, despite the babe in her belly, but our marriage was not a joyous union. The truth of your conception sat between us. She died in childbirth and I chose to raise you as my own, to preserve our family reputation." Gaston gave Amaury a chilling glance. "But since wedding again and yet again, I now have two more sons, and Philip, as you know, has earned his spurs. He will be the new Lord de Pouissance, for you are not of my lineage." Gaston's lip curled and he moved a step away, as if the nature of Jean le Beau was a contagion that could be caught from his spawn. "The time has come for a reckoning long due. You may keep the destrier you rode here and whatever else you have with you. Do not come to my gate to beg, for you have had more than your father's son deserves from me."

Amaury was stunned. He had no father. He had no coin. He had no income, no home, no shelter, no means to see his steed tended. He did not even have a squire with him, but then, that meant he had no duty to see any other soul fed. He looked up, finding Maximilian watching him, and knew his cousin understood this situation all too well.

Indeed, he might have to ask Maximilian for aid, which was not a choice for the faint of heart.

'Twas time, evidently, that Amaury's heart grew more bold.

~

CHÂTEAU DE VRIES was reclaimed by Gaston, his mother was to be dismissed to a convent and Maximilian was to be left with naught. Again. 'Twas a poor reward for over twenty years of service to his miserable villain of a father.

It seemed that both sides of his family shared a desire to see him cheated.

And what course now? He had surrendered leadership of the Compagnie Rouge, anticipating that his days leading a group of mercenaries were over. What an error. Only the temptation of Château de Vries could have tempted him to make such a mis-step. He had only four men who accompanied him, as well as five squires, intended to form the spine of his defenses here. Now he had no employ for them and no means of seeing them paid or fed.

Maximilian could perhaps slaughter Gaston if he moved quickly, but there was no telling what Amaury would do, much less the Scotsman. Would Amaury defend the man he had known as father by reflex? A man's instincts did not change that quickly, even with such tidings, and he had never thought Amaury was decisive—let alone lethal.

Mathilde meanwhile approached the stone coffin. "Here we stand, three decades later, the truth finally declared between us. You two are brothers, sons of a wicked man, wrought by force, tainted by his legacy, left with naught but each other." The situation obviously gave her satisfaction, which meant she hated Jean le Beau more than she had ever loved Maximilian.

He expected little else.

What could he claim from his ruined expectations? There was only one answer.

"What of Kilderrick?" he asked, feeling the Scotsman's surprise.

His mother was aware of it as well. She turned to consider the Scotsman. "You know it?"

"Aye. All know it in my homeland," he replied, though Maximilian did not believe that. He spoke with care, as if he was not fluent in Norman French, but he had evidently followed the discussion. He had an interest, revealed by the heat in his tone. Had this man been at Kilderrick when Maximilian had destroyed it fifteen years before? Perhaps that was why he had journeyed south. The Scotsman nodded. "'Tis a wasteland, though once it was much admired."

Maximilian knew Kilderrick was a ruin, for he had been the one to touch the flame to the tinder, at Jean le Beau's command. "Who holds it now?" he asked of his mother.

She shrugged and looked at the Scotsman.

"The wind and the rain." He smiled slightly, a little malice in his blue eyes. "The wolves." His gaze flicked to Maximilian, proof that he knew his moniker.

"And a wolf shall possess it again," Maximilian said. "I will take it as my legacy."

"But..." Mathilde began to protest.

"It was promised to me once, and I was cheated then, as well," Maximilian said. "I will have it now as my due."

"I will not contest your claim," Gaston said with a wave of his hand. "I have no desire for any holding seized by force, much less one in a distant and savage land."

The Scotsman visibly bristled.

Maximilian did not note that Château de Vries had been so

possessed, at least once. It was of no import, for this was no longer his home.

If, indeed, it ever had been.

"Yet I wager you will insist that whatever coin is in the treasury here is your own," Maximilian noted.

His uncle's smile was tight. "My forces follow me and will have entered Château de Vries by now. I instructed them to wait to reveal themselves until you were through the gates. Should you not depart by choice this very day, I will see it done. My family home is no longer a haven for mercenaries."

Maximilian had a lesson for Gaston de Vries, but he would deliver it in its own time.

"It seems you have prepared well for this day," he said mildly, noting his uncle's surprise at his tone. He put out his hand again. "I ask only for the seal of Kilderrick before I depart, if you please."

Gaston led the way to the treasury, just as Maximilian had anticipated. The others trailed behind, but most importantly, Rafael was at Maximilian's left. There were three locks upon the door to the treasury, and they waited while Yves opened them for Gaston. Gaston strode into the secured space, clearly delighted that it was his own. Maximilian saw Rafael glance toward the single high window, barred securely against intruders and distinctive in its arched shape, then smile slightly. The brothers' gazes collided for but a heartbeat and Maximilian knew his vengeance would be done.

Gaston bent over a chest as Maximilian waited beside Yves. While Gaston's attention was diverted, Maximilian took three sacks of coins, surreptitiously passing two to the châtelain he had known all his life. "At sunset, at the old place. Six only," he said, his words almost silent. "By horse or cart. Ensure the others have their due."

Yves gave no sign that Maximilian had spoken, but the two sacks of coins disappeared into his tabard just as the third vanished into Maximilian's. Both men were politely attentive when Gaston turned, the seal of Kilderrick and its leather pouch in his hand. Rafael gave every appearance of looking about himself with wonder from the doorway, though his curiosity was purely strategic.

Maximilian picked up a gold ring that glinted at him, turning it as if assessing it. Gaston's gaze dropped to the ring and Maximilian put it in his purse. His uncle's eyes narrowed but Maximilian held his gaze, fairly daring him to make an issue of it.

"A mere trinket from my home," Maximilian said.

Gaston was the first to blink, though no one was surprised by that. "A trifle," he agreed, though his lips tightened in annoyance. "Godspeed to you, Maximilian," he said coldly, handing over the seal.

Maximilian inclined his head slightly. "And also to you, Uncle."

Confusion lit Gaston's pale gaze. "But I journey nowhere."

"Of course." Maximilian smiled and bowed. "My error." He pivoted and left the treasury, then beckoned his company with a flick of the wrist. He paused beside the Scotsman who yet lingered, too watchful to be indifferent. The smell of him was rank. "Do you return to Scotland?"

"Aye."

"Then you had best ride with us." There was steel in Maximilian's tone. He would know the location of this one until he uncovered the man's scheme. He smiled slightly. "The road is not safe for solitary travellers."

The Scotsman hesitated only a moment before inclining his head in agreement. "I thank you for that invitation and will accept."

Maximilian's suspicions were unabated.

"And you," he continued, turning to his cousin, Amaury. "Will you pledge yourself to my service or have you a better opportunity?"

Amaury bristled, bitterness battling with expediency. He managed to bow his head slightly. "I thank you for your consideration, cousin."

"Brother," Maximilian corrected, watching Amaury blink. "I trust you will keep the pace. Your horse is sufficiently fine, but we shall see about your riding skills."

Amaury inhaled sharply, his eyes flashing with a resentment that would make him predictable.

Maximilian saluted his mother, who stood yet in the corridor to the chapel, her features set in stone but they did not embrace or speak. He doubted he would see her again. Then he took his leave of the keep where he had been raised, resolved that his uncle should never savor what he had stolen from the Silver Wolf.

~

Yves made haste, disguising his deeds from the new lord of the keep. He saw to the lady's departure, with her retinue and some of her possessions, feeling her surprise that he did not accompany her to the nunnery. Praise be that Lady Mathilde was not one to ask questions, for she never acknowledged a lack of certainty in any matter. By the time her cart passed through the gates, the afternoon light was waning. Yves ensured that the board was laid with the splendor Gaston would anticipate, then left the hall, complaining of a mild illness.

Word had passed through the ranks of servants like wildfire and by the time he had seized his cloak and few belongings, the chosen six awaited him in the bailey. Henri, the ostler, rode a sturdy palfrey, his young son wide-eyed in the saddle before him. His wife had died in the delivery of the boy, six years before, and his loyalty to Maximilian was beyond question.

Denis, the cook and his wife, Marie, were in the cart already, and Yves suspected their favored saucepans were in the baggage. They were older and childless and Yves did not trust the new lord to see to their future welfare. Neither, evidently, did they.

There was a maid, Nathalie, a pretty young girl who was an orphan. She would have nowhere to flee or take shelter should all go awry at Château de Vries—and Yves knew it would shortly. Eudaline, the old woman who knew all the healing herbs, was in the cart as well, for her fondness for Maximilian could not be denied. She, too, would have no defender under the new lord.

Yves took another palfrey from the lord's stables, glad beyond all that Maximilian had given him the coin to ease the hardship that might face the others. The gatekeeper raised the portcullis, coins doubtless clinking in his purse, and saluted them in silence as they passed. Yves knew he would never return to the keep that had been his home for most of his life, but he did not look back.

He looked forward.

The sinking sun glimmered on the marshes to the west of the château, but Yves led them to the east, along the road to Niort, to the rise hidden in the old forest. It had been Maximilian's favored place as a child, "the old place" where he could often be found, and it offered a good vantage of the keep. They reached the clearing as the sun touched the horizon and for a moment, Yves feared they had come too late. It seemed the clearing was empty.

Then the shadows moved and Maximilian stepped forward. He silenced them with a gesture, leading them deeper into the protective darkness of the forest. Yves saw that there were others there, Amaury and the Scotsman, more men with horses and squires. Amaury's falcon sat hooded on his fist. A trio of hounds, large hairy beasts that Yves recognized as belonging to Amaury, sat near their master, eyes gleaming in the shadows. All were silent, but the company did not ride out as yet.

The mercenary who had accompanied Maximilian to the chapel, the one with darker hair, assessed the distance to the keep below, a wooden contraption positioned on the ground beside him. It was clearly a siege engine but a smaller one than a trebuchet. A catapult then, but Yves wondered what it would launch. The other man cradled a ball in his hands, a ball knotted in a length of cloth, his gaze fixed upon the château.

They stood silent so long that Yves' knees began to ache and the chill slipped from the ground into his boots. Then they waited an increment more. Just when he feared Nathalie would ask a question, a light shone suddenly in a window of the tower below. It was the arched and barred window that Yves knew admitted light to the treasury.

Gaston had retreated to count his gains.

Maximilian nodded. The dark-haired mercenary struck a flint and there was both a flame and the scent of some fearsome concoction as he touched the flame to a cloth wrapped around the ball he had cradled. Light flared as he quickly loaded the cloth-bound ball into the catapult. He adjusted the angle with a touch, then launched it. The missile shot through the air in an arc of flame, smashing against the bars across the window. Flame erupted from the spot, fairly pouring down the wall—and likely inside the wall as well.

Did Yves hear a distant scream?

"Your aim grows better daily, brother mine," Maximilian said and Yves was startled. A third brother?

15

The dark-haired mercenary bowed in acknowledgement of the praise and reached for the reins of his destrier.

Below them, Château de Vries burned.

Maximilian beckoned to Amaury, who looked to be alarmed. "Our path forward is together, bound by blood and fury. I propose a union, between blood brothers newly found. I will claim Kilderrick and see to your futures there."

"How can that be done?" Amaury demanded, his suspicion clear.

"'Twas a rich holding," the Scotsman revealed. "With a village in the shadow of its walls and another, Rowan Fell, further away. Time was it prospered."

Yves marveled that the Scotsman knew the place.

"And now?" Amaury asked.

"The region is wild and the border contested, the hills infested with reivers as well as other predators." The Scotsman smiled. "Kilderrick is said to be a haven for witches. Better men have failed to possess it."

"And yet I will make it ours. Are you with me, Amaury?" Maximilian let his disdain show. "Or have you a better prospect on this day?"

"You know I have not." The younger knight was sullen.

Maximilian drew his dagger and slashed the inside of his left wrist so that the blood beaded against his flesh. Even in the growing darkness, it gleamed, as red as garnets in the snow. "I would swear a vow with you, as blood brothers." He passed the blade to his dark-haired companion, who echoed his gesture. Maximilian pressed their wrists together so the blood mingled. "This is Rafael, whom Jean claimed as my half-brother in the spring." He beckoned to Amaury, who swallowed, then took the dagger and sliced his own wrist, with less gusto.

Maximilian seized Amaury's wrist, rubbed the blood together, then placed Amaury's hand upon Rafael's wrist. Rafael, in his turn, gripped Maximilian's wrist. "We pledge a union to see each other defended and our cause won," Maximilian said.

Yves watched as the drops of their mingled blood fell upon the ground.

"Three together," Maximilian said. "Sworn to each other, first of all men, pledged to the reclaiming of Kilderrick. I vow I will not break this pledge before I die."

"Nor I," Rafael agreed.

Amaury hesitated only a moment. "Nor I," he vowed, then Maximilian spat on the blood that stained the ground. The others echoed his gesture, then turned to their steeds with purpose.

"We ride!" Maximilian declared and the company turned as one.

The horses took to the road, galloping out of the forest, the company of mercenaries surrounding the cart that carried the villagers. The palfreys took the mood of the destriers and raced as they never had before, the wind in their manes. They passed like the wind along the road to Niort, and thence to the harbor, leaving the keep burning behind them.

Yves felt exhilarated as he seldom had before, and knew a new chapter of his life began this very night. The quest for Kilderrick was begun. Woe to any man who stood in the path of the Silver Wolf—or broke a pledge sworn to him in blood.

On the heath, far to the north, four women gathered in darkness within the circle of standing stones called the Ninestang Ring. Alys watched as Nyssa drew her circle beneath the full moon, feeling a familiar trepidation. The wind was fey and Alys could feel change in it, even though she had no gift of foresight as Nyssa did.

The other woman unbound her hair, letting the blond length of it fly free. She murmured the charm she always invoked on the first new moon after a high quarter day and cast her hands to the sky, eyes closed. Her pet raven, Dorcha, perched on the closest stone, croaking approval of the proceedings.

The other three stood silent as Nyssa murmured and the stars turned overhead. A wolf howled in the distance and the wind gusted. The raven fluttered its wings and gave a warning cry, then Nyssa raised the witching stone to her eye and peered through the hole in its midst. She cried out, then fell to the ground, shocked by whatever she had glimpsed. Ceara and Alys crouched down beside her with concern while Elizabeth watched from a distance with alarm.

"The wolf comes," Nyssa whispered. "The wolf comes and he is hungry."

The raven cawed and took flight, the wolves howled as they drew closer, and the wind halted so abruptly that Alys shivered in dread.

Nyssa could not mean that the Silver Wolf would return, after fifteen years, could she? But Alys' wound itched as if her very skin sensed truth in Nyssa's prediction.

Woe to that mercenary if he was fool enough to return to Kilderrick. Alys would exact a hefty price from the man she hated beyond all others, if 'twas the last deed she did.

CHAPTER 1

Kilderrick, Scotland—Samhain, 1375

"Why Kilderrick?" Rafael asked, drawing his destrier alongside Maximilian's. "Surely there are other better places than this?"

They rode from the English border on a road so narrow that only two horses could walk abreast. The night was dark beyond all expectation. They should have set up camp, but they were close enough to Kilderrick that Maximilian wanted to reach their destination first. He did not like that the company straggled in a long line, even though the men rode as closely together as they could.

Their company was alone, but it did not seem that way. The forest on one side of the road rustled and stirred as if the very trees would pursue the small party. The wind snatched at their cloaks in gusts and the horses stepped high, their ears folded back. The shadows were filled with shifting shapes and strange noises erupted from the forest at intervals.

If Maximilian had been a man to believe in sorcery, he would have called this a night for witches. Instead he recognized that he drew near

Kilderrick, the place that had once struck him as the most eerie place in all of Christendom.

Fifteen years later, he still wondered how it was done. He had no doubt that the atmosphere was contrived deliberately, but that did not diminish its effect. The villagers from de Vries were watchful and uncertain and the mercenaries looked about themselves with suspicion.

The hair rose even on the back of his own neck.

This path that aspired to be a road wound northward in a valley, sides rising sharply from the broad river nestled at the lowest point. The river was sluggish at this time of year, but Maximilian wagered it would be quick and vigorous in the spring. The road was west of the river, roughly following its course, and old forest grew thickly on the eastern bank. The trees were so tall that the bare branches seemed to scratch the clouds that roiled overhead.

To the west, the land was covered only with grasses, though he could discern the furrows indicating it had once been tilled. He remembered that just south of Kilderrick's keep, the forest crossed the river, engulfing the road in shadows. Beyond that would be the ruins of the keep itself, the nearby village further to the west. He recalled how the keep seemed to overshadow all the valley and gave one a definite sense of being watched. Had he merely been young and impressionable—or was there wickedness at Kilderrick as others insisted?

"Because there are matters unresolved here," Maximilian said to Rafael. "A task left undone."

A treasure left unclaimed.

Rafael scoffed, then nodded back in the direction of Murdoch Campbell. "The Scotsman said this place was abandoned, left to the witches, the wolves and the wind." He drew his heavy cloak more securely closed and looked askance at the forest.

"I could say I have an affinity for wolves and an affection for the wind."

Rafael laughed. "What of witches?"

"They do not exist."

"I have met some..."

"Nay, you have met liars and frauds."

Rafael gave him a steady look. "Still you have not told me what you expect to find here."

"An abandoned holding, which is the kind most readily claimed."

Rafael shook his head. "For the least reward."

"I think not in this case." At his half-brother's sidelong glance, Maximilian shrugged. "I cannot believe that our father sent me here fifteen years ago to claim a worthless prize."

"Much may have changed."

"And it may not have changed a whit." Maximilian shrugged. "We had need of a destination and Kilderrick suited me."

Rafael was not deterred. "There is more to it than that."

"I desire my due. 'Twas promised to me."

"We know the merit of our father's promises." Rafael did not wait for a reply but frowned. "But he was shrewd, for all his faults. What did he say of Kilderrick?"

Maximilian recalled every word. "That the family had served the Scottish king for centuries. He said the debt between king and laird was so great that it could never be repaid, and that the laird's treasury overflowed as a result. Jean le Beau promised me Kilderrick and its treasure, if I could take it."

"Ah," Rafael murmured. "Its treasure."

Maximilian was aware of Amaury drawing closer behind him, the better to listen. He did not doubt that the Scotsman listened as well, for he was inclined to eavesdrop. Maximilian had yet to learn much of him or his plans, but doubtless now that they arrived at Kilderrick, more would become clear.

There was naught like the mention of treasure to arouse a man's interest.

"The first laird was granted the entire valley and all the coin he could gather from it as his tithe, more than a hundred and fifty years ago. 'Twas said the family prospered for over a hundred years, their fortunes doubling and redoubling again. They built a tower and a wall, first in wood and earth, then replaced it with a building of stone. 'Twas called a castle, but not one so fine as de Vries. Two structures of fitted stone, two stories on the east and three on the west, with a walled courtyard between them."

"Readily defended," Rafael noted with approval.

Maximilian nodded. "Yet when I arrived with a small company, all those years ago, I found the gate ajar and the structure apparently abandoned."

"Pillaged."

"Nay, it simply was vacant, or so it seemed. I thought the laird had ridden out, for who would assault Robert Armstrong, a man who had the favor of the king, a man worthy of both respect and fear?"

"You," Rafael said, which prompted Maximilian's smile. "And all men have enemies, especially the rich ones."

Maximilian nodded. "I thought the laird rode to hunt or visited the king's court, but that did not explain the silence of his holding."

"There should have been a castellan, and guards. Villagers."

"Aye. Nor did it explain the strange mark burned upon the wall of the courtyard, a five-pointed star within a circle."

"God in heaven," Amaury murmured. He might have crossed himself, had his falcon not been on his fist and his reins gathered in his other hand. The bird rustled its feathers, as if sensing his agitation, and gave a cry. It was hooded and tethered, but not as calm as was typical when they rode. It stirred restlessly and the bells on its jesses tinkled, perhaps because of the wind.

Rafael, meanwhile, eyed Maximilian. "I have seen that sign before."

"So had I, and many times since. There had been rumors and tales in the valley as we rode north, but I granted them little account before I reached Kilderrick and saw that mark."

"What manner of rumors and tales?" Rafael would never shirk from detail, however gruesome.

"Accounts of strange lights at the keep and mysterious visitors at odd hours. Shadows where there should be none and candles that would not remain lit. More than one peasant told me that Robert Armstrong had made a wager with the Devil himself, that his soul was forfeit, and that he had uncanny powers. He was feared and his fury more so."

Rafael made a sound that revealed that he shared Maximilian's skepticism of such claims. "Then none would dare to rob him, would they?"

"It depends who launched the tale, does it not?" Maximilian frowned. "The more practical consideration was that the crops had failed two years in a row, the same two years since Robert Armstrong had lost favor with the king. He had increased the tithes instead of granting relief to those on his land, and he had claimed the tithes collected by the church, making them his own. Amidst the tales of him secured in his stronghold, counting his wealth, there was a rumble of dissent."

"But no rebellion."

Maximilian shrugged. "My men fled when they saw the mark, leaving me alone in the courtyard of what appeared to be an empty keep. The nearby village was clearly abandoned. The sun was setting and a storm was brewing. The clouds were dark and rolling over the hills, dark with threat."

"Much like this night." Rafael gestured to the western sky and Maximilian followed his gaze. The clouds did much the same as the last time he had arrived in this place. They would have to set camp soon to keep from being soaked, but he wanted to at least see the keep first. He touched his spurs to Tempest's flanks and the destrier cantered more quickly. The others matched his pace.

"Indeed. It has always been thus when I have been in this valley," he told Rafael. "On that night, I felt that someone watched me."

Rafael shivered and glanced over his shoulder to the rest of the company. "I feel that on this night."

Maximilian did as well, but he did not admit as much aloud. "I was young in those days and impatient. I did not like the notion of a wasted journey, or even less, the possibility that my father—*our* father—had sent me on a fool's errand. I was determined to seize the treasure before I left."

"Did you?"

Maximilian shook his head. "I found an old servant, terrified and shaking, who insisted he would defend his lord and master to his last. I compelled him to lead me to Robert Armstrong. The laird was locked in his chamber at the summit of the west tower, raving about redcaps and bandits."

"Redcaps?"

"'Tis a kind of goblin, by local accounts, one that haunts places where wickedness has been done. They are said to rinse their caps in the blood of the dead."

"Whimsy," Rafael scoffed.

Amaury's trepidation was palpable.

"So one would think. But Robert Armstrong spoke to someone I could not see when I confronted him, commanding that I be seized and killed. The servant told me the goblin was Robert's familiar, summoned to serve him in unholy ways, then crossed himself in terror and fled. To be sure, I wanted only the coin. I could not imagine that Robert Armstrong had none. I thought his fortune hidden and that I could encourage him to surrender its location."

"Encourage," Rafael echoed with a smile.

"Encourage," Maximilian agreed, knowing they understood each other. He was keenly aware of Amaury's disapproval, but that the knight listened closely all the same. "We fought and I won, for he was a poor swordsman."

"I wager others fought his battles for him."

"Aye. He called upon his goblin to strike me down, but I found no evidence of that being. Certainly, no one opposed me. I bound Robert Armstrong to a sturdy wooden chair and when he would not speak, I set it alight. I thought the merest taste of the flames would prompt his confession, but he shouted and cried, summoning his goblin and becoming increasingly incoherent."

"And thus the keep burned." Rafael shook his head. "I find it hard to believe that you failed to calculate the possibility of that."

Maximilian recalled how small the fire had been, and how suddenly it had enveloped the room, as if some other force encouraged it—but that was nonsense. "The wind had a will of its own that night—it snatched the flames and spread them, from chair to carpet to bedhanging, with fearsome speed. All too quickly, the entire chamber was aflame and I watched as the fire leaped to the roof itself. 'Twas as if the keep had been struck with one of your projectiles. I knew it would burn to the ground and quickly. I could not reach Robert to free him. I had to choose between his survival and mine."

"An easy choice."

"He screamed the name of his goblin one last time, then the roof fell in. That name seemed to echo in the empty keep. In my haste to escape, I stumbled over the servant, who had expired on the threshold of the chamber. And then the symbol." He shook his head, still unable to explain what he had seen.

"What of it?"

"The pentacle on the wall of the courtyard burst into flames as soon as I stepped out of the tower, burning brilliantly against the darkness. It seared the mark upon my memory. I even thought I heard a man's laughter. My horse was fighting the tether, desperate to flee, and needed no coaxing to gallop from that cursed spot with all haste. Behind me, the keep burned with fury, the fire lighting up the night."

"It sounds as if a man should believe in the powers of that goblin," Amaury noted.

Maximilian snorted in his turn. "'Twas a ruse. Just because I do not know how it worked does not mean the Devil exists, much less that he arrived to collect his due."

"And then?" Rafael prompted.

"I found my men had set camp within a short distance. We remained the night, then I returned to the keep in the morning. I went through the smoking ruins, step by step, but there was nary a coin to be found."

"Then he was never rich?"

"Perhaps someone claimed it first," Amaury suggested.

"Or it is yet here," Rafael suggested, his thoughts following Maximilian's own as so often they did.

Maximilian, though, frowned at the darkness ahead. They approached the shadow where he knew the forest swallowed the road. It was clearly as he recalled, for the darkness ahead was nigh complete.

Save that a five-pointed star burned against the darkness, flames leaping from it and the surrounding circle to illuminate the boughs of the trees. Flame dropped from the pentacle as well, but instead of landing on the forest floor, where dead leaves might ignite, the circle was reflected in wavering darkness.

"What is that?" he asked softly.

"Sorcery," Amaury hissed. His falcon shook her wings, fighting the tether, and her agitation made Amaury's destrier prance and fold back his ears.

"Nay, the forest crosses the road here. The road is shadowed," Maximilian protested, but he could see the gleam of the river in the forest's shadows. The river was flooded, which made no sense in October.

"That sign," Rafael whispered.

"It cannot be coincidence," Maximilian had time to say before a strange tinkling sound filled the air. It came from everywhere and nowhere, and was of a pitch to send shivers down a man's spine.

The horses plunged into the river then, attempting to follow the road though it was submerged. More than a one of them stumbled, as if something was underfoot. Maximilian might have dismounted to look, but all turned to chaos in haste.

Pebbles suddenly rained down upon them and splashed in the river. The horses fought their bits as the small stones were followed by a volley of flaming arrows. Royce's destrier reared, palfreys bolted, Yves shouted as the pair of palfreys pulling the wagon left the road to race into the rough scrub to the west of the road. Maximilian's own destrier stumbled. Amaury removed the falcon's hood and released her jesses with a sweeping gesture, and the bird soared into the night sky, screaming. The party scattered in all directions.

'Twas no accident, and Maximilian would know who conspired against him. He gave Tempest his spurs and rode hard toward the burning symbol where the villain had to be.

THE FIRST PREY of the season and 'twas a large party. Their luck could not have been better. Destriers! As the party drew closer, she heard the distinctive sound of the warhorses' hooves. Ceara would fetch a fine price for them. Alys could only imagine that this company carried considerable wealth. The raiding party had made good time on their return, but perhaps they feared pursuit. And so they should, if their success had been so great. Alys was glad the preparations had been made.

Their stolen riches would soon be claimed by Alys and her

comrades. The moon was a mere sliver, but hidden behind clouds: the darkness would spark fear of what could not be seen. The men's thoughts would contrive much worse than what they saw, Alys knew.

Kilderrick, after all, had a reputation.

When Alys lit the dry branches of the symbol she had hung from the forest canopy earlier in the day, 'twas Nyssa's sign to act. All began as planned. Alys was crouched on a tree limb, hidden by the shadows, her heart racing with anticipation as wind chimes stirred. The raiding party rode into the water where the river flooded the road, splashing noisily as their progress was slowed. Sure enough, pebbles rained down in quantity upon them, sowing the first confusion. Ceara shot her burning arrows in rapid succession. Most of them fell into the water, sizzling, but they, too created consternation in the company. The men cried out and the horses bolted. A cart raced up the western slope and toppled to one side, spilling its contents. A bird screamed and flew into the sky.

But the lead horse was spurred on, riding directly toward her. The rider's cloak flared behind him and Alys saw the glint of his armor.

A knight!

In a heartbeat, she realized the truth. This was no reiver's party returning from the south. This was a different company. These men rode destriers because they were knights—or mercenaries—and more heavily armed than could have been expected. They would be experienced in the arts of war, as well. Their riches would not be claimed readily at all.

She had erred, indeed.

She gave the whistle to tell her comrades to retreat, then belatedly realized the sound had revealed her own location. That rider in black bore down upon her with purpose, undetered by water or burning sign. Alys leaped from tree to tree, her heart racing in terror now. If he caught her, she knew she would regret her mistake.

She finally landed in the stream to run the last distance, but the splash guided his course. She tried to hold up her cloak, but in her haste, part of it fell into the water. Its weight slowed her progress, possibly too much. She lunged upriver, seized the rock barrier with wet hands and glanced back.

The destrier approached steadily, its eyes reflecting the flames of the sign as if the creature was possessed. The rider was large and dark, and 'twas Alys' imagination that fed her own fears of his intentions.

She hauled herself over the rock barrier, losing her footing in the deeper water, but still managed to pull out the rock that held back the tide. The dammed water rushed through the sluice and the horse staggered backward, losing his footing and stumbling.

If she thought that would save her from the rider, though, Alys had again miscalculated.

He swore with a fury that sent ice through her veins, then leaped from the saddle, charging toward her with fearsome power as the horse regained its footing downstream. Alys tried to run, battling against the rush of water. She glanced back in horror to see him easily jump the barricade. He strode through the water, so much taller than she that he had an advantage. Alys tried to flee but stumbled instead, and fell beneath the water. She held her breath, thinking to evade him in the dark water and float past him.

Her heart stopped when the back of her kirtle was seized in a merciless grip. The knight hauled her from the water with one hand and fairly shook her, like she was an errant dog. Alys glared up at him, intending to spit in his eye, then stared in shock.

'Twas *him*. The Silver Wolf returned.

Nyssa had been right and Alys' blood ran cold.

She would have recognized him anywhere, the man who had destroyed her life, the mercenary whose face haunted her nightmares. Alys was certain her eyes deceived her, but he smiled slowly, his satisfaction clear, and she knew memory served her well. He was as handsome as she recalled, as alluring as he was wicked, as confident and merciless as his reputation.

She spat in his face and he blinked in surprise. She gave him no moment to recover, but kicked him hard in the groin. She heard him inhale sharply and tore open the clasp of her cloak, even as she twisted in his grasp. He swore again and she knew he struggled to keep a grip on her. She bit him hard, choosing the gap between the hem of his leather glove and the end of his dark sleeve. He grunted and Alys tore herself free in his fleeting moment of surprise. She left the cloak in his grasp as she jumped to the rock barrier and ran across it to the dark sanctuary of the forest.

He swore with a thoroughness that only made Alys run faster. She heard him splash as he tried to climb to the summit of the rock dam, then curse again.

The weight of his armor would slow him mightily, along with that of his wet cloak.

Alys raced onward, heart thundering, knowing she had but moments to make her escape, even as her thoughts spun.

Why had the Silver Wolf returned?

Alys did not know, but she could guess that his arrival did not bode well for her future.

How could she drive him away?

'Twas a filthy cloak and sodden with dirty river water, but Maximilian knew the weight of the cloth meant it had cost good coin. Had she stolen it? Or was his assailant of noble birth?

If so, why would she be hidden in the forest, robbing parties that passed in the night?

Sadly, Maximilian could think of several reasons. That his foe was a woman, he had no doubt. He had felt her slight curves as she had struggled against him, her lean strength and the neat indent of her waist. Her hair was wild and her hands were rough, yet she was uncommonly strong for her size. She was so dirty that the smell of her had almost made him recoil. He had had a glimpse, no more than that, of her face, but it had been sufficient to reveal her disdain. He had seen one green eye, so clear, so filled with cunning, that he knew she was both clever and sane.

He had seen her terror, as well, though he could not explain it fully. Fear or trepidation, Maximilian would have understood, but terror mystified him.

He flung the wet cloak onto the rock barrier, then cast his own after it. Only without the weight of the wet wool could he pull himself out of the river and onto what was clearly a dam. It had been built deliberately, of that he had no doubt. He wagered there was another further south, which had forced the road to flood. This one had held back more of the river, so that she could surprise him by removing a key rock and sending forth another tide of water.

In a way, Maximilian admired the feint. It had required planning to disrupt his party's progress with such effectiveness. They could not have been the target, though, for no one in these parts knew of his plans to come to Kilderrick.

Who had she expected?

Who was she?

He had no doubt that there were others in league with her, for someone had cast the pebbles from further downriver and someone else had fired the arrows of flame. His attacker had at least two comrades, perhaps more.

The tinkling sound continued overhead and he guessed that there were chimes of some kind hung in the trees.

And that symbol. Maximilian sliced it down and it sizzled as the flames were extinguished in the river. It was made of sticks and branches, woven and tied into a shape to feed fear. There was naught unnatural about it. He hauled it to one side, in case it offered a clue to her identity that he could see in morning light.

Indeed, it might already be granting him one. Had she chosen that symbol because she had seen it within the keep? Was it yet there? Did she and her comrades take refuge in the ruin?

Maximilian peered into the forest to the east, discerning only darkness and shadowed trees. He would not find her this night, for doubtless she knew the forest well.

On the morrow, the matter would be entirely different.

He retrieved his own cloak, abandoning her dirty one on the barrier. He took the charred symbol and returned to Tempest, who stamped in the shallows awaiting him. He led the horse through the forest to the point where the road emerged from the water again.

Kilderrick glowered down at him, still imposing in ruin, and Maximilian caught his breath at the sight. The lower walls had been made of stone and they remained, charred and blackened, like teeth emerging from the earth. Unlike teeth, they were regular, the shape of the two square towers readily visible to those who looked. The courtyard was a dark hole between them and he had no taste to look upon that symbol again this night, if indeed it remained on those walls.

Rafael was already gathering the company together again, and led them toward Maximilian. They were bedraggled and wet, obviously disheartened, and several of the horses limped.

"There," Maximilian said, pointing to the spot. "We set camp in the vale beneath Kilderrick's very shadow. I hope Denis yet has some soup."

"You are not alone in that," Rafael said grimly, issuing instructions to the squires. Some would pitch tents, others would gather firewood. They had a system for setting camp as quickly as possible, the mercenary's tents around the perimeter, the villagers and horses in the midst.

Maximilian considered the brewing skies. It would rain before dawn, he would wager.

But he would hunt down his opponent, no matter the weather, and do as much at first light. He pulled back his cuff and considered the bruise appearing on his forearm.

Maximilian and this virago were far from done.

"HUNDREDS OF THEM," Elizabeth said, her dismay clear as she sank to her pallet in the small hut shared by the four women. She fingered the worn hem of her velvet cloak and her hands trembled.

The most recent addition, Elizabeth was not yet accustomed to their life in the forest. She jumped at every sound and saw threat in every shadow. All the same, she was resolved to remain with the other women. Alys knew Elizabeth would never return to her father's abode, wherever it was, no matter what the price. She also knew Elizabeth would not sleep this night, not with so many men in close proximity.

Alys might not sleep herself. She was soaked and chilled, but that was naught compared to the terror that kept her heart hammering even once she'd reached their sanctuary.

He was back.

"Perhaps two dozen in total," Ceara corrected with a snort, setting her bow aside with care. "And not all warriors." She tossed her red braid over her shoulder and folded her arms across her chest to confront Alys. She was pragmatic, as ever, and unafraid to share her views. "The horses would have sold for a good price. They still would if we could claim them." There was a challenge in her tone, which Alys knew was intended for her.

"They were too many."

Elizabeth clicked her tongue, noting Alys' wet garments. "You are soaked!" The other woman urged a dry kirtle and chemise upon Alys. "'Tis too cold for that."

Alys shed her wet garments, letting Elizabeth wring them out and hang them to dry, then rubbed herself down with a dry length of rough cloth. The motion brought welcome heat to her skin. Her boots were sodden but would stay that way until they had a fire.

They dared not light one this night for it would betray their location.

At least he had not taken her cloak. It was dripping with river water, but she had found it and it would dry. She tried to wring the water out of it and Nyssa helped her.

"You should not have ended the foray." Ceara was adamant. "I could not believe you whistled! We could have had four palfreys, and readily. Perhaps five."

Alys stood up. She was taller than Ceara and needed every advantage in this dispute. "But I feared for your welfare."

Ceara scoffed. "I had my bow."

"They are knights or mercenaries," Alys explained. "They are skilled in warfare and the destriers are their own. They would not have suffered the creatures to be stolen, not without using their blades. You would have paid with your life for trying."

Elizabeth shivered, her eyes wide.

"Impossible," Ceara replied. "Why would such men be here? They are brigands, such as we always surprise, albeit with better spoils than most."

"And so numerous," Nyssa murmured, shaking her head. "When did we last see such a large party?" Her raven, Dorcha, croaked and whistled, as if in agreement. Nyssa fed him some of the last of the bread they had taken from a previous company.

"You were deceived," Ceara insisted. "In the shadows and darkness, they looked to be more than they are. I am not even certain they were two dozen." This last she addressed to Elizabeth. "The horses might not have been mounted."

"They are warriors," Alys insisted. Ceara opened her mouth to argue, but Alys held up a hand to silence her. "I recognized *him*."

The other three stared at her in silence, awaiting her explanation.

Alys touched her scarred cheek. "He did this." She pointed in the direction of the burned ruin of Kilderrick. "And that. He is the Silver Wolf, the Loup Argent." Even Ceara caught her breath at that name and its repute. "Fifteen years ago, he killed my father and razed Kilderrick. He is back, though I know not why."

"You cannot be certain," Ceara protested, but her voice did not have its usual heat.

"I will never forget his face," Alys said with conviction. "He is older, but he is the Silver Wolf."

Elizabeth began to whisper her prayers under her breath. Ceara's lips tightened and she dropped to a crouch, poking at the hearth as if she would lay a fire. The wind howled with greater vigor, making the tree branches rattle high over the hut and driving itself through the chinks. Alys shivered from more than cold.

She realized that Nyssa was frowning. "Have you seen him?" she asked the other woman. "Was that the wolf you saw?"

Nyssa had the gift of second sight. She'd been born to the caul and often had dreams that hinted at the future. Ceara was skeptical of these portents, but Alys had grown to trust them, at least as warnings.

Nyssa averted her gaze. "Perhaps. I saw a silver wolf howling at the moon. I saw the wolf draw nearer. I saw that it had blue eyes and a hunger that would not be readily sated." She fell silent with a shudder. Dorcha made a clicking sound and nodded, as if he too had shared the vision.

Ceara snorted.

Alys wondered.

"Do we dare risk a fire?" Elizabeth asked quietly.

Alys shook her head. "Not this night."

"Let them pass on," Ceara said. "To whatever their destination. We will be able to set the trap again before more reivers arrive."

Nyssa shook her head. 'I do not think they pass on."

"Nor do I," Alys agreed.

"Whyever not?" Ceara asked Nyssa. Nyssa had been the last one to return to the hut, for her position in their scheme was the furthest away.

"They set a camp below the walls of Kilderrick," she said.

"But if he is the one who burned Kilderrick, why return?" Ceara asked with exasperation. "There is naught left there but the ruin. What advantage could he seek?"

"They set camp," Nyssa insisted. "I saw them begin to pitch the tents."

Alys felt a chill to her very marrow. "Naught good came of the Silver Wolf's arrival the first time," she said. She expected less good of him fifteen years later.

"We cannot tolerate a company of men so close," Ceara said. "They may claim the bounty from the road that sustains us."

Nyssa nodded. "They might drive us from the forest."

"Or worse," Alys said.

Elizabeth caught her breath. "What can we do?" she whispered, eyes wide.

A wolf howled in the distance, as was typical of an autumn night. The sound was chilling as always, but the beasts usually kept their distance from the hut. The women had defended themselves repeatedly with fire, and the wolves remembered.

But the women were not the sole prey available this night.

Alys' gaze fell on the hares hung behind the hearth. Nyssa had checked her traps after they had labored all day to replace stones in the two dams. Nyssa had managed only to clean the carcasses before Ceara had warned of the arrival of the villain's party.

They were nearly fresh.

"We can encourage them to leave sooner," Alys said with purpose. She reached for the hares.

Elizabeth made a little moan of dissent, but the others were quick to agree.

"Wolves," Ceara said with a nod.

"They are already hungry this autumn," Alys said, handing a hare to each of the other women. "Perhaps we can invite them to dine at a certain mercenary's camp."

Ceara smiled. "Such an attack might convince the most stalwart man to move on."

"You remain here," Nyssa said to Elizabeth, her tone more kindly than Ceara's would have been. "Alys can borrow your cloak that way."

"You will hasten to return?" Elizabeth asked, her hands twisting together as soon as she had surrendered the cloak. "I would not be alone this night."

"We will be back as soon as possible," Alys said, flinging Elizabeth's cloak over her shoulders and leading the way.

The sooner this rout was begun, the sooner it would be finished.

CHAPTER 2

*S*he had *bitten* him.

His foe was a woman, but with the nature of a feral cat.

Maximilian considered the mark on his forearm in the better light inside his tent. There was a crescent left by her teeth that was rapidly darkening from red to purple. It had a mate on the other side of his arm. She had sunk her teeth into his flesh just above the wrist, past the cuff of his glove, and he had to wonder whether the mark would endure forever. 'Twas the sole place he was not protected and she had found it in the blink of an eye.

She had bitten hard, as if her intent was to tear his hand from his body or rip free a chunk of his flesh.

Yet she had not been mad or terrified. There had been a shrewdness in her gaze, one he associated with cool planning. She was fierce but not savage. Cunning in pursuit of her advantage, and relentless in exploiting a discovered weakness.

Like a wolf.

The realization made him smile. Perhaps they were two of a kind.

He was in his tent, which had been set up by the squires in the company. The five boys worked together to set and strike camp, always beginning with Maximilian's tent. There were three tents of roughly the same size, one for Maximilian, one that had been Rafael's and which he now shared with Amaury—and that knight's hounds, a choice of much contention—and one shared by Royce, Matteo and Victor, the three mercenaries who had chosen to follow Maximilian when he had surrendered command of the Compagnie Rouge.

A larger and plainer tent completed the circle of their camp—it was set up by Yves and the servants from de Vries for their own use. The horses were brought into the middle of the arrangement at night, and the squires slept in the open air to watch over them. That arrangement would not suit for the winter, but Maximilian had made plans for the construction of better shelter.

For the moment, 'twas a relief to be out of the wind. A brazier emitted a welcome heat from its position in the middle of the tent. Maximilian had cast his gloves and cloak atop his trunk and was still considering his new bruise when Rafael swept open the tent flap and ducked his head inside.

"The Scotsman warned of witches here," he said, flinging himself into one of the pair of folding chairs. He lounged there with familiar ease, his gaze fixed on Maximilian.

"He did not say they bit." Maximilian pulled back his sleeve to display the mark and Rafael's grin flashed.

"Finally, you meet a woman immune to your charm."

"Who is she?" Amaury asked. That knight was lingering just inside the flap, doubtless awaiting an invitation to enter. Maximilian doubted his half-brother would ever lose his formal manners. He gestured and Amaury entered, securing the flap against the wind, but did not sit down.

"Who can say?" Maximilian said, wondering much the same thing.

"Did your falcon return?" Rafael asked Amaury.

The knight shook his head and frowned. "'Tis probably too windy for her to hear my summons."

"And a good night's sleep will be had by all as a result," Rafael said. "I do not suppose that you might contrive to lose the hounds before we retire?"

Amaury glared at Rafael. "Nay," he said, biting off the word.

"I do not know why you released her in the first place," Rafael complained. "You might as well have cast her to the wind."

"Do you not release the reins when you ride down a steep hill?" Amaury demanded.

"Of course. It is always better to let the horse find its own way. They take care of themselves first, which incidentally can save the rider."

"And so 'tis with a falcon. She was hooded and tethered, and all went awry. "Twas better for her to be unhooded and released, that she might fend for herself."

"Even though you might lose a valuable asset in so doing."

"I will find her," Amaury said with resolve. "I will seek her in the morning and I will continue to do so until I find her."

"I wish you luck with that quest," Rafael retorted. "She might be halfway back to de Vries by now."

Amaury's expression set to stone, his annoyance palpable but restrained. "You should wish me success, for I will not hunt without Persephone, which means you will have no meat until she is retrieved and rides upon my fist again."

Rafael rolled his eyes. "You assume that I am reliant upon you to eat," he said, eyes darkening as they did when he was irked. "Do not imagine, *brother*, that I never ate a morsel of meat before you joined our party."

The pair glared at each other, the tension fairly making the air crackle. Maximilian did not imagine how either of them managed to sleep in the same tent as the other—but then, perhaps their tempers were the result of a lack of rest. He cleared his throat pointedly. "The woman," he said. "And her allies."

"Two?" Rafael asked. "Three?"

"At least two, perhaps more."

"One with the stones and one with the arrows," Amaury agreed.

"Or two acting in concert with both tasks. There could be more." Maximilian paced as he thought it through. "They dammed the river, flooding the road, then dammed it again upstream that they might release a tide on demand. They created and strung the symbol, intending to disconcert the arriving party, and they hung chimes in the forest, to tinkle and whistle in the wind."

"But how did they know we approached?" Rafael asked. "Such preparations would take at least a day."

"Perhaps we were not their intended victims," Amaury said.

Maximilian turned to face him. "But this road is not so heavily traveled. Weeks could pass without a rider approaching."

"If naught else, it is an inefficient trap," Rafael said. "But then, women are not always keen of wit in matters of strategy."

Maximilian shook his head. "Nay. This one is. I would wager my steed upon it. There is a detail we do not know."

"More than that," Amaury said. "We do not know who the women are."

"Witches," Rafael said with an elaborate shiver. "Just as Murdoch foretold."

"But why here?" Maximilian asked. "And why that same symbol?"

Rafael shrugged. "You said it was on the wall of the courtyard within the keep. If it remains, those in the vicinity will know of it. Using it might encourage others to believe that they are witches, perhaps even that they know Robert Armstrong."

"Or they have made a similar wager," Amaury suggested.

"Or they share his familiar, the—what was it?—the redcap goblin," Rafael added.

"Or they want their victims to think they are unholy," Maximilian mused. "I saw naught that could not be explained in a most earthly way. I think they practice deception for their own reward. I would know why here."

Rafael chuckled. "I would wager you will not catch that one readily to ask her," he said, nodding toward the mark on Maximilian's arm. It was so purple that it was almost black.

"But if you did," Amaury said softly, his eyes gleaming blue as he stepped forward. "If you did, the sheriff could identify her by how closely her teeth matched that mark. You have evidence in that scar, Maximilian."

Maximilian eyed his half-brother. He was less interested in the pursuit of legal justice than the idea Amaury had given him. "The sheriff," he echoed. "He will know all the tales of the region, the gossip and the facts."

"Is there a sheriff in this wilderness?" Rafael asked. "We seem to have ridden beyond the bounds of civilization."

CLAIRE DELACROIX

"There was a village, doubtless there still is, called Rowan Fell. It was under the command of Kilderrick. It was sited about a mile and a half to the west, just over the rise." Maximilian nodded. "I will visit the sheriff on the morrow, if only to tell him that Kilderrick has been claimed anew."

"A town," Rafael mused. "Does one dare hope for wine and wenches?"

"Ale and daughters," Maximilian said. "If you accompany me, 'twill not be to find your leisure. Kilderrick is not to be plundered."

Rafael grimaced but nodded agreement.

"And you?" Maximilian turned to Amaury. "Will you hunt on the morrow?"

"If I can retrieve Persephone. Her welfare is my first concern."

"And the survival of this company is mine. If you cannot hunt, I will send Matteo and Victor to do so."

Amaury's disapproval showed. "They do not hunt: they slaughter. 'Tis not sporting..."

"Then you must see your way clear to hunting, to ensure it is done as you see fit. Otherwise, you may find another place to shelter." Maximilian let his voice harden. "In this camp, you follow my command."

Amaury's lips tightened. "Aye, my *lord*." He put emphasis on the last word and bowed crisply before leaving the tent.

Rafael sighed and rose to his feet, then stretched like a great cat. "Now there will be no peace this night. He will march about the tent with impatience, brow as dark as thunder, then toss in his pallet like a very tempest."

"You will survive."

"Only because the dogs have not eaten so well of late. When last we feasted, they let such wind that I feared to take a breath all the night long. I thought I would not see morning."

Maximilian laughed and would have clapped his companion on the back, but a wolf howled at startling proximity. Amaury's hounds took up the cry, then began to bark avidly in warning. A woman screamed, the dogs began to snarl in earnest, and a horse whinnied in terror.

"Wolves," Rafael said. "The fiends."

"The women, it seems, are not the sole ones to prey on new

arrivals," Maximilian agreed. The two brothers darted out of the tent as one, daggers drawn.

～

ALYS WENT first to learn more of the camp. The three women moved like wraiths, emerging from the forest in silence, then fanning out as they crossed the valley and approached the camp that had not been there earlier. The ruins of Kilderrick were faintly lit by the sliver of moon, and a cracking bonfire sent a flurry of sparks into the night sky.

The camp was larger than she had expected. Perhaps Ceara was wrong and the arriving party was as large as it appeared at first glimpse. Alys counted four tents, circular structures with peaked roofs, which made her guess there was a central pole in each holding the roof aloft. They looked to be made of plain cloth, not striped silk like the tents of champions in the tales and songs. The tents were arranged in a circle and a fire burned on one side of it. She could see no openings and guessed all of them faced the middle.

She could hear voices as well as the nicker of horses. The wagon she had noticed earlier had been righted and was near the fire. People moved back and forth with purpose.

Who had been in the cart? Prisoners? Slaves? By the fire, a man with silver hair laughed, accepting a steaming bowl from a stouter man. He was a slavemonger, then, in a position of comfort and authority. Two women chatted, then also drew closer to the fire to take bowls. Perhaps they had reconciled themselves to their captivity. Perhaps they earned better conditions with the sharing of their favors. Alys could smell food, perhaps a soup or stew, and the scent made her belly growl with its emptiness.

Aye, a hot meal each day would do much to tame the most reluctant prisoner.

Wolves howled, the sound coming from the west. They were yet at a distance, but the company by the fire fell silent, turning to look. A dog within the camp howled, answering the wolf cry, then others barked. Perhaps three dogs in total. The sentry revealed himself as he stepped out of the shadows to look toward the west and Nyssa took advantage of his inattention to move swiftly up the hill on the far side of the camp.

'Twas as if the Silver Wolf moved a household to Kilderrick. Surely he could not mean to stay?

But what else could be his destination? To the immediate north were several towns, none of which were particularly rich or undefended. To the west were the wild isles, where Ceara had been raised. Far to the north was Inverness and Sutherland, Nyssa's homeland, but there were easier routes to reach that territory. And the riches of Carlisle and the borders were behind them.

What was his scheme? Alys knew he had to possess one.

Though truly, the details would be of no import once Alys evicted him from her family holding. The sentry returned to his post, and she considered him. He was large, bearded and blond, with rings glinting upon his fingers. A stout man brought him a bowl and they chatted together, though Alys could not hear their words.

Ceara was in the shadow of the ruins, waiting and watching. Nyssa had disappeared near the summit of the hill. Alys slipped behind the camp, avoiding the ruin of Kilderrick and strode quickly up the hill after Nyssa. Elizabeth's cloak was dark enough to hide her from view.

The wolves howled again, closer already. Perhaps they sensed Alys' plan.

Once over the crest of the hill, Ceara cut the hares into pieces. Nyssa listened then pointed into the distance, locating the pack of wolves. She and Ceara ran toward the wolves as Alys watched. She spotted the first stealthy silhouette, then eyes flashed in the darkness as the wolves turned to fight. Ceara raced forward, flinging raw meat into the distance. She pivoted and ran back, dropping pieces of meat as she raced toward Alys. The wolves sprang forward to devour the meat, then howled again before they gave chase.

Nyssa also ran toward Alys, dropping meat at intervals and creating a trail toward the Silver Wolf's camp. Alys waited until her companions reached her, almost breathless, then they ran in opposite directions. They had no more meat and would give the camp a wide berth to return to the hut.

Alys stood her ground, waiting for the wolves to draw nearer. She had to ensure they fell upon the camp and had the last hare to encourage them to do as much. Her heart was racing as their silhouettes became more clear. Their howls became louder. The dogs in the camp behind her barked in a frenzy and men began to shout to each other in alarm.

She waited until she could see the gleam of the lead wolf's eyes. Then she dropped a piece of meat and pivoted to run directly toward the camp. One wolf stopped to claim the hare, another lingered to fight him over the prize, but the others flowed down the hill after Alys. She dropped another piece of meat and then another, almost stumbled as she drew near the camp, then flung the last piece so it landed between two of the tents. There was blood on her hands and on her kirtle, and she knew the wolves would not care about its source.

A man must have heard the sound of the meat falling, for he appeared in that gap, his figure illuminated by the fire's light. Alys did not have to guess who he was. Indeed, she saw the silver wolf on his tabard and her heart nearly stopped.

He raised a hand and shouted at her, but Alys' feet might have been winged. He had a dagger in his other hand, after all, and his intentions could not be good. She raced toward the river, plunging into the water to rinse the blood away. She stood in the icy water, heart racing, and stared back from the shadows as chaos erupted in the Silver Wolf's camp.

Then she smiled, knowing the wolves would give him the welcome he deserved.

～

MAXIMILIAN STOOD IN THE DARKNESS, watching the summit of the surrounding hills against the night. The howls of the wolves were growing louder and Amaury's dogs were barking, straining at their leads. The horses stepped with agitation, and Maximilian had his dagger in his hand. Royce had gruffly insisted that Yves and the villagers take refuge in their tent, leaving the stew over the fire. The men had fanned out, each taking a position to watch the perimeter.

The wolves came ever closer, though Maximilian could not fathom why.

Then he saw her.

The woman came over the hill from the west, the sway of her hips prompting his guess of her gender. She wore a long cloak that flicked behind her and she was running. Was it the same one who had bitten him? He could not see her face at this distance, but she was of the right height. Maximilian did not imagine there were many women in this wilderness, but there were already more than he might have expected.

She ran down the hill toward his camp, something in her hand. He narrowed his eyes but was unable to tell what it was. Was she fleeing from the wolves? His instinct was to defend her, regardless of her identity or what she might have done to him. When he might have called out, she halted, spun and flung something behind her. It was perhaps the size of his fist. It fell into shadows, then the wolves howled again, dangerously close.

Maximilian saw them crest the rise in pursuit of her, half a dozen shaggy beasts in momentary silhouette. They were larger than he might have expected, and doubtless more ferocious. He could fairly see the glow of their eyes in the darkness.

The woman raced toward the camp. Maximilian took a step closer, intending to call her to safety. The wolves howled and barked, then bounded after her. Amaury's hounds went wild. Maximilian could hear the woman's running footsteps now and her anxious breath.

He heard her stumble and gasp, then he took a step closer. Would he simply put them both at risk if he tried to help her? There were a dozen wolves behind her, perhaps more. She dropped something, something the wolves found of interest. One pounced upon it then another fought with the first over the prize. The others followed the woman.

She halted abruptly, her breath heaving as the wolves streamed toward her. Despite her raised hood, Maximilian knew her eyes had to be clear green. To his astonishment, she came no closer to sanctuary but turned, as if assessing the progress of the wolves. What madness was this? Suddenly, she flung something at him. The projectile landed wetly at his feet and Maximilian saw by the firelight that it was the hind leg of a hare, raw and bleeding.

He glanced up but she was fleeing toward the river.

Then the first wolf was upon him, lunging into the camp, teeth snapping, its goal obviously the meat at his feet.

"Wolves! Bring fire!" Maximilian roared and lunged at the creature, his blade sinking into its shoulder. The creature snarled and bit, twisted away then came for him again, clearly so hungry that it did not consider the risk or the injury.

Maximilian heard Rafael and the others shout as they fought the wolves and someone banged the cook's treasured pots in an attempt to drive the predators away. His gaze was fixed on the wolf before him, blood on its jowls and its shoulder, eyes filled with intent. It was calculating, just as he was, seeking an advantage to exploit. When it lunged for him again, teeth bared as if to make its attack count, Maximilian was ready.

He buried his dagger in the creature's chest, shoving it between the creature's ribs to the very hilt. He held the massive beast aloft on the blade, watched its eyes die, then cast it aside.

The woman, of course, had vanished.

She had led the predators to his camp, luring them with fresh meat, endangering all those who followed him. Maximilian had to respect her forethought. She lived in the forest, without defenders, perhaps even without weapons, yet she used what was available.

Clearly, she wanted him gone. Just as clearly, he had no intention of leaving. As much as Maximilian admired her resourcefulness, such a deed could not be allowed to occur again.

Which meant he had to either ally with the so-called witch, drive her away or kill her.

Maximilian much preferred the first option. He wanted to know more of this audacious woman who challenged his claim. He had never encountered a woman who had dared so much.

He went to check upon the battle, knowing from the sound that it had ended. Rafael had killed a wolf and so had Matteo. The three wolves' carcasses were cast into a pile by the fire and the other wolves circled the camp slowly before retreating. The villagers were distressed, Denis was outraged by the abuse of his pots, but the hounds were already calming down. Maximilian gave orders for the wolves to be skinned, for the pelts would be welcome in the coming winter, and the meat given to Amaury's dogs.

"'Twill be useful for them in this place to have a taste for wolf," he said. As others scattered to follow his orders, Maximilian returned to his tent, feeling cheated of something he could not name.

The woman, of course. Already, she fascinated him.

"But why did they target our camp?" Amaury demanded, trailing behind him. "Are wolves so bold as that in these parts?"

"Or so hungry?" Rafael asked. "That is a poor portent for the winter ahead."

"They were led to us," Maximilian said, retrieving that hind quarter of hare and tossing it to Amaury's dogs. It scarce hit the ground before it was gone.

"Did you see who did it?" Rafael asked.

Maximilian nodded and held up his wrist, displaying the bite mark.

Rafael laughed. "The lady *is* immune to your allure," he teased.

"And I wonder why," Maximilian mused. "Let us hope the sheriff can shed some light upon the situation."

It was later, after the others had retired and the camp was filled with the sounds of slumber, as Royce paced steadily around the perimeter, that Maximilian wondered. Rowan Fell had once answered to the Laird of Kilderrick. If there was no laird, who gathered the taxes for the king?

And more importantly, who kept the laird's share?

He would seek Robert's hidden treasure, but there might be funds rightfully his that could be accessed more readily.

The sheriff would know, though Maximilian wondered whether that man would confide the truth in him. He smiled as he drifted off to sleep, knowing that the Silver Wolf could be most encouraging.

ELIZABETH HUDDLED IN THE HUT, telling herself not to be fearful. The mercenaries were in their camp. No one could readily find the hidden hut, especially in darkness and without a fire to reveal its location. Her own advice was difficult to take: she was cold and hungry and she was never at ease in the forest as the other women were.

She never would be. She missed walls and guards, gates and moats, and the protection of warriors. She missed comfort, too, the softness of a feather mattress instead of a straw pallet or a bed of cedar boughs. She missed being clean and she missed pretty kirtles. She missed having more than one garment to wear. She missed hot meals at regular intervals and sunny afternoons in the garden. She missed the luxury of an afternoon of embroidery in the garden and the surety that a fine meal was being prepared for her pleasure.

But Elizabeth had learned that the price of those luxuries was too high.

She shivered and paced the length of the small hut again and again, fairly wearing a trough in the dirt floor as she fretted. How long could it take for the others to return? How long had they been gone? Dorcha watched her, his eyes bright, and she supposed it said much for her state that she was glad of the companionship of a raven. She stretched out a finger to stroke the gleaming feathers on his chest, but he pecked at her and she hastily withdrew her hand.

Dorcha only suffered Nyssa's touch. She should remember that.

At first, Elizabeth thought she imagined the hawk's cry. It was higher pitched than typical of a hawk and unusual to hear at this hour. Owls would be more likely, and small woodland creatures who hunted at night. The cry came again and she knew it was not her imagination.

Indeed, it sounded like one of her father's peregrine falcons.

But there were no knights and ladies in this forest, and even if there had been, they would not hunt at night. She could not imagine that falcons were common here in the wilderness: she had never yet seen one and her father had always said they preferred lands with rocky outcroppings for breeding.

But it cried again, and indeed, she heard bells, like those hung upon a prized falcon's jesses. It was not a wild bird then, but a trained one—and it could not be with its master.

The bird had to be lost.

If her jesses were caught on something, she might not survive.

That was sufficient motivation for Elizabeth to try to help. She opened the door of the hut and looked out into the darkness. The forest was in shadow and the wind rustled through the bare branches overhead. It was colder than it had been earlier. The bird called again and she wondered where it might be. She did not want to startle it.

Then she recalled Nyssa cleaning the hares. She hadn't had time to burn the innards and the falcon would be drawn to the scent. Elizabeth went back into the hut and retrieved a small purse and a piece of leather. She considered the purse for a moment, then cut a slit in it. She wrapped the leather around her forearm, wished she still had her cloak, then hurried into the darkness.

She moved stealthily toward the place where Nyssa always cleaned her prey. It was so dark that for a moment, she thought her guess was wrong. Then something rustled and flapped, the falcon cried again and the bells jingled.

The falcon was on the ground!

Elizabeth moved closer. She crouched down, spotting the bird on a fallen branch near the mess. It tugged at its leg, making the bell sound, and Elizabeth guessed that the jess was tangled. The bird stretched toward the innards, but couldn't reach them and tugged on its tether again, with more agitation. The more upset the bird became, the harder it would be to capture. On the ground, though, and tethered, it could become prey instead of predator.

Elizabeth wished she knew what songs the falconer might have used with this bird. For lack of choices, she sang the feeding song taught to her father's falcons. The bird was in the act of stretching again, but hesitated, tilting her head and peering into the shadows. Her next cry sounded more like a question than a plea and Elizabeth moved steadily forward, singing softly all the while.

When she reached the falcon, Elizabeth moved quickly, putting the inverted purse over the bird's head like a hood. The falcon's beak protruded from the slit which was just the right length. The bird shuddered, but Elizabeth sang a little more to calm it.

She also gave it a piece of liver from the hare.

The falcon gobbled it up, ruffled her feathers and settled a bit more.

Elizabeth sang the feeding song again, then carefully released the snared bell from the tree. She held fast to the jesses as she coaxed the bird to her arm, the leather keeping its talons from digging into her skin. Another piece of liver settled the bird, who evidently believed that matters had returned to routine.

Elizabeth took a bit more liver, remembering how careful her father's falconer had been about quantity, and sang to the falcon as she returned to the hut. Dorcha watched with interest, but remained on his perch at the other end of the hut. Elizabeth found a branch, braced it in the corner and encouraged the bird to the perch, tying her jesses securely.

Elizabeth exhaled with relief that the creature was safe. The jesses were of fine leather and she could feel that they had been embroidered heavily. The bells sounded like they were silver. She knew the falcon was prized and even if its owner had lost it forever, Elizabeth might be able to help Nyssa with the hunt this way.

Indeed, she felt as if a tiny part of her former life had returned to her with the falcon and she stroked its feathers with gentle care. She also did not feel so alone in the hut, waiting for the other women's return.

MORNING DAWNED DARK AND COOL, and the scent of rain was in the wind. The clouds churned overhead as they grew ever darker. The wind was stronger than the night before and the storm, when it came, would be powerful.

Alys, who had barely slept, was up at dawn, intent upon witnessing the departure of the Silver Wolf. His visitors of the night before would have ensured that he and his followers understood the perils of Kilderrick. She fully expected his company to break camp and ride away— inclement weather would not keep her from witnessing that happy event. She and the others would have time to set their trap again in preparation for the company of border reivers who still had to return.

Her cloak was not quite dry but it was stiff. She could not keep Elizabeth's cloak, so wore her own anyway. Her boots were yet damp, but she was accustomed to such discomforts—and truly, if it rained this day, they would be wet again. She looked forward to a blazing fire this night after the Silver Wolf was gone and would check that there was wood sheltered from the pending rain. She left the other three women sleeping, Elizabeth's new falcon slumbering under its makeshift hood, Dorcha watching from the opposite end of the hut with disapproval.

No doubt Ceara would continue her complaints about the falcon's presence. That woman already disliked the presence of Dorcha, but as Nyssa consistently reminded her, Dorcha had been in residence before Ceara had arrived. It would not disappoint Alys to miss the next instalment of that argument.

She took a meandering path toward the river, listening all the while for intruders in the forest she knew so well.

There were none.

Alys crossed the river well downstream where there was a line of rocks that kept her feet dry, her mood optimistic. The wind was from the west, so she would remain to the east of the camp's location, to ensure the hounds did not catch her scent in case they were still there. She hurried to the point of the forest where it covered the road, then climbed the biggest tree near its perimeter. She held her breath, fully expecting an empty plain, and looked.

The camp had not changed a whit.

If anything, it seemed to have grown a little larger. Squires led horses around the field on the river side of the camp, checking their hooves, brushing their coats and their manes. The boys laughed together, joking with each other as they worked. They did not appear to be making preparations for a departure. They might have been in the courtyard of a keep, so secure that they did not even post a sentry.

Only one destrier, a chestnut with a white star on his brow, was being harnessed, and Alys watched a man emerge from the camp, tugging on his gloves with purpose. He was tall and broad, but his hair was a darker gold than that of the Silver Wolf. His manner was imperious, though, and he was well armed. He wore chain mail and a hauberk beneath his cloak. He gestured and spoke, then two of the boys ran to saddle palfreys.

The departure of one man and two boys was hardly what Alys had hoped to achieve. The man strapped a quiver on his back, checking first upon the bolts, then accepted a crossbow from one of the boys. He had no other baggage and she had to conclude he rode to hunt.

Aye, a company of such size would need to eat.

That could only mean they intended to stay. Alys frowned.

A stout man who could be no warrior came out of the camp, hailing the mounted knight. He might have been the one who had brought the bowl to the sentry the night before. His hands flew through the air as he gesticulated and Alys wondered what he said. It seemed to amuse the mounted man who smiled and nodded, then beckoned to the boys. When he whistled, three dogs came barking, cavorting with each other as they ran before the horses. They were large and hairy beasts, all hues of dark grey, although the largest one was black. Alys could have told him that the deer favored a clearing well to the east, but perhaps the dogs would discover that. The party rode directly toward Alys, granting her no chance to run and no choice but to remain in her perch and hope she was not seen.

The small party made sufficient noise, though, that the other women would hear their approach. Alys did not need to fear for them. Nyssa and Ceara were always vigilant and they would have awakened by this time. She watched as the rider led his party beneath her, as cheerful as a nobleman seeking his sport. At closer proximity, she could see that his tabard was dark blue and heavily embroidered with gold along its hem and neck, but there was no crest upon it. His garb and harness were as fine as his steed. Was he a knight? Was he the owner of Elizabeth's falcon? Alys could not imagine where else it might have come from. But why did a nobleman with such a fine steed have no insignia?

Why was he at Kilderrick?

Why did he ride with the Silver Wolf? Alys had no explanation for his presence. He should have been visiting the king's court in Edinburgh, not keeping company with a mercenary on the borders.

He whistled repeatedly as they rode into the forest, his head tilting back as if he sought something in the sky. Even though he had ridden past her, Alys froze in place, for the barren branches of the trees would not disguise her if he glanced back. He was looking ahead, though, whistling in summons. It was a different whistle than the one he had used with the dogs, and they ignored it.

It had to be the call for the falcon. Would the bird reply? Alys knew little of hawks and hounds, and she feared that Elizabeth's kindness might bring trouble to them all. Before she could move, though, one dog bayed and the others raced after it. They raced hard to the east, following what was almost a trail through the forest, and Alys knew the dog had caught the scent of the deer. The knight spurred his horse, his anticipation obvious, and in a matter of moments, the sound of the party had faded from earshot.

Alys looked back at the Silver Wolf's camp. That fire still blazed on one side of the group of tents. The sight made her more keenly aware of the coldness of her feet. Could she smell broth? Her hollow belly growled as if to confirm that. Women laughed, apparently content with their lot, though they must be slaves or whores. A large man with dark hair came into the field to stretch what had to be a wolf hide upon a frame. He had cast something at his feet in a grey pile, so several of the wolves had not survived their foray.

There could be no mistaking the identity of the tall man who appeared next, for all those in the camp straightened to attention. His black cloak flared behind him and the sunlight danced in the dark gold of his hair. Alys' mouth went dry as she remembered his handsome features and his cursed confidence. The Silver Wolf could not see her from this distance, but when his gaze swept over the forest, Alys shrank back, peeking around the trunk of the tree. He stroked the nose of a black stallion, likely the one he had ridden the day before for there was no other horse so dark of hue in sight. He gave instructions to two of the boys, then strode toward the ruin of Kilderrick.

He would find little there but ash and ruin. Even the mark on the courtyard wall had washed away years before and Alys had not etched it there anew. There was no point, as no one entered the ruin any longer. Even the most curious had been driven away by her ploys.

She watched the Silver Wolf all the same, reluctantly admiring his agility as he leaped to the summit of the walls. There was a vitality about him that was not shared by the men in the village of Rowan Fell, or even the reivers they robbed in the night. He walked around the perimeter, looking down into the old cellars, then jumped into the ruin.

The boys meanwhile saddled the black destrier, then two others as well. Three men stood outside the camp, one of them tugging on his gloves with his helms tucked beneath his arms. They wore swords and daggers, hauberks, too. One was the huge blond man with the rings she had seen the night before. The second was almost as large and swarthy, with a robust laugh. The third was sleek and dark and 'twas he who donned his gloves. They jested with the one who cleaned the hides, who abandoned his task and washed his hands.

A man who had to be a Scot joined them, his hair russet and his beard full. The length of woolen cloth belted around his hips identified him as such, but Alys could not figure out why he was in the company at all. Was he a guide? But surely, the Silver Wolf knew his way to Kilderrick. She studied the Scotsman, but could not have said whether she knew him or not.

What a curious company. Were they all mercenaries? Why would such a group of men come to Kilderrick where there was neither wealth nor warfare? Alys could not figure it out, but she doubted that the Silver Wolf did any deed without a plan.

How could she discover the truth?

When finally the Silver Wolf returned from the ruin, two men were mounted and ready to ride. She recognized the one who had been cleaning the skins, and the dark one. The sun was higher in the sky, though Alys could not fathom what the Silver Wolf had found of such interest in the ruin of the keep to have spent so much time there. The other two mercenaries remained with the Scot, saluting the Silver Wolf as he and his companions turned their steeds and galloped away from the camp with purpose.

They rode west toward Rowan Fell, armed, and Alys could only wonder why.

CHAPTER 3

*T*he sheriff of Rowan Fell sat down to a midday feast of roasted duck. He inhaled deeply of the scent of the rich gravy and smiled with approval at his wife, Jeannie. She knew it was his favorite and raised the birds specifically to prepare this meal at regular intervals.

He surveyed the table, set with their two prized pewter plates, giving the moment its due appreciation. Life was good for them since the death of Robert Armstrong and he prayed as he often did that there might never be another Laird of Kilderrick.

The situation suited him well as it stood.

Eamon carved the meat with care, having sharpened his knife earlier for the task. He stole a piece of the crackling and Jeannie giggled at the way he rolled his eyes in pleasure. He laid a perfectly roasted breast on his plate and a leg on hers, just as she insisted she preferred. She added dumplings, then took the pot of sauce from over the fire to ladle a generous amount over the meat.

"There can be no finer meal in all of Christendom, Jeannie," he said to her. "Thank you for your labor in this."

"I like it, too, Eamon. 'Tis good that we cannot have it all the time, my lord," she said, as practical as ever. "For you might become too stout for your pony." She smiled, dimpling, and he knew better than to comment upon her own ample proportions.

"I cannot resist it," he said, then raised the first bite to his lips.

Instead of watching his pleasure, Jeannie frowned and averted her gaze. "Horses," she murmured then glanced over her shoulder. "Someone arrives."

"No one arrives in Rowan Fell." Even as he said the words, Eamon put down his knife. He heard more than one horse, not even ponies, and felt a trickle of dread.

The steeds stopped outside his door and Jeannie met his gaze with alarm. Eamon frowned in his turn and made to rise, hesitating even so to leave his meal. The door was kicked open before he got to his feet, causing Jeannie to squeak in fear and retreat to the shadows by the hearth.

Two men strode through the door, men so big that they filled his cottage to bursting. They wore helmets and were heavily armed, with chain mail, tall boots and long cloaks.

Swords and daggers, too.

Warriors. Were they knights or mercenaries? Eamon swallowed. He had little experience of either and was not sure. Had they come from the king?

Was his reckoning due?

When they doffed their helmets, he saw that one was fair and one was dark. The fair one, who was strikingly handsome, surveyed the sheriff, then sauntered toward him, sheathing his sword then drawing his dagger. The dark one cornered Jeannie but did not touch her, his predatory smile sending a chill through the sheriff.

The fair one stabbed his knife into the meat on Eamon's plate and lifted it, biting it as he held the sheriff's gaze. His own steely expression fairly dared the sheriff to protest. The sheriff swallowed, his gaze lingering on the wolf rampant on his visitor's black tabard.

The Silver Wolf had returned.

This was no good thing.

Eamon had been a young man—and a much slimmer one—when the mercenary had ravaged Liddesdale fifteen years before. He had been fighting in the north but had heard the tales. All knew the mercenary's repute: the face of an angel and a heart darker than that of Satan himself.

"Delicious," the Silver Wolf said, finishing the meat. He eyed the carcass. "Uncommon in these parts, I believe."

"My wife is a good cook, my lord."

"And you are not without comfort, are you?" The Silver Wolf cast a glance over the contents of their home, then raised a brow. He helped himself to the other breast. Instead of eating it from his dagger's blade, he claimed Eamon's plate and rolled the meat in the gravy before consuming it neatly, taking each bite from the tip of his knife. "You prefer the dark meat, do you not, Rafael?"

His companion guided Jeannie to the table, compelling her to sit beside the sheriff instead of in her usual place. The Silver Wolf turned to the other warrior—Rafael—presenting Jeannie's plate, with the drumstick, to him.

That man tapped the pewter plate on the table then turned it, assessing the thickness of the metal and the craftsmanship while Jeannie bristled. "Nice," he said, before he picked up the drumstick and tore into it with his teeth.

They stood, eating the sheriff's dinner, their gazes locked upon the unhappy couple. When they smiled, Eamon's dread redoubled.

"It has been a long ride," confided this Rafael, then cast the bone on the table. The pair exchanged a glance and the Silver Wolf carved the other drumstick for his comrade. "I don't suppose you have another? Matteo would appreciate it."

Eamon realized there was a third mercenary, likely outside his door.

"Not plucked and roasted, sir," Jeannie confessed, her words breathless.

"Ah well," the Silver Wolf said. "This one will have to suffice for this day." He considered the carcass, finding more meat to add to the plate he had claimed. He looked askance at it, for there was no gravy, and Jeannie hastened to fetch more for him. "So long as you add all you know of Kilderrick." He met Eamon's gaze, his eyes a startling clear blue.

"Kilderrick is burned," Eamon said without thinking.

"I know, for I touched the flame to it myself," his visitor agreed easily. He held out the plate and Jeannie ladled gravy upon the meat. He turned a smile on her that left her blinking. "I thank you, madame. You are indeed an excellent cook." He turned back to the sheriff, his gaze cold.

"'Tis abandoned these fifteen years, sir, for the laird is dead."

"I know this, as well, for I killed Robert Armstrong."

The Silver Wolf did not appear to suffer from any regret over this— and truly there was no cause, for Laird Robert had been wicked to his marrow.

Eamon's visitor bit delicately of the meat. "But the holding is not abandoned in truth, is it?"

"You mean the witches, sir?"

The Silver Wolf granted him a pitying look. "I do not believe in witches."

"Yet many do, sir. There are...incidents at the ruins of Kilderrick."

"Incidents?"

"Fires, sir. Tales of goblins and ghosts. Curses made and spells bought. People avoid the ruins, unless they have need of the witches' assistance."

"Errant lovers and unwelcome children," the mercenary said, almost under his breath. He then flicked a look at Eamon, so intense that it might have bored to his very soul. "Who tells these tales?"

'Twas not the time to reveal Jeannie's gusto for gossip and rumor.

Eamon faltered, but Jeannie did not. "They are witches and harlots, those three! They were taught by that old witch, Morag, and though she is dead, her wicked ways endure in her minions. Women go to them for aid with their maladies, men go to satisfy their lust, and none dare to challenge them outright."

The Silver Wolf nodded. His gaze rose slowly to meet that of the sheriff, who found himself flustered. "As I recall, Rowan Fell was part of Kilderrick and Laird Robert's holding. The village looks most prosperous."

Eamon blustered. "The taxes are collected, sir, and the royal due delivered to the king as is right and proper. It is my responsibility to ensure..."

"Who keeps the laird's share, since there is no laird?" the Silver Wolf demanded, interrupting him smoothly.

"It...it is kept in trust, sir, for the future."

The Silver Wolf smiled and it was a chilling sight. He deliberately set aside his knife, reached into his purse and conjured an item that the sheriff had never thought to see again. He set it deliberately upon the board between them and the sheriff blinked.

'Twas the seal to Kilderrick.

Eamon swallowed. His day of reckoning had indeed arrived.

"I come to claim my legacy," the Silver Wolf confided, watching the sheriff so closely that the man in question dared not show his horror at those tidings. "I mean to be a most excellent overlord."

His companion guffawed, then cast the other leg bone on the table. He stabbed his knife into a dumpling and consumed it whole.

"I will accept the laird's share now." The Silver Wolf's tone was dangerously low, as if he knew the sheriff no longer had the coin. "After fifteen years, the sum must be considerable."

Eamon felt sweat trickle down his back. The notorious mercenary watched him, so utterly still that he did not even seem to breathe. This man would cut out his heart and feed it to him, of that the sheriff had no doubt.

"I cannot surrender it, sir," he stammered. "Not without the approval of the rightful heir to Kilderrick."

"Robert Armstrong had an heir?"

"Heiress, sir, to be sure. Alys Armstrong leads the witches."

The mercenary was suddenly more taut than he had been. His lashes swept down to hide his eyes but his mouth was a hard line. The sheriff sensed that he was keenly interested in this tale. Why? Had he encountered the women already? "Alys Armstrong," he murmured, apparently savoring the name.

"Aye," the sheriff agreed. "She is Robert's daughter, the sole survivor of the family."

"I left every soul dead in that keep before burning it to the ground," the Silver Wolf said, as if that was a feat worthy of merit.

Eamon replied quickly. "You missed one, sir." Then he regretted his words, in terms of his own fate, that of his wife, and even that of Alys herself.

The Silver Wolf's eyes flashed and he rose abruptly to his feet. "How fortuitous," he said, startling Eamon again. "Do you like weddings, madame?" he asked Jeannie, barely glancing her way.

"Aye, sir," Jeannie said, clearly startled by the question. Her gaze flew to her husband and back to their unexpected guest. "Everyone does, my lord."

"Bring her," he commanded his companion. "We shall need witnesses."

The Silver Wolf reached across the table with lightning speed and seized the sheriff by the back of his vest. He quickly divested the sheriff of his weapons and bound his hands behind his back, while the companion did the same to Jeannie. They were pushed out of their home in the blink of an eye, where a third mercenary waited with three stamping steeds.

They were massive beasts, destriers the like of which the sheriff had only seen at the king's own court. They snorted and stamped, impatient to run, their eyes flashing as if they were possessed of demons themselves.

The Silver Wolf shoved the sheriff toward the third man, who reached down and hauled him up by his belt, flinging him across the back of his destrier like a sack of grain. It was cursed uncomfortable, but Eamon dared not complain, not once he felt the mercenary's knife upon his neck. Jeannie rode similarly before Rafael, her eyes wide and her horror clear.

The Silver Wolf himself swung into the saddle of a black destrier, a beast that looked as dangerous as his master. The horse's nostrils flared, his tail and mane flowing behind him as the mercenary touched his spurs to the horse's flanks. The Silver Wolf rode out of Rowan Fell, cloak flaring behind him, companions galloping in his wake, and headed directly for Kilderrick. Jeannie loosed a low moan, one that stopped suddenly, likely at the touch of a knife blade. The third mercenary said something to the second that the sheriff did not understand but when they laughed together, his blood ran cold.

Eamon was well aware of the villagers peering out of their homes as the company passed and knew the tale would quickly be shared with all. The Silver Wolf had returned like a hunter come to claim his prize.

And thanks to the sheriff's loose tongue, his first victim would be Alys Armstrong.

Eamon, the sheriff of Rowan Fell, feared he would be next.

~

SHE WAS ALYS ARMSTRONG.

How had Maximilian never known that Robert had a child? His father, he now recalled, had said that the Laird of Kilderrick had no son, which was not the same thing. But Maximilian held the seal to Kilderrick. Wed to Alys, the blood heir to the holding, his claim could not be disputed, even by the king. The sheriff's wife declared Alys to be a harlot, but Maximilian cared even less about that than the suggestion that his intended was a witch. Her past was of no import, for he had a plan for her future.

He would wed her.

They would have a son.

They would rebuild Kilderrick. Aye, their shared knowledge would lead to success. She would know what had been and he knew what could be. Together, they would triumph. The solution was so neat that it might have been destined to be. Maximilian knew better than to let such an opportunity elude him.

And indeed, he was sufficiently honest with himself to admit that the prospect of meeting ferocious Alys abed set his very soul afire. She would not lie back and endure his caress. Nay, she would meet him touch for touch. She might fight him, she might have to be seduced, but their mating would be magnificent.

Aye, they would suit each other well.

And she might know more of her father's hidden treasure. There had been no hint of it in the ruin, but then that had been a remote possibility after so many years. He had sought a hidden nook, a loose stone, a place where a prize could have been locked away for years, but had found naught. Had another found it in the years since Robert's death?

Had Alys herself claimed it? She was the most likely to know her father's secrets.

There could be more than one advantage to taking this woman as his bride.

Maximilian did not imagine for a moment that the virago in the forest would quickly agree to his suit, however.

In truth, he could scarce await the challenge of matching wits with his intended.

If not more than that, and both this very night.

ELIZABETH WAITED until Ceara and Nyssa left the hut. Ceara did not like the falcon in the hut any more than she liked Dorcha, though Nyssa had allowed that Elizabeth was kind to keep the bird safe. Alys did not care either way and had left by the time Elizabeth awakened.

Elizabeth knew though that this bird could be key to her contributing her share to their survival. She was aware that the others did more to ensure their welfare than she did. She knew she owed them much. She had hunted with a hawk at Beaupoint, and if she could train this falcon to return to her, she could help to provide them with food.

Ceara would see.

When she was alone, Elizabeth carried the falcon to a small clearing, murmuring to it all the way. She remembered the falconer training a bird to the lure and surely this one had been trained thus. She had no fresh meat, but the bird had come to her once.

The only way to discover whether the falcon would do as much again was to release her, then summon her anew. Elizabeth chose the clearing so the falcon would be able to see her. She sang the song that had brought the bird to her fist the night before, then she sang it again. She removed the bird's hood and sang it once more.

The falcon considered her, its eyes bright.

How she wished for a long training lead, but there was none to be found.

Elizabeth took a deep breath, sang the song again, then launched the bird. With a mighty flap of her wings, the falcon soared high. She gave a cry of exultation and circled the clearing. Elizabeth watched her with awe, then raised her fist and sang the song.

The falcon cried. She circled and she dove toward Elizabeth's upraised fist, talons extended. Elizabeth had a heartbeat to believe she would succeed, then the bird called, swooped past her and soared into the sky again. She spun and sang, but the falcon flew on.

"Nay!" Elizabeth cried, then ran in pursuit. She would never catch the creature but she might be nearby when the bird landed. She might be able to help the falcon again.

She had to try.

~

THERE WERE days when the hunt seemed to be destined for success. There were others when no number of hours trudging through the woods would yield results. Amaury had possessed doubts from the outset of this day's venture into unfamiliar forest with a storm obviously brewing. He would never have hunted, if Maximilian had not insisted upon it. When the dogs had taken a scent and led the party further into the forest than his plan, Amaury's doubts redoubled.

But he had been mistaken.

The dogs found game aplenty, so unaccustomed to hunters that 'twas easy to succeed. Indeed, his bow might have been enchanted. His shots were true, each and every one, and by midday, they had as much to take back to the camp as they could carry. Two deer, large and healthy bucks both of them, half a dozen partridge and a dozen hares. Those in the camp would eat well for a few days. Amaury retrieved his bolts and cleaned them in the scrub as the boys trussed the deer. He flung the liver to the dogs, wishing he might find Persephone. She would have had the first morsel. The squires, Oliver and Louis, were rhapsodizing about roast venison and venison stew, about Denis' famed dumplings, when Amaury heard a familiar cry.

He held up a hand so Oliver and Louis would fall silent, then he listened.

It came again, unmistakably the cry of a falcon. Oliver's eyes rounded. Amaury whistled, using the tune that Persephone had been trained to heed. He saw a shadow pass overhead and his heart leaped with joy.

"Persephone!" he roared and crashed through the undergrowth to a clearing. He held his gloved fist aloft, seeking another glimpse of her, and whistled anew.

She cried out, then swooped down, eyes flashing, to land heavily on his fist. He seized her jesses, relief nearly taking him to his knees. She ruffled her feathers and considered him, as composed as ever.

As if he had been a fool to doubt her return. Amaury exhaled in relief.

She had to be starving. He retrieved a piece of liver and held it for her, but she sniffed it and turned her beak away.

How could she not be hungry? What had she killed?

He checked her talons and her beak but she was so clean that he knew she had not made a kill. What had she eaten then? How could she have eaten?

He shed his other glove and hooded her, then ran a finger over her figure. She did not feel leaner and her feathers were as glossy as ever.

A twig snapped in that moment, the sound coming from the opposite side of the clearing from where the boys worked. Amaury pivoted and the barest glimpse of a woman in a dark green cloak. Her hair was deep auburn and loose over her shoulders. She was the most lovely creature he had ever seen.

He froze, staring.

She sought something, her gaze trailing upward, inattentive to her own path. Then her toe caught on something and she tripped. She caught herself before she fell, then saw Amaury and froze. She gasped, her eyes widening, then her gaze dropped to the falcon on his wrist.

Time stopped as she stared in awe.

She flushed the most alluring shade of pink, and he thought that perhaps he might be so fortunate as to see her smile—but then she spun to flee. She was faster than a deer and so much quieter that Amaury could not hear her at all. He lost sight of her with cursed speed.

He paused to listen but could only hear the boys and Zephyr stamping with disgust at the smell of blood.

She was gone.

Amaury retraced his steps to where he had first seen her and noticed something on the ground. He bent to pick up a red silken purse, the kind a wealthy noblewoman might dangle from her wrist at court. It was mired but otherwise very fine.

And it was sliced up one side. He turned it over, wondering why that should be. It looked to be a recent cut. There was naught within it and it was when he held it upside down that he guessed.

She had used it as a hood for Persephone. She had tended to the falcon, keeping her safe through the night. This maiden might live in the forest, but she knew of hawks and hunting

Amaury smiled. Such a deed should be rewarded.

To do as much, though, he would have to know where to find her again.

He returned to the boys, entrusting Persephone to Oliver and instructing the boys to remain where they were with the horses. He snapped his fingers for Bête, the largest and most loyal of his hounds, and also the one with the sharpest nose. He held the cut purse beneath the dog's nose and whispered his command. "Find her, boy. Find her."

'Twould not be merely deer that Amaury hunted this day, but the maiden who had stolen his heart with a single glimpse.

"WE COULD DAM the river and flood the field," Ceara suggested. She and Nyssa had joined Alys, having guessed her destination. The three women huddled behind trees and studied the camp Alys wished would simply vanish.

The Silver Wolf showed no indication of complying with that desire.

"It would take too long," she said to Ceara. "He has chosen high ground for his camp, curse him."

"He is not a fool, that is for certain," Nyssa acknowledged, her tone grudging.

"We could invade the camp at night and set fire to a tent," Ceara suggested.

"We might be caught, and he would have no mercy," Alys said.

"We could summon the sheriff." Even as Nyssa suggested as much, her tone made it clear she had doubts about the merit of this plan.

Alys scoffed. "And Eamon would have to leave his cozy hearth."

"To face these men and drive them away?" Ceara laughed. "I think he would not dare to try."

Alys leaned back against the tree, thinking furiously. "If only we had an ally."

"One with an army," Ceara agreed, then heaved a sigh. "Why have they even come to Kilderrick?"

Alys shook her head, mystified. "Why did he ride out and where did he go?"

They shrugged in unison.

"Wait! They return," Nyssa whispered, as if the Silver Wolf would be able to hear her from the other side of the camp. Alys and Ceara looked around their chosen trees. Alys' heart gave a little skip at the sight of the three warriors riding over the distant hill, the Silver Wolf in the lead on his black destrier.

"They brought something," Ceara said.

"Two sacks," Nyssa said with confusion. "But of what and from where?"

The horses cantered into the field where the boys tended the others and the members of the Silver Wolf's company gathered around. The two sacks were dropped from the backs of the two horses and proved to be a man and a woman. They struggled to their feet with visible effort.

"'Tis Eamon and his wife," Ceara whispered with no small measure of delight. "They must be prisoners."

The Silver Wolf rode around the company and gave instructions as Alys stared.

"Aye, their hands are bound," Nyssa agreed.

Ceara chuckled. "And Jeannie, that wretch, looks most unhappy." The sheriff's wife staggered to the perimeter of the group, bent over and vomited. Ceara's smile broadened. "I could like him for this."

Alys nudged her hard. "You will not like it when you are next."

"Nay, but Jeannie is a venomous toad. You cannot blame me for being glad to see her get at least a measure of her due."

Alys ignored Ceara's comment, for the Silver Wolf rode directly toward them. He halted his destrier some twenty paces from the river and the beast tossed its head. The storm clouds rolled ever closer and lightning cracked in the distance.

The Silver Wolf turned his horse in place then, and his warhorse arched its neck, prancing in place. The steed was black, as black as midnight, his coat glossy with good health. "Such a steed," Ceara whispered in admiration.

The destrier was perfectly beneath his rider's command, but Alys was not surprised that the Silver Wolf was an experienced horseman. Let Ceara admire his skill.

She admired naught about this man.

She could see more of him than had been possible the night before. She had known his garb was dark, but he wore black, an expensive hue. That long black cloak flared behind him, he wore tall black leather boots and his black tunic was emblazoned with a silver wolf rampant. She did not doubt that he wore a chain mail hauberk—indeed, she thought she could see it glimmer. Every element of his garb spoke of wealth, which Alys knew was ill-gotten gains.

He had pushed back his mail coiff, for his hair gleamed dark gold. Was he as handsome as she recalled, this man whose heart was filled with evil? Did his eyes truly burn with pale blue fire, or was it the terror of a young girl that tinged her recollection?

She recalled his fearsome strength when he had held her the night before, the hard contours of his arms locked around her, and she felt something other than fear. Something unwelcome, indeed. She recalled the taste of his skin, the clean masculine scent of him, and frowned at her own shiver of awareness.

Nay, not this man. Never this man.

"Alys Armstrong!" he bellowed in the voice that haunted her nightmares and Alys' heart stopped cold. "Show yourself!"

Alys flattened herself against the tree, her heart galloping. It could be that day again, the sky roiling, a storm brewing. She had run to hide then and she would run to hide now. She was not a child any longer, though her heart pounded as it had that day. Her fists clenched at her sides.

He would not hurt her this time.

She would not permit as much.

"How does he know your name?" Nyssa whispered, standing straight behind her own tree.

"The toad told him." Ceara muttered. "Faithless wretch that Jeannie is."

"If she meant to gain his goodwill, it did her little good," Nyssa noted.

Ceara scowled. "Someone should cut out her lying tongue and silence her for good."

As ever, Ceara was harsh, but then she had an old grievance against Jeannie. In this moment, Alys was more concerned with the Silver Wolf.

"Alys Armstrong, I would parlay with you!" he roared. He had a slight accent, as if French was his mother tongue, but Alys understood him well enough.

His voice was louder, as if he had moved closer.

"Not on your life," she whispered. As if she would reveal her presence to the man who had destroyed her family home, slaughtered her own father and nearly killed her.

Never.

Her heart skipped and her mouth went dry.

Nyssa peeked around the tree again, then caught her breath. "They mean to hunt us down," she whispered, prompting both Ceara and Alys to risk a look.

Three mercenaries had mounted their destriers and formed a row behind the Silver Wolf. In between them, three boys waited on palfreys. Alys understood immediately. Seven of them would ride in formation, charging into the forest in an attempt to flush Alys and compel her to that parlay. At least the Silver Wolf did not have command of the dogs, which were still in the forest with the one who hunted.

"Do not surrender," Ceara said fiercely.

Alys shook her head. "Elizabeth," she reminded them softly.

Nyssa nodded once. "We will find her. Save yourself."

"I have need of a wife, Alys," the Silver Wolf shouted to Alys' astonishment. "As I have claimed Kilderrick for mine own, only Robert Armstrong's sole daughter will do."

Ceara's mouth dropped open and Nyssa turned to Alys with horror. Alys stood blinking in shock. "'Tis a trap," Ceara whispered and Alys could only agree. "Woe to you if you are in his power."

The Silver Wolf's voice dropped low. "I believe we may be well-matched, Alys."

Oh, she would slice out his wicked tongue for even making such a foul suggestion.

"Never!" she cried, even though it would give him a hint as to her location.

"Nay, Alys," he replied with intent. "This very day."

So this was his scheme. Alys would rather die. Her lips set in a grim line. "Net," she said, claiming one of the women's established means of evading unwelcome intruders.

"Thicket," Nyssa said, claiming a second.

"Then the fen is mine," Ceara said with a smile of anticipation, claiming the third.

They nodded once at each other with resolve.

"Goddess be with you," Nyssa said.

"And with you," whispered Alys. Ceara nodded and their gazes clung for a potent moment.

The Silver Wolf gave a shrill whistle. "I will find you, Alys Armstrong," he shouted. "And we will wed this very day. Rely upon it, lady mine."

She would not be his lady.

He shouted a command, then hoof beats echoed on the field. The line of horses charged toward the forest, their riders bent low over their backs. One man gave a hoot and another laughed at what he obviously saw as a game.

The women ran.

As Alys lost sight of Ceara and Nyssa, lightning cracked, drawing a vivid white line across the sky. The hair tingled on the back of Alys' neck, then the lightning struck a point not very distant. The ground jumped as the thunder drowned out the sound of the approaching horses. The wind howled, tossing the trees in a frenzy. All seemed to take a breath, then the skies burst open and cold rain beat down hard, soaking all within a heartbeat. The storm made no difference to Alys or her predator. She heard the horses charge onward.

The net.

She ran with all the strength she had, knowing her survival depended upon reaching the trap in time.

MAXIMILIAN HAD EXPECTED a challenge and indeed, the conquest would be all the sweeter for it. He rode Tempest hard, guiding the beast in the direction of Alys' voice. He spotted her and spurred the horse on, then let Tempest choose his own path through the tangle of the undergrowth.

The rain fell in sheets, the timing so wretched that he halfway gave credence to Alys' reputation as a witch. She might have summoned the storm to hinder the chase, but that was whimsy. Even so, the wind made the deadened branches of the trees shake, and Alys was cursedly difficult to spot through the falling rain. She ran an irregular course, ducking beneath low branches specifically to hamper the horse's path, and he respected her cleverness.

Her cloak was sufficiently dirty to be of a hue with the woods and it was only her motion that allowed him to spy her at intervals. She was quick, too, and sure of foot, obviously knowing her path. She did not hesitate, which meant she had a plan and a destination. He understood her well enough to guess that.

It would not be one to his benefit. She had survived in this forest for fifteen years, and not simply by evasion.

Aye, she led him toward a trap.

Maximilian would not comply with her scheme. Alys might have no compunction about injuring him or his horse, but he had other plans.

He slowed the steed to a halt and listened. Beyond the heavy drumming of the rain, he heard his own party dispersing through the forest. Someone—he thought perhaps Rafael—gave a shout and he knew that man had found his prey. Amaury's dogs barked, but at a great distance.

He heard someone running through the forest, someone too noisy to be Alys. Someone smaller and lighter than one of his men.

Someone whose breath caught in fear.

Alys had allies in this forest, and he knew there were at least two other women.

His thoughts flew like quicksilver. He could only imagine that she felt some loyalty to her comrades. He would have done so in her place.

The footsteps became louder, the woman drawing closer. Clearly she was unaware of his presence. Maximilian slipped from the horse's back, holding a hand over the destrier's nose. Tempest, well accustomed to his master, stilled, understanding the silent command.

The woman caught her breath and made a little cry that confirmed both her gender and her fear. Maximilian saw her silhouette, not twenty paces away. She sat down hard and put her face in her hands, apparently in despair. He dropped the reins and moved like a shadow through the forest, silent and quick, the patter of the rain disguising any sound he might have made. He circled around, noting that she was still unaware of his presence, then snatched her up from behind. One arm he locked around her waist, holding her arms against her sides, and the other he clapped over her mouth.

The woman froze, then she fought against his grip frantically. Her hood fell back as she struggled against him and her long auburn tresses tumbled over her shoulders. Her cloak had once been fine, wrought of dark velvet, embroidered down the front and around the hood. Now it was worn and dirty.

And wet. They were both soaked to the skin.

She exhausted herself all too soon and stifled a sob as she shuddered. Maximilian had a very good idea then what incident had driven this one to hide in the forest, for her heart raced like that of a wild bird and her breath caught in terror.

He had no intention of savoring her charms, but she did not have to know that as yet.

"Call Alys," he whispered, his lips against her ear.

She shook her head furiously, shivering convulsively.

"Then we shall be compelled to find another amusement." Maximilian trapped her against a fallen tree, imprisoning her between it and his hips. He moved his hand from her mouth, letting it slide down to cup her breast.

She panicked anew then, and he knew he had guessed aright that she feared men. Perhaps she had been raped. Perhaps she had been assaulted and had fled into the forest, ultimately finding a haven with Alys. Maximilian did not particularly care.

"Nay!" she whispered, fighting against him with new strength. "Nay, nay, nay." Her voice broke and he saw her tears fall on his glove as she wept.

"Call her," he commanded, his whisper hard. "And I will release you."

"You lie." She bit out the words with hostility.

He crushed her slightly beneath his weight, wanting only to get out of the rain as soon as possible. "I never lie," he said softly. "Call her."

She inhaled sharply, trembled, then shouted. "Alys! Help me, Alys!"

"Louder."

His victim called again, and yet again.

"Well done," he informed her and stepped away from the tree. Her relief was a tangible force and she stumbled as her knees weakened. Still he held her before him, still she was captive, but he was not pressed against her or cupping her breast.

"Again," he insisted.

As anticipated, the small reward gave her more encouragement. She shouted for Alys with greater vigor, her voice echoing through the forest.

The rain fell in torrents. The sound of the other men faded completely. There was just the sound of the rain on deadened leaves, the wail of the wind, and the wait for Alys.

Maximilian had no doubt that she would come.

CHAPTER 4

*R*afael was fast behind the woman he had chosen to pursue, and found himself admiring that she ran with the agility of a deer. She wore chausses and there was a quiver slung over her shoulder, but Rafael did not imagine for a moment that he gave chase to either man or boy. The curve of her hips made her gender most clear.

And to be sure, that sight fed his interest in the chase. It had been a long ride from Château de Vries and one devoid of the pleasures that Rafael liked to savor frequently. An agile wench would suit him well.

The rain fell with vigor, soaking him to the skin with its cold onslaught, but for once, Rafael was oblivious to the weather. He spurred his destrier on, smiling as the woman dodged a fallen tree branch in the last moment. His destrier leaped over the barrier elegantly, not losing its stride in the least, and nickered for the sheer joy of it.

The woman glanced over her shoulder and her hood fell back, revealing that her face was fair and her long hair was a vivid hue of red. Saints above, she was a beauty! Her expression was filled with resolve, though, a warning to Rafael. She halted, pulled an arrow from her quiver as she spun to face him, loaded her bow with astonishing speed and loosed it at Rafael. He was so surprised that he ducked only in the last moment, fairly feeling the arrow part his hair.

That had been no fortunate shot. Nay, her aim was deadly accurate.

His admiration swelled and he urged Phantôm onward. The woman ducked behind a tree, disappearing into the shadows and the scrub.

Rafael slowed his destrier, listening but there was no hint of her presence. Where had she gone?

The second arrow grazed his right shoulder, ripping his tabard and leaving a line of blood across his flesh. He should have worn his hauberk this day, but he had not anticipated a battle. The wound was not deep, though he would ensure it was tended all the same. He still did not see where she was, until she ran onward again. Rafael muttered a curse and urged the destrier to follow.

He came suddenly upon a sparkling stream that had to feed into the greater river far behind. The stream was almost completely hidden by the trees, which grew to its very banks. Their branches interlaced overtop. Phantôm strode through the water unimpeded by its shallow depth or the pebbles on its bed. The land dipped ahead of them and Rafael could see a feminine silhouette at intervals. The forest thinned and he guessed that there was a clearing in the distance, perhaps in the shelter of a valley.

The horse thundered onward but the woman did not fire another missive. Rafael's suspicions rose, then redoubled when he spotted a cloak discarded on the barren shrubs to one side of the path. He halted the horse beside it, but there was no doubting it was her garment.

Why had she abandoned it?

Could their expectations be as one? Rafael dared to hope as much.

The sheriff's wife had said the women were harlots, which meant they plied their trade somewhere. Women did not like to couple outdoors, in Rafael's experience, even those who made their living doing so. They might have a shelter nearby for such liaisons. She could have led him to it apurpose.

Aye, there was promise in this choice of hers.

Rafael smiled, his anticipation rising, and slipped from the saddle, tethering the horse under the shelter of the forest. He eased closer to the clearing ahead of him, and saw that it was extensive, fading into silver mist in the distance as if it continued forever. Some plant grew to about the height of his waist, obscuring the ground, but he was more interested in the woman. She could not be two dozen steps away from him, her back turned to him. Her hair was loose, hanging in a wet tangle down her back, its flamelike color darkened by the rain.

As he watched, she tugged her chemise up to her waist, then pulled it over her head. Her bare back gleamed as pale as alabaster, rainwater streaming over it, and Rafael took a step closer. She turned to face him and he saw the ripe curve of her breasts, the taut darkness of her nipples, the invitation in her smile. She was magnificent! That resolve was banished from her expression and there was only allure. Her skin was slick and wet and he took a step closer, wanting to touch her.

She smiled a little more and crooked a finger at him. "Leave your weapons behind," she said in a husky voice. "I meet you willingly but will not be at your mercy."

Rafael unbuckled his belt and put his sword aside. "I will not leave the dagger, lest I have to defend you."

She laughed. "Then you will not have me." She lifted a brow. "You have need of only one blade to meet me this day."

Rafael grinned and set his dagger aside, still in its scabbard. There was no one to take his weapons or his destrier in this place, and he had been so long without a woman that the mating would not take long.

He strode into the clearing, ignoring how the mud underfoot sucked at his boots. The woman turned to watch him, that smile unwavering, those pert breasts inviting his caresses. She even raised her hands to her own nipples, teasing them to taut peaks before his very eyes, and he moved more quickly to claim the prize. The mud churned beneath his boots, sucking at them, rising to his ankles and impeding his progress.

He looked down with alarm as his boots sank into the mud so that his feet were hidden. He took another step with an effort and sank to mid-calf.

What was this place?

He glanced up again and the woman had vanished. The rushes stirred and Rafael saw her again, at much closer proximity. The ruthless light in her eyes told him that she had plans other than seduction.

Then she lifted her bow. She was so close that she could not miss. Rafael raised his hands in appeal, but she loosed the arrow. He ducked quickly, losing his balance, and felt the arrow pass by him. He took a step to steady himself but the ground beneath his boot seemed to disappear. He might have stepped into a hole, one with no apparent bottom, for his boot sank into the mud and kept sinking lower. Rafael struggled to free himself and only sank deeply, the mud apparently intent upon devouring him whole.

Rafael shouted and flailed but that only made his situation worse. He snatched at the reeds on either side, but could not halt his own progress.

"Help me!" he cried as the rain pounded down upon him, driving him down into the mud. He was up to his waist, the mud sliding into his boots and beneath his tabard.

What foul madness was this?

And where had the woman gone? He could not see her, but he heard footsteps as she ran around the perimeter of the clearing. The rain pelted down, but being wet was the least of Rafael's troubles.

Then he heard the nicker of his own horse. It was the sound Phantôm made when meeting a new acquaintance.

One he liked.

"Do not steal my steed!" Rafael shouted, but heard only an answering laugh. He twisted in time to see her, the reins in her hand, bend to claim his dagger. She smiled as if to thank him, then pivoted and leaped into the saddle in a single graceful move.

She meant to rob him, as well as leave him to die. Rafael was outraged, but his determination to free himself only made him sink deeper. He roared, snatching at the plants on either side, which simply pulled loose of the ground in his hands.

"Do not leave me, witch!" he bellowed, fearing even as he shouted that she would do just that.

The rope landed a footstep away from him. It was his own rope, the one he kept coiled upon one side of the saddle. Rafael recognized it well, including the knot at the end. He prayed that she had bound it securely to a tree, then gave it a tug. The rope pulled taut. It seemed that this witch had some mercy in her soul after all.

Perhaps she was not done with taunting him.

Rafael gritted his teeth at the sound of fading hoof beats, then hauled himself from the mud, hand over hand. By the time he reached solid ground, he was soaked and filthy, far from the camp and without either horse or dagger.

Rafael seized his sword, which was yet there, coiled up the rope and began to walk back to the camp. His boots made the most terrible sound as he walked and he was aware of the filth that covered his skin.

Maximilian would laugh.

Rafael would find this witch, sooner or later, and she would pay for her audacity.

One way or the other.

～

AMAURY RETURNED IN DRENCHING RAIN, only to find the camp nigh deserted. He settled Persephone on her perch in the tent he shared with Rafael, brushing her dry and hooding her there. She ruffled her feathers and fell asleep, as if tired from her adventures and glad to be back in his care.

Oliver was brushing down the horses and the dogs ran alongside Amaury when he went to check on the meat. There was no evading the fact that the camp was quiet, and the tents he peeked into were empty.

Where was everyone? The quiet made him uneasy.

He made his way to the clearing where the fire burned. The wooden framework they carried with them had been set up, and the length of canvas stretched far overhead. The contraption ensured that there could be a blaze, no matter the weather, and Amaury had never been more glad of Maximilian's foresight than on this day. He held his hands to the fire to warm them and shook the water out of his hair. The rainwater already gathered in footprints, turning the trodden paths between the tents to mud, and he knew the situation would have been far worse without the fire.

Denis, the cook, was not just pleased with the results from the hunt but nigh bursting with some secret tidings. Amaury recognized his expression well, and his wife was nigh the same. They said little, though, save for admiring his skill, which meant Yves had instructed them to hold their tongues.

Amaury did not have to wait long for the appearance of that man, who managed Maximilian's camp as if it were a massive keep. Yves, the former châtelain of Château de Vries and a man Amaury knew to be inexplicably fond of Maximilian, joined them promptly. Amaury thought 'twas to take an accounting of the kill, but Yves was uncommonly animated.

Perhaps he, too, hungered for a hot meal.

"Roast venison for the wedding feast," that man said with pleasure and much to Amaury's surprise. "'Twill be most appropriate."

Who would be wedded?

"I have yet some peppercorns and juniper berries," Denis confided. "The sauce will be magnificent."

"And there is a measure of flour still," his wife agreed. "Fresh bread for the trenchers. I can begin the dough tonight." The three of them beamed at each other and then at Amaury, whose efforts were making this special day complete.

"What nuptials?" he was compelled to ask.

"My lord Maximilian intends to take a bride," Yves said, his satisfaction most clear.

Amaury blinked. "He will wed?"

Who would Maximilian marry? There were few options. The maid, Nathalie, from de Vries was the sole candidate, to Amaury's thinking, but Maximilian had expressed no interest in that maiden thus far. Amaury was not even certain that his half-brother had noticed the younger woman—the notion that Maximilian suddenly felt compelled to marry her was inexplicable, if not irrational.

While Maximilian could be inscrutable, he was never irrational.

"Aye, and this very night," Yves confided. "He has ridden to collect the bride."

Amaury felt as if he been absent for far longer than part of a day. "From where?"

To his dismay, Yves gestured toward the forest.

Amaury could only recall the maiden with the dark auburn hair who had cared for Persephone. His heart clenched at the inevitable conclusion. Surely she could not be compelled to become his half-brother's wife?

And how did Maximilian even know of her presence? Maximilian was cursed perceptive, but this seemed too much, even for him.

"From the forest?" he echoed, as if he had not encountered a lovely damsel there himself and could scarce imagine women to live in such circumstance. He thought of the hut he had located with the aid of the dogs and the cut velvet bag yet secreted in his own leather purse and could not believe 'twould be as he feared.

"The one who defies him is Alys Armstrong," Denis provided, falling silent at a piercing glance from Yves.

"She will defy him no longer once they are wed in truth," that man chided. "'Twould be most unsuitable. The match, however, is *parfait*. She is the daughter and sole child of the last laird, and my lord holds the seal. Together, they will rebuild Kilderrick."

"But that would mean that Maximilian killed her father," Amaury protested. "Surely she will not welcome a match with him." This, he felt, was an understatement of the greatest magnitude, but Yves waved it aside.

"If she is keen of wit, she will see that she has little choice. Even if she is not keen of wit, she must recognize that her life will be better as my lord's wife than as a savage in the forest." Yves' silver brows drew together. "Yet I think she is not a fool. That feat of last eve that interrupted our journey was most cleverly contrived."

Amaury frowned, unable to reconcile an intent to rob with the caring nature of the maiden who had sheltered Persephone.

Oblivious to the knight's concerns, Yves gestured to a plump couple of middle years who watched them avidly. They were so still and silent that Amaury had not noticed them earlier. They were seated on the far side of the fire, yet not quite beneath the protective canopy. Their backs had to be in the rain, yet they did naught about it. Amaury guessed by their postures that their hands were bound behind their backs. The woman was rounder than the man, while he was ruddy with outrage. "My lord brought the sheriff and his wife to witness the nuptials," Yves said. "As is right and proper."

How like Maximilian to show concern with key details like the legality of the match but disregard both his intended bride's perspective and that of this couple. Clearly, they had been brought against their will to provide service to the newly declared Laird of Kilderrick.

How like Yves to believe that Maximilian could do naught amiss.

The couple looked between the group, their suspicion and lack of comprehension most clear.

"They do not speak Norman French?" Amaury asked Yves.

"He seems to understand more, though he contrives to hide as much," Yves said. The man averted his gaze with haste, proving the truth of that. "She speaks only that vulgar tongue with him."

Gaelic, the language of the isles and Ireland to the west. Amaury nodded. He found it incomprehensible, but then he had never tried to learn, even as the sound of it became more prevalent on their journey.

"Have Murdoch listen to them," he advised Yves in an undertone, turning his back upon the couple. "Without revealing himself."

Yves smiled. "He is already hidden in the tent behind them, at my instruction." The older man took a deep breath, disapproval emanating from his every pore. "'Twas time enough, to my thinking, that the Scotsman earned his place in this company."

"He has a place because Maximilian invited him."

"But I know not why, sir." Yves shook his head. "I know not why."

Amaury did not know why either, but he had long ago ceased to try to understand Maximilian's choices. His half-brother treated life like a game of chess, and any objective could be years in the future.

He lingered a little longer, but learned no more about Maximilian's intended bride. Concerned for the fate of the maiden and unable to do much about it, Amaury went to tend his steeds and await Maximilian's return, all the while wondering what he might do to save the damsel with the auburn hair.

MAXIMILIAN DID NOT KNOW how much time passed before he discerned a footfall. The sky was darker, the rain having settling into a steady downpour, and the thunder having moved east. He heard a second step and his blood quickened.

Alys had come.

There was a faint movement in the forest, a shadow against the shadows, and Maximilian smiled.

"Elizabeth?" a woman asked softly. Her voice was low, a little husky, and he suspected it was more sultry than she realized.

"I am unhurt, Alys. I am sorry! He said he would release me if I called you."

"You are not free of him yet." Alys was wary, and rightly so. Maximilian respected that she had the wits to understand his trade and his likely choices. She had a slight accent to his ear, an echo of the north in her vowels, though she spoke the Norman French of the English aristocracy to this Elizabeth.

Robert Armstrong must have seen his daughter educated. The tidings improved with every passing moment.

Maximilian tired of standing in the rain, though, and wished to hasten events to their inevitable conclusion. He pulled his knife and touched it to his captive's throat. She gave a very satisfying and audible gasp of fear. He moved closer to Alys, into a small clearing, this Elizabeth captive before him. Though the rain drummed upon him with vigor, he knew his blade gleamed at his captive's throat.

Though Alys did not utter a sound, the air became taut.

"How much will you surrender to deny me, Alys?" he asked, appealing to the loyalty she must feel to her comrades. She had come to Elizabeth's aid, after all. "I have no care for this one's life, if that is the price you would pay." He let his voice drop low. "Or we could savor other pleasures first."

"Alys!" his captive cried in panic.

"What do you want?" Alys demanded, still disguised in the shadows.

"I have told you. We will wed. I will rebuild Kilderrick with you as my wife."

"Why?" She was clearly skeptical of his claim.

"Because a man has need of a home." He paused then continued. "And a son."

She spat then and he fought a smile when he heard the projectile land.

"I will not wed you and I will not bed you," she said with cold fury.

"I will not conceive a child by you and bring another demon into this sorry world."

"And I grow weary of the rain. Surrender, Alys."

"Nay!"

"I do not lose, Alys," he informed her. "You of all people should know that."

"And I do not surrender to villainy."

"But if you cede to me now, your friend will survive unscathed. Otherwise, I can make no guarantee." He moved the knife slightly, letting it nick the woman's skin and draw a bit of blood. Her gasp was filled with unmistakable terror, but Alys did not move. He could feel her outrage, crackling across the clearing, and if she had truly possessed dark powers, Maximilian knew he would have been struck dead already.

"Villain and cur," she muttered, clearly caught between her desires.

"The choice, my Alys, is yours."

"I am not your Alys," she said hotly as she stepped into the clearing. He surveyed her cloaked figure, greedy for details. She was tall for a woman but shorter than him. She was slender, too, and her voice echoed with a resolve he admired. "I will never be your Alys, yet you will not injure my friends." She marched toward him, so fearless that his heart leaped, then halted when she stood four steps before him. "Release her," she commanded. "Release her *now*."

"Nay, Alys. Those are not my terms." Maximilian let his voice harden. "You will agree to be my bride and then I will release her."

"I will never be your wife," she retorted. "But declining the match will be *your* choice."

Maximilian did not understand. He frowned and shook his head.

Alys leaned closer, her voice dropping low, but he could not discern her features within the shadows of the hood. "Even you will not want me once you see what you have done. Release her now or I will leave her to you."

"Alys!"

Intrigued by her feint, Maximilian released his grip upon the other woman. Elizabeth seized the opportunity and ran, her footsteps crashing through the forest as she fled to safety.

"Show me," Maximilian commanded of the cloaked figure before him.

Alys flung back her hood, revealing herself to him for the first time. She stood straight, chin high, challenge in her posture, eyes snapping.

Her hair was bound back, but Maximilian could see it was as dark as a raven's wing and wavy. Her eyes were clear and green. On her right side, she was a beauty, her features perfectly formed, her lips full and her gaze steady. The other side of her face was deeply scarred. There was no avoiding the truth of her wound. She had been burned and badly, her cheek and temple disfigured by the injury. The flesh remained red and puckered. Maximilian guessed that the injury extended beneath her clothing. She was both beauty and monster, and part of him wanted to shudder and retreat.

But that was exactly what Alys expected. He could tell by the challenge in her gaze.

The better part of him admired her valor. She was unarmed. She faced him with only her bravery and her wound, for the sake of her comrade's survival, and Maximilian was both surprised and impressed. He had never met a woman of such spirit and resolve—but he understood this one as well as if he had known her a lifetime. She would use any means to gain the end she desired, yet she was loyal to those she defended. Principled, fierce and bold.

She was like him.

Aye, Alys Armstrong would suit him well as a bride.

He sheathed his knife, then stepped forward to catch her face in his hands. He felt her astonishment, but looked deeply into her eyes as he drew her closer, ensuring that his expression was filled only with the admiration he already felt for her.

"You gambled and lost," he said softly, seeing the flicker of trepidation in her gaze. "You will be my Alys, and I will ensure that you come to be glad of it."

Then he kissed her, a conquering and triumphant kiss intended to set her blood afire.

It certainly lit a flame within his own.

∼

He was undaunted.

The Silver Wolf did not care that Alys was scarred.

He did not care that she was disfigured, much less that she was filthy.

Indeed, he kissed her as if he intended to claim her right then and there, in the clearing, in the rain. Alys was so shocked by his reaction that she did not step away, then his mouth was locked over hers and she was nigh overwhelmed. She had never been kissed by a man, not like this, not a seductive, bewitching kiss that melted her knees and drove all reason from her thoughts.

There was only pleasure, glorious, irresistible pleasure. God in Heaven, who had known that a man's kiss could be so wondrous as this?

He held her captive to his embrace, his gloved hands framing her face. The leather was cool and wet against her skin, his grip perfectly calculated to hold her but not to injure her. It was curious indeed to feel treasured, no less to have this man be the one to treat her as a prize. The Silver Wolf lifted her slightly, so that she was on her toes, and feasted upon her mouth as if she had been wrought for his pleasure. She found herself responding to his touch before she had another thought—then realized his ploy.

She *was* a prize, one he would use for his own satisfaction.

Alys tore her mouth from his with an effort, found that she backed into a tree, and glared at him. "Fiend," she spat. "Despoiler and blackguard."

His pale eyes gleamed, so pale a blue that they might have been silver, and his mouth curved into a smile of satisfaction. Aye, he was handsome, wickedly so. Those eyes seemed to peruse the depths of her very soul. Alys felt as if all her secrets were revealed to him—and knew he would use them against her. She averted her gaze, her breath coming quickly.

"A fine beginning, my Alys," he murmured, reaching to pull her close again.

Alys struck him before he could repeat that loathesome endearment, and the crack of her palm echoed in the clearing. She shoved him hard, then watched him warily when she realized she could not retreat.

A little too late, she was horrified at what he might do in retaliation for her impulsive move. A little too late, she wondered why he had allowed himself to be pushed aside. There could be no good reckoning from this. The rain poured down, cold and relentless, as their gazes held.

She braced herself for a blow but his eyes only darkened. His lips tightened into a line of resolve that sent fear through her, then he snatched at her with astonishing speed. He seized her elbow and spun to march her back toward the camp, half dragging her beside him. He was taller than she and lifted her, ensuring that she could not get a good footing—or wrench herself free. Alys was keenly aware of his power and strength, yet also that he did not hurt her.

He must not like his women bruised. It could not be that he had a care for her welfare.

She struggled against his grip, even knowing it was futile, as thorns tore at her ragged kirtle. He moved with resolute purpose, undeterred by either her lack of cooperation or any obstacle before them. He marched directly through the thickest tangle of undergrowth, then strode into the river, undeterred.

"Wretch and cur," she muttered, trying to wrest her arm free of his grip. "You do not mean to wed me. You will despoil me before your entire cursed company, then compel me to watch as they do the same to my friends."

"I have told you my intention," he replied. His tone was calm but Alys sensed that he spoke through gritted teeth. There certainly was a tension within him. "I am many things, my Alys, but I am not a liar."

She did not believe him. "Vermin and devil-spawn. Of course, you lie."

"'Tis as if you believe you know me already," he agreed easily and she spun, striving to kick him. He was not surprised: indeed, he might have anticipated her move. He swept her off her feet in one smooth gesture and cast her over his shoulder, as readily as if she were a small child or a sack of grain.

"All know your repute, and I know its truth better than most," she said vehemently, wriggling with all her might. He held her in place so easily that she fumed all the more.

"Do not make me bind you," he continued with the even tone that already infuriated her. He forded the river as he held her firmly. "It offers a poor prospect of our future happiness."

"There is *no* prospect of future happiness," she retorted, aiming a kick at his groin. Her knee instead struck his chain mail hauberk and it was every bit as hard as she should have expected. "Not if I am compelled to wed a villain such as you."

"And yet for all my dark repute, you do not fear to provoke me," he mused. "It appears that you do not believe me to be so wicked as that."

"Or I am convinced that I have naught to lose."

"But so much to gain, my Alys." He swung her down into his arms as he reached the other bank, his gaze boring into hers. "You live in dirt and squalor, undefended and likely hungry most days."

"I—" she began to argue, but he continued, his tone steely.

"I have sufficient wealth to rebuild Kilderrick, and for you to live in comparative comfort with regular meals. Surely that has some appeal."

He lied about rebuilding the keep, Alys was certain of it. The cost would be exorbitant and she could not believe he meant to stay in this one place for the remainder of his days.

But she guessed that if she challenged that, he would simply insist that he told no lie.

Time would prove her right—if indeed, she had time.

"You demand too much in exchange for food and shelter," she protested, her panic rising even as she strove to disguise it.

"I offer more than that. No one touches what I claim as my own and lives to tell of it." His eyes flashed with a resolve that sent an unwelcome thrill through her. "As my wife and mother of my children, you will be safe, safer even than a queen."

"And now there are children," Alys said, unable to think immediately of another protest. "But moments ago, you wished only one son."

His smile flashed, brilliant and unexpected. God in heaven, he was a handsome brute—and he knew it well. His gaze lingered on her warmly, as if he found her pleasing, although Alys knew that had to be a lie. "Aye, I suspect that our union will be a most fruitful one, in many ways."

Alys seethed that he mocked her so. She glowered at him, even as he carried her toward the camp in triumph. What could she do? He whistled and his black destrier whinnied. It cantered after him and halted, nostrils flaring, ears flicking. Its reins were trailing but it heeded his call, nuzzling him with obvious affection when it drew near. It was a fine steed, and she recalled her father's conviction that horses were the best judges of men.

She would not be swayed.

The rest of his company emerged from the camp with their steeds, all sodden to their very skin. They looked as if they had recently returned from the forest. She could smell something delicious, perhaps a roast pheasant, and her stomach growled a reminder of its emptiness.

"Ceara?" she shouted. "Nyssa?"

"Your friends have not joined us this night," her captor said smoothly.

"Good."

"Would they not have liked to witness your nuptials?" he murmured, and she glanced up to find those eyes shining in the darkness.

He made a jest at her expense and Alys knew it. Once again, anger replaced her fear. She was the one in peril: her companions would be safe this night in the hut.

She alone could see herself saved.

The sheriff and his wife were led to the clearing, their expressions disgruntled though they appeared to be unhurt. The company of men awaited the Silver Wolf's command, half mounted on horseback, half standing beside their steeds. They were garbed in dark cloaks and clearly armed. Most had a helmet beneath their arm; all wore chain mail that fell to their knees. They all had to be wet and cold, but they stood at attention, waiting.

As did the group of villagers or common people, the ones who had ridden in the wagon. They were not armed or guarded, and seemed to be led by a tall, slender man with silver hair. They were not bound or shackled, but Alys had to guess that they were captives. To what end? Would the Silver Wolf ransom them or keep them as slaves?

"Did I not promise you a wedding?" he asked of Jeannie, the sheriff's wife, his tone amiable. Jeannie was pale, but 'twould take more than uncertainty to silence her wagging tongue.

"Aye, my lord," that woman replied.

"There must be a more appealing location for the exchange of marriage vows."

"There is a chapel in Rowan Fell," Jeannie said. "Though the priest is likely asleep at this late hour."

The Silver Wolf shook his head. "Nay, I will not return there just yet."

"Then there can be no nuptials for we have no priest," Alys reminded him.

He lifted a brow, managing to look both charming and diabolical. "Marriage is the sole sacrament that does not require a priest, my Alys. Surely I do not know the catechism better than you? We have need only of witnesses, which I have supplied. We can seek a blessing at a later date."

She was sorely tempted to do something to surprise this man, to shake his confidence if not destroy him. He smiled at her, so confident that she despised him, so alluring that it was obscene he possessed a nature so wicked.

Could she lure him to a trap? Alys had to try. She truly had naught to lose.

"The Ninestang Ring," she said. "It is a place of majesty and power, as befits the making of a vow." She met his gaze, ensuring there was a dare in her expression.

"A place of sorcery and wickedness," Jeannie fumed.

Alys smiled at the Silver Wolf. "If you dare to force a witch to take your hand there."

"The Ninestang Ring 'twill be," her captor agreed. He lifted Alys to the front of his steed's saddle and the destrier stamped. Alys clutched at the beast, unaccustomed as she was to riding, but noted that he kept a firm grip on the reins. Doubtless the creature would not move without his command.

Doubtless even the horse feared his retaliation.

The Silver Wolf then swung into the saddle behind her. He locked an arm around her waist, holding her tightly against his muscled strength. Despite herself, Alys recalled that kiss and felt an unwelcome reaction to his touch. "The sheriff and his wife, of course, are cordially invited to attend as witnesses, as well as Yves." The silver-haired man bowed, and Alys wondered again at his role in this company. The Silver Wolf pointed to two others. "Amaury, you will ride with us, and you, Matteo." The first, Alys thought, was the fair man she had watched ride to hunt that morning. The second was the slender one with dark hair who had accompanied the Silver Wolf earlier in the day, evidently to Rowan Fell. "Bring the witnesses." The dark-haired mercenary turned and barked what were clearly commands. He might have spoken Norman French but his words were so quick and clipped that Alys could make no sense of them.

Two boys loaded the sheriff and his wife onto palfreys so that they rode like sacks of grain. Jeannie moaned, but no one paid her any heed. If she had ridden all the way from Rowan Fell slung over a saddle, Alys could imagine the reason for her pallor.

The rain fell steadily but with less vigor and the skies rumbled overhead. The brunt of the storm had moved east, the lightning cracking now in the distance.

When all were assembled, the Silver Wolf touched his spurs to the destrier's flanks. The creature galloped to the north at unholy speed and Alys clutched at his mane.

The ring of ancient stones was not far away and soon, soon she would be liberated from this man. Their traps were not solely in the forest, for there was one at the Ninestang Ring. Soon she would be free again.

Would she offer the Silver Wolf a deal in exchange for his freedom? The very notion was so audacious that it made her smile. 'Twas tempting to match wits with him, but Alys knew that would be a dangerous game.

Nay, she should just leave him to die, as he had once abandoned her to do.

This wretch deserved no less.

CHAPTER 5

*A*lys had a scheme.

Maximilian would have wagered his right hand upon it. Nay, he would have wagered his soul. Her sudden compliance could mean naught else. He was intrigued and curious, and guessed it had something to do with this Ninestang Ring. The sheriff had sharpened to attention at the mention of it, as well, so there was some detail known to locals but not to Maximilian.

He guessed any discovery would not be to his advantage.

He doubted it had much to do with witches or sorcery.

He rode ahead of the others, ignoring the rain and the darkness. The choice appeared reckless or confident, and would convince Alys that he was persuaded of her willingness. In truth, he trusted Tempest to find a path. And he would not sleep in this woman's presence in the foreseeable future. Her hatred of him ran deep and he wondered what her wound had cost her. A specific suitor? Any marriage at all? A life better than the one she led in this wilderness?

Maximilian did not know but he would find out.

The Ninestang Ring proved to be a circle of standing stones, not unlike many others he had seen in his days. This ring was large in diameter, though, so large that he might not have realized it was a ring, especially on a rainy night. The stones were broad and tall, though he could only discern five of their jagged peaks pointed at the sky.

"Before that one," Alys said, indicating the largest one, which sat on a bit of a rise. "It is the leader."

"The leader of the stones?" he asked, letting his tone turn mocking.

She stiffened slightly. "It is the focus of power. It is the place to exchange a vow or make a pledge. We have a local custom in that."

"I see. Then it is a most fitting choice." The ground was rough underfoot, rife with ragged growth mixed with stones and fallen leaves that must have blown from the nearby forest. The air seemed colder in the midst of the circle, the wind was suddenly still, and the rain fell with greater intensity. A superstitious man might have felt a foreboding, but Maximilian thought only of the welfare of his horse.

He dismounted, aware that the others were approaching, and lifted Alys from the saddle. He took her hand in his and watched her lips set with fury at his familiarity. The very fact that she did not recoil from him or try to pull away was another hint that she plotted against him. All the same, he enjoyed the weight of her hand in his as they walked together toward the stone. It could have been companionable, had she not hated him to her very marrow.

This conquest would be sweet indeed.

Maximilian let her lead slightly, fairly inviting her to show him the trap. As they approached the stone, she halted suddenly and stumbled, her hand slipping from his grasp. "Ah! A sharp pebble!" she said, bending to feel beneath her boot. She clearly expected him to take another step, but Maximilian was not fooled. He scanned the distance between them and the large stone, but saw naught amiss.

Then he noticed that the scrub was flatter before the stone, as if it had been placed there apurpose. And the ground was dry in the stone's shadow, as if the rain could not form a puddle.

He heard a faint drip and knew there was a pit trap.

His intended grew more fascinating with every passing moment. What a clever and scheming creature she was!

How perfectly they were matched.

Maximilian made to take that step. Alys suddenly jumped to the left, jerking her hand from his grip. Maximilian grinned that he had guessed her intent. He moved like lightning, seizing her around the waist then taking the next step. If he fell into a pit, she could accompany him.

They might come to terms in the darkness.

There was nothing under his foot but a layer of dried plants. It gave way immediately and Maximilian tumbled into the hole, Alys fighting his grip furiously as he bore her down into the darkness with him.

"Nay!" she cried. "*Nay!*"

He held her weight above him, even as she beat her fists on his chest, and grunted when he landed on his backside at the bottom of the hole. There was straw there, but not enough of it to soften the fall. A dank puddle of rainwater splashed as he landed and soaked the back of his tabard. He winced at the impact and knew that he would have another bruise as souvenir of this courtship. The cold water slid under his garb to touch his skin and he shivered.

Alys was perched atop him, which was not objectionable, though she scrambled to her feet and moved away from him. "Wretch!" she spat and kicked at him, sending another volley of cold water cascading over him. Maximilian fought the urge to laugh at her outrage.

The patch of light, such as it was, was far above their heads. They must have fallen more than twenty feet. The impact felt as if it had been at least that far. He stood, brushed himself off, then reached out to explore their prison. There was smooth stone on all sides. It had been built a long time before. The water rose to his ankles, so it must drain somehow. That was a relief, given the intensity of the rain.

"Cur!" Alys cried, flailing in the darkness in his general direction and managing only to strike his arm. "Look at what you have done."

"I understand I was to be here alone."

"Of course, you were." She took a shuddering breath. "Fiend."

"Are you injured?"

"Nay."

"You knew this was here."

"All know it," she said with scorn. "'Tis an old burial pit."

"And an efficient trap." Maximilian doffed his gloves, tucking them into his belt. He found the flint in his purse by feel and struck it, touching it to a twist of cloth he also carried. In his trade, it was best to be prepared for all contingencies.

The flickering light was sufficient to illuminate their prison, though it would not last, for the cloth was small. 'Twas intended to be a wick not a lantern. The space was perhaps as wide on a side as a man was tall, made of fitted stone. Above the highest point he could reach, it was packed earth, so smooth that it would be impossible to find a foothold and climb out of it.

Maximilian walked around the perimeter, avoiding the deepest puddle in the middle, aware of the sound of Alys' breathing. There was no way out, save the way they had entered the pit, and he suspected the pile of debris in one corner included the bones of an unfortunate creature. He held up his makeshift candle and saw that Alys' eyes were wide, then the flame touched his fingertips and he cast the cloth into the puddle. The light went out and she inhaled sharply.

Was she afraid of him or of darkness?

Thus far, she had shown little fear of him. Maximilian guessed that darkness was the culprit—and then he guessed why. "Where were you?" he asked.

"When?" she demanded with suspicion but he thought she understood.

"That night at Kilderrick." He stood opposite her, leaning back against the wall, confident that she could not flee. "I did not intend to leave a single soul alive."

"You erred." 'Twas clear that pleased her.

"Where were you?" he asked again.

"In the cellar," she confessed.

"I checked the cellar."

"Not well enough," she said in that challenging tone.

Maximilian recalled the cellar, the casks of wine, the vessel of oil that had been so very useful in lighting the blaze, the walls that had been similar to these. He revisited it in his memory, the details as clear as if he stood there anew.

"The sack of cloth," he said finally. "The one the old castellan insisted was empty." Aye, Maximilian recalled that the man's vehemence had made him doubt that statement, but then the laird had screamed from the chamber above.

Perhaps they had acted together to defend the laird's daughter.

Perhaps it had been only coincidence.

"It was not." Alys' hostility seemed more vehement in the darkness.

He nodded. "I secured that door from the outside, because I did not believe him."

"I know." Her tone was bitter. "And his name was Rupert."

Maximilian recalled the fury of the fire, the brilliant flames licking against the night as he stood and watched. "How did you survive?"

"Does it matter?"

"I am curious."

"Because you failed."

"Because you challenge expectations. I should like to know how."

For a moment, he thought she would not reply. He could feel the crackle of her anger with him, and could not blame her for it.

"The ceiling collapsed," she said finally. "The floor above burned through and I managed to crawl out." She exhaled shakily, perhaps revisiting that night in her own memory. It must have been an inferno. He was impressed by her bravery yet again. "I had to climb so far. I did not think I would live to tell of it."

"But you did," Maximilian said quietly.

"But everyone else was dead," she replied. "I saw my father's corpse the next day."

Ah, it had been burned to cinders, barely recognizable. That was no sight for a child, and Maximilian would have spared her, if he had known she lived.

What would he have done with Alys if he had found her? He had not been much more than a child himself, not even twenty summers of age, filled with his father's venom and rage.

Perhaps it was better for her that he had not discovered her, but he doubted Alys would believe that readily. Her disfigurement troubled her and again he wondered at its price.

"How old were you?" he asked.

"Ten summers."

He felt his brows rise, so impressed was he with her endurance. At ten summers, though, she would have been womanly enough to tempt some of his father's company who had ridden with him. The burn might have been the lesser price. "Who tended your injuries?"

"Where is it writ that anyone did?"

"I doubt you would have survived otherwise."

"Do not assume my weakness."

Maximilian smiled. He would never do that. "Do you believe in Fate, my Alys?"

She laughed, a harsh sound. "Nay."

"But I do."

"Then you are a superstitious fool."

"But you are the one pretending to be a witch."

"I do not pretend."

Maximilian shrugged. "I do not believe in witchery, but I believe in Fate."

She snorted.

He continued, knowing she could not see his smile. "I see purpose in events that others believe to be chance. I find intention in the world."

"How can you see purpose of any kind in this situation?"

"I suggest to you that you survived that night so we might wed on this night, that I might make amends to you for the rest of my days and nights."

She scoffed. "'Tis no secret that I hope they are few in number."

Maximilian laughed. "Nay, it is not."

"Indeed, if you insist upon this folly, I will do whatsoever I can to end your life with all haste." There was fury in her voice, fury and hatred, but that audacity again intrigued him.

"I would expect no less."

"But you do not fear my vengeance. Is that because I am a woman?"

"Nay." Maximilian did not tell her all of the truth. "It is simply that I take the conquest of your heart as a challenge, my Alys. You should be warned that I always triumph."

"Then you should be warned that you will soon learn to accept defeat," she countered. "My heart is not available to be conquered by you."

Maximilian smiled, thinking that a kiss would seal their respective threats well. He took a step toward his intended and could fairly feel her steely glare.

Sadly, a bit of dirt crumbled down from the opening above in that very moment and he knew they had company.

"Maximilian?" Amaury called, his silhouette appearing in the square of the hole. "Are you hale?"

"Hale enough," Maximilian replied heartily. "My intended is also hale."

"I thought you might have climbed out by now."

"But the company is superb."

Amaury audibly stifled a laugh. Alys fairly seethed.

"I have sent Oliver back for a rope," Amaury supplied.

"Excellent. And in the meantime, I see no reason to delay the exchange of our vows." Maximilian reached for Alys in the darkness and found her hand, pulling her toward him so that they faced each other in the darkness. Her left hand was in his right, his left in her right.

"Not here," she muttered.

"Aye, here," he insisted. "'Twill pass the time most amiably."

"I think not."

"Then we shall agree to disagree, my Alys."

'Twould be an unconventional exchange of vows for a match that Maximilian suspected would be unusual indeed.

He could not wait to embark upon this adventure.

❧

FATE.

Justice.

The Silver Wolf sounded like Morag, which had to mean that he tried to deceive her—despite his insistence that he did not lie.

Of course, he lied. His trade was in falsehood, theft and violence. That he was handsome meant naught about his character: that he was clearly affluent meant he excelled at his chosen trade. His deeds spoke more loudly than his words, and he had captured her to force her to wed him. It seemed a whimsical choice for a man of war, but who knew how many women he had claimed thus. And what happened to them once they were despoiled? Did he cast them aside? Or did he wait until 'twas clear whether his chosen prey would bear him a son or not?

Alys did not want to know.

Maximilian. What a name he possessed. It sounded princely, almost noble. She was surprised to realize that she knew little about him other than his moniker, the Silver Wolf. How had he become a mercenary—and why? Where was he from? Why had he returned to Kilderrick? Indeed, why had he come in the first place all those years before? Who were these men who followed him—and why did they do as much? Alys knew it was folly to be curious, but told herself it was best to know her enemy. It might provide her a notion of his weaknesses.

If indeed he had any.

The sheriff recited the wedding vows from above their prison, his reluctance resonant in every word. The Silver Wolf repeated them, then Alys did as well, having no other choice. Maximilian de Vries was his name, as lordly a name as might have been held by any baron. Alys blinked at that, but held her tongue.

The marriage had to be a farce. It had to be a jest, and one at her expense. But the Silver Wolf removed something from his purse when their vows were made, locating it by touch. He slid a cool circle of metal onto the middle finger of her left hand, as surely as if he could see her fingers.

A ring. He carried a ring, evidently prepared for the taking of a wife. He did not even flinch at her ravaged flesh, though he had to have felt that her left hand could have been that of a dragon.

How many predecessors did she have in this?

"Do you always have a wedding ring at the ready?" she asked sweetly and he chuckled.

"I took it from my father's treasury, along with the seal of Kilderrick."

"Why?"

"A bride and a son, my Alys. 'Tis not complicated."

She itched to look at the ring. She could feel that it was broad and when she ran a fingertip across it, there seemed to be an inscription. It was heavy, an unfamiliar weight on her hand, and a most unwelcome reminder of her newfound status. She would not see Fate in the fact that it fit her perfectly, much less imagine that their match was destined to be.

Alys knew what had to follow the ceremony to make the marriage complete.

Her destiny was not sealed yet.

She turned away from his inevitable kiss, but the Silver Wolf caught her chin between finger and thumb, compelling her to face him. She could fairly feel his gaze boring into hers, though the warmth of his hand sent an awareness through her that she could have done without.

"I have never forced a woman, Alys," he said softly and she wished it might be true.

"I doubt as much," she whispered.

"Then let me convince you to meet me halfway," he said, touching his lips to hers. She caught her breath, fully expecting him to catch her close in a crushing kiss like his previous thrilling one, but he teased her with a light touch.

That startled her and once again, her delay made his ploy possible. He brushed his mouth over hers, once, twice, three times, his caress as soft as a butterfly in the darkness. Alys felt herself shiver with anticipation, then he kissed her temple with gentle heat. He kissed her ear, the fleeting touch of his mouth against her skin heating her anew, the quick flick of his tongue making her catch her breath. The darkness seemed to make it possible to surrender to temptation, to commit a secret deed without any soul knowing of it. When his mouth returned to hers again, Alys found her lips parting, seemingly of their own volition, opening beneath his as if to invite him onward.

She softened to him, but told herself it was wise to let him believe her to be tamed. In truth, she could not have denied either of them the kiss that followed.

It was exquisitely pleasurable and fed a shocking desire within Alys for more.

"Hoy there!" someone shouted from overhead, a rougher voice than the first mercenary. A rope suddenly came tumbling down from above, and the Silver Wolf stepped back, letting the knotted end fall into the puddle.

Alys found herself yet clinging to his shoulders and snatched her hands away.

His chuckle made her yearn to strike him anew.

"It is secured to the stone," that man said from above and the Silver Wolf gave it a tug.

The rope smelled of a familiar mix of mud and mire, reminding Alys of Ceara's choice.

"It smells of the fen," she said.

"Aye, the rope is wet, but it will still suffice."

"You said my friends were not captive," she said, thinking to catch him in a lie. She fairly felt the sharpening of the Silver Wolf's attention.

"Why is the fen of import, my Alys?" he asked in a dangerous whisper, one that made the hair stand up on the back of her neck.

"Where is Ceara? If she has been injured, I will grant you naught," she said with fury. "If you have lied about her captivity, I will surrender naught."

The air simmered between them, then she felt the Silver Wolf step back. "Rafael!" he shouted. "Tell me the fate of my lady wife's comrade."

The man swore softly. "She led me into a swamp and stole my destrier."

"Did you catch her?"

"Nay, she was as slippery as an eel," Rafael admitted with obvious annoyance. "And as lovely as the dawn."

"Then it is clear how she lured you," the Silver Wolf said, prompting his companion's reluctant chuckle. "It appears that Ceara is fine, Alys, and in possession of a fine steed."

Alys could not halt her smile of satisfaction.

The Silver Wolf's voice dropped low. "But I warn you that if any harm comes to Phantôm, I will not be able to halt Rafael's revenge."

Alys shivered. "Ceara knows much of horses."

He was silent for a long moment and she could fairly feel his gaze upon her. "And now the choice is yours, my Alys."

"Suddenly, I am offered a choice?"

She heard him chuckle. "I told you that I would ensure your comfort and security, and told you also that I do not lie. Choose whether you will climb or whether I will carry you.

The prospect of him touching her was enough to make Alys reach in the darkness in search of the rope. "I can climb."

"Of that I have no doubt," he said mildly and guided her hand to the rope. It was taut, as if he stood on the end to steady it. Alys felt the knots, which were at regular intervals.

"Will this Rafael betray you?" She had to ask.

"He is my blood brother, sworn to my cause, so, nay, he will not."

Brothers. Alys would never have guessed as much but her new husband's confidence was total. Perhaps they had saved each other before. Perhaps even a mercenary had to trust someone. She gripped the rope and began to climb, locking her ankles around it as she pulled herself upward.

The sole good detail was that her newfound spouse could not look up her skirts.

FINALLY, they would escape this infernal rain.

Maximilian was glad to see the fire burning with gusto when they approached the ruin of Kilderrick, for he knew there would be a hot meal. He would be glad even of clear soup after this night, so long as it was hot, but he could smell roasted meat, which was better. He was aware of Alys' surprise but uncertain of the reason for it. Was she surprised that they had the means to nurture a blaze in the rain, or by the beguiling scent of food being prepared? Maximilian could have eaten an entire boar himself after this day—and he had eaten the day before. Had Alys?

"But..." she began, then fell silent.

Reynaud appeared and Maximilian dismounted, aware that Alys took note of the bustle of activity in their makeshift village. Rafael, 'twas clear, had only a minor injury—beyond the more considerable blow to his pride.

He argued briefly with Maximilian about encouraging Alys to admit the location of the women's refuge, his word quick and rough in dialect that Alys clearly did not follow.

"You will not touch my lady wife," Maximilian said coldly, speaking so that Alys would understand. She turned to him in alarm, her gaze flicking to Rafael in obvious trepidation.

"I could convince her to tell..."

Maximilian drew his dagger and lowered his voice. "You will not touch my lady wife."

Rafael exhaled and stepped back, eyes flashing. "I will return the sheriff and wife to Rowan Fell, then, if you will spare me a steed."

"Aye."

Rafael departed with Matteo, purpose in his step.

"How good to know that I will be defended like a valued possession," Alys said with vexation. "Will that still apply if I fail to grant you a son in time?"

"'Tis good for you to know," Maximilian agreed, ignoring her second question. "Rafael is most adept at torture."

"Are not all of you?"

He shook his head. "I do not share his gift of persuasion with force, although I can be encouraging."

"'Tis reprehensible," she muttered in disapproval. She considered her surroundings with obvious distaste.

Maximilian let the comment pass. He could have argued with Alys at every turn, but would try to choose his battles. He led her toward his own tent and Nathalie met them at the opening with a smile and a curtsey. Yves, it seemed, had anticipated them. The maid carried folded garments on her hands, then offered them to Alys with another curtsey.

"'Tis the best I possess, my lady," she said. "And I pray it will be of use to you."

Alys did not move.

Maximilian did not admire bad manners or a lack of grace. "She offers her best garb to you, as you are now her lady," he said with quiet heat. In truth, Nathalie would have expectations in return, but he would discuss that later with Alys if she failed to realize as much herself.

"I cannot take them," Alys said with pride. The maid's gaze flicked between them worriedly. "She does not owe me a gift..."

"Yet she offers it of her own choice and you will not insult any soul in this camp," Maximilian said softly. "Surely you do not wish to don your own garb again after your bath when it so needs to be cleaned?"

She turned to look at him, surprise lighting her features. "What bath?"

Maximilian smiled as he swept open the flap of his tent. As anticipated, two braziers burned, emitting golden light and a palpable heat. The bed was piled with furs, and before it was a leather tub, filled with steaming water. "Perhaps Nathalie could be of assistance to you," he said, indicating the maid. The maid smiled and curtseyed again, her gaze fixed worriedly upon Alys.

Alys blinked rapidly, obviously trying to hide her surprise. "I thought you would sleep on the ground."

"I am no barbarian, my Alys."

She swallowed, her gaze dancing to the girl. "Nathalie?" she said, attempting to pronounce the name in the French way.

"*Oui*, madame," the maid replied, her delight clear. She began to chatter, explaining how she hoped the temperature of the water was right, for she had been compelled to guess both her lady's preference and the timing of her return. Alys took a step across the threshold, clearly drawn by the lure of the bath.

"I suggest your garb be burned," Maximilian said, even more aware of its filth now that they were in slightly better light.

"But I could not take her garments..."

"You will buy her better garb."

"But I have no right..."

"She offers it," Maximilian said, interrupting firmly. "We are a company, who survive because we share our resources and labor together. These people are neither my vassals nor my servants."

"Slaves," Alys hissed, her eyes flashing. She was magnificent, even in squalor. Maximilian could not wait to see her garbed fittingly.

"Nay," he said. "They each have their place, but they have chosen willingly to join my company. I defend them, I see to their welfare to the best of my abilities and they, in turn, contribute to our survival and our success. On this night, you have need of clothing. Nathalie has offered her garb to my bride. You will accept and repay her kindness as soon as possible."

Alys blinked. She looked between the two of them, apparently skeptical, then was evidently reassured by Nathalie's smile. "I thank you," she said, bowing her head to Nathalie, whose smile broadened when Alys took the garments. She ran an admiring hand across the pale blue wool of the kirtle. "Very pretty."

"*Jolie*," Maximilian contributed, to Nathalie's obvious pleasure. "*Très jolie*."

This launched Nathalie upon another lecture, about the cloth having come from Ghent. She urged Alys into the tent, shaking a playful finger at Maximilian, then closed the flap against the night. He heard her comments upon Alys' dirty kirtle and worn boots and thought it likely a good thing that his feisty bride could not fully understand the extent of the maid's disdain.

He resolved to discover what Denis had concocted for the evening meal while his lady bathed.

He would have need of sustenance for the night ahead.

Maximilian smiled. Aye, so would his lady wife. He could not help but anticipate what skills she possessed as a seductress and imagined their first coupling would be satisfactory indeed.

The prospect was almost sufficient to make him want to whistle.

IN THE HUT hidden in the forest, there was a rousing argument about the destrier. All three women were agitated and it was a cold night. They had already agreed that they dare not light a fire, because the smell of it might attract the attention of the mercenaries camping at Kilderrick. Elizabeth almost desired the comforts of her father's keep enough to pay whatever their price might be.

That said much of the cold.

"He is a valuable steed," Ceara insisted. "We cannot leave him out in the rain. He might become ill."

"A horse in the hut," Nyssa replied, propping her hands upon her hips. "What madness is this?"

"A stallion," Elizabeth corrected quietly. "A *destrier*."

Nyssa rolled her eyes and continued. "There is scarcely sufficient space for us, and you would bring a horse inside?"

"Only for the night," Ceara said, surveying the hut interior. "He could be tethered there."

"And you complained about the falcon last night," Elizabeth noted with a sniff. "*She* sat quietly on her perch above my bed and slept. The horse will likely stomp, fart and defecate."

"Defecate," Ceara echoed. "You mean he will crap. What if he does? There is no scent more bracing than that of fresh manure."

Nyssa and Elizabeth exchanged a glance, each of them knowing no living soul could adore horses so much as Ceara did.

"He will stamp and he will sniff," Nyssa said. "He might eat anything. Or everything." Dorcha cawed and bobbed his head in apparent agreement.

Ceara was incensed. "He is not a goat. He is a fine and noble creature that will fetch an excellent price in Carlisle, if he does not die of neglect before I can get him there."

"And if he becomes aroused..." Nyssa shuddered and shook her head. "Absolutely not." She turned to Elizabeth as Ceara went to the door to look upon the tethered destrier. Elizabeth could see that the beast appeared to be dejected. His ears were folded back and his back was slick with rainwater. He was a dapple, with a charcoal mane and tail, and truly a splendid creature.

"Where do you think the Silver Wolf took Alys?" Nyssa asked.

"Back to his camp, of course. He said he meant to wed her."

"Do you think he lies?"

Elizabeth shrugged. "All men lie when it suits them."

"He did release you when she came. He kept his word there."

Elizabeth winced, having to cede that and not liking it a whit.

"We forget the dispute! We have a prize to defend," Ceara insisted. "Look at the gloss of that destrier's coat. Look at how muscular he is. How can you consign him to a night in the rain?"

"The mercenary might steal him back," Elizabeth noted. "It is likely he has naught else of such value."

The women exchanged glances of trepidation.

"He could not find us," Ceara insisted. "Especially if the horse is not visible. We will not have a fire until I ride to Carlisle."

"And how will you ride to Carlisle without them seeing you depart?" Nyssa demanded.

"Through the forest, of course." Ceara had no lack of confidence. "There is sufficient incentive to see it done. I have sold horses there before."

"Aye, stolen from thieves who left Kilderrick on foot," Nyssa countered. "There was no chance of them seeing you or following you."

"Or taking vengeance upon you," Elizabeth added with a shiver that was not entirely due to the cold.

"What can we do to aid Alys?" Nyssa asked with impatience.

"I had a notion," Elizabeth said and indicated a collection of charms. She had been busily creating them since her return and the sight made Ceara laugh.

"A curse upon them," she said.

Nyssa did not laugh. "Aye, we might frighten them away," she said, fingering one of them. "A fine idea, Elizabeth."

Elizabeth smiled and flushed a little.

"We should wait until they sleep." Ceara sat down heavily. "You should have seen him," she murmured. "He was furious!"

"Your strategy was effective," Nyssa noted.

"He followed his prick. Temptation was the best lure." Ceara shrugged. "And he was not truly injured."

"That may prove to be an error," Nyssa said under her breath.

"He was rather handsome, in a dangerous way," Ceara admitted. "Dark hair and flashing eyes. Tall and broad." She sighed and smiled a little. "Perhaps it would not have been so bad if he had caught me."

"Ceara!" Elizabeth was shocked, but the other woman just laughed.

"It matters little now. He will hate me forever, and that is probably best for all." Ceara smiled to herself. "Do you think he might acquire another destrier? I could enjoy stealing horses from him in succession."

"He will retrieve this one and make you pay for the insult," Nyssa predicted.

"Did you see that? Or do you simply try to frighten me?"

"You underestimate his resolve," Elizabeth said. "Men do not like to be denied."

"You know naught of him!" Ceara complained.

"But you tricked him, and a man has been cheated of pleasure does not forget the insult easily," Nyssa said.

Elizabeth nodded wisely.

Then the horse nickered, as if in greeting, and all three women fell silent in unison. The rain drummed on the boughs overhead, some of it seeping through the layers of branches to drip on the hard packed dirt of the floor. The forest rustled and the destrier stamped. Ceara opened her mouth, no doubt to say that it had been naught at all, when a man cleared his throat at close proximity.

Elizabeth thought her heart would stop.

They remained motionless, eyes wide, Nyssa's hand on the hilt of her knife. Ceara had her bow and silently nocked an arrow. They were all listening with care and Elizabeth doubted she was the sole one to notice the sound of retreating footsteps. The horse blew out his lips and stamped, digging at the undergrowth restlessly.

Ceara opened the door slowly, revealing the shadows of the forest, gleaming wetly. There was no sound of any intruder and Nyssa moved to her side to look. Elizabeth stayed on her bed, arms wrapped around her knees in fear. Nyssa pointed, Ceara nodded, then the pair slipped out of the hut like shadows.

No one even asked Elizabeth to come along and that was fine to her thinking.

They returned in moments with two bundles, each tied in a length of linen. The contents were warm, a rich scent of it filling the hut as soon as they entered.

"'Twas a man," Ceara said. "He disappeared into the forest as quietly as he came."

"We did not see him," Nyssa said. "Not clearly."

"Was it your mercenary?" Elizabeth asked.

Ceara shook her head. "Nay, he was more slender. His hair was fair, I think."

Elizabeth dropped her gaze to hide her response. Her heart was in her throat. Any suspicion that she had been followed back to the hut by the knight who owned the falcon would not be well received.

"And he did not retrieve the horse," Nyssa noted. "So it cannot have been that one."

"Did you hear a dog?" Ceara asked and the other woman nodded.

"I think so, but not close."

It had been him!

Ceara frowned at the bundles. "As if it had been commanded to stay." She leaned closer "Smells like roast partridge." She opened the bundle and they all stared at the perfectly roasted partridge nestled in the napkin.

How long had it been since they had eaten such fare?

"It could be poisoned," Nyssa said, unable to keep herself from leaning closer to take a deep breath of the scent.

Elizabeth doubted that she was the sole one salivating. She untied the other cloth to find a loaf of bread wrapped within it. It was a bit hard, but again, they did not bake bread themselves. Bannocks baked on hearthstones were not the same.

"What shall we do?" Ceara said. "A hot meal would be most welcome, but not if it is our last."

Dorcha hopped down to the floor of the hut, as if he, too, were curious. He made the trilling sound that Elizabeth always thought was like a question, then tilted his head to look at her.

Elizabeth lifted the bread and smiled when she spied what was hidden beneath it in the cloth. She picked up the falcon feather and turned it, displaying it to her friends. "It is a gift of gratitude," she said, feeling her cheeks heat as she recalled the sight of the knight with the falcon on his fist. "For giving shelter to the falcon. This is one of her feathers."

"How do you know?" Ceara asked but Elizabeth gave her a look.

"I can distinguish a falcon feather," she said.

"How did he know where to find us?" Nyssa demanded with suspicion.

"I saw him today when she flew to him. She answered his summons."

"Then what?" Nyssa asked.

"I fled," Elizabeth admitted.

"And he followed you," Ceara concluded with disgust. "I should leave with the destrier this very night to avoid detection."

Nyssa had taken a knife to the partridge and closed her eyes as she savored her first bite. "If this is the reward they bring for the care of a falcon, we might fare so well with the return of the destrier that you do not even have to ride to Carlisle."

"I am *not* returning the destrier to him," Ceara began to protest, but Nyssa pushed a drumstick in her direction to silence her.

The tactic worked admirably. Elizabeth tore the bread and the three women sat together, devouring the knight's gift. It was not simply the meal that warmed Elizabeth to her toes but the memory of the knight and his expression of wonder when he met her gaze.

He had followed her, but not to harm her.

To thank her, and that was wondrous indeed.

CHAPTER 6

*T*he bath was hot and deep, the tub itself made of heavy leather that had been sealed along the seams. Alys guessed that wax had been used on the outside, though she had never seen the like. It was clever, for it would be comparatively light and flat for transport—she guessed she was not the only one who appreciated the pleasure of a bath. How long had it been? She would not think of it.

And she would not become accustomed to such luxury. As soon as she could free herself from this mockery of a marriage, Alys would return to the hut in the forest and the life she knew best.

Even so, she found herself unable to refrain from enjoying the luxurious treat. The water was blessedly hot and was so deep that she could sink up to her chin. There was even a piece of soap from Paris. Evidently, the Silver Wolf had ridden north intent upon courting a bride. Alys did not imagine she was his first choice. Still, it was a pleasure nigh forgotten to scrub her skin clean, to have the maid wash her hair and comb it until it shone. She had not bathed since summer, when the sun heated the river.

But what price this pleasure? Alys feared she knew.

A son.

She took the opportunity to consider her ring as she soaked in the hot water and Nathalie fussed. The ring was wide and gold, filling half the depth of her knuckle. The letters engraved upon it were deeply etched but made little sense to her. Had the ring been the gift of another man, she might have thought it a family piece or a legacy. As a token from the Silver Wolf, Alys could only assume it had been stolen from the treasury of another.

All it said of her spouse was that he had an eye for plunder.

And how did that explain her presence by his side? What was his scheme? She could not believe he truly desired a wife, or that she would be his choice even so.

He had looked upon her and had not flinched. That fact was startling.

Indeed, he had kissed her. The memory sent heat through Alys and another kind of pleasure, too. He had chosen her, even seeing her truth.

He must truly believe he had need specifically of her and over-looked his aversion to see his goal achieved. Alys felt a chill at that. He could not possibly know the truth.

Could he?

The tent was round, perhaps a dozen paces across, and made of heavy cloth of solid brown. A central pole held the roof in a high peak. She had heard once that the courtiers and kings had tents of striped silk, but this was a more servicable structure. The cloth was thick and the rain did not penetrate it. Perhaps the tent even disappeared against the forest, due to its hue. It had a floor of heavy canvas which was dark but dry, with a fine rug cast across it. The tent was not as small as Alys might have expected, and she wondered whether the Silver Wolf often lived in such conditions. It made sense that a man at war would not take his leisure at an inn, or that there might not be accommodations to be found where battles were fought.

An oil lantern filled the interior with a golden glow. A brazier stood near the tub, emitting a welcome warmth, and a second was on the opposite side of the tent. There was a bed at one side, a short wooden structure laced with rope, furs spread atop it. A pair of trunks were placed on one side of the flap that served as a door, one large and one small, and a trestle table was on the other side. The rain beat on the roof but the chill of the night seemed distant. It was a haven without being luxurious, a practical refuge providing shelter and some comfort.

Alys was reminded of Morag's hut and was struck by the similarity between the living conditions she knew and those of the Silver Wolf. Doubtless, he had slaves to cook for him, though, and to heat the water for this bath. Morag—and Alys and her companions in turn—had done all the labor for survival without aid.

The maid, Nathalie, had to be a captive or a slave despite the Silver Wolf's insistence, but not one who expected better. She was very pretty and perhaps a decade younger than Alys. She was lithe with dark brown hair so wavy that it escaped her braid and curled in tendrils around her face. Alys did not imagine she could have traveled in this company and remained a maiden, but her good cheer could not have been feigned. Her eyes were sparkling blue and the kirtle she had given to Alys would have favored her coloring well.

Nathalie must have a protector within the camp, or a mercenary who treated her with some kindness. She did not seem to be abused, but a person could accustom herself to any situation as Alys well knew. Nathalie chattered constantly, her changing expression giving Alys a hint at what she was saying. She spoke Norman French, but her words were too quick for Alys to understand readily, and her accent was unfamiliar. Alys caught a word for every six or so but they managed to convey much with gesture.

Would Nathalie aid her to escape? Alys suspected not—she was certain that her new spouse would have ensured she had no ally.

Was the tent surrounded? It would certainly be watched. Alys heard the occasional cough or muttered comment despite the sound of the rain, which meant the Silver Wolf's men were nearby.

She would have to wait until they slept.

She would have to wait until *he* slept.

There was no chance the Silver Wolf would do that before he was sated, which meant her maidenhead would be claimed and she would be his wife by any reckoning.

Unless she could repel him and destroy his interest. He had not minded the sight of her in the rain and the darkness, but perhaps the light would be her friend.

The very prospect had Alys rising from the bath with impatience to see the matter behind her. The bath water was dark when she stepped out of it and Nathalie's disapproval was clear. The maid rubbed Alys down, hesitating only slightly before gently brushing the water from her scarred skin.

Nathalie bowed as she offered the chemise, which appeared to be new. It was a plain garment of clean white linen, gathered at the neck. It fell full and past Alys' knees, the sleeves reaching her wrists where they were gathered on cords. The cloth was softer than any Alys had felt in years and as light as gossamer. The shadows of her body could be seen through the sheer cloth. Nathalie fussed and adjusted the draw-strings, clearly proud of the garment. Alys knew it had been costly.

Perhaps it had been intended for the maid's wedding night. Their gazes met and held, Nathalie smiling even though her eyes glimmered with tears. *"Si jolie,"* she said, her voice husky, unable to keep from a quick caress of the cloth. *"Parfait."*

Somehow Alys would see her kindness repaid. She nodded and smiled, trying to show her gratitude, and thought she had succeeded when Nathalie blushed.

Nathalie gestured to the bed, smiled mischievously, then clasped her hands beside her cheek. "Le Loup Argent," she whispered then sighed with apparent rapture. Apparently, the maid admired him, against all expectation, undoubtedly because he was handsome.

Nay, Nathalie would not aid Alys to escape.

Was the maid his concubine? Alys frowned in recollection of his beguiling kiss and knew that many a woman might be seduced by his touch, if not his appearance. Aye, a man who was fine of feature and gifted with charm could do much to disguise a dark nature.

Did Nathalie give a reference to the Silver Wolf's amorous abilities? The notion was troubling. Alys did not desire any husband she was obliged to share. She stepped away from the maid, pacing the width of the tent in her agitation. Nathalie watched her, eyes wide, finally silenced.

Maid and mistress both jumped when the tent flap was swept open with an imperious gesture.

Of course, it was Alys' captor and spouse, looking as resolute as ever. Her heart skipped as his gaze swept over her and his own expression grew more intense. He seemed taller and broader within the confines of the tent, more masculine and vital. Raindrops glistening on the shoulders of his dark cloak and shone in his hair. He shed his gloves and cast them onto the larger trunk, his gaze locked upon her all the while.

Alys' mouth went dry as appreciation lit his eyes. Why could he not find her repulsive? How was it that *this* man did not find her scar objectionable?

How was it that his admiration sent such pleasure surging through her? Alys cursed herself for tingling in awareness of his presence. He was finely wrought. That had to be the root of it. She had never glimpsed a man so handsome, let alone one bent upon charming her.

Her pulse leaped when he swept off his cloak, then stepped closer to cast it over her own shoulders. He smiled down at her as he fastened the silver clasp at the neck. The cloak was lined with silver fur and warm from his body, and it surrounded Alys like a cocoon. The weight of his hands lingered on her shoulders for a heart-stopping moment, his steady gaze close to her own, the scent of his skin rising to tease her.

"Si jolie," he said, his voice a low purr of approval. He echoed Nathalie so perfectly that he might have been listening—but Alys knew the compliment was a lie.

She spun away from him, prickly and annoyed. "'Tis not so cold that I need your cloak."

"But you will need a little defense against curious gazes, my lady wife. I defer to your modesty."

Alys might have argued but he lifted her left hand in his, again ignoring the scarred flesh. He planted a hot kiss on the finger now graced with his ring, his gaze unwavering, and her throat tightened.

She was a possession, no more than that.

Alys spun away from the Silver Wolf and retreated to the more distant brazier, raising her hands to the warmth.

Her new husband spoke quickly to the maid, perhaps praising her, for she blushed and bowed low. She glanced back at Alys, offering a smile of encouragement, then she was gone. He had not given the maid a touch or a glance. Did they have no intimate relationship? Why did the maid not despise him for capturing her thus?

There was a sound outside the tent flap and her husband called a summons. A boy stepped into the tent and bowed low before the Silver Wolf, his gaze flicking to Alys in open curiosity. It was the same one who had taken the reins of the destrier on their return. He had seen perhaps fifteen summers and was lanky, nigh as tall as the Silver Wolf but much more slender. His hair was dark and wavy, his eyes deep brown and thickly lashed. He carried a bucket of steaming water.

"This is Reynaud, my squire," the Silver Wolf said to Alys. "Reynaud, my lady wife, to whom you will show every courtesy at all times."

Reynaud bowed and the back of his neck reddened, his greeting almost incoherent.

Alys inclined her head slightly and was glad of the cloak. She pulled it more closely around herself, hiding the sheer chemise from the boy and felt a tiny wave of gratitude toward her husband for his foresight.

"I have told him that he must knock from this day forward," the Silver Wolf informed her. "For a man of merit never surprises a lady in her chamber."

"How would you know?" Alys asked, unable to stop herself.

Reynaud looked at her in alarm, but her new husband chuckled. He unbuckled his belt and Reynaud laid it atop the trunk, taking particular care with the scabbard and sword. The boy returned to unlace the back of the Silver Wolf's tabard, then the Silver Wolf shed it with impatience. Reynaud folded it and set it beside the scabbard, brushing some dirt from the hem with fastidious fingers. The Silver Wolf bent over at the waist then, his chain mail hauberk falling toward the ground. There was a lace at the back of it as well, and the boy deftly assisted in its removal.

How could her husband look bigger without his armor? His hair was tousled and he wore only his chemise, chausses and boots, the neck of the chemise open to reveal the tanned length of his throat and a tangle of golden hair on his chest.

"I can manage the rest," the Silver Wolf said and the boy bowed again. He took the hauberk, along with sword and scabbard with him, bowed again, and ducked out of the tent.

Alys swallowed, aware that she was alone with her husband. He pushed up his sleeves and washed noisily in the bucket of water, splashing the water as he scrubbed himself clean. Alys could not help but notice the two purple crescents on his forearm, the bruises resulting from her bite the night before. Would he retaliate for that insult?

"I will not take the second water on this night," he teased, to her surprise, gesturing to the tub.

There was another rap and two men appeared to fetch the tub. Their gazes, too, were quick and curious. The Silver Wolf bade them dump the water then refill it for Rafael. There was a jest about this Rafael's muddy state and they were quickly gone. Her husband rubbed himself dry, watching Alys with a smile, and she wondered at his intention—then there was another sound at the tent flap.

The place was as busy as a great hall.

In a way, Alys supposed it was his great hall.

This time, 'twas a couple, a plump man of middle years and a slender woman of similar age. The man dropped his gaze politely but the woman stole a dozen glances at Alys. She spread a length of cloth upon the trestle table, followed by a pair of bowls and two crockery cups, two spoons and two napkins. The man placed a plate and a bowl upon the board, the plate nigh filled with a roast partridge that Alys could smell, and the bowl brimming with a steaming soup. The woman added a loaf of bread, tied in a napkin, then they stood back. The smell of roasted meat weakened Alys' knees and she gripped her hands together under the cloak, struggling to hide her hunger.

They did not appear to be abused, which made Alys wonder anew. Could it be possible that these people followed the Silver Wolf willingly? Why would anyone who was not a warrior choose to join a company of mercenaries? Did they have their freedom? Did he compensate them so well as that?

How much coin did he possess?

What would happen to him when 'twas all spent?

"My lady, this is Denis, my cook, and his wife, Marie," the Silver Wolf said. "They have served my family faithfully for many years and now grace me with their service."

Alys inclined her head in greeting and spoke with care. "I thank you for this repast."

"I apologize that the wedding feast will not be prepared until the morrow," Denis said with what seemed to be concern. Alys wondered whether it was fear of repercussions that made him anxious. "My lord Amaury only obtained the deer today and there is much to be done in preparation..."

"There will be fresh bread and dumplings as well," his wife contributed.

"I have spices..."

"I am certain it will be delicious, Denis," the Silver Wolf said, interrupting them. "Your fare is always most fine."

The cook bowed again to Alys. "Our every felicitation on the good fortune of your marriage, my lady."

As much as Alys might have liked to argue the extent of her good fortune, she could not be churlish with people of such kind intentions. She could not explain how they came to serve her husband, but she would unearth the truth.

She inclined her head and thanked them.

The pair bowed and left.

"Amaury?" Alys echoed.

"My other blood brother, the one who looks most knightly. He accompanied us to the stones."

"The fair one."

He nodded agreement. "He hunts with a hawk and his hounds, in lieu of seeking the favors of fair maidens at tournament." There was a slight disdain in his voice at this.

Amaury had to be the owner of the hawk Elizabeth had sheltered.

"We are seven," he continued, then counted on his fingers. "Myself, my brother Rafael, and my brother Amaury. In addition, there are three mercenaries who have served with me in the past, Royce, Matteo and Victor. Finally, there is a Scotsman, Murdoch Campbell, who has chosen to ride with us."

Alys gave no sign that she recognized the name. It could be another Murdoch Campbell and not the one she had once known. "Why?"

"We rode to Scotland and so did he. I fully expect him to leave us soon."

"And Reynaud is squire to all?"

He shook his head. "There are five squires in all: my own, Reynaud, as well as Mallory, Oliver, Louis and Nicholas."

"And Nathalie."

"She is one of six from Château de Vries, my childhood home, as well as Yves, formerly the châtelain of that keep."

"Denis and his wife are from there as well, then."

"Aye, and Henri the ostler, with his young son. There is also Eudaline, an elderly healer."

Alys was surprised that an elderly woman would choose to travel with his company, but then she wondered what had occured at Château de Vries to compel them all to leave. A châtelain did not often leave a holding in his winter years.

Perhaps the Silver Wolf had razed it to the ground, as he had burned Kilderrick, and they had escaped—leaping from the fat to the fire, so to speak.

The Silver Wolf invited her to the table with a gesture, and Alys had no ability to stay away. He moved the lantern to one end of the table and Alys chose the side that would put her scar in the light, leaving the undamaged side of her face in shadow.

Let him look upon what he had wrought. He might like it less well when he could see it fully.

Her husband gave no indication that he noticed. Alys was seated in the sole chair, and he moved the smaller of the two trunks that he might sit opposite her. He served her neatly, carving the bird with his dagger and arranging a meal of the choicest morsels on her plate, which was pewter. There was a napkin at Alys' place and a crockery cup, which he filled with what smelled like ale.

It took all within Alys to keep from falling on the meal like a starving dog.

Perhaps he would find her curiosity offensive.

"Why does Amaury ride with you, if he is a knight and not a mercenary?"

"Because he has no coin and no legacy. At my father's funeral, Amaury learned that the old cur had been his father, as well." The Silver Wolf's brows rose, his attention fixed on the filling of his own cup. "As a result, Amaury was cast out by the man who had raised him, my uncle

Gaston finally being freed of the threat of my father's retaliation. Amaury has naught but his hawk, his hounds and his horse, but he is my brother, as well. I could not abandon him."

Was it true that he felt such loyalty? Alys had to concede that having one who hunted in the company was useful, for they would eat better.

"What does your mother say of this union of brothers?" Alys asked.

"She has retired to a convent." He flicked a glance at her, his gaze very blue. "But we three all have different mothers, to be sure. My father was not known for his restraint."

He held her gaze, fairly daring Alys to ask the obvious question.

"And you?"

"The sole trait my father and I ever shared was our effectiveness at war." The Silver Wolf toasted her with his cup. "For he trained me young and war is all I have ever known. Indeed, I surpassed him years ago in that matter."

"You will find no war at Kilderrick." Alys sipped the ale then took a piece of meat. It was glorious, the skin rubbed with salt, the meat tender and flavorful. She closed her eyes despite herself and savored it.

When she looked, the Silver Wolf was smiling at her and she hated that she had been predictable. "I may find sufficient battle in my chamber to suit my needs," he said silkily. "Matching wits with my lady wife."

She might have conjured a cutting retort, but the Silver Wolf held up a finger.

Sure enough, there was another sound at the tent flap.

He called a summons and the silver-haired man entered. This had to be Yves. His gaze flicked over the interior of the tent as he confirmed that all was as it should be and Alys knew she had guessed aright. "My lord? Is there aught else?"

"My lady, this is Yves, formerly the châtelain of Château de Vries. He will be our castellan at Kilderrick."

Again, there was that insistence upon his remaining at her family holding. Alys wondered why he was so intent upon it.

"I am most honored to make your acquaintance, my lady," Yves said briskly, his crisp French easy for her to understand. "If I can be of any service at all, please do not hesitate to summon me."

Alys was tempted to ask if he might annul her marriage, but the steady watchfulness of the Silver Wolf convinced her to refrain from doing as much. She simply bowed her head and thanked the older man.

"I shall see that you are not disturbed, my lord," Yves said, then he was gone. Alys heard a murmur of male voices beyond the tent, guessed that there was a sentry, then her husband moved closer.

"Alone at last," he murmured, then rose smoothly to his feet. He prowled around the table to pause behind her, then bent to whisper in her ear. "Do you find it sufficiently warm?"

Alys shivered at his proximity. "I am fine."

"Nay, you will be too warm." He lifted the cloak from her shoulders and she heard him catch his breath when the chemise was revealed again.

She glanced down and could see the shadows of her breasts beneath the cloth, the lantern light creating shadows where her nipples strained against the cloth.

She should not be shy. This was her chance to repel him.

He cast the cloak across the other trunk, then sat down opposite her again. When he met her gaze, the hunger in his expression made her mouth go dry. His lashes swept down to disguise his thoughts, though truly it was a challenge to read them in any moment. Alys pulled her braid to drape over her shadowed shoulder, baring the scar upon her neck to his view. He did not so much as blink.

"And so I see the truth of my lady wife," he murmured, taking his place anew.

Alys was snared by the heat in those blue eyes. "You can see the damage wrought upon me," she said, pushing up her left sleeve. The scarred flesh looked worse in the light of the lantern, rougher and more ravaged, and she could only hope the sight would quench the desire of her newfound spouse.

Sadly, the cursed man was proving inclined to challenge her every expectation.

～

ALYS TRIED to use her scar as a weapon.

Maximilian could only admire the ploy, though it was doomed to be ineffective. He was aware that she had chosen her seat so that the lantern's light would fall upon the damaged side of her face, for the challenge in her eyes had been unmistakable. She must have been spurned for her looks, though 'twas too late for Maximilian to be dissuaded by them.

He was too beguiled by her intellect and her resolve.

That her expectation was otherwise only meant that those who came to her and her companions for satisfaction did not linger. Those men did not take the time to become intrigued, to learn of her nature, to see the ferocity of her will.

Or perhaps they feared her.

Perhaps they coupled in the dark, never looking upon her.

Maximilian did not care about the past and he did not care about fools who failed to value what was before them. He would build a future with this woman, which meant he had to win her trust. He made no effort to hide his admiration and watched as his manner discomfited Alys more with every passing moment.

He pushed aside his meal, sipping only his ale, watching her with undisguised pleasure. He smiled. She flushed. Her gaze flicked to him repeatedly, her uncertainty growing. She pushed aside her plate as well, her serving unfinished even though she had to be famished. She eyed him with the suspicion that already made him smile.

"I see you have a hunger for more than the pheasant," she said, that dare in her tone again.

"No man of wit could blame me. 'Tis our wedding night."

She wiped her fingers on her napkin, then untied the lace of the chemise and bared more of her throat to his view. Her movements were seductive, though there could be no hiding the angry truth on her flesh.

Maximilian looked. He had done this. Inadvertently and without a plan, yet 'twas his doing all the same. He wondered anew what the scars had cost Alys, knowing she would not confide that tale in him soon. He sipped his ale, hiding his thoughts from her, and acknowledged a twinge of guilt.

He had never felt regret in his choices before. He never atoned for any deed. He did what was necessary and did not look back.

But he surveyed his new wife and wondered whether the burning of Kilderrick had been necessary. What had been the point? He had found no treasure and he had, at the very least, adversely affected the life of a woman who had been a bystander. He knew the death of the laird had been unnecessary—it had been an accident, just like Alys' injury.

That did not mean it could be undone, though.

"Do you have a preference for the maimed?" Alys asked in a hot whisper.

If she thought to disgust him, she miscalculated. All Maximilian could see was the audacity in her expression and the brightness of her eyes, and his body stirred in anticipation of her touch. "I have a preference for women of wit and vigor, for women who speak their thoughts aloud, for those who are bold. You will suit me well." He turned the full weight of his approval upon her and watched her flush. He let his voice drop low. "We will suit each other well, my Alys."

Her lips tightened and she averted her gaze. "You assume much."

"I recognize the signs. Surely you do, as well."

She frowned and tore the bread, taking a bite he was certain she did not desire. She was stalling, though he could not imagine why. He would make the interlude pleasant for her. Perhaps others had not done as much.

Perhaps there was something good he could teach her.

Maximilian resolved to try. "Of all the men in all the world, you must realize that I would know appearances can be deceiving," he said gently.

Her glare was hostile. "You would mock me."

"On the contrary, I would cherish you."

"You lie!"

He shook his head with resolve. "Never, Alys. Your scar will not make me turn aside from my goal."

"Why me?" she demanded in vexation. "Take another woman as your prize!"

Maximilian put down his cup with deliberation, holding her gaze.

"But you are the sole heiress of Kilderrick. Our match resolves any and all questions of inheritance."

"But the holding is worthless."

"Not to me."

She eyed him. "You cannot mean to live here like a landed baron."

Why did the notion surprise her? "What if I do?"

"But you are a mercenary. You set camp wherever you must and travel constantly, seeking employment from the highest bidder."

It was a fair assessment of his former life. "Who better to defend Kilderrick than a man experienced in the arts of war?"

"My father..."

"Was not a warrior, which is why he lost both his holding and his life."

"The keep is ruined."

"'Twill be rebuilt."

"By whom?"

"The masons should arrive from Carlisle in the next day or so. Assuming the state of the keep had not changed and knowing that winter would soon be upon us, I took the liberty of securing their services."

"'Twill cost a fortune."

Maximilian winced. "I daresay."

She glared at him, tossing the bread onto her plate. "And how many women will you have?" The fire in her words told her that this query mattered most of all.

"I have need of only one, my lady wife, and we will meet abed daily —or nightly—until you conceive."

"And then?"

"You will bear a child."

"And then?"

Maximilian leaned closer, biting off the words. His patience thinned. "You will bear another and it will be mine."

"How many?"

"Who can say?"

"I will not be your brood mare!" She pushed to her feet, her cheeks flushed.

"Nay, you will be my wife and in every way." Maximilian took a breath, schooling his temper. "You do not have a choice, my Alys. We are wed." He cast his napkin on the board, tiring of the game. "'Tis time to see the matter done."

She cringed when he moved around the table, but Maximilian did not believe she feared him, not for a single heartbeat. She had provoked him and challenged him and stared him down. Perhaps she thought he would strike her. But he knew that she simply sought a point of weakness—and also that she would not find one.

Nor would he prove himself a brute. Maximilian took a steadying breath, then listened to his wife's quick breathing.

He smelled the fear she sought to hide.

It appeared his reputation had preceded him.

The mating would be better if he could dismiss her concern. He paused behind her, watched her flinch, and lifted the end of her braid slowly in one hand. The hair was thick and wavy, long enough to fall to her waist. The braid was fat and glossy. "As dark as ebony," he murmured, noting the set of her shoulders. She sat as straight as a warrior and unless he missed his guess, she held her breath.

"I would not know."

"With the glimmer of silk." He untied the ribbon at the end, moving slowly, as if she was a wild creature. She was unpredictable in her ways and readily frightened. In this moment, Maximilian was keenly aware of her, the scent of her skin, the ripe curve of a breast beneath the chemise, even the pink skin of her scar.

"I have never seen silk." The hostility in her tone was slightly diminished.

"Then I shall have to remedy that." When he had untied the ribbon, he undid the braid steadily, moving with deliberate gestures. She trembled. Aye, others had been quick about it. He would enjoy teaching her that there could be pleasure when man and woman met abed.

When her hair was loose, he speared his fingers through her hair, savoring the feel of it between his fingers, and spread it over her shoulders. It was dark and lustrous, a splendid curtain that might have been a cloak.

"Or like a raven's wing," he whispered, then bent to touch his lips to her cheek. 'Twas no accident he chose the cheek in the light, the one that was scarred, and he felt her jump at the brush of his lips against her skin.

"How fitting for a witch." She spun to look at him in alarm and their gazes met, so close that he could feel her breath.

"You are no witch. You are magnificent."

"You mock me," she said, her voice breathless.

Maximilian shook his head slowly. "Never that." He leaned closer, touching his lips to hers. As before, she stiffened in anticipation of some injury, then when his touch was gentle, her eyes closed and she shivered ever so slightly. The taste of vulnerability, however fleeting, made him feel protective of her. He claimed her lips, slowly deepening his kiss, granting her time to welcome him.

She nearly did, then pulled herself away from him, the battle in her eyes anew.

"I will kill you in your sleep," she threatened and he chuckled.

"Aye, you said that was your scheme." He had prepared for that eventuality, but Alys did not need to know of that as yet. He pulled back the chair and swept her into his arms before she could flee, striding toward the bed with purpose. "Few surprise me, Alys, though I invite you to try."

Her eyes flashed and she would have clawed at him, but Maximilian dropped her on the bed and seized her wrists. She struggled, battling in futility against the weight of his knee upon her hip. "I could bind you. I could force myself upon you," he said in a tight whisper. "But it would be a poor beginning, Alys. I would make this night sweet."

"It cannot be sweet."

"It does not have to be bitter."

She twisted beneath his weight to glare up at him. "It will be, no matter what lies you tell me."

Her words struck a chord within him and his temper flared, despite his desire to remain calm. "I do not lie, my Alys," he informed her again.

She writhed, apparently boneless, pulled her hands from his grasp and tore his ring from her finger. She flung it at his face but Maximilian did not so much as blink as it bounced off his cheek. It fell to the ground and rolled beneath the table, but he would fetch it later.

"Enough," he said through gritted teeth and held her down with one hand. He knew his fury showed, because there was a flicker of fear in her eyes. She bared her teeth but he had ensured she could not reach to bite him again. He seized her wrists and bound them to the frame over her head with the length of ribbon that had been in her hair.

"You cannot do this," she protested hotly.

"I have, because you granted me no choice."

"I do not welcome you."

"You will, because I will make it so." Maximilian bent to retrieve her ring, then shed his chemise. She looked at him, her gaze dancing over him, as if she had not seen a man nude before. Perhaps her visitors had remained in their garb. He shed both chausses and boots, letting her see all of him.

She swallowed and curled her fingers to hex him, though her wrists were yet bound. "I curse you," she hissed, her voice low and filled with intent. "I curse you, Silver Wolf, by all the power within me, I curse you to be barren and shriveled, to shrink to naught and leave me untouched this night."

Maximilian did not laugh. He did, however, glance down at his erection before meeting his wife's gaze. "You see why I do not believe in witchery," he said in a low voice. "Your spell does not appear to be working."

"I place a hex upon you," she began, but Maximilian lay down beside her, leaning slightly atop her. She caught her breath and stared at him as he bent to capture her lips in another kiss of dizzying power.

There was something about this woman, something that told him he would never tire of her or her touch, that he could feast upon her all the night long and still be unsated. He kissed her slowly, thoroughly, cajoling her to join him until she made a little moan of surrender. She already came to rely upon the pleasure in their kisses.

Just as Maximilian did.

Without lifting his head, he put his ring back upon her finger, then braced his weight on his elbow. "Did you read it?" he asked, turning the ring on her finger.

"I cannot."

"*Vous et nul autre*," he said in a low murmur. "You and no other. 'Tis a wedding ring, inscribed thus for another couple, but again Fate guided my choice. I sense, Alys, that you are like no other, and that we will only suffice for each other."

"You are mistaken in that," she said, eyes flashing.

Maximilian shook his head. "Nay, I must only convince you." He stared down at her as he slid one hand down the length of her in a possessive gesture. He moved his fingers under the hem of the chemise, then swept it back to her waist, taking the cloth upward and baring her to his view. She was smooth and strong beneath his hand, soft—and yet he felt her muscled strength.

"Never doubt your beauty," he whispered, sounding nigh as fierce as she could. She gasped aloud when he cupped her breast, her mouth working in silence for a moment, before he felt compelled to kiss her again.

This time, his kiss was a little rougher, a little more demanding, and to his satisfaction, Alys rose in response to his touch. She kissed him back, her hunger growing with every moment. She arched beneath him as he teased her nipple, her breath coming quickly. He could feel the thunder of her heart and when he finally abandoned the nipple, easing his fingers between her thighs, she was slick and hot with need.

The feel of her reaction sent that fire through him, for it could not be contrived. She desired him, just as he desired her. Here there was truth. When he rubbed his thumb against her, his caress making her gasp aloud, he could not have resisted her to save his life. He untied the ribbon, releasing her wrists, and, as he had anticipated, she reached for him.

She locked her hands in his hair as he bent to capture that nipple with his lips. He suckled upon her and she trembled with pleasure, so incoherent in her need that he knew it was time. He eased between her thighs and thrust, only to feel an unexpected barrier. He had time to meet her gaze, then he was within her heat, the barrier banished.

Alys cried out beneath him in dismay and the truth could not be ignored.

"You are a maiden," Maximilian whispered in shock. "How can this be?"

CHAPTER 7

The Silver Wolf insisted he did not believe in sorcery, but Alys had no other explanation for the tumult he conjured so easily beneath her flesh. His kisses dissolved her objections to him and his touch. His caress drove all protest from her thoughts, leaving her burning with a need she could not explain. She knew he could sate the desire he awakened within her, though she knew not precisely how. She hated how she forgot her resolve to fight him, how she became pliant and welcoming, how she met him touch for touch.

But this hunger he awakened was undeniable, irresistible, and she could think only of having more.

Until he pierced her maidenhead and froze.

Without his beguiling caress, her objections returned with a vengeance. She was abed with her husband atop her because her determination to fight him every moment had been banished like dust in the wind.

And she despised him for it.

"A maiden no longer," she snapped.

"But..." He was clearly astonished. His throat worked and his body was taut. Alys recognized the power of will that kept him from finishing what he had begun. His eyes blazed sapphire when he looked down at her and he shook his head. "But they said..."

"Aye, they said we were harlots and witches." She shook her head, aware that the sheriff's wife said that and more about the four women. "You were prepared to believe me a whore but not a witch."

"I do not believe in witches," he said yet again. "But any man with eyes in his head knows there are whores aplenty."

"Not me." She held his gaze steadily, again daring him.

He appeared to be astounded.

In truth, she wondered what he would do.

If he had asked her to choose, Alys realized she could not have done so. On the one hand, she was determined to cede naught to him. On the other, that taste of pleasure left her wondering whether there might be more, whether he had a means to relieve the tension that still coiled within her.

"Nay, not you." He exhaled and bowed his head, leaning his forehead upon her shoulder. He sounded contrite when he continued, which surprised her. "And now I owe you another debt, my Alys, that you may be sure I will repay."

To her astonishment, he retreated and rolled to his back beside her, one arm over his eyes. His mouth was a taut line and the press of him against her was not unwelcome. He was solid and warm, and she liked the scent of his skin. It fed that tingle of awareness, the one she both enjoyed and wished she could ignore.

She had noticed his hands earlier, so much larger and heavier than her own, and studied them while his attention was diverted. They were strong and tanned, long fingered and had moved with both grace and precision. There was an old scar on the back of the hand closest to her, one that had been sufficiently deep to heal as a white line and it was a telling reminder of his trade.

Her gaze trailed down the length of him, lingering on the patch of golden hair upon his chest and the hard curves of his muscles. He was all tanned power, his skin smooth and unblemished, its golden hue a hint that he had recently been in warmer climes. Alys had seen boys swimming in the river, young men with new beards, and she had hidden in the forest to look, but none of them had looked like the Silver Wolf. He was man, not boy. There was a shadow of whiskers on his chin and he was all corded strength and lean sinew. She could not keep from studying him, noting the differences between their bodies.

Alys risked a glance downward and saw blood upon his prick, which still stood erect. It seemed he had not lost interest, after all.

"You have seen five and twenty summers," he said, his voice strained. "How can you be a maiden?"

"By never having coupled with a man," she replied and he chuckled unwillingly.

He moved his arm away and turned his head to face her, his eyes dancing with unexpected merriment, his mouth so close that she was startled. "Aye, that would be the strategy." She was so entranced by his smile that she did not pull away when he pushed her chemise over her head and cast it aside. She was nude beside him and did not know what to do—save flush as his gaze swept over her. Yet again, his admiration was clear—or he was adept at pretending to think what he did not.

Alys recalled his insistence that he did not lie. What if her husband *did* find her pleasing? The notion was thrilling in a most unwelcome way, but when his hand slid down the length of her in that possessive gesture, she found herself arching to his touch.

She watched as he captured her nipple between finger and thumb, then teased it to a point once more. 'Twas curious that he knew how to give her pleasure better than she might have guessed. She had the strange notion that her body had changed allegiance, then caught her breath as pleasure surged through her anew.

"You would train me like a hound," she whispered.

"I have never trained a hound thus," he informed her solemnly, though that glimmer of laughter lingered in his eyes. Alys fought a smile as their gazes met, then he bent to take her nipple in his mouth again. This time, he teased her more slowly, coaxing her response, using his tongue and his teeth to give her pleasure. Alys found herself rubbing against him, trapped beneath his weight and unwilling to evade his touch. He stirred that restless tumult to greater power again, and she cursed herself for her curiosity.

Aye, she wanted more.

"You would teach me to rise to your touch," she accused breathlessly.

He did not reply, but turned his attention to the other nipple. Meanwhile, his hand slid lower again. She caught her breath, expecting pain, but instead, his fingers slid across her gently. She gasped aloud when he touched her with surety, then found herself making an incoherent sound of pleasure.

It felt so very good.

He caressed her slowly and steadily, and when he slanted his mouth over hers once more, Alys met him with newfound hunger. Her heart raced, her breathing was quick, and she was flushed from head to toe. His kiss nigh made her swoon, combining with his touch to make Alys dizzy with need. She clutched at his hair and his shoulders, mimicking him, and felt that tumult rise to intolerable intensity.

There was naught in her world but his mouth and his hand, his weight against her, the feel of shoulders beneath her hands. She wanted more. She could not name her goal, but she trusted him to satisfy it. The fever rose, growing hotter with each passing moment, making Alys yearn with vigor. She heard herself moan, she found herself caressing him, she returned his kiss with a fervor she had not known she possessed.

Abruptly he pinched her in that most private of places and Alys cried out as fire shot through her body. She roared in her release, uncertain what had happened and trembling in its wake. She clutched at his shoulders and arched against him, not as if she would escape but as if she would meld their flesh together. Indeed, she rode a wave of pure pleasure and the heat surging through her body in its wake left her languid and satisfied.

Maximilian.

His name was Maximilian.

She struggled to catch her breath, falling back against the bed and meeting his gaze. He was smiling in truth now, a warm light in his eyes.

"Now, 'twill be easier," he murmured and she believed him. He moved atop her, bending to claim her lips anew. She watching him inhale, his nostrils fairly pinching shut as he eased within her again. It twinged this time, but did not hurt so much. He was taut, but moved with deliberation, their gazes meeting as he slowly buried himself within her.

Alys had never felt the like.

"I will not last," he whispered, his voice strained. "Perhaps 'tis better thus." He moved only several times, the motion making Alys catch her breath and grip his shoulders. She could feel the heat rising within him and guessed he would find a similar release. She supposed it was only fair that they both had satisfaction on this night.

But his eyes shone with resolve and he rolled abruptly to his back, carrying her with him. Alys found herself straddling him, his satisfaction with the situation most clear as he smiled up at her. He eased his hand between them, caressing her with surety there again, and Alys gasped.

"I would wager that you, my Alys, would prefer to set the pace," he growled. He touched her hips, giving her a hint, and she braced her hands upon his broad chest, then lifted herself. 'Twas a marvel to see her effect upon him, to watch his pleasure increase and know that she was responsible.

He might have been her captive. There was a seductive notion.

Alys' hair fell over her shoulders and she looked down upon the Silver Wolf, liking that she could so readily command his reaction. His gaze brightened as he watched her and she recalled his assertion that she was magnificent. She felt like a beauty when his eyes glowed thus and again, she wanted only more.

He teased her with his fingers as she tormented him, the two of them finding a rhythm together that surely could not endure. Alys moved faster, unable to do otherwise when his fingers fairly provoked her to dance. She felt that tumult again and this time, she knew her goal. Their gazes locked, his a fiery blue, the entire bed rocking until he whispered her name and pinched her again.

Alys cried out along with her husband, then collapsed atop him, shuddering in her release. His arms closed around her tightly and she could hear the thunder of his heart beneath her cheek. 'Twas only then that she realized her scarred side had been toward the light again, and it had not deterred him a whit.

"Aye, Alys, we will suit each other very well," he said finally, his voice husky, and she could not halt her smile.

THE SHERIFF and his wife found themselves home again when the night was dark as pitch. The fire on the hearth had gone out and their cottage was cold. The rain had slipped beneath the door to form a puddle on the floor. As the sound of hoof beats faded and the mercenaries left Rowan Fell, the sheriff stirred himself, as if awakening from a bad dream. He struck a flint and lit a lamp, then surveyed the remains of the meal they had not shared, still upon the board.

Jeannie, who had feared she would not survive the night just moments before, was annoyed once the danger had disappeared. Her cottage was dirty and cold, the smell of duck fat lingering in the air. She had worked hard to prepare a fine meal and had only the cleaning to do, her own belly growling with hunger. She stirred the fire with impatient gestures, finding a few coals still glowing in the ash by some miracle, and set it to burning merrily again. The sauce upon which she had used her last peppercorns was congealed in the pot; the duck carcass was nigh picked clean. She was chilled to the bone, so she moved briskly, scraping the remains of the meal into a bowl for the smith's pig. 'Twas a waste of fine fare and she resented it bitterly.

At least they had arrived home so late that the neighbors were asleep—or too daunted to knock on the door at this hour. She had time to contrive a tale that showed her to better advantage than the truth.

"Curse Alys Armstrong," she said under her breath. "And curse the Silver Wolf."

Her husband bit the silver penny he had been granted as his wage and she knew by the way his brows rose that it was genuine.

"That was Murdoch Campbell," she continued, speaking quietly lest the Silver Wolf could hear her words even at such distance. "He has grown his beard since last I saw him, but 'twas him."

"Aye," her husband agreed, sitting down heavily at the table. "I feared you might reveal him in your surprise. 'Twas good you did not."

"I should have done so. I should have called him out!" Jeannie was outraged. "How could he willingly join the ranks of the villain who killed his own father? It does not bear consideration. Rupert would have been dismayed beyond all."

Eamon shook his head. "Do you not recall, Jeannie? Murdoch vowed vengeance upon the Silver Wolf for Rupert's death."

"That was years ago! He was but a boy."

"And a boy no longer." Her husband picked a bit of meat from the carcass, wincing that it had dried to a sinew and casting it back at the carcass. "And now he is within the wolf's very den, awaiting the moment he will deliver his reckoning."

Jeannie blinked, her assessment of Murdoch completely changed with just those few words. "I should like to witness that," she said, turning to face her husband.

"Not I!" Eamon surveyed the cottage with a frown. "'Tis good that we are not so close that I will be expected to intervene in the name of justice."

"I doubt the Silver Wolf has need of your aid, husband."

Eamon grinned and tossed the silver penny in the air, catching it with a flourish. "He already did, wife. He already did." He rolled the coin between finger and thumb, holding it up as if it would replace his eye.

Jeannie could not smile at his antics. Indeed, she disliked that he made his peace so readily with the change. "Why would he desire your aid again?"

Eamon shrugged. "He needs the appearance of legitimacy, for some reason of his own. The seal and the heiress are his, but I wonder if his seat is as secure as he believes."

"Mark my words, husband, he will demand a settlement from you." Eamon's frown deepened as Jeannie watched and she wondered whether he had a scheme. If so, he would not share it, for he thought money was his to manage. She shivered. "I would not be Alys Armstrong this night for all the riches in Christendom."

Eamon pursed his lips. "And I would not be the man who sought to tame Alys Armstrong. She is wild and she is bitter. The Silver Wolf may have made a worse wager than he realizes." He tossed the coin in the air and caught it with a flourish. "'Tis a fair price for witnessing a wedding."

"Do not forget the duck," Jeannie reminded him, still disgruntled that they had not tasted a bite.

"Do not forget the tale we now possess," her husband countered. "There will be many wanting to hear every detail, again and again, on the morrow."

"Aye, so you will have your ale," Jeannie said. "What I desire is another fine plump duck." She shook a finger at her husband before he could suggest the obvious. "And you will not be spending that penny upon one. The Silver Wolf owes me a duck and I will not forget as much."

Her husband shook his head. "I welcome you to collect it, wife of mine. I have greater concerns than a mere duck, to be sure."

His tone was thoughtful and Jeannie turned to face him. "What will you do?"

"I think the king should know that the Silver Wolf has returned to claim Kilderrick." Eamon shed his boots, then stretched. "It cannot be a good situation for the people of Rowan Fell to endure a mercenary so close at hand, can it?"

"And you have paid the king his due each year."

"I have. That must carry some weight."

Jeannie bit her lip, wondering whether the king's word would be sufficient to persuade the Silver Wolf to abandon fifteen years of tithes due to the Laird of Kilderrick.

The coin was gone, so she had to hope for the best.

MAXIMILIAN DOZED for only a moment or two, but it was sufficient time for Alys to have left the bed. He rolled over immediately upon awakening and found her washing herself again. She jumped a little at his movement and he wondered what her scheme had been. His dagger was yet on the board and his purse, with the vial of poppy powder within it, was still on the trunk. He thought both were untouched, but he was wary all the same.

"The water must be cold," he said, rising to his feet.

"Warmer than the river," she said and dried herself. She pulled the chemise over her head again and began to braid her hair once more.

When she passed him to retrieve the ribbon, she gave him one of those challenging looks.

Maximilian only smiled, taking his turn to wash up. He, too, donned a chemise but not his chausses. The chemise he had worn earlier had been cast aside and he left it for Reynaud to wash, getting a new one from his trunk. That gave him the opportunity to drop a few grains of the poppy powder into the cup he had left there. By the time he turned, Alys was seated at the board, picking at the carcass of the partridge with a hunger she had not shown before.

"It is good," she said at his glance.

He had to distract her so that she drank the ale.

"You have devoured it all," he complained, trying to sound disgusted. He turned the plate, one way and the other, studying the bones in apparent disbelief. There was not a morsel left.

Her smile was so impish that he would have forgiven her far more than that.

"It has been years since I have tasted a roast partridge so succulent." Alys licked her fingers noisily, enjoying the horror of his expression. "Your cook *is* talented."

"And the bread?"

Alys put the last bite into her mouth and chewed with gusto. "I was too troubled earlier to have an appetite." She flashed him a smile that startled him with its brilliance.

Maximilian was not so startled that he failed to notice the disappearance of his dagger.

She *had* warned him.

"I have an appetite after lovemaking," he said.

"You will have to summon your cook then," she replied, unrepentant.

"'Tis too late to trouble him." He lowered himself onto the trunk opposite her and set the cup down heavily on the board, apparently despondent. Hers was empty and he checked the pitcher, then poured the last of the ale into the cup with the powder. He pretended to be surprised when there was no more ale to fill her cup. "You might as well have the rest of the ale, as well." He ensured that he sounded disgruntled and granted her the cup with poor humor.

Alys drank the ale in a single gulp. She put the cup down with a flourish. "Lest you change your thinking," she said triumphantly, those eyes dancing with challenge.

Maximilian watched her as he let his triumphant smile dawn slowly. Rafael always said 'twas a smile of pure wickedness and supreme satisfaction.

Alys sobered as she watched, then pushed away from the table. "What did you do?" she asked with a suspicion she should have shown earlier.

"I ensured that you would sleep." Maximilian stood up, then braced his hands on the table before leaning toward her,. "You have led me on a merry chase, my lady wife, and I have need of rest this night."

Her eyes flashed then she looked puzzled.

She yawned, clearly unable to stop herself, a yawn that stretched her mouth wide open and lasted long. She blinked then, as if her eyelids had become weighted. She shook her head, fixing her gaze upon him. "What have you done?" she demanded again, her words slightly slurred.

"I augmented the ale," he confessed. Her gaze darted immediately to his purse on the trunk.

"You would poison me!" The words were almost impossible for her to utter as sleep began to claim her.

"Never that, my Alys," he said gently. "I merely would sleep this night in safety."

"Fiend," she charged but the word was no more than a whisper. "Blackguard and villain."

"Aye, all of those and more," he agreed.

"You lied to me."

"Nay, but neither did I tell you all of the truth."

"Cur," she said, but the word was merely a drawl. She slumped against the table, fighting the poppy powder with all her might. He moved to her side to pick her up, knowing she would not be able to walk to the bed. She had not eaten enough to delay its action much. His dagger fell to the ground from her lap and he glanced down at it, then smiled at her.

"And you believe we are not well suited," he mused with a shake of his head, then carried her to the bed. She poked him in the shoulder once, even as her head lolled against his shoulder.

"I will have vengeance..." she said, her words trailing to silence.

"Ah, Alys," Maximilian murmured as he settled her on the bed. "May you always declare your intent so clearly in advance." He tucked his cloak around her, ensuring that she was warm, and watched her slide into a deep sleep.

He might have joined her there, but Rafael murmured a word from outside the tent. Maximilian swept open the flap to admit his brother, who surveyed first the sleeping Alys, then the carcass.

"Not a shred of meat," Rafael said with a shake of his head and sat down heavily. "It is true, then, that the demands of a wedding night feed other appetites."

"I earned that meal and more in winning this bride," Maximilian said.

Rafael chuckled. "Aye, I know of your bruise."

"Call it two. The drop was long to the bottom of that hole."

Rafael laughed aloud. There was no question of their conversation awakening Alys. She breathed deeply and steadily.

"I doubt I shall sit with comfort for a week after that fall into the hole this night." Belying his own words, Maximilian sat down at the board again.

Rafael shook his head. "How did you enjoy bedding a harlot?" he asked, reaching for the cup Alys had emptied. "That is not your usual choice, after all."

Maximilian knew the others jested about his preference for widows, but he had no desire for the pox.

"Do not touch that," he warned, just as Rafael would have lifted the cup to his lips. It was empty, but Rafael had a tendency to check every cup to be certain. Maximilian inverted it on the board so there could be no error.

Understanding dawned in Rafael's dark eyes. "You still have that powder of poppy."

"Eudaline gave me a measure more," he admitted.

Rafael nodded. "So your bride will sleep deeply and until morning. I thought you might have taken the entire night to tire of her skills."

"She has none," Maximilian said flatly. "She was a maiden."

Rafael stared at him, aghast. "You jest."

"I assure you, I do not."

Rafael swore softly, his gaze trailing to Alys. "I wonder about the others, then."

"They are not witches. Why should they be harlots? In truth, I feel a fool for accepting even half the rumor." Maximilian surveyed his comrade, noting that Rafael had changed his garb after his bath. His long dark hair was still wet. He had lingered for a reason after reporting that the sheriff and his wife were home, and it had not been to ask about Alys. "What did you come to tell me this night?"

"Just the gossip of the camp, as usual." Rafael leaned back, toying with the other empty cup. "First a matter of great import: there is no ale." He gave Maximilian an intent look. "Not a single drop remaining."

"Perhaps we can buy some in Rowan Fell on the morrow."

The other man nodded. "Second, there is a fierce argument between Amaury and Denis."

"What is this? Denis was pleased with the deer when last I spoke to him."

Rafael wagged a finger. "But a partridge is missing, to hear Denis tell of it. He says there were six and insists that Amaury took one before the meal was served. Amaury denies doing as much and says there were always five. Denis says he knows what he cooked. Amaury says he learned to count as a child and has not yet forgotten the lesson." He raised his brows. "I thought they might come to blows. I am surprised you did not hear their dispute from here."

"I was otherwise occupied."

Rafael nodded then continued. "Marie concurs with Denis. Oliver insists that Amaury counted aright. The dogs did not have it, the air is thick with distrust, and that cursed bird is back." He tipped the other cup, as if ale would magically appear within it. "I would slaughter a village for a sip of ale in this moment."

Maximilian, understanding his brother's hint, retrieved a wineskin of *eau-de-vie* from his trunk. He claimed the empty cup that had not contained poppy powder, poured a measure into it and pushed the cup across the table to Rafael.

His brother grinned. "Tell me you do not expect me to leave you a taste."

"That portion is yours," Maximilian said. "To ensure that you do not fall ill after your interval in the fen."

Rafael sobered then, a deadly glint lighting his eyes. "I will slaughter *her* if any harm comes to Phantôm," he said darkly. "Though perhaps first I will find out whether she is a harlot or nay."

"Best drink it soon," Maximilian advised and Rafael emptied the cup in one swallow. He closed his eyes and grimaced, no doubt as the fiery liquid burned in his throat. "What bird?" Maximilian asked.

"Amaury's falcon."

Maximilian was surprised. "He recovered her? In this wilderness? I thought her gone forever."

"Aye, but he found her. Oliver said Amaury whistled and the falcon answered the cry, then landed on his fist. Came without a lure."

"She must have been hungry."

Rafael shook his head. "Oliver said not. She must have killed on her own."

"With her jesses and bells?" Maximilian was skeptical.

His brother shrugged and stood, then stretched. "Who can say? Perhaps she found something dead to feast upon. I do not care, for now I shall be blessed with the sound of her fussing and chirping and jingling all the night long." He shuddered elaborately. "Tell me that you will build a falconry in this keep where the falcons can nestle with their own kind, and a stable where the dogs may roll in the hay and fart at will, so that a man can sleep with his own kind and no others."

"I thought you would want a woman."

Rafael's smile flashed. "Aye, there is one I would like, to be sure."

He had no opportunity to elaborate on that, for there was a shout and then a ruckus. Both men straightened and pivoted, looking toward the river. Men shouted in the distance, horses neighed and Maximilian smiled in understanding.

"Her comrades have baited the trap again," he said with approval. "They are most enterprising women."

"But who rides through the valley?" Rafael asked.

"Make haste and we shall see!" Maximilian dressed quickly, tugging on his chausses and boots. He snapped his fingers but Reynaud was already arriving with his hauberk and sword. He spared one last glance at Alys, who was still asleep, then called for Nathalie to watch over her new mistress. With that, he raced toward the river, curious to see what the women did—and who their intended victims might be.

ELIZABETH WAITED until the Silver Wolf's camp had nearly emptied of occupants. She counted the men who raced toward the river, where Ceara and Nyssa had surprised reivers returning home. It was the party the women had believed to be returning the night before. There was a lot of shouting in the darkness and dogs ran barking from the Silver Wolf's camp, ahead of the men. It appeared that they did not even leave a sentry behind, which suited Elizabeth well.

The rain had slowed and she had not much time to work her trickery. She had blackened her face and her hands with soot and had brought her tokens. She hastened into the camp on silent feet and set to making mischief.

She only hoped the knight with the falcon did not catch her.

ANOTHER SYMBOL WAS hung over the river, just as it had two nights before. Maximilian recognized the shape of it and the location, as it burned in the darkness. As before, the fire was reflected in the water— and just as before, a company of men shouted as their company fell into disarray.

Who were they and why did they ride through the valley of Kilderrick at night? Whoever they were, the women had anticipated them. Maximilian saw the volley of stones and heard them splash in the water. He saw burning arrows launched at the party from a second point in the forest.

That made two of Alys' companions who caused this disturbance.

Where was the third?

On impulse, he pivoted and ran back to the camp. He ducked

between the tents on silent feet. If this was a distraction, the plan might be to aid Alys. He swept open the flap to his tent and Nathalie spun to face him in alarm, eyes wide.

"What is amiss, my lord?"

Maximilian touched a finger to his lips, listening. There was a crack as someone stepped on a twig, then a slight splash. He followed the sound stealthily and finally emerged in the clearing where the canopy was erected for Denis' fire.

The fire had burned down to glowing embers but a copy of the large pentacle blazed against the night, suspended from the canopy. It, too, was made of twigs bound into the shape and its flames cast a shadow on the far side of the makeshift hearth.

Even though he knew it was a ploy, the sight sent a shiver down Maximilian's spine.

A cloaked figure was yet there, the silhouette almost lost in the shadows.

"Alys," that woman whispered and Maximilian recognized the cloak Alys had worn when she had led the wolves to his camp.

He had found her third companion. He steadily moved closer, intent upon capturing this intruder and putting her folly to rest. He realized that the woman was drawing a pentacle on the side of the tent in soot. She whispered again, more urgency in her voice, then glanced furtively over her shoulder. Her face was dark, perhaps smeared with soot, but her eyes widened when she spotted Maximilian.

He lunged toward her but she fled, scattering something behind her as she ran. She was gone in a heartbeat, lost against the shadows, even as his companions shouted near the river. A horse neighed and he guessed it might be Phantôm. He dropped to one knee to retrieve what the woman had dropped and found a collection of small pentacles.

Evidently, she'd planned to scatter them throughout the camp, as well as draw more in soot like this one—all while she located Alys. He gathered them with disgust, and flung them into the slumbering fire, then cut down the large pentacle so it, too, burned. He kicked up the coals so the fire blazed brighter again, then realized he was no longer alone.

The villagers from Château de Vries were gathered, their fearful faces lit by the fire. Marie held one of the charms, her trepidation clear. Even Yves appeared to be shaken. Eudaline was muttering to herself and wringing her hands.

The ostler, Henri, invariably a stalwart man, held fast to his wide-eyed son with one hand and crossed himself with the other. "'Tis a wicked place, my lord," he whispered. "We should leave."

"That is exactly what someone is trying to persuade us to do," Maximilian replied. He stepped forward and plucked the charm from Marie's nervous fingers. "Where was this?"

"On the threshold of the tent we share, my lord. It is a sign."

"It is a taunt, no more and no less." Maximilian flung the charm into the fire and Marie recoiled. "It is only straw and vine and a quest to see us gone."

"The sheriff's wife said they were witches," Yves contributed in a low voice. "I understood as much as that."

"My lord, have you wed a witch?" Marie demanded. She fell to her knees before him, her hands clutched together. "Do not keep such a woman as your wife, sir, I beg of you. She will steal your very soul."

"She will do no such deed," he said sternly. "There are no witches. There is no sorcery. There are people, however, who would prefer I leave Kilderrick. They are doomed to disappointment." Maximilian could see that the cook's wife was not convinced and shook his head at the whimsy of it all. However much he thought it foolery, there were those in his company who believed.

Curse Alys and her comrades in this. They were too experienced in fostering fear.

This could not be allowed to continue.

"There *is* a demon in this place," Marie whispered. "It took the partridge..."

"I told you," Denis said with impatience. "Amaury took the partridge."

"But..."

"Demons seldom have an appetite for partridge, in my experience," Maximilian said with resolve.

"Because they would feed upon our souls," Marie whispered and buried her face in her hands.

Maximilian exchanged a glance with Denis, and knew his impatience showed by the way the cook spoke with haste. "I will speak with her, my lord."

Rafael strode into the camp then, wet to the thighs, his eyes flashing. "They repeated the trick with the river again," he informed Maximilian. "Just as with us. 'Twas a company of men on ponies or on foot, laden with baggage, they targeted."

"What happened to them?"

"The men abandoned much of it and fled north." Rafael turned and pointed. "They scattered so they were not readily pursued. The women seized three of the ponies, but we retrieved the others. The others are bringing the goods to you." He frowned. "I had a glimpse of Phantôm and the temptress who seized him." His tone turned wistful. "She rode bareback. God only knows what she has done with my saddle."

"And Phantôm? Is he hale?"

Rafael glared. "Faithless beast. He barely spared me a glance." He shrugged. "But then, if she rode me bareback..."

Yves inhaled sharply in disapproval but Maximilian turned away, thinking.

Three women, a destrier and three ponies.

"They have a haven," he said. "Hidden in that forest. It must be destroyed."

Amaury returned just then and seemed to be startled by Maximilian's words. He put down a small chest that was clearly heavy and opened it. Coins spilled from it.

"Plunder," Maximilian murmured, bending to push his hand through the treasure. "I heard it once said that these valleys were full of bandits and raiders." He remained in a crouch, glancing toward the river, as he thought. "If the raiders have a routine, then Alys and her companions would know of it."

"Perhaps they see them ride south," Rafael suggested.

Maximilian nodded. "And they prepare for the raiders' return." 'Twas brilliant, in his view. Alys had effectively put a toll on this road, one that only was collected when the northern residents journeyed south to raid along the English border. When they returned, laden with goods and coin, the trap on the river surprised them into surrendering a measure of it. No doubt, this was how the group of women survived.

Maximilian would do the same, but he would not rely upon surprise. He would build a gate and demand a toll each and every day of the year. He had paid tolls himself when he had need to use a road, and he delighted in the knowledge that he would soon commandeer this entire valley.

"Robbing thieves." Rafael grinned. "Few men are vigorous in the defense of what they have stolen."

"Especially when they fear for their lives. It is a kind of a toll, one we will continue though we will simply bar the road and demand our due, no matter the day or the hour." Maximilian straightened as the other mercenaries returned, bearing another trunk of coins and a tangle of gems, a collection of weapons and a wagon with three barrels within it. They spread what they had seized beside the fire to be admired.

"Easiest day of pillaging in my life," Matteo said with a laugh. "They simply dropped the goods and ran."

Maximilian knew he would have to divide the spoils, ensuring that his men were rewarded for their efforts. "Each of you, choose a weapon for your own," he said to the mercenaries. "I will keep most of the coin for rebuilding the keep."

"I thought you had coin for that," Rafael noted.

"Aye, but such tasks always consume more than one expects," Maximilian said, then raised his hands. "And now we must add a toll gate to the road."

Rafael laughed at that, and bent to examine the weapons. He discussed the merits of a pair of daggers with Victor, and the company began to chatter.

Denis scrambled to check the barrels in the wagon and laughed aloud. "No demon would bring Burgundy wine for my lord's wedding feast," he said to Marie with undisguised delight. "One of wine and two of ale, Yves, for your inventory."

"Duly noted," Yves said primly, his gaze flicking to Maximilian. "What will you do, my lord?"

"Eliminate the women's sanctuary this very night," Maximilian said, his plan made. "And with luck, retrieve Phantôm." He raised his voice. "Rafael, Matteo and Royce, with me. Amaury and Victor will take the watch. Nathalie, please ensure that my wife remains in her bed. The boys will guard the steeds. We go on foot, the better to surprise our prey."

The three mercenaries nodded and armed themselves. The others secured the gains for the night and the villagers retired, whispering. Within moments, Maximilian led his company toward the forest, intent upon seeing the matter resolved with all haste.

CHAPTER 8

"e make the preparations and he claims the takings," Ceara said with disgust. "I could despise this man and his company."

The three women were in Morag's hut again, their mood uncertain. Even Dorcha was subdued on his perch.

There had been no indication of the Silver Wolf's company dispersing, despite Elizabeth's ploy.

And they had claimed the plunder from the raiding company, too.

'Twas clear to Ceara that they would not be able to survive so long as the Silver Wolf's company remained—and that he had no inclination to leave.

"What of Alys?" Elizabeth asked.

Nyssa sighed. "She will have been forced by now."

"We failed her," Ceara concluded, then rose to pace the confined space. "We must free her from him somehow."

"But how?" Nyssa asked. "We are vastly outnumbered and they are warriors as well."

"They do not frighten easily, that is for certain," Ceara said, then pivoted to confront the other two. "We may have to kill him."

Elizabeth gasped and paled.

Nyssa frowned at the dirt floor of the hut. "That will not be easily achieved. He is surrounded by his men all the time."

Ceara dropped to a seat beside her. "Alys could do it, if she had a weapon. I wager she would, as well." She did not say more but knew the other women understood. If Alys had been raped, she would be glad to bury a dagger in the heart of her assailant.

Nyssa glanced up, considering. "They would have ensured she had no weapon for their wedding night, but might not confirm as much again. They will simply ensure that she cannot claim one from them."

Elizabeth nodded with enthusiasm. "And she is Lady of Kilderrick now," she said with excitement. "If the laird dies, she can claim all as his widow."

"Trust Elizabeth to see the legalities of it all," Ceara whispered.

The women exchanged glances, the atmosphere in the hut improving with this prospect. "We must find a way," Ceara had time to say before Nyssa caught her breath and spun to look in the direction of the camp.

"They come to rout us," she whispered with urgency. "Seize what you can and flee!"

"To the old shelter by dawn," Ceara said.

"Leave the horses," Nyssa commanded. "That may give us time."

Ceara grimaced but she saw the merit of that plan. She untethered the horses, smacked their rumps to send them fleeing in different directions, then fled into the forest herself. The three women disappeared into the shadows as silently as wraiths but Ceara's resentment of the Silver Wolf and his men redoubled.

They must see him gone and soon.

ALYS AWAKENED when sunlight was shining through the roof of the tent. Judging by the angle, the morning had half passed already. She felt groggy, having slept harder than was her habit, and her thoughts were unclear. She frowned as she recalled who was responsible for that, and swung her legs out of the bed in annoyance. How could she have been cursed to wed such a man?

The previous night would teach her to keep her guard high against her spouse. He had given her a sleeping draught against her will and without her knowledge. He was vile, fixed on his own objectives regardless of the price, untrustworthy and a villain, as well. A mercenary and a scoundrel! A ruffian, to be sure.

Although, it was not all bad to be clean and fed, and to have slept in a dry bed piled with pelts. She was warm and comfortable, well-rested, and her belly did not complain that it was empty. Alys pursed her lips, acknowledged that the comforts of her husband's life had some redeeming qualities, then peeked out the flap of the tent. There was no chance of escape, even barefoot in a chemise, for a massive swarthy man stood guard outside. She ducked back inside as he began to turn, then she heard him shout to the Silver Wolf.

Alys paced as she reminded herself of her spouse's shortcomings. She would not admit that she was buttressing her resolve against the power of his presence.

For he would come to her and soon.

Was there any merit in the man who had taken her to wife? He had wedded her against her will, bedded her against her will—nay, worse, he had persuaded her to meet him halfway when it came to pleasure. The man knew her body better than Alys knew it herself and she vehemently distrusted his ability to make her forget her objections. They were married in truth now and no one could argue the matter, for Alys would not lie.

She declined to admit that she shared that trait with her spouse. Nay, he simply said he told no falsehoods, but that in itself had to be a lie. Indeed, he admitted that he might not surrender all of the truth, if that situation suited him.

Irksome man.

He had given her pleasure beyond her experience. Alys had to cede that. He had coaxed her response when he could have simply taken his due. He had not bound her—for long—or hurt her. He looked upon her scarred flesh without flinching.

But he had murdered her father and the castellan who had raised her. He had burned her home. He had caused her scars and changed her life, eliminating the value of the holding that should have been her dowry and leaving her penniless in the forest. Aye, she had plenty of blame to lay at the Silver Wolf's feet.

But their match could not be annulled, not now. They were bound together until death did they part. 'Twas a chilling truth.

Did Alys have the audacity to kill him? Did she have the cunning to succeed? 'Twould not be a deed to attempt and fail, not if she wished to live long herself.

She paused to consider the possibilities of how she might best become a widow, her gaze flicking over the contents of the tent. There were no weapons within view, which was the first consideration, but that did not mean there were none at all. He was a mercenary. He had to have daggers and knives aplenty. She doubted she would have much time alone. Her husband was disinclined to trust her.

Alys acknowledged that she had given him no reason to trust her.

In that moment, the man in question swept open the flap, granting her an intense glance before he stepped into the tent. He wore his hauberk and tabard just as previously. The tabard had been cleaned, though, and his boots were polished to a gleam. He leaned outside and called to Nathalie, then fixed his gaze upon Alys again. His eyes were so very blue and she wished he had not been so fair of face. She found him alluring, which was perilous indeed, and foolish, given what she knew of his nature.

"I trust you slept well," he said when the flap had dropped and they were alone together. Alys' heart was skipping, just because of his proximity, but his tone was level.

Because he was indifferent to her presence. Truly, her existence would be wretched if she could not resist his touch while for him, any woman would suffice. But then, what more could she expect? She was a means to an end, no more, and the sole blessing was that he did not know all of the truth. He would bed her until she conceived, then likely abandon her bed.

How vexing that the prospect did not sound as inviting as Alys knew it should.

"Of course, I did," she said tartly, folding her arms across her chest. "You ensured as much."

"The poppy powder was expedient."

148

"I would ask you to refrain from giving it to me again."

His gaze flicked but he gave no such assurance. "If you swear to kill me in my sleep, you cannot truly expect otherwise."

Alys had no argument for that. In future, she would give no warning of her plans.

That he had given her the same advice was only more irksome.

The Silver Wolf did not seem to expect a reply. "It is good that you are awake. There is much labor to be done this day."

"And I expected the wife of the Laird of Kilderrick to live a life of leisure. Should I not be cultivating my skill with embroidery?"

He seemed to be amused. "Do you have any such skill?"

Alys shook her head. Her expression must have conveyed her opinion of such activities because her husband smiled. "I despise embroidery and never was even competent."

"Alas, we shall have to find some other labor for you to do. Perhaps you could tell me the truth of our neighbors and those who would petition me."

"Do any petition you?"

"They will." He perched one hip on the table, so masculine and vital that the sight of him stole her breath away. She felt warm, recalling his caresses of the night before, and knew from the glint in his eyes that he had guessed as much. "Did the Lady of Kilderrick live in leisure previously?"

His tone was light but his words prompted an unwelcome memory. Alys averted her face and chose not to answer him directly. "My father did not trade in slaughter and thievery. He had not the riches that you must possess." If she thought this might be an invitation for him to brag of the weight of his purse, she was doomed to be disappointed.

He pursed his lips. "We should go to church in Rowan Fell this morn and seek the priest's blessing."

"I doubt that is the sum of your quest there."

His smile was slight but his gaze warmed. "I do like that my wife is clever."

Alys felt her cheeks heat and knew she flushed crimson.

"You guess aright," he continued. "'Tis time that those of Rowan Fell know that there is a new Laird of Kilderrick. We shall attend the mass, request a blessing, and you will dispense alms."

Alys stared at him. "No one has given alms at the chapel in Rowan Fell for twenty years."

"Not even your father?"

"Not in his last years. He was destitute, and raised taxes instead."

The Silver Wolf's brows rose. "A poor strategic choice, when one is reliant upon the goodwill of one's tenants. What was your mother's counsel in this matter?"

"She had none, for she was dead." The words sounded harsh, but they were true all the same.

The Silver Wolf looked up at that, his gaze sharp. "When did she die?"

"In the birthing of me." Alys eyed him. "You missed only one hidden in the keep, not two."

The barb did not seem to strike him. Indeed, there was curiosity in his gaze. "Then you were raised by your father alone?"

"There was a nursemaid for a while, but she departed. And the castellan, of course, but you must recall him." She lifted her chin in challenge, for she could blame him for old Rupert's death, as well.

"Aye, Rupert," he agreed softly. "A most loyal servant." The Silver Wolf eyed her for a long moment and Alys wondered at his thoughts. "Your list of my crimes is long indeed."

Before she could consider a reply, he glanced over his shoulder in expectation. Nathalie came into the tent and bowed, the sentry having opened the flap for her. The man could hear the most minute sound!

Nathalie carried a steaming bucket of water, and had Alys' old garments over her other arm. It looked as if she had cleaned and mended them to the best of her ability during the night, and Alys was surprised both that she had done as much and by her success. They were nearly rags and had been filthy beyond all. She was touched by the girl's efforts, especially when Nathalie laid the old garments out with care on the bed.

She thanked the maid, hearing that her own words were husky with gratitude. Nathalie smiled at her, cheerful as previously, her twinkling gaze darting between husband and wife. Did she anticipate a confession?

The Silver Wolf cleared his throat. "If you will fetch something for my lady wife to break her fast, Nathalie."

The maid hesitated, glancing at the bucket of water, and Alys knew she had intended to help her wash and dress first. They looked at the Silver Wolf as one and he raised a brow, his expression so commanding that no further word was necessary. Nathalie hastened away, leaving Alys with her inscrutable spouse.

What *was* he thinking?

'Twas only when Nathalie was surely out of earshot that he spoke again, his voice low. "I have tidings for you. While you slept, your former companions traded in thievery," the Silver Wolf said and Alys blinked. She knew he did not miss her reaction. "Aye, there was a party on the road, headed north. They are gone, but abandoned many of their possessions, as I am certain was the plan."

Alys could not help but smile that Ceara and Nyssa had managed to keep to their scheme even in her absence. She was glad that her friends had managed to steal from the reivers, nearly beneath the gaze of the Silver Wolf. He had been cheated of those spoils, and she could not regret it. Surely his pride would be pricked, at least.

He continued, his tone firm. "The survivors will blame me, of course, for word of the Silver Wolf's arrival will have reached their villages by the time they arrive home. Is there a schedule for such parties to journey through Kilderrick?"

"Why do you ask?"

"I would know whether there are additional gains to be made."

Alys shrugged. "I cannot say. We saw this party ride south five days ago." She chose to surrender half of the tale. "We knew they would return."

"At night?"

"They travel more slowly with their plunder and tend not to camp on their return."

"They anticipate pursuit and wish to return home with all haste," he guessed. "You thought we were this party."

Alys nodded. "It is better when they reach Kilderrick at night." She bit her tongue then and fell silent, realizing she had said too much.

"For it is easier then to surprise and frighten them." The Silver Wolf nodded once and stood with purpose. "I ask again, is there a season for this or does it occur all the time?"

"Because you would seize any additional spoils?"

He granted her a sidelong glance that made her sizzle, as did the low timbre of his voice. "You cannot blame me for that, Alys. You would do the same. Indeed, you have done so."

Again, she found herself flushing. "They first head south to raid once the harvest is in, but they will halt when the weather is poor." She met his gaze in triumph, savoring the truth she had to share. "The raid around Samhain is the largest raid of the year and you have just missed it."

Her husband smiled then, one of those smiles that she already knew to distrust. "Nay, Alys, I missed naught. Your companions interrupted the party's progress, but they did not capture the greater part of the spoils."

"How can that be? You said the reivers had abandoned their spoils," Alys asked but her vexing spouse held up a finger.

Two squires came then, both carrying trunks that were clearly heavy. Again, he had heard their approach and she had not. Alys knew she should recall how observant he was for future reference.

One of the squires was Reynaud and he bowed his head to her, still blushing. The other stole a glance her way and she wished she might have been wearing more than the chemise. An imperious glance from the Silver Wolf had that boy averting his gaze. A third appeared with a selection of daggers and knives, dropping them on the board with a clatter, never glancing up before he retreated again.

When they were all gone, the Silver Wolf gestured, inviting Alys to sit down. He lined up the daggers and knives, choosing one at intervals to take it from its scabbard then replace it alongside the others. She was certain he had already examined the blades. His manner was so casual she guessed he meant to confide some detail of import.

Some detail to his advantage.

Could she seize one without his notice? Did he intend to tempt her? She could not say.

"What happened?" Alys asked when he did not speak.

"Your former companions seized three ponies and some coin." He sat down opposite her, his eyes vividly blue. "We claimed the rest."

"You did more than that," Alys guessed.

"You should know that one sought you here in the camp while we were diverted."

Alys could not look away from his intent gaze. Her heart leaped that her companions had tried to aid her—though their scheme had failed because of the poppy powder. "How do you know this?" she asked, fearing for whoever had entered the camp.

"The symbol," he said with a dismissive gesture. "Left in charms, marked in soot, left burning over our fire." He shrugged but Alys saw his annoyance and was glad of it. "When your companions retreated, I knew they must have a refuge in the forest." He arranged the daggers, as if seeking something to do with his hands. "They had to have retreated to a specific haven."

Alys' mouth went dry and she stood up. "What have you done, wretched man?"

At that, she had the Silver Wolf's full attention. He leaned forward, eyes snapping. "What did they do first?" he demanded and she glimpsed his fury for the first time. He then counted off their offenses on his fingers. "You are not alone in keeping a list, Alys. You and your companions attacked my party when we arrived. You and your companions led a pack of wolves to our camp with raw meat, urging them to attack. You and your companions deliberately led me and my men into the forest to traps that you had set, causing Rafael to lose possession of his destrier. Your companions set upon this party of men —although, granted, they are thieves in their own right—and robbed them. At the same time, the fourth of your companions entered this camp, hung one of your pentacles over the fire, drew more in soot on the tents and left charms on thresholds, in an attempt to frighten my company." He closed his fist, his gaze steely as his voice rose. "I will not endure this, Alys. I am the Laird of Kilderrick and you, the heiress, are my wife. I will not suffer thieves on this holding, nor will I allow anyone to frighten those I defend."

She had never seen him so angry and Alys feared the import of that —but she refused to retreat. "What have you done?" she asked again, this time in a whisper.

He inhaled sharply and pushed to his feet, leaning over the table so that they were eye to eye. "I have ensured that there is no refuge in the forest any longer and I have retrieved Rafael's destrier," he said crisply. "Despite provocation, I have shown restraint." He glared at her. "And even anticipating your reaction, I have confessed the tale to you, for I would have truth between us."

Alys seized his sleeve, unable to remain still in her uncertainty. "I would have more truth. What of my friends?"

The Silver Wolf made a sweeping gesture with one hand. "Gone. With any fortune, we are rid of them forever. There is no place for witches and harlots at Kilderrick any longer."

Alys knew where the women would have fled, but that place would not give them sufficient shelter for the winter. That structure was small and derelict, which was why they chose to live in Morag's hut.

Which her husband had likely destroyed. Anger rose within Alys again, mingling with frustration and a growing sense of her own powerlessness. This man would take all from her! "They are my friends and companions!"

"No more." He was as cold and impassive again, as if he had been carved of stone. "As Lady of Kilderrick, you have no need of such acquaintances."

He was so calm, so dismissive, that Alys could not disguise her temper. How could he cast her companions aside, as if their lives were of no merit at all? How could he give no care for her fondness for the women who had nigh been her kin? She flew at him with her hands outstretched, hoping to gouge out one of his eyes.

The Silver Wolf seized her wrists, his eyes flashing as he easily overpowered her. "You will not strike me," he said in a low growl. "And you will not defy me."

Alys despised him in that moment, for being larger, for being stronger, for being triumphant—for his conviction that he alone would decide her fate. "And you will not bed me again this night," she said through her teeth, fairly daring him to try.

He took the dare with gusto. He seized her and lifted her, but she twisted and managed to drive her heel against his groin. He grunted and she smiled with satisfaction, but triumph was short-lived. He swore with a thoroughness that surprised her, then rolled her to her back. He pinned her against the table, still holding her wrists, though now they were against the board. He looked taut and furious, his face a mere handspan from hers and his eyes blazing sapphire. "I told you, Alys, that we would meet abed nightly until you conceived."

"Perhaps I have already."

"Until we both know that you have conceived," he clarified. He was furious with her and she knew it by the vivid hue of his eyes, but she was too angry to care.

"Perhaps you will kill me," she taunted. "Perhaps that is my escape from this marriage I did not desire."

"Do not make the prospect so inviting, my lady," he murmured, but something changed in his manner as they glared at each other. Once again, the air seemed to crackle between them, their battle of wills a tangible force. Despite herself, Alys thought of his caresses of the night before and was aware that he held her firmly—again—but did not hurt her. She inhaled sharply, vexed by him anew, and her breasts pushed against his chest by the move. He glanced downward, and when he lifted his gaze to meet hers again, his eyes were simmering with a different heat.

The very sight set her traitorous body aflame.

He smiled, the blackguard, knowing his effect upon her well. If Alys could free herself and seize one of the daggers, she might see this matter ended with haste.

"Kiss me, Alys," he invited in a low whisper. The very sound made her shiver and a tingle slip to her toes. He was still and intent, holding her captive between his muscled strength and the board.

"I would rather kill you." She spoke through gritted teeth.

He lifted a brow. "With pleasure? I would wager that you just might succeed, my bewitching bride."

"I am not..." Alys began to argue hotly, but he bent and touched his lips to the corner of her mouth.

Once again, his gentle caress undermined her fury. Alys fought against her impulse, but he took his time, touching her so tenderly and deliberately that he awakened that desire within her once again. She shuddered, her eyes closing as she recognized he would compel her to forget her own principles.

She was weak. There was no other explanation. They said women were weak and it was true, for this man could turn her thoughts to intimacy with the slightest caress. He brushed his mouth over hers, launching an army of shivers over her flesh. He murmured her name, an ache in his voice that made her wonder whether he, too, found the desire between them irresistibly powerful.

Alys opened her eyes to find him surveying her with that familiar heat. Their gazes locked for a moment during which her heart stopped, then his lashes swept down as he looked at her mouth. He caught his breath then leaned closer, as if unable to resist her, and closed his mouth gently over hers.

Knowing that he, too, felt compelled to touch her, to kiss her, to caress her was a realization that changed all for Alys.

They were both in thrall to this strange and potent attraction, to this fire that burned within and demanded to be quenched.

When he released her wrists with a groan, Alys found her hands in her hair, her mouth open to his seductive caress, her skin afire with a need that only he could satisfy.

When the Silver Wolf deepened his kiss, Alys could not care for anything but his touch. Perhaps he was the demon who would claim her very soul.

HE SHOULD NEVER HAVE WED her.

Maximilian had the conviction in the same moment that he knew he could never have done otherwise. Once he had seen Alys, once they had met—once he had touched her—he had known that she would haunt his dreams forevermore. No other woman had ever challenged or infuriated him so readily. No other woman tempted him without intending to do as much, and none launched an inferno through his veins. No other woman surprised him, sparred with him, challenged and provoked him—or might succeed in outwitting him. No other woman was worthy of being his partner and his mate.

No other woman kissed him back, learning more of the seductive arts herself with each encounter and astonishing ease. She had been a maiden but was rapidly becoming a temptress, as fearless in provoking his fury as his desire. He was tempted to take her on the board, knowing full well that anyone could enter his tent at this hour. He was shocked that he, a man most concerned with appearances and protocol, did not care.

Maximilian did not surrender control to any force, even temptation. Until Alys.

There was no reassurance in that realization.

But Alys sighed and softened, tempting him to deepen his kiss yet more and he could not resist.

Suddenly, Nathalie caught her breath, a waft of chilly air revealing that the flap had been opened. Maximilian lifted his head, abandoning the pleasure Alys offered, and stood. He did not want to risk a glance her way, for he knew her dark hair would be disheveled and her lips swollen from their embrace. Her cheeks would be slightly flushed, her eyes glittering with need, and her chemise might be loosened to reveal the ripe curve of her breasts. He could imagine the sight perfectly and then he had to look, if only to verify his suspicions. The sight of Alys just as he had expected, though now she stood, retying the lace of the chemise at her neck, sent a hot thrill through him and left him clenching one fist.

Alys and no other.

"I will meet you after you have dressed," he said to her, inclining his head as he counted the daggers on the board. They were all yet there so she had not hidden one away. "Nathalie, my lady will have need of my short cloak and your kirtle this day. We ride to church in Rowan Fell."

"Aye, my lord."

Alys' gaze flicked to the daggers, but Maximilian gathered them, counting them aloud, then placed them in the larger trunk. The chests of coins fit within it as well and he locked it securely as she watched.

"At your leisure, my lady," he said to Alys. He bowed then left before he was seduced into touching her anew.

Maximilian was simmering. He had to calm himself before they rode to the village. There might be provocation there, indeed he expected it, and he must be temperate.

He left Victor standing sentry outside his tent, and beckoned to Oliver. The squire whose service he had granted to Amaury was more clever than most, adept with languages. He could stalk nigh any creature, and his skills would be ideal for Maximilian's assignment. Oliver followed, keeping pace with Maximilian. The boy also was inclined to silence, which was welcome.

Maximilian climbed to the rise to the south of his camp, Oliver behind him, and found it to be an excellent vantage point. He could see the sweep of the river toward the south, a wide and lazy stream that was readily forded. To the east of both river and road was that dense forest, which came to the very banks of the river. At that one point, the shadow of the trees swallowed both river and road, the trees on the west bank as well.

To the west, the land rose higher in undulating hills. They were covered with scrubby growth and occasional trees. He noted again the furrows where crops had once been tilled and the cluster of more than one abandoned cottage beyond the ruined keep. He would have to see how many of them could be readily rebuilt. In the distant west, a plume of smoke rose from the village of Rowan Fell. Maximilian wondered whether all in that town knew the tale of the sheriff's adventure already and smiled. The sky was fiercely blue in the west and the wind from that direction had the tang of the sea.

Maximilian exhaled slowly, regaining his usual composure with an effort. Kilderrick was a fine holding and it would be his stronghold.

What was it about Alys that vexed him so greatly? He considered her concern for her former comrades and acknowledged that it was no bad thing to possess such loyalty.

If he could reassure her as to their welfare, she might be appeased.

Or she might not.

Maximilian would try. "You ride to hunt with Amaury this day?" he asked.

"Does he hunt? It is Sunday."

"He must hunt, for we are numerous."

Oliver nodded. "Then I will ride to hunt with him, my lord."

"I would have you become separated from him, perhaps even to lose yourself in the forest."

Oliver smiled. "I am never lost, my lord."

"But you have the wits to give that appearance." Maximilian turned to meet the boy's gaze. He was almost as tall as Maximilian but still slender. He was stronger than he looked, but Maximilian would rely upon him being underestimated. "You track well, better than most. I would have you find the women who were my lady's companions. They cannot have gone far. Perhaps they have another refuge."

"And then, sir?"

"And then you might contrive to be captured, the better that you might listen. I would know more of my lady wife, her alliances and her past. How has she endured in this place? To whom does she owe a debt? Who, if anyone, has betrayed her? Has she any remaining kin? She will not surrender such truths willingly to me, but her companions will know all of it. If they think you do not understand them, they may talk freely."

"I could feign sleep, sir."

"Whatever you deem appropriate."

"I have learned some of their tongue from Murdoch, sir."

"Excellent."

Oliver bowed. "I will return in two days or less, sir, with whatever I have learned."

Maximilian nodded and the boy strode down the hill, making a course for Amaury's tent. Denis was at work, because the fire was burning—the venison would be roasted for the evening meal, the wedding feast. Marie would be baking bread this morning and that would be a welcome addition as well.

It was impossible to believe in sorcery on a clear cool morning like this, but Maximilian knew that those from Château de Vries, and perhaps the squires, had not forgotten the women's feat of the night before.

He would invite them to attend church in Rowan Fell. Some might find their hopes restored thus.

He saw Rafael step out of the area where the horses were sheltered and head toward him. Maximilian had a notion, and he would compare it with his brother's observations.

And for a few moments perhaps, he might cease to be consumed by thoughts of his fetching wife.

Alys might as well be a witch, given the spell she had cast over him. Maximilian reminded himself that witches and sorcery did not exist.

Even he, though, was beginning to acknowledge Alys' ability to beguile him.

CHAPTER 9

*T*hat man.

Alys wanted to kick something or shred it, to beat upon her husband with her fists. Instead she paced the width of the tent and back like a caged beast. In truth, she was as furious with herself as with him. How could she surrender so readily to his touch? How could she forget to despise him, even for a moment? One gentle kiss and she melted before him.

Curse him!

Nathalie reappeared and bowed low before putting the bowl of stew on the table. Civet of hare, unless Alys missed her guess, with a large piece of bread alongside. She had to admit that there were advantages to being in her husband's camp. The fare was excellent and plentiful, and having been hungry for years, she could only appreciate that.

But at what price?

The maid could tell her.

She indicated that she would wash first, and clearly Nathalie was in agreement with that strategy. The maid fussed over her nails this morning, trimming them neatly, making them cleaner than they had been and buffing each to a gleam. Alys spoke slowly, for her Norman French was not so fluid as Nathalie's and she wanted to ensure that she was understood.

"How long have you been with the Silver Wolf's company?"

The maid smiled. "But two months. Since he came to Château de Vries for the funeral of his father."

Was it of import that his father had died? "And he captured you there?"

Nathalie glanced up, puzzled. "It was my home for years, that is true, but I was not captured, my lady. I was invited to join the company."

"At what price?"

The maid shrugged. "None, save loyalty."

Alys feared that she was not truly understood. "How is your loyalty shown, Nathalie?"

"Like this," the maid said and buffed Alys' nails with a flourish.

"Are you compelled to meet any of the men abed?"

Nathalie was visibly shocked. "Nay, nay, my lady. I am a maiden and I will remain thus until I wed." She blushed a little and lowered her gaze. "To be sure, I am encouraged that I now have a lady, for a lady finds husbands for those maids in her service." She spared a shy smile at Alys. "I would ask that you find me a good husband, my lady, and perhaps soon. I have seen seventeen summers and 'tis time I wed."

Alys was astonished. "Is there not a man in the company who enjoys your attention?"

Nathalie was dismissive. "No warrior for me, my lady. I desire a man with some trade who is honest and labors hard, a man who sleeps in his own bed each night, who will give me children and go with me to church on Sunday." She looked up. "A warrior must leave to pursue his trade, oft for months." She shook her head, convinced of her reasoning. "No warrior for me."

"I am surprised that none of them here desire you."

"Oh, the one, he looked at me often, with a hunger. Victor is his name. He is large and strong, but missing a finger." Nathalie indicated the smallest finger on her left hand. "'Tis not so bad as that but I do not desire a warrior. I told Yves, and Yves told the Loup Argent, and Victor, he does not look any more." Her smile turned impish. "The Loup Argent is a man, hmmm? Your wedding night was fine?"

Alys found herself blushing, which made Nathalie laugh. "So, you would have a husband, too?"

Nathalie sighed. "I would have a family, my lady." She gestured as if she patted the heads of half a dozen children who surrounded her. "*Les enfants.* Many of them."

"Did you have a big family?"

The maid sobered and shook her head. "I do not know. I was given as a child to the convent, for my parents either died or did not want me. They gave no donation, though, simply left me at the door. The nuns take only those who are offered with coin. Yves took me to Château de Vries, and asked Lady Mathilde to allow me to serve in the kitchens."

"Lady Mathilde?"

"The mother of the Loup Argent. She did not care, but Yves did and so I stayed. He was good to me, as were Denis and Marie."

It was difficult to think of the Silver Wolf having a mother, much less a home. Alys found herself listening avidly to the maid.

"When Yves said six of us could leave with the Loup Argent after the funeral of Jean le Beau, Denis and Marie were first to agree."

"Jean le Beau?" Even Alys recognized the name of the mercenary who had led a company of mercenaries for hire, though she was uncertain of his role in this tale.

"The father of the Loup Argent! My lady, you do not attend the tale!" Nathalie shook her head, smiling as she chided Alys. "I knew Yves would go, so I also joined the company. I never thought to see England or journey so far." Her dark eyes lit with pleasure. "And now you will find me a husband in this land, and I will have a family again, and I will serve you as my lady to the end of my days. *Bon!*"

"And in those years at Château de Vries, you knew the Silver Wolf?"

Nathalie shook her head. "He came at intervals, but he did not live there. He brought coin from his father for the treasury. Yves said the father of the Loup Argent came for him when he was twelve years of age, to teach him the arts of war."

"He must have yearned to go."

Nathalie bit her lip. "I do not think so. Yves said always that father and son were so different, but then Lady Mathilde did not treat him as her son." She paused as if it would be inappropriate to speak the truth. "She never had a kind word for anyone. I was glad to leave her home." She smiled winningly as Alys considered what the Silver Wolf's childhood must have been like.

She would not feel compassion for him, though.

"It is much better here," Nathalie concluded. "And now we go to church!" She spun and lifted the chemise again, but Alys reached for her old garments.

"You have washed and mended these so well, Nathalie. Thank you. I will wear them this day."

"But you must wear my kirtle to church and to your wedding feast. I entreat you, my lady. You must be splendid, as a bride should be."

"I will never be splendid, Nathalie." Without intending to do as much, Alys rubbed the scarred skin of her left arm.

The maid's lips tightened, then she removed the small crockery vessel from her pocket. "The Loup Argent said it might give you pain still. He asked Eudaline for a salve and she mixed this for you." Nathalie curtseyed. "It is honey with finely ground herbs. She said it might be of aid."

Despite herself, Alys was touched by this consideration. "It was honey and herbs that healed my skin this much," she admitted.

"How did you know to do this? I thought you were a child when you were burned." The maid rubbed a measure of the salve into Alys' arm, the scent bringing back memories of Morag.

Alys realized the others in the camp must speak of her. "I did not. There was healer in the forest who took care of me."

"Like Eudaline! Did you learn her trade? For Eudaline is curious about the plants here. Some are different from those she knows, and she is uncertain where to find the ones she uses most."

"Does she speak French?"

"Aye, but her accent is stronger than mine!"

"Will you help me to talk to her?"

Nathalie smiled. "Aye, my lady. And you will break your fast now, and you will wear the blue kirtle this day."

Alys laughed, charmed despite herself. "And I will find you a good husband, Nathalie."

The maid was so delighted that she kissed Alys' hands repeatedly. As Alys sat at the board and ate the delicious stew, she wondered at the tale the maid told of the Silver Wolf. She did not doubt that the maid believed it, though she wondered whether Nathalie knew the entire tale.

Still, Nathalie was a maiden after two months in a company of mercenaries, because the Silver Wolf had defended her choice. That was unexpected, as unexpected as his concern for her own scar.

Perhaps there was more goodness to her spouse than she had realized.

Perhaps she could learn more of him this day.

First, she would discover what had happened to Morag's hut, and her companions. She had to know that Ceara, Nyssa and Elizabeth were well.

Woe to her spouse if they were not.

~

"TAMED THE BRIDE?" Rafael asked as he reached the crest of the rise. His smile was teasing and Maximilian almost laughed.

"'Twill be years, if even I succeed then." In truth, he did not mind the prospect of matching wits with Alys each day, and seducing her each night.

"Then why take the trouble?" Rafael turned to look over the land, his eyes narrowed against the sunlight.

Maximilian considered his words. "I like her wits and her spirit."

"And you like the challenge."

"Aye, there is that."

Rafael had been in the act of handing him an apple, also having one for himself. The two moved in unison, having no idea that their movements were the same. Each considered the apple; each polished it on his tabard; each took a bite, oblivious to the actions of the other. "There will be soup at midday," Rafael confided and Maximilian nodded. "The wolf pelts are curing well and will be warm this winter."

"All the comforts of home," Maximilian said lightly.

"A few of them at least." Rafael grinned, then gestured to the north. "Where does this road lead?"

"North to the end of the valley, to Hawick and Jedburgh, beyond that to Galashiels."

Rafael chewed and nodded. "What manner of men live there?"

Maximilian shrugged. "The ones who came through Kilderrick last night, I wager."

Rafael nodded, then gestured to the camp. Another man appeared outside the circle of tents, readily identified by his garb, even at a distance, as Murdoch Campbell. He wore a length of woven wool belted around his hips, having abandoned his chausses when they left England behind. He wore a boiled leather jerkin over his chemise as well as high boots, and his chemise was a golden hue. Maximilian realized that his garb echoed the shades of the land, and even the cloth might disappear in the distance.

"What do you make of the Scotsman?" Rafael asked, his own suspicions clear in his tone.

"I do not trust him," Maximilian confessed. "Do you?"

Rafael shook his head. "Nay." There was no doubt in his tone.

"Why?" Maximilian liked to hear Rafael's assessments of others. They noticed different details but oft reached the same conclusions.

"He does not meet my gaze. He has a secret, I would wager."

Maximilian nodded in agreement. "If not two."

"And you?" Rafael asked. "Why do you distrust him?"

"I do not like his tale."

"How so?"

Maximilian watched as Murdoch spoke to the squires, then helped with the brushing of the horses. "Consider two possibilities," he said. "The first is the tale that Murdoch himself recounted. While pursuing his business—"

"Unspecified business," Rafael contributed.

"—he discovered the corpse of a man. He believed the man to be a mercenary, even though the dead man had been robbed."

Rafael snorted and took another bite of his apple. His gaze was fixed on Murdoch.

"That would mean the dead man's coin, his weapons, his armor and even his clothing had likely been stolen, leaving little means to identify the corpse. Yet, Murdoch knew the name of the dead man or guessed it."

"How?" Rafael asked.

"How," Maximilian echoed. "Perhaps he had seen him before. Perhaps he knew the man was in the area. Perhaps he recognized our dear father." He shrugged, finding all those explanations inadequate.

"Perhaps he sought him out."

Maximilian shook his apple at his companion. "That is not part of this tale!"

Rafael grinned.

"And so, knowing the name of the man, and the location of his holding—" Maximilian nodded as Rafael snorted again "—Murdoch took it upon himself to deliver the corpse to the mercenary's widow."

"Why?" Rafael asked.

"Why?" Maximilian echoed. "Perhaps he wished to ensure that a man who has done so much evil has his Christian burial. He knew our father's identity, remember."

Rafael chuckled.

Maximilian knew his skepticism was fully shared. "Perhaps he hoped for a reward."

Rafael shrugged and finished his apple. "But there was none to be had."

"Nay, there was none to be had, for the eldest son, who would gladly have granted the man a coin for his effort, was cheated of his inheritance. And yet when that son insisted that the man journey to Scotland as part of his company, the Scotsman agreed."

"Why?" Rafael asked again.

"Because it was his destination, perhaps." Maximilian finished his apple and wiped his hands. "Or perhaps because the tale of Murdoch Campbell was a lie from start to finish."

Rafael nodded agreement.

"Consider an alternate version," Maximilian invited. "Murdoch knew the identity of our father because he hunted him. He followed Jean le Beau; he confronted him; he demanded something from the old cur and he was denied what he saw as his due. They fought and Murdoch killed his opponent."

"No small feat. Jean was a wily old scoundrel. He did not fight fair."

"Then we must consider that Murdoch either is skilled or unscrupulous."

"Or both."

"But still Murdoch did not have whatever he sought. So, he took the corpse to Château de Vries, hoping it would grant him admission and at least tidings of his objective."

Rafael nodded. "But he only learned that his prize was not there, so he accompanied us north, hoping that you knew more."

"Or simply planning to betray me."

"Or to challenge you and kill you."

"He should be so fortunate as to injure me and live to tell of it," Maximilian said and Rafael laughed.

"Aye, I would not take that wager. But what does he seek?"

"I do not know," Maximilian admitted. "Though I find the second tale more compelling than the first."

"'Tis more plausible."

"Especially as the sheriff's wife recognized him."

Rafael turned in astonishment. "Nay!"

"Aye." Maximilian nodded. "She knew him and well. She was shocked to see Murdoch in our company, so shocked that it took a precious moment to hide her reaction. She had to look and look again to be certain. He has been absent a while, or was not expected to return."

"He gave no sign."

"He was not surprised. Indeed, if he is of these parts, he likely expected to see those he recognized. I wonder who he truly is."

Rafael took another apple from his purse. "Does your new wife know him?"

Maximilian chose to keep his suspicions to himself. "I do not know, not yet."

"But you will find out."

"Aye."

"Because it would be of interest to know his connection to Kilderrick."

"It would indeed, if there is one." Maximilian smiled. "Be sure to continue the ruse that neither of us have any understanding of their tongue."

Rafael chuckled. "To be sure, I only understand the occasional word."

"Then it will not be hard to feign a complete lack of comprehension. I wonder whether he will leave us now or find an excuse to linger in the company."

"We should know soon."

"Aye." Maximilian turned to his longest companion and brother. "What say you to a new position?"

Rafael raised his brows. "What do you mean?"

"I would have a sheriff I could trust, and one who can defend the town if necessary. I thought, naturally, of you."

"So long as I do not have to take the sheriff's wife as my own."

"Nay, but you would be able to wed, if you so chose."

Rafael shook his head. "Not I." His gaze turned shrewd. "What of the sheriff you already have?"

"He will have to find another situation shortly." Maximilian strode down the hill then. "I envision a toll upon this road," he said and Rafael nodded. He pointed to the place where the road disappeared beneath the trees, where the women had seen the river flooded. "There."

Rafael grinned. "Indeed. 'Tis an ideal choice."

Maximilian nodded, reminded again that his new wife was keen of wit. Loyal, as well, for she had been fearful of the fates of her former companions. He had yet to decide whether to bring those three within the camp, if indeed that feat could be done.

It would be complicated, given Rafael's experience of at least one of them.

"You will use such tricks as the women did?" Rafael asked.

"Nay, we have our own tactics." Maximilian turned to his half-brother. "I am certain the Dragon knows how best to impede their progress." He watched Rafael's eyes light with anticipation.

"Aye. I must keep in practice lest my skills erode."

"Indeed," Maximilian agreed, then noticed his wife emerging from the camp, Victor like a large shadow behind her. She wore the blue kirtle from Nathalie, as well as his shorter cloak. He suspected that she wore her own boots. She looked tidier but the purpose in her stride was unchanged.

He raised a hand to salute her, knowing she could not fail to see him.

If she did, she gave no sign. Instead, she turned to march in the opposite direction, heading for the forest. Victor looked between her and Maximilian, then pursued Alys. He looked to be calling after her, but Alys ignored him completely.

"And what of your skills?" Rafael asked, amusement underlying his tone. "There was a time, brother mine, when a woman you seduced would unfailingly return with a desire for more. Perhaps *your* talents have eroded."

"Perhaps my lady has not yet been truly seduced," Maximilian countered.

"Either that or they have moved Rowan Fell during the night," Rafael jested.

Maximilian did not reply but strode in pursuit of his wife, leaving Rafael laughing behind him. He could not wait to discover how she would challenge him before the day was through, and did not fail to note an unfamiliar anticipation lending speed to his steps.

Perhaps he should not have wed Alys, but Maximilian knew he could have done naught else.

And he was not a man to nurture regrets.

'Twas Elizabeth who decided their course, against every expectation.

Ceara and Nyssa were debating the merit of taking the three ponies to Carlisle immediately or waiting to see whether there would be more spoils from raiders to be claimed. They had recaptured the ponies but not the destrier after the destruction of Morag's hut, and Ceara was notably disappointed. Nyssa had dreamed of the wolves again and wished to travel immediately to sell the ponies. The three women trudged through the forest, leading the ponies, making their way toward the old refuge where Alys had once lived alone.

Elizabeth halted, well and done with the discussion. She was not inclined to speak up, for Ceara had a much more commanding nature, but she could not let her companions make a poor choice—not when the right one was so obvious to her. "We should set a trap," she said. "Perhaps the net trap could be put to use."

Ceara and Nyssa turned to stare at her, but of course, it was Ceara who protested. "A trap? To what purpose? We have no time to be hunting game."

"A trap for whoever is sent in pursuit of us," Elizabeth said, sinking to sit on a log. She had not slept well in several nights and was tired beyond all.

"What is this?" Nyssa said, sitting down beside her.

"The Silver Wolf will not suffer us to remain here," Elizabeth explained. "We have attacked his party, we have set wolves upon his camp, and we offer a refuge to Alys. He will not rest until we are routed."

"I hear no invading army," Ceara said with a smile.

"He already destroyed Morag's hut," Nyssa reminded her.

"And that will not suffice." Elizabeth shook her head. "He will send one person alone, a hunter and a spy. Perhaps a woman or a boy. 'Twill be someone we do not fear. And that person will discover us, then return to him to tell of our location and condition. Then the Silver Wolf will see us driven from this forest, but you will not hear his approach."

The other two women exchanged a glance.

"How do you know this?" Ceara asked.

"Because it is what my father would have done. He was a warrior and a laird like the Silver Wolf, and he oft told me that prizes have to be defended. The Silver Wolf sees Kilderrick as his prize and we threaten his possession of it."

"Not so much as that," Ceara protested.

Elizabeth met her gaze. "He will tolerate no risk. If we are left to survive, we might find allies. We might build a union against him. We might aid Alys to betray him." She shook her head again. "There will be a spy, and he or she will probably ride out with the hunter. We already know of the hunter and may overlook his presence in the forest." She bit her lip. "My father always used the assumptions of his foes. I would wager that there will be someone in the hunter's party who will leave that party in pursuit of us."

"A different hunter," Nyssa said.

Elizabeth nodded. "And so, if I were my father in our situation, I would anticipate that ploy. I would set a trap and I would set a lure within it, and I would ensure that the spy returned to the Silver Wolf with the tidings I wished him to take."

Ceara laughed aloud at that and sat down on Elizabeth's other side. "'Tis brilliant. I did not think you had such scheming within you."

"I survived as a prize in my father's domain," Elizabeth informed her, her tone cool. "I have been both bait and boon, which is why I am there no longer."

She saw Ceara straighten slightly, surprise lighting her eyes, then the other woman drew away. "The net trap, then. Where shall we place it?"

"Away from Alys' refuge," Nyssa replied. "That location should remain a secret between us."

The women nodded agreement, then rose with purpose to prepare for their expected visitor.

"Rowan Fell and its church are in the opposite direction," the Silver Wolf said from behind Alys as she approached the river.

She had expected him to follow and also to disapprove of her curiosity about her friends. She had known he drew near when the other mercenary halted his steps. She would never be unobserved so long as she was wed to this man, and already she chafed for freedom.

Alys spun to find the Silver Wolf immediately behind her. "It seems you have guessed my destination."

"You voiced concern for your former comrades."

"I would know the fullness of what you have done."

Her declaration did not seem to surprise him, or her defiant tone.

He gestured and they marched onward in silence, each step taking them closer to Morag's hut. That his steps never wavered meant that he knew its exact location.

Any hope that he had been deceived was lost.

"There is not much time," was his sole injunction.

Even though Alys tried to brace herself for the worst, still she uttered a cry when she saw what was left of the hut. Her husband paused and folded his arms across his chest as he grimly watched her reaction. Alys ran toward the shelter she had once shared, initially with Morag, then with Ceara, Nyssa and Elizabeth.

Just the day before, it had been a hut made of branches and boughs, buttressed and patched over the years, almost disguised in the forest. Now the boughs that had been on the roof were ripped asunder, the walls torn open so that they were barriers no longer. The stones from the makeshift hearth had been kicked into the forest, and the few household implements there had been cast out. Their beds had been cut down and torn apart, the destruction so complete that no one could take shelter there again.

Alys circled the hut several times, seeking some sign that would encourage her.

"They have fled," the Silver Wolf said finally.

"Have they? You have had time to dispose of their corpses, if they were dead," she retorted.

He smiled that maddening smile and she wished she had a dagger to hurl at his black heart. "I do not assault women."

She gestured to the destruction of Morag's hut. "This is not assault?"

"This is encouragement to find another abode, one further from my camp and my wife."

Alys pivoted so that he might not glimpse the depth of her anger. Ceara's bow was gone as well as her quiver. Dorcha was gone, and his favored perch. The earth had been marked by horses' hooves, though she could not have guessed whether the Silver Wolf's claim that he had regained his companion's destrier was true: the tracks were too numerous and too muddled. Ceara would be furious if that had been the case. She had likely been counting the coin that beast would fetch in Carlisle.

There were no weapons left in the hut. Although she and her companions had possessed few, Alys would have been relieved to know that Nyssa and Ceara had taken them, rather than the Silver Wolf and his men having claimed them. At least they had not been amongst the daggers he had displayed that morning. Any game that had been hanging was gone, and the rabbit pelts Ceara had been curing were torn from their frames. The drying herbs had been scattered to the wind.

The willful destruction of any item of value shook Alys.

She should have been there, or at least been able to warn them.

Perhaps Nyssa had known in advance of the assault. She had forecast many an attack on them before and her visions had seen them prepared for the worst. There was one way to know for certain.

Aware that her husband watched her, but also that he was at a distance, Alys bent to look. The hearth stones had been at one end of the hut and behind them, there had been a hiding place beneath the earth. She saw that a small vial had been crushed to splinters on the ground there. This had been part of Morag's legacy, four small treasured bottles, each containing some herbal remedy. All but one were empty in these times, and Alys reached beneath the last stone and into the hidden hole, her heart in her throat.

The other vials were gone, as was Nyssa's witching stone. Nyssa must have taken them. That was a good sign.

She turned to her husband and lifted the broken frame with the hide of the hare. "No one in your company will have need of warmth this winter?" she asked and cast it to the ground. "You had to destroy this place." She surveyed the damage with disgust. "You had to assert yourself over three helpless women and drive them into the wilderness before the sun rose again." She shook her head and walked past him. "You have much to confess this day, it seems."

"They are far from helpless."

"They will die this winter," Alys countered.

His gaze flicked. "They will find another haven, no doubt."

"I doubt that utterly. Did you not hear that they were witches and harlots? Such women are not welcome in every village and keep."

"You are welcome enough in mine." He claimed her arm, but Alys pulled free.

"For the moment, because I am potentially useful. It is possible that I will bear you a son." She turned to confront him. "But if I fail to do so, what then? Will I be abandoned in the wilderness while you take a more suitable bride? Or will I meet a more dire fate than that?"

Once again, his gaze was steely. "You assume much about my nature."

"I assume naught. I merely know your repute. I would know your truth, before 'tis too late for me." She gestured in the direction of the ruined hut. "That does not offer reassurance."

His mouth set in a grim line. "I defend what is mine. I defend those who follow me. A laird guarantees protection and stability to those sworn to his hand, as well as justice."

"A laird also offers mercy."

"I have little experience in that."

"I know." Alys pivoted, intending to return to the camp. She was unsettled and uncertain, not knowing what to believe or how she would fare in future. She would not think of him being raised by a noblewoman Nathalie said was cold. She would not think of his father being a legendary mercenary or the Silver Wolf being collected to serve his father when he was deemed of age. She would not think of him inviting six from his childhood home to accompany him north, even though his company would have ridden more quickly without them.

She would not think of the orphan Nathalie being defended instead of abandoned.

They were tales told to soften her resistance to the husband she did not desire, no more than that.

Alys wished she could be certain that Nyssa, Ceara and Elizabeth were well, but she could not leave to seek them out—for she would not lead her husband to their likely refuge.

She was sorely tempted to flee from this man, then she heard something in the distance. It might have been a cry of dismay.

It made Alys think of Ceara's net trap. It must have been moved from its location of the previous day, which was encouraging in itself. That someone stumbled into it was even more so. The sound gave her hope that Ceara and Nyssa were well. Alys moved away from her spouse, ensuring that she stepped on every possible twig and branch, in order to make as much noise as possible.

She had to ensure that he did not notice the distant cry.

She prayed he had not already done as much.

He matched his steps to hers with some impatience and she risked a sidelong glance, noting no sign that he had heard anything amiss. Perhaps he had mistaken the cry for that of a bird. "What would you have me do, Alys?" he demanded. "They defy me and frighten those under my care."

She met his gaze, assuming he mocked her, but found consideration in his expression. "Offer them shelter. Ensure their welfare."

He shook his head. "I fear that would be like bringing wolves to our hearth. Or is this your scheme to see me driven away?"

Alys opened her mouth and closed it again, thinking there was no shortage of distrust between them. "I have no scheme," she admitted wearily. "But I would see you gone."

"Aye? Because I do not do what you wish in every matter? What else did you expect from marriage?"

"A choice."

He scoffed. "You are more clever than that, Alys. Women in all lands are claimed for their beauty and their ability to bear sons, no more and no less. It is the way of the world."

"It has not been the way of mine. Recall that I have seen five and twenty summers yet was a maiden." She met his gaze. "I am no beauty."

He smiled ever so slightly. "I would argue that with you." He touched her cheek. It was the barest flick of a finger but the gesture seemed affectionate.

Alys' cheeks burned. "You mock me!"

"I admire you," he said, his voice so low that it launched that cursed awareness of him again.

"'Tis not the same."

"The same as what?" His eyes narrowed. "Had you no wish to wed?"

"Does it matter?"

"I ask," he said with heat.

Alys nodded once, knowing the one thing she could demand of him that he would never be able to grant her. She halted on the bank of the river, turning to face him. "Then I will tell you. My mother said a man who loves his wife would treat her with honor and dignity, no matter what ill fortune might befall them. She said a woman was only truly safe when wedded for love. That had been her choice and she wanted the same for me."

He blinked and she was snared by his bright gaze. "But you said she died in the birthing of you. How can you know what she desired for your future?

"My father told me."

He raised a brow.

"There was a letter. She wrote it to me while I was in her womb."

"Where is this letter?"

"Burned," she said, inviting him to realize when and where.

He frowned. "And your father agreed with this counsel?" At her nod, the Silver Wolf continued. "But what is the merit in wedding for love?" he demanded, as if she spoke of folly. "Just because a man declares his affection, that is no guarantee that he will defend his bride or provide for her welfare."

"But love is of merit in itself. My father had every comfort. He was wealthy. He had land and noble blood, but without my mother by his side, he saw no reason to live."

Once again, that blue gaze sharpened as he studied her. "Not even for his daughter?"

Trust this perceptive man to find the heart of the matter.

Alys shook her head, a lump rising in her throat at the truth of that. "He wanted no other woman. He desired only my mother and he would have done any deed to regain her company."

The Silver Wolf raised a brow. "Even sell his soul?"

"Even that and without hesitation."

He nodded. "Is that not a warning about the price of love?"

"It is one I would willingly pay were I to love a man with all my being."

He considered her, as if she was incomprehensible, then shook his head and straightened. "Not I. In your place, I would desire a husband whose deeds were louder than his words, a man who would defend me and see me in comfort."

"But one who might eventually love another?" Alys shook her head. "One who might expect me to share his attention? Not I, sir—but then, I did not have a *choice*." Their gazes locked and held, the air fairly crackling between them once again. They disagreed as before, but there was a new awareness, a knowledge that they could please each other with a touch. It shook Alys to her marrow, for she had long believed that only love made marriage sweet.

'Twas clear she had underestimated the power of desire.

When he might have moved closer, Alys held up her left hand, challenging him. "Why do you think these words were inscribed on this ring?"

"Not by me," he said quickly.

"Nay, but at the command of some man who wed for love."

He frowned and Alys turned away, planning how she would cross the river. There were rocks here that could be used as stepping stones. Once she would have simply waded across, but she appreciated Nathalie's kindness too much to see the kirtle ruined.

She realized then that she had never shared the tale of her mother with anyone and stole a glance at her attentive spouse.

Of course, he was yet watching her, his eyes vividly blue. "And you would have followed her dictate and wed for love?" He glanced at the sun, then swept her into his arms and strode across the river. Alys found herself pressed against his strength, her body responding even to this contact.

The realization made her tone sharp. "If it had been my choice, but you stole that from me."

The Silver Wolf shook his head, skeptical. "At five and twenty summers? Who was your choice? There are few men who would wed a maiden of such advanced years, my Alys, never mind one who has hidden herself in the forest and lived as a brigand. I stole naught from you, but brought you opportunity."

The notion was so outrageous that Alys glared at him.

And then, as was so oft the case with this man, she confessed too much.

CHAPTER 10

$\mathcal{T}$here was such a man pledged to wed me a decade ago," Alys admitted with heat, then could have bitten her tongue for making the confession.

The Silver Wolf was clearly intrigued. "Indeed?"

"I will not tell you of it."

He halted in the middle of the river, the water swirling around his boots. The squires had saddled the horses and the gathered company awaited them in the field before the camp, watching them. "I will wait," he vowed softly and Alys knew he would.

Vexing man!

Alys admitted the remainder in a rush. "My father made a match for me when I was a child. I was betrothed to the son of a comrade. This man had three sons and the eldest was to inherit his father's holding. The middle son was to gain something from his mother's side but the youngest had no legacy. When it was clear to my father that I would be his sole child, he and his comrade made an agreement that the third son and I should wed, and Godfroy would then be Laird of Kilderrick upon my father's death. We pledged our troth in the courtyard of Kilderrick on Midsummer Day when I was seven years of age. The nuptials were to be performed eight years later, when I was fifteen."

The Silver Wolf was very still, so intent upon her words that he did not seem to breathe.

No doubt he disliked the suggestion that he had competition.

Alys felt the urge to prick his pride by embellishing the truth—if that deed could even be done.

"Godfroy was five years my senior, so kind, so clever, so fine a swordsman. I lost my heart in truth and could not wait for the day our nuptial vows would be exchanged." Alys sighed, trying to give credence to her tale of a lost love. There had been no love between her and Godfroy Macdonald. His affection had been solely for Kilderrick. She had been as much of a trophy to her betrothed as she was to the Silver Wolf—but her husband did not like this tale of her being pledged to another.

Any tidings that irked him were those Alys would share.

Fortunately, most of the next part was true. "But then you arrived, and Kilderrick was burned, and my father died, and I alone was left to stand witness to the truth." She held up her ravaged left hand and for the first time, saw something like guilt touch his expression.

"I am sorry, Alys. Had I known you were there, I would have ensured your safety."

The confession shocked Alys, all the more because it rang with sincerity.

"I was only a child and a girl." She knew that both of those traits had made her less valuable to her father and expected the Silver Wolf would share that view.

But he shook his head with resolve. "A knight pledges to defend those weaker or more vulnerable than himself. I hold myself and my men to that same code of honor. There is sufficient bloodshed in war to see the innocent defended from harm."

Alys was alarmed to feel her heart touched. Surely this man could not win her over? She turned away from his piercing gaze. "On the fated Midsummer Day, I awaited my beloved with the healer, Morag. I was fifteen and not the pretty maiden I once had been. My father's comrade and his son came to Kilderrick. They knew my father was dead. They knew the keep had been burned, but Godfroy believed that

I would keep my pledge and be here to greet him on that day. I *was* here."

She watched the flowing water as she lied. "I was prepared to make my vows and so was he, but his father took one look at me and broke the pledge. He insisted that I was no longer worthy of his beloved son and they left as one, abandoning me beside Kilderrick's ruins." Alys swallowed, recalling the rejection well, though it had not been precisely thus. "My last sight of the man I loved was of him looking back, powerless against his father's choice, for he was reliant upon that man to survive. Godfroy's heart was in his eyes, though, and I knew that I was not the only one devastated by what had come to pass."

In truth, it was not Godfroy's father who had broken the agreement: it had been Godfroy himself. Alys would never forget the revulsion in his expression when he had seen her scarred flesh or how he had recoiled.

The Silver Wolf nodded. "I wondered if your wound had cost you a suitor."

"A suitor?" Alys echoed. "It cost me my beloved! It cost me the man wrought to put his hand in mine, to love me for all eternity, to father my children and hold me close for all my days and nights. It cost me happiness and it cost me love and I will never forgive you for that loss." She was vehement, too vehement, and she knew it well. She thought he would recognize that she was not as bereaved as she claimed, but the Silver Wolf was silent.

She dared to glance at him, only to find his expression somber. He shook his head and strode to the bank, then set her on her feet. He raised a hand to her cheek and she could not look away from him. "Love," he said softly. "I had not expected you, Alys, of all women, to believe in such folly."

"It is not folly. It is the greatest force in all the world."

"Hardly that." He studied her, the gentle caress of his finger upon her cheek holding her by his side as securely as a bond. "If love is all a woman can rely upon to see her future secured, she is doomed to misfortune. Bear me a son, Alys, and you will live like a queen for the rest of your days."

She spun away from him, once again annoyed with herself for being tempted to trust his word. "Until you become infatuated with another woman."

"I am not so feckless as that." He matched step with her and claimed her elbow as they approached the company. "We will be late to church."

"I will never love you," she said hotly. "You have wed me and you have bedded me, and you may compel me to bear you sons, but I will *never* love you."

The Silver Wolf was unperturbed. "It could not matter less to me, Alys. Only loyalty is of import."

"Loyalty?"

"Aye." He stopped and looked down at her, his countenance stony. "Be so fool as to betray me, and I will carve out your heart myself." There was no doubting the truth of that, not when his gaze was so chilling.

Alys pulled her elbow from his grasp, striving to hide how his claim had shaken her. "There is no horse for me."

"That is because we will ride together." He gestured to his destrier. "I will not give you the means to flee from me as readily as that, Alys."

"Not even if I am loyal?" she asked sweetly and he chuckled.

"We have yet to see whether that is the case. Rafael, however, will have his due today. You will see how I reward those loyal to me."

"What is this?" Alys was lifted to the saddle without ceremony. She knew the Silver Wolf had heard her question but he gave no sign of it. He swung into the saddle behind her, wrapped an arm firmly around her waist, then mustered the company with a nod.

What did he plan to do? Alys had until they reached Rowan Fell to discover his plan.

'Twas just as Maximilian had suspected: Alys had been betrothed yet cast aside because of her scar. She blamed him for the loss of what would have been a life of greater comfort and security than the one she had lived in the forest, and he could not fault her for that. Curiously, there was more of this matter that troubled him. Did that man still hold Alys' heart? The very notion troubled Maximilian, as he knew it should not. Love was a tale and a lure—deeds were the true measure. He would be a good spouse. He would provide for Alys, protect her, and if all went well, they would have sons. He would defend their children as well.

But Alys placed great weight upon love and Maximilian suspected that the import of this tale could only be that she would never surrender her heart to him.

It should not have mattered.

Maximilian feared that it did. Would this woman challenge all he knew to be true?

The weather was fine, the wind brisk and the skies clear. Denis had given many instructions to the squires aiding him with the feast, but he rode in the wagon with Marie—likely at Marie's insistence that he attend the mass. Nathalie and Yves were also in the cart. Henri, the ostler, rode his palfrey, his son before him, though Eudaline had remained in the camp.

Of the Silver Wolf's men, only Rafael accompanied the party. Amaury had ridden to hunt, as expected, with Oliver, and Murdoch had remained in the camp along with Victor, Matteo and Royce. Maximilian saw import in that—no doubt Murdoch did not wish to be recognized. Who was he, in truth?

Of the squires, only Reynaud rode to Rowan Fell, for Mallory, Louis and Nicholas had been charged to tend the roasting deer in Denis' absence. They were a party of good size but not so large as to be threatening, with only two warriors among them.

If he had thought to ride to Rowan Fell in silence, with only the sweet distraction of his wife in his lap and the prospect of another night abed with her, Maximilian was to be mistaken.

They had not even reached the ruin of Kilderrick when Alys twisted around, a challenge in her eyes. "What do you intend to do?" she demanded, evidently expecting him to confide his every secret in her.

Maximilian was affronted. "Whatever do you mean?"

"You say you will reward Rafael for his loyalty this day. How?" Her suspicion was a tangible force, but Maximilian could see no reason to deny her curiosity in this.

Indeed, she would soon witness the way he rewarded loyalty.

"I mean to make him sheriff of Rowan Fell."

"Rowan Fell has a sheriff, unless Eamon has met his demise in the night and I have heard naught of it." She held his gaze, clearly thinking him capable of ensuring such a situation.

"So far as I know, he is well. He was returned home with his wife and compensated for his inconvenience."

"I would wager *she* did not think the price sufficient, whatever it was."

Maximilian took note of the heat in Alys' tone. "There is bitterness between you and Jeannie."

"There can be naught else. She did her best to make my life as bad as it could be and I am not inclined to forgive the past."

"Then you should not be troubled that I would have a sheriff I can trust, and this very day."

To his astonishment, Alys shook her head. "You cannot do this!"

"I can do whatsoever I desire. I am Laird of Kilderrick."

Alys shook her head again, as if he spoke nonsense. "You are not a king and this is not a court. Nor is it a battlefield where all are obliged to accept your command."

"They will accept..."

"You have need of them, and they have need of you," she said sharply, interrupting him as no one had in years. Maximilian blinked as she continued. "Village and keep must rely upon each other, and that bond must be protected with good will and fairness."

"I suppose you will tell me that your father taught you of that."

"His castellan did, when he complained to me of my father's choices. I do not remember my father being fair or just, but Rupert did and he bemoaned the change. He said naught good would come of it."

"And?"

"And, my father declined to see to the welfare of those in his household and they fled. Only Rupert had stayed, and he told me once that he feared for my survival if he left. My father increased the tithes when there was famine, and his tenants abandoned both him and their fields. My father's treasury was robbed, yet no one came to his defense. Then you came and burned the keep, and no one came to his aid or that of Kilderrick."

Rupert had been the castellan, the one who had died outside the door of the laird's chamber. Maximilian had not raised a hand against him, but the man had been elderly. Perhaps the shock of a mercenary's arrival had been too much for him. Whether Maximilian was directly responsible or not for the castellan's death, 'twas clear Alys blamed him.

It was doubtless on her list.

"This is not an impulse or injustice," he informed her. "I must have a sheriff I can trust, and one who can defend the village, if necessary."

"And you cannot dismiss a sheriff who has held his post for years without just cause, not if you wish to keep the good will of those beneath your hand."

"They are not beneath my hand as yet. I will have them swear fealty on this day."

"And if you dismiss Eamon, a man they know, a man they count amongst their allies whether they like him or not, many will not so swear. Where will you be then? Who will pay your taxes and tithes if the villagers leave?"

Maximilian exhaled, noting the good sense in her words. "I will not have a sheriff who steals from me."

"Then prove his crime. Show the evidence to them, and then you may dismiss him with their full understanding."

"And if it cannot be proven?"

"Then you must suffer Eamon as sheriff."

Maximilian caught his breath.

"You would be laird, not brigand," she informed him. "That means you are the voice of justice, and it must govern your choices as well."

"I *am* laird!" he insisted.

"Only if you act as one," she retorted, then turned her back upon him. She even contrived to put some distance between them, no small feat given Tempest's steady canter.

Maximilian fumed. No one questioned his judgment or challenged his command. No one dared to do as much.

Save his wife.

Yet as his temper cooled, Maximilian was compelled to admit that she might be right.

～

WHEN OLIVER SPOTTED the bent branches, he ducked under the scrub, letting the trickle of the stream disguise the sound of his movements. Amaury charged on in pursuit of a deer, obviously assuming that Oliver was fast behind him. The dogs raced onward, barking, disinterested in any creature beyond their prey.

Oliver waited in the shadows until he could no longer hear Amaury's horse and the dogs were distant. He waited yet longer, his gaze picking out a sequence of broken twigs and indentations in the soft ground.

Someone had passed this way, and done so since the rain had stopped.

More than one person by the indentations, and people lighter in weight than his armed companions. They were accompanied by several ponies, perhaps three.

Oliver had found evidence of the women.

When there was only the sound of the forest, he emerged slowly from his hiding spot, then followed the trail. It wound in a tortuous path through the forest. The route bent back on itself, crossed itself, went around trees and across the river several times, but always it tended in the same direction.

Eastward and slightly uphill.

Oliver followed the path diligently as the sun rose higher overhead. The day became warmer, especially since the wind had stilled.

The forest was unfamiliar to him but not so different from others he had known. So quiet was his progress that the wild creatures came close to him, the birds landing on branches near him and surveying him with apparent surprise. He heard the scuttle of mice beneath the dried leaves on the ground and saw the silhouette of more than one large bird overhead. He noticed hares and partridges and a pair of does, then a sudden stillness caught his attention.

He was being watched. Oliver was convinced of it, though he dared give no sign of his awareness. The women were near and they must have a scheme. He recalled the pit trap that the Silver Wolf had fallen into and that Rafael had been led into a fen. This might be his opportunity to be captured.

Oliver halted and looked about himself, as if confused or lost, but actually seeking some sign of a trap. He spotted it finally, an area in a small clearing in which the fallen leaves were too artfully arranged. Another pit trap? He supposed the woman had time aplenty to dig them. Tree boughs bent over the clearing and he suddenly spotted ropes between the ground and the trees. When the trees were in leaf, they would be completely hidden but on this bright day, he managed to discern them.

Though he pretended otherwise.

'Twas a net trap. Oliver approached it, striving to look oblivious. He turned in place, as if overwhelmed by the forest's unfamiliarity. He pushed a hand through his hair, giving the appearance of choosing between various directions. Then he deliberately stepped into the area where the net had to be hidden.

He cried out as the net was hauled suddenly into the trees, leaving him both trapped within it and swinging above the ground. He flailed and shouted as if shocked beyond all. It took all within Oliver to stifle his smile as the two maidens laughed in triumph beneath him.

He soon would learn their location and plans, then report back to the Loup Argent.

He had time to congratulate himself on a ploy well executed, then the trap swung hard and he hit his head on the trunk of a tree. Oliver saw stars, then knew no more.

ROWAN FELL WAS QUIET, for all were within the chapel. Seeing it for the first time in daylight, Maximilian surveyed the small village. There were a dozen houses in a rough circle, the chapel in the middle. The chapel was stone and built between two old trees, their gnarled branches stretching for the sky. Maximilian had to assume that they were rowan trees, and indeed, the portal and the trees had practically joined together, for they had been thus for a very long time.

A stream that ran into the river at Kilderrick passed to the north of the village, at the bottom of a sloping hill. The village was peaceful, though not overly prosperous. He could see walled gardens behind the houses, heard an ox low from an outbuilding and looked upon the neat furrows that ran down toward the river. The harvest would be in by now, and he wondered whether it had been good.

He knew little of agriculture, but supposed he had until the spring to learn more.

The priest's voice could be heard as he sang the mass. Chickens scattered as the horses cantered into the midst of the village and two dogs barked from the safety of their respective huts. When the horses halted, the priest fell silent as well.

Maximilian swung out of the saddle, reaching to lift down Alys. She drew up the hood of his dark cloak, hiding her features from view. Was she still annoyed with him, or was she shy? He should have asked her when she had last been to the village or chapel, but now 'twas too late. He escorted her to the chapel door, Nathalie following close behind. The villagers from Château de Vries followed, then Rafael was last. Reynaud remained with the horses, one hand on the hilt of his dagger.

The villagers of Rowan Fell pivoted to stare as the Silver Wolf's company marched into the shadowed interior of the chapel. There was more than one glimmer of fear on the faces that turned to confront him and Maximilian was not surprised by how many dropped their gazes. They knew better than to defy him openly, but Alys' words made him wonder whether they might rebel against him more slyly, if given the provocation.

He was bound by the same justice he was obliged to administer. That was new and he was glad of Alys' reminder. Though Maximilian was not an unfair man, he had never needed to tend to subtleties or ensure the loyalty of those who were not warriors like himself. The Compagnie Rouge arrived, did what they had been paid to accomplish, then left—over and over and over again. Being laird was different for he would stay at Kilderrick.

Alys gave him good counsel.

He was glad she had dared.

There was no glass in the openings for windows, not in this remote land, and the worshippers stood in rows upon the stone floor. The sole item of furniture was the table at the altar, a white cloth upon it, as well as a cup and plate. The priest stood behind it in his simple robe and a crucifix was mounted behind him on the wall. He was tall and angular, his tonsure white, his gaze assessing.

Alys held her chin high as she walked toward the altar. Her footstep faltered on the large stone there, then she recovered quickly and genuflected to the cross. Maximilian saw that there was a name upon the stone and realized there had to be a grave beneath it—'twas only after Alys had moved aside that he read the name and realized whose grave it was.

Robert Armstrong.

It defied belief that the man who had been accused of sorcery in his lifetime had been laid to rest at the very altar of Rowan Fell's chapel, but perhaps a donation had overwhelmed any objections.

Or perhaps Robert's sorcery had been as much a ruse as that of his daughter.

But who would have made the donation? And who had seen to his funeral? Alys had been a child, gravely injured, and the servants had gone.

Had she even known the stone was here? Maximilian would have guessed that she had been surprised, given how her step had faltered. She could not have attended the funeral. She might not have even known that her father had been laid to rest in this chapel.

Maximilian bowed his head and genuflected, his thoughts spinning. He noted the other stones to Robert's left and right, undoubtedly Alys' forebears. He led Alys to the front of the company at the right side, then realized the truth.

She must have read the name on the stone.

His new wife was literate, or at least she had recognized enough letters to know it was her father's grave.

There was a marvel, to be sure.

And perhaps a skill of great use. Maximilian would have to think upon it. In the meanwhile, he was well aware that the sheriff and his wife had to move out of the primary position to accommodate himself and Alys, and he did not miss the poisonous glance that Jeannie granted to his lady wife.

In that moment, he knew what he had to do. Alys might well be right about the folly of deposing the sheriff without cause. Either way, it was clear to Maximilian that any retaliation on the part of the sheriff —or more likely, his wife—would rain down upon Alys.

Maximilian would not tolerate as much. He would defend Alys, which meant he would take her advice.

Rafael could wait for his post.

He nodded to the silent priest, who began his service anew, though his manner was flustered. Maximilian was aware of the whispers in the company, of Rafael's motionless silhouette at the doors, and knew that the townspeople expected little good from him. There was agitation amongst them and he felt the weight even of Rafael's expectation.

How would Alys respond when he showed his trust in her judgment? Maximilian did not know, which meant he could only hope for the best.

His lady wife, to be sure, might always keep him guessing.

That realization made Maximilian smile.

ALYS HAD NOT BEEN in the chapel in years, not since her childhood. She had not known that her father was buried here, although it made perfect sense. In truth, she had not thought about it. It had taken the better part of a year for her to recover from her burn and his corpse had been gone from the ruins by then. If she had guessed then, she might have concluded that Morag had buried him somewhere, with no marker left upon the spot.

'Twas better he was here. The truth of it relieved Alys. Her mother lay to his left, her parents and grandparents also having resting places of great esteem. Morag must have seen it done somehow. Their family line could be traced all the way back to the first of Alys' kin to be granted custody of Kilderrick, all of them buried in this church, and Alys clutched her hands together, fearing that the Silver Wolf would read the names and discern the pattern.

The treasure of Kilderrick ran in her veins, in the truth of her lineage. Should the Silver Wolf ever guess the truth, he would never let her go.

She felt on the verge of exposure and kept her head bowed, as if she could hide from that piercing blue gaze.

It felt strange to see the stone with her father's name engraved upon it and she had a strong sense of his presence in the shadowy chapel. Would he have approved of this match? Not given the destruction of Kilderrick, but he would have understood the Silver Wolf. Perhaps he had understood his assailant even then.

Alys could not fail to note Jeannie's sweeping survey or that woman's disdain. Truth be told, there was some satisfaction to be had in the Silver Wolf's decision to replace the sheriff, though it must be done properly to ensure that he did not lose the support of all in Rowan Fell.

Would he heed her advice? Alys could not say and that made her clench her hands even more tightly together. She was aware of the villagers staring and whispering and was glad her husband's cloak had a hood. She did not wish to see them recoil or grimace in revulsion.

In that moment, she realized her husband had never done as much. Indeed, she had nigh forgotten her appearance in his company. How did he manage that?

The sheriff himself stood beside Alys, restless in his uncertainty. He must wonder at the reason for the new laird's presence. She could smell the sharp tang of Eamon's fear, as a predator might have done, and she was sufficiently wicked to revel in it.

Of course, she owed naught good to Jeannie and her husband. The sheriff's wife had spread—if not instigated—the vile rumors about Alys and her companions. She had sent men to the forest, men made dangerous by their desperation for physical satisfaction. One had hurt even Ceara, though he had paid for his transgression with the loss of an eye. Worse, Jeannie had sent women to Alys and her companions, women in search of charms to bring them love or take an unwanted child, women who were trapped by their circumstances and much to be pitied. Those women had been warnings of Alys' potential fate if she ever left the forest, and she thought of them now, the Silver Wolf silent by her side.

Eamon was not the sole one who suspected that her husband had come to Rowan Fell for a reason. The gathered company fairly twitched with uncertainty. Alys did not know many of them, or no longer recognized those she had once known. There was the sheriff and his wife, the priest, the woman who kept goats and sold their milk and cheese, the smith and his two sons. The elder son had evidently wed, and his wife held a babe in her arms. There was Nerida and her granddaughter, who kept bees and grew flowers, who had been friends of Morag as well as suppliers. There were another half dozen others Alys did not know or recognize, mostly older, and she supposed that the lack of a laird had affected the fortunes of Rowan Fell adversely.

The mood was not helped by Rafael, who looked most fearsome and unpredictable, guarding the portal. He also looked jubilant, as if his dreams were about to come true. One might think he had been granted permission to slaughter all of them, for he seemed one who would savor that task. None would leave while he stood there, hands braced on his hips, eyes flashing, more weapons on his belt than any man should possess. No wonder the villagers were unsettled. Even the sound of the horses outside the doors would be unusual in this quiet village, where there was a single ox to be shared for the tilling.

The villagers who had followed the Silver Wolf from Château de Vries were possessed of a different mood. They were pleased to receive the blessing of the mass, Marie in particular, and the smiles they granted to the Silver Wolf were radiant. It seemed absurd that Alys had ever thought them slaves or captives. They trusted him completely, and yet again, she wondered what she did not know of him. Their happiness and confidence was in striking contrast to the doubts of the villagers.

Alys noted all this as the service continued, stealing glances at those gathered, then down at her interlocked hands.

When the service was done and the priest bade them go with God, the Silver Wolf stepped forward. He faced the company and raised a hand for their attention. There was no need, for they were in awe of him already and fell silent.

"I am Maximilian de Vries," he said with authority. Though he spoke Norman French, he spoke slowly and clearly that he might be understood. "Known in many lands as the Silver Wolf, now Laird of Kilderrick. My lady wife is Alys, the daughter of Robert Armstrong, the last Laird of Kilderrick, and his sole child." There was a slight stir in the company and Alys knew that more than one person strained for a better look at her. She kept her head bowed.

The Silver Wolf continued. "Together we will rebuild the keep of Kilderrick and restore the prosperity to this holding that has been lost. Rowan Fell remains within the jurisdiction of Kilderrick and will be defended by me from this day forward. Court will be held monthly at Kilderrick, including all issues from Rowan Fell, on the day after the new moon. Taxes will be collected annually at Michaelmas."

Alys smiled to herself that he was so practical, summarizing the matters of greatest concern. There was some whispering about this and Alys felt his gaze upon her.

She went to his side and repeated his words, but in Gaelic.

"You are welcome to bring any and all concerns to my attention, at Kilderrick," he continued. "The village there will also be rebuilt, and those of you wishing to serve the keep more immediately are invited to speak to me about moving there. You may need to assist in the rebuilding of the huts. I expect the fields to be tilled again, beginning in the spring, and will ensure both that there is a healthy ox for the plow and seed for the sowing. Again, you are welcome to share your knowledge of what grows best in this land and I rely upon your counsel in this."

There was a murmur of interest after Alys' translation, though they were still wary.

"On this day, I invite you all to Kilderrick to pledge your fealty to me as the new laird, then to share in the feast celebrating my marriage to Alys Armstrong. You will need to bring your napkin, bowl and spoon, but there is fare aplenty for all."

That roused more interest.

"The deer roasts as we speak!" Denis said and the company began to whisper.

"The first court will be one week from Wednesday and I invite you all to attend." The Silver Wolf turned to the priest. "I thank you for the service this day and would ask you to bless my match with my lady wife."

The priest looked discomfited. "I did not witness the exchange of your vows," he began to protest but the Silver Wolf gestured graciously to Eamon and Jeannie.

"Fortunately, the sheriff and his wife were so kind as to do as much."

"Aye," Eamon acknowledged. "The vows were exchanged as is proper, though no banns were called."

"All know that my wife has no spouse already, and I give my solemn pledge that I do not either. My brother will swear to it." He gestured and Rafael bowed, all turning to survey him before their gazes returned to the Silver Wolf.

The priest clearly discerned that protest was futile before the Silver Wolf's implacable will. He raised his hands and blessed them both as they knelt before him. Alys was aware of the hostility radiating from Jeannie but did not grace that woman with so much as a glance.

God in Heaven, she prayed that her husband did not humiliate the sheriff before the entire village as well as take his post. The villagers might not be warriors but resentment of a perceived injustice would not be left unavenged.

"And now I will have the ledgers," the Silver Wolf said to the priest, who blinked in surprise. He flicked a glance at the sheriff. "Do you not keep the ledgers for the holding? I would expect you to be one of the few with the ability to read and write."

"I do, my lord. Of course." The priest stammered.

"And the court records, if you will. I would review the local customs and traditions."

The priest shuffled and bowed. "Of course, my lord. I must fetch them from the sacristy, where they are stored."

"I will accompany you," the Silver Wolf said smoothly. "Perhaps you might come to Kilderrick this day as well, to record the names of those to pledge fealty." It was not a question and the priest nodded quick agreement. The Silver Wolf turned to Alys. "Dispense your alms, my lady, and I will meet you outside."

"I thought you had another errand this day," she said, watching him closely.

Her husband smiled. "As did I, but I have been given good counsel I choose to follow." His gaze clung to hers for a moment, his expression so intense that Alys' heart fairly stopped.

He was heeding her advice. Her knees weakened at that and she could not help but smile back at him. The Silver Wolf blinked, as if astonished, then pivoted quickly to follow the priest.

Rafael swept open the doors and Nathalie was quick behind Alys with the small sack of coins. She pressed them into Alys' hands, one at a time, and Alys gave them away blindly, at least fifty silver pennies that were surrendered to grasping hands. More than one recipient stole a look beneath her hood and she found herself a little shaken by the way they seized the coins. How badly did the people fare in Rowan Fell in these times?

When the coins were gone, she found herself beside the great black steed, Rafael close beside her in her husband's absence. The mercenary seemed a little less triumphant than he had been earlier, but Alys held her tongue. The Silver Wolf strode out of the chapel with two trunks, one smaller and one larger, both of which he entrusted to Yves. Once they were in the cart, he lifted Alys to his saddle. In a heartbeat, the entire company was mounted or in the cart, and they rode out of Rowan Fell in a thunder of hoof beats. The villagers stood outside the chapel, clutching their pennies and staring after them.

"That went well, I think," the Silver Wolf said. "If naught else, my lady wife smiled at me for the first time."

Alys twisted to look at him, hearing the satisfaction in his voice. "You listened to me."

"Aye. Does that please you?"

"It does," Alys admitted, unable to hide that truth.

His arm tightened around her waist, drawing her against him again. "I told you we made a good pair, my Alys, and you prove me right again." He gave the destrier his spurs. They raced toward Kilderrick, the wind in Alys' face, her husband behind her, and she felt a rush of pleasure.

It was not just his touch or even that he had listened to her. What if he truly meant to rebuild Kilderrick and restore her legacy? The prospect made her heart soar. How she would love to see those towers against the sky again, and feel the protection of those walls around her.

Even if the Silver Wolf's sole objective was his own power, Alys did not care.

She hoped that in this matter, his vow would be the truth.

CHAPTER 11

*W*retched woman.

Jeannie had not believed that the Silver Wolf would bring his ruin of a wife to the chapel for the Sunday service until that cursed pair walked through the door. What a couple they were: the warmongering mercenary and the witch from the woods. Both more fearsome than the most terrifying demon, both with hearts so dark and evil that their very presence made her shiver. She had nigh expected the roof of the chapel to fall when they crossed the threshold or for lightning to strike the roof, coming out of a clear blue sky without warning.

To her dismay, she also felt her husband's resistance to the new laird diminishing. He was losing his audacity in the face of power and Jeannie knew that unless she bolstered his will, Eamon would be entirely under the heel of the so-called new laird.

Jeannie watched the Silver Wolf and his disfigured bride ride away, his company of followers fast behind them, and spat on the ground. "Can this be endured?" she demanded of her husband. "A veritable monster, with the stare of a basilisk, yet looking down her nose at me. A harlot and a witch, she is not worthy of being Lady of Kilderrick!"

"Yet the laird has chosen her," said Rona, the goat woman. She would never have challenged Jeannie's words even a day before. "I like that he sees past her scar."

"Aye," agreed the young smith's wife. "'Tis the measure of a good man."

Nerida nodded with enthusiasm, her grand daughter's eyes filled with stars. "And he is so handsome," said that maiden with a sigh.

"Handsome is as handsome does," Jeannie scoffed. "A good man? Is that what we will call the Silver Wolf now? He is a mercenary and a thief, the very man who burned Kilderrick to the ground and killed its last laird. He has an audacity to stand on that man's grave and demand a blessing for his marriage to the old laird's daughter!"

There was a ripple of unease at this.

"I was there!" Jeannie reminded them. "She had no desire to wed him. But he rode that whore for a single night and now she is in thrall to him." She spat again. "They are as dirt, filthy people to whom we owe naught at all. We should not tolerate them in the old keep. We should drive them out!"

To Jeannie's dismay, there was no agreement with this very sensible plan.

"He rides with a dozen warriors," was one protest.

"They are armed and trained for battle," was another.

"He has claimed the keep and the heiress, and he has the seal. He cannot be cast out. The law is with him."

There was a lengthy pause.

"And we have been invited to the laird's board for dinner," contributed Rona. "How long has it been since you ate your fill of roast venison?"

"Since the last time the smith stole a deer," came the jest that made them all laugh.

"But it will be a feast," Rona insisted, likely unaware that she licked her lips. "A wedding feast as in the old days. I will go and drink the health of the new couple. I would not be saddened to see Kilderrick rebuilt."

"Nor I," agreed a farmer name of William.

"I will go," said the young smith's wife and nudged her husband.

"I as well," he said, for he had little choice. His younger brother,

Tynan, nodded with resolve. Nerida brushed off her skirts as if she meant to dance at the king's own palace.

Glances were exchanged and glances cast toward the ruined keep.

"Do not show your support to him," Jeannie urged, but she had lost them and she knew it. The villagers headed home to fetch their bowls, spoons and napkins, to don their best cloaks, and secure their chickens. Then they filed out of the village in a line that trailed toward Kilderrick keep. William even took his harp.

"You cannot go," Jeannie said to Eamon when he appeared with his cloak. "You owe him fifteen years of tithes and he will not forget it."

"And we do not have the coin any longer. I will have one fine meal, even if it must be my last."

"He will not injure you!"

"He has every right to do as much." Her husband sighed and licked his lips. "Roast venison. 'Twill be a fine feast, I am sure."

"He owes me a duck."

"Perhaps there will be one on the board. Come along, Jeannie. It has been long indeed since we have shared the laird's bounty."

Jeannie's lips tightened in vexation. Her husband would not challenge the Silver Wolf himself, and the king might not reply to Eamon's summons, but surely some man would challenge the new Laird of Kilderrick.

Jeannie could only hope that day came soon.

"HE WILL BE HALE?" Elizabeth asked worriedly, circling the unconscious squire. "For if we kill one sworn to the Silver Wolf, that man will not rest until we are dead ourselves."

"'Twas you who warned that there would be a spy," Ceara reminded her with scorn. Sometimes, she could not bear the noblewoman's timidity. If she had been born to riches, she would have known the world's bounty was hers to claim.

"Aye, but I thought we would send him back with a falsehood to share," Elizabeth said. "I did not think he would be injured."

"No one planned for him to hit his head," Nyssa said.

Ceara and Nyssa had released the net and were busily removing the boy's garments. He had only a dagger on his belt and no jewelry that would fetch a good price. His boots were worn, but they fit Ceara and were better than the ones she possessed. She claimed his boots and put hers in the pile of his garments. "The chemise is fine," she said and kept it aside as well.

Nyssa spared Elizabeth a pointed glance. "You could be of assistance. Begin with the woad. We must be done before he awakens and there is no telling when that might be."

Elizabeth grimaced then pushed her fingers into the salve that Nyssa had prepared. It was a thin paste of fat colored with woad roots that had been dried and ground. It was blue. She began to rub the salve into the boy's skin, beginning with his arm closest to her.

Ceara, not nearly so shy, put the salve on his face, pushed it into his hair, and spread more down his chest. "How young he is," she said with a smile. "Nary a hair on his chest or his chin."

"But..." Nyssa said and pointed. Ceara laughed with her while Elizabeth blushed.

"In a way, it is simpler that he struck his head," Ceara said. "He knows naught at all."

"But how can we keep him? He will awaken sooner or later," Elizabeth said, beginning on his leg.

"We will return him," Nyssa said with satisfaction. "Naked and blue from head to toe, a pentacle hung around his chest."

"And another in ash drawn on his forehead," Ceara said.

Nyssa nodded. "They will be terrified." She surveyed the boy. "And something else, I think, to startle him."

"Like what?" Elizabeth asked.

Nyssa smiled. "A surprise from a witch, of course." Elizabeth looked mystified but Nyssa did not say more. Ceara could readily imagine what the other woman might do. Once she had tucked a new brood of snakes in the boot of an intruder left similarly naked but otherwise uninjured. His shout upon discovering them must have been heard all the way to Edinburgh. That had been before Elizabeth had joined them.

"I can make a sling from his cloak," Ceara said. "And leave him swinging in the forest as he sleeps, like a babe in a cradle."

"Keep his dagger," Nyssa advised.

"Of course, though 'tis not as fine as that of the mercenary." Ceara had already put the dagger in its scabbard in her belt, beside the mercenary's blade. She admired the two of them. "I shall soon have a collection."

"Let us hope the Silver Wolf's company leave before then," Nyssa said and they hefted the weight of the boy together.

Ceara wondered whether he would ever leave, but chose not to say as much aloud. Nay, it was better to try to think of some way to encourage him to depart.

Even if she could not think what it was as yet.

MAXIMILIAN WAS PLEASED. The villagers came, a long line of them marching over the hill toward his camp, the setting sun behind them. They were silhouetted against the orange sky but already he knew the identities of some. He was relieved when he saw Eamon at the end of the company, Jeannie trudging behind him.

His chair had been brought from his tent and he sat upon it, already anticipating the day that he would have a great hall in which to welcome his guests and his villagers for the greater feast days. Amaury had returned from the hunt with more hares and partridges, as well as some quail eggs. He was troubled that Oliver had been lost, but Maximilian reassured him, knowing the boy followed his own command.

All went well.

"You have changed your scheme?" Rafael asked, clearly having waited until they were alone. He spoke in Venetian, his mother tongue, and his words thrummed with anger.

"I merely delay it," Maximilian said.

"Why?"

"I must prove that he does not deserve the post," he explained. "So his replacement is seen as justified, not merely my impulse."

"Does it matter?" Rafael demanded. "You are laird and your command is law."

"We are not at war, though, and tactics may need to be altered in times of peace."

Rafael swore and rolled his eyes. "Does your wife make you timid? Does she already have you in thrall?"

"She made an argument for delay that I thought was sound. She knows more of this holding than I." Maximilian eyed his brother, who bristled with impatience, and thought the lesson might be good for both of them. "I will not break my word, Rafael. You will have your due."

"You have broken your word," that man said, lifting his arm to display the scar from the mingling of their blood. "And you have been the one to shatter our alliance."

"I will grant you the post..."

"I do not believe it, *brother*." Rafael flung out a hand. "I have followed you to the ends of the world in the hope of some reward, but there is to be none. Even that post was a meager offering for my years of loyal service to you, and naught compared to what you will claim and possess. You do not share, Maximilian. You conquer. You claim. And in the end, you will be the sole wealthy man among us." He sneered and scoffed. "I did not surrender my role in the Compagnie Rouge for this! I was to be Captain-of-Arms at Château de Vries!"

"And in time, I will see you rewarded here."

Rafael scoffed. "You had best so do, or I will take my due from you. So far in this endeavor, I see only that you benefit. That must change and soon." He spun on his heel before Maximilian could reply and marched away, just as Alys and Yves approached.

Maximilian watched Rafael's furious retreat, considering his outburst. Rafael had need of a woman, to be sure. His temper always flared when he was long celibate. Perhaps that would be addressed on this night, for there were several comely wenches at Rowan Fell.

And he knew that Rafael would keep his vow, no matter how much he argued about the terms. All would be well.

With a gesture, Maximilian beckoned Alys to his left side. She pulled up the hood on her cloak, but he halted her with a touch. "Do not hide your truth, Alys. It is only when you cower that others perceive you to be weak."

She cast him a glittering glance, her doubts clear, but left the hood down, her hair lifting slightly in the wind. She stood tall by his side, a woman he was proud to call his wife, and Maximilian watched as the approaching priest from Rowan Fell recoiled at the sight of her face.

Alys' expression did not change and she did not retreat. She simply eyed the priest, daring him to comment upon it. Maximilian knew she was more stiff, but she did not cower and she did not hide her face again.

That man stammered, his gaze flicking from Maximilian to Alys again, then he spoke to Maximilian. "My lord, I will keep the list as requested."

"And tell us the name of each man, if you please."

"Of course, my lord."

"I would be reminded of their occupations, if you will," Alys said, her voice soft but her tone resolute. Maximilian almost smiled at the priest's discomfiture, but he looked at her again and this time, he did not flinch.

"Of course, my lady."

"And you may speak the tongue of the Isles," Maximilian said. "I know it is your mother tongue and my wife will translate all for me."

"Of course, my lord," the priest said, his surprise almost as complete as Alys' own. He turned and beckoned to the first of the villagers and Maximilian captured Alys' hand within his, holding it upon his left shoulder. He watched the reaction of the first man, so much like that of the priest. That man's wife, one step behind him, paled and looked at the ground.

'Twas intolerable. Maximilian would not suffer that Alys be insulted.

They must look upon her and see her merit.

The priest spoke and Alys asked a question, then spoke to Maximilian.

"This is Niall Carter," she said. "He owns the ox, and his wife, Beth, is a brewster."

"Pledge to my wife first," Maximilian commanded, steel in his tone, and when Alys translated, Niall was compelled to look at her again.

His gaze did not waver this time. "Aye, my lord," he said carefully, then swallowed and made his pledge.

⁓

ALYS THOUGHT the swearing of fealty would never end. She had found it difficult to endure the reactions of the villagers, but she understood the Silver Wolf's order. By compelling them look at her, he diminished their fear of the sight of her scar. The horror in their eyes died, especially when she spoke to them.

The Silver Wolf's command that they should speak Gaelic was the strategic choice, and one she knew he made for her. Indeed, it pleased Alys to be given a task and his trust, for it was not her way to be idle. And this showed her role as his wife, as Lady of Kilderrick, as his partner in this endeavor.

God in heaven but she hoped he did not deceive her about rebuilding the keep.

She asked after the villagers' occupations, their children, their chickens and their gardens. There was some measure of affection, especially from Nerida, who clasped Alys' hand and blinked back tears of joy. She knew the Silver Wolf listened and memorized all that she translated for him.

And truly, the exercise diminished her own dread of their reactions. By the time Eamon and Jeannie were before her, Alys felt no desire to hide. She knew she stood taller and she met Jeannie's gaze steadily.

'Twas the sheriff's wife who faltered, not Alys.

Once the pledges were made, the mood became merry. Tables had been brought from the tents, including the one that was usually in the Silver Wolf's own tent, and makeshift others were set up from stumps and logs. There was even a contraption of wood that Rafael fussed over that was pressed into service, much to his disapproval. There were pots of stew, slices of venison, trenchers of bread, and yet more. The bowls brought by the villagers were filled, cups overflowed with ale and wine, and much laughter filled the air as those beverages were consumed. Amaury's dogs wound through the throng of merrymakers, in hope of a stray morsel or two, and the ostler's young son aided the squires in ensuring that all were served.

Alys had not attended a wedding or a feast since her father's death. It had even been some years before that and her recollection was dim. She was surprised by how merry they all were, being comparative strangers, but perhaps the wine and ale were at work. The Silver Wolf was constantly on the move, making a jest here and calling for a cup to be filled there, patting a dog, admiring a child, asking a question. Alys knew his choice was deliberate and doubtless a plan to win the support of the villagers, but she was charmed all the same. She found herself laughing, well aware that her husband's gaze followed her as if he were truly smitten. When she glanced up, he smiled, just a little, and Alys felt alluring.

She also could not fail to note how the villagers watched the two of them, and how the women whispered and smiled. Clearly, the tale already spread that the new laird was enamored of his wife. Alys knew it could not be so—he insisted he did not believe in love, after all—but she enjoyed the weight of his gaze upon her.

Indeed, she felt a flush in anticipation of the night ahead. Would his touch summon the same tide of pleasure within her? Or had it been novelty at work?

William began to play his harp and another man sang a ballad which was vaguely familiar to Alys. The Silver Wolf returned to her side to listen, the heat of his arm against her own, and Alys strove to hide her reaction to his very presence. The sun set in a final blaze of orange and gold, the flames of the fire licked against the darkening sky, and the stars slowly emerged.

And then the Silver Wolf stood, bowed before her and invited her to dance. "My lady?" he said, his hand outstretched and his eyes fiercely blue.

Alys was well aware that the entire company watched, their expressions ranging from indulgence to curiosity.

"I do not remember the steps," she whispered, feeling herself blush.

"You are the lady," he said with quiet heat. "You may dance however you like." There was a challenge in his expression, one that Alys could not resist. She put her hand in his and let him lead her into the middle of the group as the tune turned lilting. The villagers began to clap in time, the Silver Wolf caught her hands in his and they spun around together. The beat was infectious and she matched his steps, finding herself laughing aloud with the pleasure of it. She was keenly aware of the strength of her husband's hands and the warmth of his gaze. Though he barely touched her, she felt all a-shiver, both hot and cold at the same time.

She was breathless when the tune wound to a close, then he spun her into his arms and kissed her soundly. The quick embrace sent more heat flooding through Alys, and she was a bit dizzy when she realized the music began again. The villagers applauded the embrace. The mercenaries had lined up to ask the bride to dance, Rafael at the first.

As Alys should have expected, her husband's stern eye meant that none of them touched more than her hands. Rafael was an elegant and energetic dancer, and Alys guessed that some of the village women watched him keenly. Amaury led Nathalie to join the dance, Denis and Marie danced as well, and all clapped in time as they watched. The smith's son led his wife to join in, and even Eamon and Jeannie danced.

Alys danced and danced again, her confidence in her steps growing with each tune. The next mercenary introduced himself as Victor, the one Alys recognized as having been sentry. He was a large swarthy man missing a finger on his left hand. He also was missing a tooth, a fact that was inescapable when he laughed aloud as he often did.

The next mercenary to lead her in the dance was named Matteo. He was the one who had ridden to Rowan Fell with the Silver Wolf. He was as sleek as a great cat, his hair touched with silver at the temples and his eyes gleamed. He had a scar on his cheek and limped slightly as he danced, though that did not slow him down.

Royce was the last and largest of them all, a bearded behemoth with hair that hung down to his waist and a ring on every finger. He might have been a great bear but he danced better than any bear might. He was missing an eye and Alys thought perhaps part of one ear, but he was a vigorous dancer who left her short of breath.

It was only after they had each spun her around that she realized the Silver Wolf's company had never looked upon her wound with horror. She wagered they had seen much worse in their time.

When Royce spun her back to her seat, he bowed to Marie, who giggled as she took his hand and began to dance. The Silver Wolf danced with Nathalie, though he kept such a considerable distance between them that Alys doubted her earlier suspicions of their relationship. The music was infectious and the ground fairly jumped with the vigor of their stamping feet. Alys was fanning herself, watching the Silver Wolf change partners to dance with Eudaline, when Yves approached her and bowed low.

The older man, it was clear, had enjoyed too much of the wine. He was flushed and much more cheerful than Alys had ever seen him before. She caught his elbow and coaxed him to sit down. "Perhaps you are unaccustomed to the wine," she said gently and he grinned at her.

"There is that, my lady, but the greater truth is that I am relieved."

"About what?"

"About Maximilian. I feared so greatly for his future when he was a boy. Did he tell you that he grew up at Château de Vries?"

"Nathalie did."

Yves nodded, his gaze snared by Maximilian and Eudaline. "I served in that keep since my own boyhood, when I was sent to aid the châtelain as a clerk."

"Were you born in the village?"

The older man shook his head. "I was sent, from the monastery. I learned my sums and my letters, but there were too many of us. The châtelain from de Vries came regularly to the monastery, for that establishment had been endowed by the family, and he took a liking to me. I owed my place at the château to him and knew it well. I endeavored to do the same in my time, and brought many children to the keep to serve."

"Including Nathalie."

"Indeed. Though few worked as hard as she has done." He braced his hands on his knees, smiling as he watched Maximilian and Nathalie dance.

"She is a good maid," Alys said. Though she knew little of such duties herself, she suspected that Yves would be glad that she was pleased.

He bowed slightly. "I am honored that she serves you well, my lady."

"Why are you relieved?" she asked when he fell silent, unable to say her husband's Christian name aloud.

"I used to think that he was the most unfortunate child in all the world," Yves said. "I feared no good could come of it."

Alys was startled. "But you were given away to the monastery and could be said to have been unfortunate yourself."

"Maximilian would have been better for it, had his family made that choice," the older man said, to her astonishment.

"But he was the son of the house, was he not?"

Yves winced. "Do you know how he was conceived?"

"In the usual manner, I would expect."

The older man laughed a little. "'Twas not a miraculous conception. That has only happened once, to be sure." He sobered. "But 'twas cruel. I was there. I saw." His throat worked and he fell silent again.

"What did you see?" Alys finally prompted, her curiosity making it impossible to remain silent.

"The keep was assaulted by the notorious mercenary, Jean le Beau. Have you heard of him in these parts?"

"Aye, he was in the employ of the Percy family when I was a child, then sought his due from others. I assume it was at Jean le Beau's command that the Silver Wolf first came to Kilderrick."

"Aye. Jean le Beau was not one to serve any master for long, for he cared only for himself." Yves shook his head. "He was a handsome man, the bastard son of a duke, a man of relentless greed and one capable of such violence. He was strong, proud and ruthless. The sole mercy is that men of his ilk are so rare."

Alys did not mention Jean's son or his reputation, for she guessed that Yves was fond of the Silver Wolf—though she could not fully explain why. "And Jean le Beau came to Château de Vries?"

Yves nodded. "The Lord de Vries was a nobleman of great lineage, a knight in his own right, and a man of firm opinions. He declined to surrender his holding to the mercenary at his gates. He thought he had the power to resist an assault, but he was wrong—and Jean ensured that he paid for his error. Jean not only took the keep but he hunted the lord down afterward, his men destroying all they touched and willfully so. He found the lord in the chapel, with his priest and his sole daughter,

Mathilde. The lord's son, Gaston, a knight in his own right, was abroad. Several of the household, like myself, had also taken refuge there. The old lord truly believed that the barbarian who attacked his holding without cause would honor the law of sanctuary." Yves shook his head at the folly of that.

"I will wager that he did not," Alys guessed.

"Not Jean. He and his men broke down the doors. He demanded the hand of Mathilde in marriage, for he would declare himself the new Lord de Vries. The old lord was so insulted that he drew his sword to defend his honor, that of his family and that of his daughter. He had not a chance. He was struck down, his sword hand sliced from his arm. He changed to the other hand, having trained to use both, and his left hand suffered the same fate."

Alys could not evade the similarity in her situation and that of Mathilde, but before she could remark upon it, Yves continued and proved the differences.

"Jean then sliced the old lord from groin to his chest, halting the injury before it killed him but leaving him powerless all the same. Jean kicked the priest aside, then raped Mathilde before us all. 'Twas savage, for he took pleasure in hurting her."

Alys stared at Yves, shocked.

"Aye, 'twas an act of war, to be sure. The old lord was horrified, but Jean had left him alive to watch. The priest declared their vows, Mathilde held before him by Jean. Jean took her again, like a dog, after the pledges were made. He then cast her aside—I remember how she landed on the floor, stunned—before plucking the seal of the keep from the old lord's purse. I saw him smile as he ended that man's life." Yves took a shaking breath. "'Twas the only time I ever heard Lady Mathilde weep. She had always been a woman of composure and reserve, but after the humiliation of that day, she was never the same. She cared for naught, as if he had shattered her heart forever."

Alys stared at Yves, appalled by his story. It confirmed what Nathalie had told her, but included so much more detail.

Yves glanced up and held her gaze. "Maximilian was the fruit of that union."

Alys was shocked and could not hide it. How could a child

conceived thus not be a monster? She felt sympathy for the Silver Wolf then, which startled her with its vigor.

"Jean le Beau was a plague upon the land," Yves continued. "It was God's mercy that he left Château de Vries that day and only returned once a year, for the tithe. Lady Mathilde always ensured that she was locked within her chamber when her husband arrived."

"And what of her son?"

"She could not look upon him without recalling that day. A fine healthy boy, but one who might have been invisible for all the care anyone expended upon him."

Alys' heart squeezed. Her father had lost his wits but she remembered the years when he had doted upon her, and Rupert, too. And she had had Morag, as well—gruff and a little addled, but protective and affectionate, to be sure.

"He spent his childhood ignored by them both, at least until his father came for him in his twelfth summer." Yves smiled in reminiscence. "He was such a clever boy. Quiet and thoughtful. Observant. He did not play like other children, but then, he did not have the opportunity. I could not abandon him. He had need of some attention."

"All children do," Alys agreed.

"He could have been my own son, for we were that close. I taught to him to play chess, the game of kings, for I thought it might suit his nature. He soon excelled at it."

Alys could believe that. "But then his father came for him."

"Aye, he did. Though it would not have been Maximilian's choice, he fulfilled his duty—perhaps I had taught him that a man of merit fulfills his responsibilities, and truly, all men have a duty to their fathers."

"Even when that father is Jean le Beau," Alys said softly.

"Aye, and he served that demon for years."

Alys did not doubt that he had learned much from his father in those years and she found her opinion of him diminishing again.

"'Twas all for the legacy of Château de Vries, but when Jean le Beau was dead, Maximilian's uncle, Gaston, cheated him of his due." His brows rose. "Though the blame for that, too, could be laid at Jean's feet."

"I do not understand."

"When Jean seized Château de Vries, Lady Mathilde's younger

brother, Gaston, was betrothed to a lady of good family. That is where he was when the mercenary attacked, at Château Pouissance. The lady in question, Lady Florine, had no brothers and Gaston was to become her father's heir upon their wedding."

Alys was well familiar with this strategy, for her father's plan had been similar for her own marriage and Kilderrick.

"Lady Florine was a kind woman, generous of nature, and she came to Château de Vries for the birth of Lady Mathilde's child by Jean le Beau. At the time, I thought it a wise choice, for I was uncertain what Lady Mathilde might do on first glimpse of her child, given her hatred of her spouse and humiliation at her nuptials. In the end, though, the price was high for Lady Florine."

"How so?"

"She was pretty." Yves met Alys' gaze. "Jean came for the birth of his child, so anxious was he for a son. He saw Florine, of course, and desired her. It did not matter that she was not his to claim. He had her, perhaps repeatedly, undoubtedly by force, and she, too, conceived." Yves sighed. "Gaston was livid and humiliated, but he still wed Florine."

"For her father's legacy," Alys guessed. The Silver Wolf should be ten times the villain he had shown himself to be, given the history of his family.

But then, Alys had only been wed to him for a day. What did she truly know of him?

"We were all sworn to secrecy, but Lord Amaury is that child. He, alas, was not told the truth until Jean's funeral." Yves frowned. "Gaston seized Château de Vries, denying Maximilian as penance for his father's crimes, and also denied Amaury, who he had raised as his own son, for being Jean's bastard. I am not entirely certain that Maximilian was shocked, for he had learned to distrust all from his father, but Amaury was shaken beyond all expectation."

"The Silver Wolf said he had only his horse, his falcon and his hounds."

"Not so much as a squire or a silver penny," Yves agreed.

"He must not like that he is beholden to the Silver Wolf."

"I would wager that he does not. He cannot like that the luxuries of his life are in the past either. I suspect he intended to wed a beautiful heiress and host tournaments at Château Puissance, not ride to hunt alone in Scotland and sleep in a tent."

"He is not the only one whose life is other than might have been expected," Alys felt obliged to observe. She did not feel sorry for Amaury with his many years of leisure and affluence, even if his situation had changed.

"Nay, my lady, he is not, but I pray it does not make him bitter." The older man beamed at her. "Sometimes, there is unexpected treasure found upon the road one would not have chosen to travel. Bitterness can keep one from seeing merit when it appears."

Alys wondered what he knew of the treasure of Kilderrick. But Yves simply smiled at her, as if his had been a chance remark.

When Alys did not reply, Yves rose to his feet. "I thank you for your attention, my lady," he said, bowing to her, his tone formal again. "I wish you and Maximilian much happiness and many children."

"He desires sons."

Yves chuckled. "All men desire sons, until they have a daughter who steals their hearts. Do not fear for the gender of your first child, my lady." He winked, then strode away, leaving Alys with much to consider.

Despite herself, she felt sympathy for the Silver Wolf, given his childhood. But no tales of injustice served to the Silver Wolf would diminish the truth of what he had inflicted upon her.

Aye, no doubt he had commanded Yves to tell her this tale, in the hope of softening her resistance to his charms. Alys shook her head at the whimsy of that and accepted another invitation to dance.

CHAPTER 12

"hat now?" Ceara asked. She and Nyssa had hung the squire's cloak from the trees near the place where they routinely left the large pentacle. He slept, but no doubt would be discovered by morning.

They had heard the song and laughter from the Silver Wolf's camp and noticed that the fire blazed high. They had circled the camp to the south and lay now on the hill, looking down at what had to be a celebration.

"A wedding feast," Nyssa murmured.

Ceara spoke with disgust. "The entire village is in attendance. Look! There is Jeannie, gorging herself by the fire."

"They must have pledged fealty to him," Nyssa said, bracing her chin on her fists. "He would not have fed them a meal otherwise."

"And so he makes an ally of every soul within the valley." Ceara was clearly outraged. "With every passing moment, our chances of sending this wretch away diminish."

There was a sound behind them as Elizabeth approached. She dropped down to lie on the hill beside Nyssa, her curiosity evidently sufficient to make her bold. "Dorcha is in the shelter," she said. "I added more boughs to the roof and he took to his perch."

"I shall sleep a month when this company is banished," Ceara said. "I thought you would remain hidden," she said to Elizabeth.

That maiden's lips set with resolve. "I will not return to my father's house. This is our home and we must defend it."

"Agreed," Ceara said. "But we have need of a plan."

Nyssa, however, was thinking. "The entire village is there," she repeated softly, feeling Ceara's sidelong glance.

"And so?"

"And so they are not in Rowan Fell." Nyssa rolled to her back and looked up at the stars overhead, calculating. "I wonder whether all in the village have slaughtered their pigs as yet."

It was typical in Rowan Fell for those villagers of means to buy a suckling pig in the spring, feed it in their garden all the summer long, then slaughter it between Samhain and the Yule for the meat. Most would salt the meat and have ham for the winter when game was scarce and produce more so.

"What is your scheme?" Ceara asked.

"Only that the Silver Wolf's new allies should be turned against him. They must blame him for some deed, a crime committed in the village."

"We will not kill anyone!" Elizabeth protested with alarm, and was hushed by the others.

"Of course not," Nyssa said. She reached out and tapped the two daggers on Ceara's belt. "You can choose who to blame."

Ceara grinned in understanding. "When there is a choice between that handsome rogue and a boy sent on an errand, there is no choice at all." She pulled the mercenary's dagger from her belt. "And he left the celebration with that woman from the village," she added with a heat that indicated she cared more than she would admit. "Did you not see them go into that tent? It has been a long time."

Nyssa smiled. "Perhaps he is a thorough lover."

Ceara sniffed. "I do not care. It means only that the others do not know where he is, so he can be blamed."

"Fair enough. Give me the other dagger," Nyssa said. "There may yet be a way to deliver it to Alys."

Ceara eased down the hill, out of sight of the Silver Wolf's camp. "Let us hasten to Rowan Fell."

"What of me?" Elizabeth asked.

Ceara shrugged and continued down the hill. Nyssa could not turn her back on the other woman. "The choice is yours. If you would prefer to return to the ponies and guard them, that would be of use, as well."

To Nyssa's surprise, Elizabeth squared her shoulders. "Nay. The ponies will be fine. We must aid Alys and soon."

∼

ALYS WAS WINDED when she took a seat after her dance with Amaury. She was surprised to find Rafael appear by her side. She had noticed that he had been absent from the dance for some time, perhaps since he had first danced with her.

Where had he been?

And what did he want of her?

Naught good, given his sly expression. Alys braced herself for another tale about the merit of the Silver Wolf and greeted Rafael warily.

They were brothers, after all, and united in this endeavor.

Rafael carried two cups of ale and offered one to her. Mindful of her experience the night before, Alys plucked the other from his grasp. He was likely the Silver Wolf's emissary, after all.

The mercenary grinned and saluted her with his cup of ale. "Felicitations on your match." His tone was mocking, as if he saw as little good in the marriage as she did.

"Have you come to tell me a tale of my husband's merit?" she asked, sipping of the ale. It was cool and crisp, the perfect refreshment.

"You sound amused by that."

"Yves was intent upon defending the Silver Wolf's nature."

"Ah, the sad tale of his lonely childhood, no doubt." Rafael rolled his eyes. "For yours and mine were so much finer." He saluted her with his cup and drank while she wondered at his wry tone. He flicked a glance her way and she was reminded of a serpent, poised to strike. "Have you not wondered why he led us here?"

"Aye, I have and I asked him of it. He said Kilderrick was once promised to him."

Rafael nodded. "Yet he did not attempt to collect on that promise for fifteen years. Why is that? What has changed?"

"His father died and denied him?" Alys guessed.

"There was that." He sipped his ale. "But consider that Maximilian surrendered the leadership of the Compagnie Rouge to attend the funeral of Jean le Beau. Consider that he expected to be entrusted with the seal to his childhood home, Château de Vries."

"But his uncle denied him, and Amaury, from what I heard."

Rafael leveled a look at her, one that chilled her to her marrow. "And so instead of de Vries, he chooses to journey past the edge of the known world, to exist in a cold clime, distant from all he knows well, and to take you to wife. It makes no sense."

Alys bristled. "He says that wedding me secures his claim."

"What claim?" Rafael cast out a hand. "Kilderrick is a ruin. He could spend every coin he possesses to rebuild it and at best it will be a fortress or a sanctuary. It will never be a palace like de Vries. It will never be at the intersection of the world we know best. Kings and courtiers will never come to his hall, and no one will ever ask his counsel or request his aid. Maximilian has spent his life in Jean's service, but also in influencing the world. He has made kings. He has destroyed duchies. He has undermined or buttressed the ambitions of powerful men throughout all of Christendom. Yet you believe that he comes here to live for the rest of his days." Rafael scoffed, shaking his head as he quaffed his ale.

"He says he tells no lies."

Rafael laughed. "Which might in itself be a falsehood." He turned slightly to face Alys, his manner intense. "Maximilian triumphs. Maximilian conquers. Maximilian has had every luxury at his fingertips and he is an excellent warrior. He does not come to Kilderrick to retreat from the world forever. He comes here for a pause, to reassure Gaston before he strikes again. He will come from the north with an army, like an avenging angel, and he will seize what he has always expected to be his legacy."

"Château de Vries," Alys said, her mouth dry. "I thought it destroyed."

Rafael was dismissive. "A fire in the treasury. No doubt it has been repaired and is finer than before.

She had to ask. "And what of Kilderrick?"

Rafael grinned. "You can only believe this holding is desirable because you have not seen the majesty of de Vries. It is magnificent, a holding fit for a champion—a holding any man would do much to claim." He slanted a look at her. "And Maximilian always claims his desire in the end."

Alys dropped her gaze, finding herself reluctant to believe that the Silver Wolf deliberately deceived her.

Rafael's voice dropped to a whisper. "I thought you were keen of wit," he whispered. "I thought you were not susceptible to Maximilian's charm. But even you must know that no man—much less a man who has had whatever he desired whenever he desired it—could truly want this forsaken ruin of a holding and a monster for a wife." Alys glanced up, her lips parted to defend herself, then the malice in Rafael's eyes silenced her. "He will leave Kilderrick and he will leave you, perhaps with his babe in your belly. It will not be a bastard, but there will be no real legacy for that child. Will your life truly be better, alone in the forest with a newly born babe?"

Alys tried to hide her horror of that prospect but Rafael's smile told her that she failed. He plucked the other cup from her hand, drained it, then rose to his feet. His bow was as mocking as his tone. "As I said, felicitations to you on your match."

Then he was gone, striding across the clearing toward the barrels of ale. He hailed one of the other mercenaries as Alys considered his words, fear of the future rising hot within her.

Rafael was not just the Silver Wolf's brother but had been his companion in arms. He must know the Silver Wolf's intentions better than anyone—or at least better than she could. She was alarmed to find that she was already inclined to think him less than evil.

It had been only a day and she already forgot herself.

That was the Silver Wolf's ploy.

He lingered at Kilderrick to muster his forces, as Rafael said, and he would leave. In the meantime, he did not relish a cold bed each night.

But Alys would not bear him a child. She would not find herself abandoned with a babe in her belly. She would deny him and his touch.

And perhaps, refusing him the marital debt might hasten his

inevitable departure.

She could only hope.

~

WHAT HAD Rafael said to Alys?

Maximilian would have wagered his last coin that his brother had made trouble, in compensation for the delay to his new post. Alys was avoiding his gaze and her lips were set. When they retired to his tent, he found himself impatient with Nathalie and also with Reynaud, wanting only to be alone with Alys and get to the root of the matter.

"Did you dance with every man?" he asked lightly when Reynaud finally left. The great fire had died down to embers, the villagers had walked home—singing—and several of the men were already snoring loudly in their tents. The sentries were posted and all was well. He had no doubt that Oliver learned more of the other women's location and that he would soon be able to make a change there. He was both invigorated and exhausted, buoyed by the successes of the day.

It was the prospect of another night with Alys that made Maximilian forget how long the day had been. His very blood was afire, but she did not seem to share his anticipation.

Curse Rafael!

Alys toyed with the drawstring of the chemise, then flicked a hot glance his way. "Yves told me of your childhood," she said, a challenge in her tone. "I suspect he wanted me to know your merit."

She said this as if the goal was not possible.

"And you decline to believe him?" he asked, striving to keep his annoyance from showing.

She impaled him with a look. "Rafael insists that you will return to claim Château de Vries, that you only linger here to disarm your uncle Gaston."

Maximilian folded his arms across his chest. "I have not lied to you, Alys."

"I think you omit the truth on occasion, which is similar to a lie. It is a deception all the same." Her voice was hard.

"How have I deceived you?" he asked, his own voice silky.

"I think you do not intend to rebuild the keep," she said, rising to her feet. "I think you do not mean to remain here." She closed the distance between them and met his gaze, anger simmering in her own. "And I will not be the next woman abandoned with a babe in her belly by you or your kin."

Praise be that Alys was not shy in confessing her thoughts.

All the same, Maximilian was stunned by the implication of her words. He raised a hand to her cheek, but she retreated, fire in those eyes. "But we are wed."

"And the match is consummated. I cannot change that, but I can decline to meet you abed again."

If she wanted a battle of wills, she had found one.

"Nay, Alys, 'twill not be thus. We will meet abed and we will conceive a son."

"We will not." She flung out a hand. "Take a woman in the village. I do not care!"

"I do!" Maximilian's temper flared, though he knew that would gain him little. "You are my wife and will be so in every way."

"Will you hold me down and rape me?" she demanded with hostility. "As your father claimed your mother? Will you show me the truth of your nature now that I decline to be charmed?"

Maximilian inhaled sharply. "I am *not* my father."

"But you are his son. And what courses in your veins is his legacy. He chose you to follow him and his trade. He trained you. I wager he recognized that you were two of a kind." She lifted her chin, eyes flashing. "I invite you to show me your truth, sir. There should, after all, be no secrets between man and wife."

If she was trying to compel him to strike her, she aimed her barbs well.

But Maximilian would not stoop to that.

"Aye, then, I will," he vowed in a low voice and saw her flash of fear. "Victor!" he shouted, stalking Alys across the tent as he untied the lace of his chemise. He kept his gaze fixed upon her, aware of the pulse that fluttered at her throat.

"Aye, sir?"

"Please ignore any cries from my wife this night," Maximilian said, watching Alys' eyes widen slightly. "She is in need of a lesson of the most intimate kind."

Victor chuckled. "Aye, sir."

Maximilian tugged his chemise over his head and cast it aside. He was raging for Alys and she flicked a quick glance downward, inhaling sharply when she saw the truth of it. She was nigh backed into the wall and he knew that she would have to make her attempt at flight soon, if she meant to flee at all.

She ducked and darted but he was prepared for her. He seized her around the waist and lifted her from the ground, ignoring the blows she rained upon his head and shoulders. He managed to evade her kicking feet and flung her to the bed, landing atop her and pinning her there. She would have scratched at his face but he seized her wrists and held them down, letting her thrash against his weight. She exhaled finally at the futility of her efforts and glared at him, her breath heaving.

"Barbarian," she muttered. "Wretch and cur."

"You forgot 'husband.'"

Alys inhaled sharply, the move driving her breasts against his chest in a most delightful manner. "I despise you," she said with heat.

"It does not matter, Alys," he murmured, though her words sent a pang through him.

She fought against his grip, but he held her firmly. "Release me!"

"I promised you that we would meet nightly until we both knew that you had conceived a child," he reminded her, keeping his tone temperate.

"That was no promise I sought."

"Yet it was the one you had. I also vowed to ensure your pleasure in those matings."

Alys glared at him. "You cannot do it. Not this night."

Maximilian smiled. "I like a challenge, Alys, and you offer a considerable one. On this night, I will seduce you, but it seems I can only use my mouth to do so."

"Do not take me by force," she said through gritted teeth.

Maximilian met her gaze. "I am not my father, Alys. You will invite me."

Her eyes narrowed. "You will wait long for that invitation."

"Let us see." She stared at him as he bent to take the lace of her chemise in his teeth. Slowly, he untied the bow then flicked his tongue against the cord to loosen it completely. He kissed the point where her pulse fluttered, his lips touching her soft skin ever so gently, and she shivered. Already he felt the fight slide out of her body, but he would ensure that there was no doubt who summoned him. He slowly drew the neck of her chemise open with his teeth. Her breasts were bared to his view, the nipples so taut that he knew she was aroused, and he paused to admire her.

"Beautiful," he murmured.

"Blackguard," she replied, then swallowed as he held her gaze and eased lower. He trailed kisses down her chest, then around the nipple, finally taking it gently in his mouth. She gasped when he suckled a little, then he flicked his tongue across that taut tip and she shuddered to her toes. She opened her mouth to protest but made no sound, her throat working and her fingers now clenching his hands. He watched the flush rise over her skin, heard her moan softly, and knew conquest would be his this night.

And yet, he had barely begun his amorous assault.

ALYS WAS SHOCKED anew by how readily her body responded to the Silver Wolf's touch. She could not believe that after a single night in his bed, she was already so hungry for his caress. As before, it was his gentleness that shook her resolve: it should not have been unexpected, not now, but she was unprepared for tenderness again.

And his kisses melted her very bones.

She felt her flesh warm and her heart skip as he teased first one nipple with his kisses and then the other. He did not relinquish his grip on her wrists, but he moved ever lower, drawing her hands down as he went. She was surprised that he could take so long over the task of pressing a kiss against her flesh. She was amazed by the playful flick of his tongue at intervals and the thrill that sent through her. She found her eyes closing as he moved ever lower, bracing his weight between her thighs and holding her hands at her hips. She felt his breath upon her thighs and could not believe he would kiss her there, but he did. He moved with surety, his mouth closing over her and Alys gasped aloud at the pleasure that surged through her.

That was as naught compared to his intimate kisses, the periodic touch of his teeth, the mischievous play of his tongue. She found herself writhing beneath him, her fingers winding into his hair, her back arching as she surrendered to a pleasure beyond any expectation. Once again, he awakened that fever beneath her flesh. Once again, he conjured a storm and coaxed it to a tempest. Once again, he made her forget any inhibitions and all her resolve to reject him. Alys did not know how many times he urged her higher, then retreated just before she found her satisfaction. She did not know when he released her wrists and grasped her hips instead. She had lost her sense of every anchor in her world save the Silver Wolf's seductive kiss.

And when the heat rose again, summoned by his touch, she hoped only for release. She said something, and could not even understand her own entreaty, but the Silver Wolf understood. He moved with greater surety, fairly commanding her to abandon herself to sensation. Her heart raced again, his kiss demanded again, her breathing caught and the fire slid through her veins. This time, he did not stop but urged her on and on and on, until Alys felt she had stepped into the heart of the sun.

She screamed as she reached her release, screamed and thrashed and shuddered to her very marrow. When she opened her eyes, she thought her heart would burst out of her chest, so vigorously did it pound. She heard Victor clear his throat and flushed even more deeply, then looked into the Silver Wolf's sparkling gaze. He was yet braced between her thighs, his hair tousled, his smile confident.

"You are proud of yourself," she managed to say and he grinned, looking much younger than the man who had claimed her as his bride.

"Should I not be?" he asked but did not await her reply. To her surprise, he left the bed and went to his trunk, taking out a wineskin and pouring a measure of its contents into a cup. He stood nude, and she admired the lean strength of him, even as she noted the sign that he had not had his satisfaction.

"I thought you would claim your own satisfaction," she said.

He cast her a simmering look. "I am not my father," he said, his voice tight. "I must be *invited.*"

Their gazes clung across the distance, his desire as tangible a force as his restraint, then he turned away from her—as if the view of her might tempt him to forget his noble intentions. That was remarkable. He did not feign his response to her, and Alys liked that well. Despite herself, she could only feel admiration for him. There was much of merit in repudiating his father's habits and any traits he might have inherited or been taught.

And 'twas seductive to have a warrior like this man grant the choice to her. He could have taken what he wanted of her. He could have compelled her to surrender. But instead, he gave her pleasure and stepped away.

His choice was seductive indeed. Alys acknowledged that her satisfaction was not complete. Truly, it grew within her again, just by her awareness of his arousal.

Could she truly share a bed with the Silver Wolf and not surrender to his caress? Alys realized that she could not. His touch was too alluring and the pleasure he gave her was too addictive. She knew he would make the same amorous assault each and every night and she recognized that she would not be able to refuse him. She yearned to learn more and ached to feel that tumult again.

What if she could negotiate with him?

The Silver Wolf turned slightly and offered the cup to Alys, as if belatedly recalling his manners, but she shook her head. She saw his eyes glitter as his gaze flicked over her, his nostrils flared, then he sipped of the cup, as taut and controlled as ever. His throat worked and his jaw clenched.

He still burned for her.

Alys felt powerful, as if there was a balance between them she had not realized before. This was her moment for that negotiation. She rose from the bed, aware that he studied her from the periphery of his vision, and slowly began to unbraid her hair. The Silver Wolf turned then to watch her openly, his expression inscrutable and his gaze hot.

"I have yet to invite you," she said.

"I have noticed the omission." It seemed he could not tear his gaze away from her. "And now you will taunt me."

"You cannot be taunted by your monster of a bride, can you?"

"You are no monster, Alys," he said, his words low and hot. "You are magnificent. Let no man tell you otherwise."

Even if it was only desire fueling his words, they gave Alys satisfaction. She shook out her hair, then picked up the comb and began to comb its length anew. The Silver Wolf watched her stroll closer as if she was the most alluring seductress in all of Christendom.

"Will you leave Kilderrick?" she asked when she was within an arm's length of him. She was certain she could feel the heat radiating from him, but he did not touch her.

"'Tis not my plan."

"Not even for Château de Vries?"

He took a breath and looked away, his lips in a grim line. "I suspect that Gaston's possession of that holding means that it will pass to one of his sons upon his demise," he said, his words measured.

"Amaury?"

"Amaury is not Gaston's son," he reminded her. "Gaston wed twice more and has two more sons. He granted Château Puissance to the elder of them, Philip, at my father's funeral. Whether it is Philip who claims de Vries after Gaston's death or the younger son, Gaspar, is of no interest to me." He met her gaze steadily once more and sipped of the cup. The air crackled between them, his gaze clinging to her face with a hunger Alys recognized.

She wanted to believe him. She was inclined to believe him. But she would have a guarantee.

Alys took a step closer and placed a finger upon the Silver Wolf's forearm. She felt a tremor of desire pass through him and the evidence of the power in her own touch thrilled her beyond reason. "I will make you a wager."

"Will you?" There was a thread of humor in his tone.

Alys met his gaze steadily, the intensity of blue startling her. "If you pledge to leave me the seal of Kilderrick and the contents of its treasury whenever you depart, then I will meet you abed each and every night."

He shook his head slightly, his eyes narrowing, as if he did not understand.

"Rafael said I would scarce be better off if you left Kilderrick and abandoned me, for I would be living in the forest again, but with a babe at my breast. I will not conceive a child who might be compelled to survive thus for I know the challenge of it."

"I told you I will not leave."

"That remains to be seen."

His lips tightened with impatience and she knew it was because she implied that he might not keep his word. "And if I do not leave?"

Alys lifted her chin. "Then perhaps that child will have a sibling."

She saw the light in his eyes and watched the corner of his mouth pull up in a smile. "And if I agree to your terms?"

"Then I will entreat you to meet me abed, husband," she said, letting her fingertip slide up his arm to his shoulder.

The Silver Wolf's eyes flashed and he fairly cast the cup down in his haste to turn to her. "I swear it, Alys. I swear it upon all that is holy and much that is not. In my absence, Kilderrick will be yours, seal, stone and treasury. I pledge it to you now."

Alys leaned closer, letting her breasts collide with his chest, and slid her hands up his arms to his shoulders. She felt bold and brazen, but the Silver Wolf did not seem to disapprove. Indeed, his eyes were glowing and Alys found herself smiling, not just at her success. "Then come to bed, husband," she murmured. "We have a bargain to keep."

She had no chance to say more, for he speared his fingers into her hair. He framed her face and held her captive to a possessive kiss that astonished her with its power. Without breaking his embrace, the Silver Wolf swept her into his arms and carried her to the bed, seating her atop him.

"I am yours to conquer, my Alys," he whispered, his voice husky. "Ride me until you can bear no more."

ALYS! She exceeded Maximilian's every expectation and his hope. She took him to the highest heights and demanded yet more. She tested him and she provoked him and she aroused him beyond the bounds set by any woman before her—indeed, snared in her embrace, Maximilian forgot that there ever had been other women. Every caress, every posture, every pleasure was all new to Alys and in that, he discovered it all again.

When she explored him, learning the shape of him with her hands and then her mouth, it was such sweet torment that Maximilian knew he would not last. Her touch launched an inferno within him and her rare smile made his heart thunder. He loved that she was curious and liked that she had found a boldness.

He did not even mind that she had demanded a due from him, for he would gladly pay it. Indeed, he would do that and more for Alys, though Maximilian knew he had yet to convince her of that.

The truth of it surprised even him, but the heat that was aroused between them was so potent that already he could not imagine his nights without it.

Without Alys.

When he could not bear her touch any longer, she straddled him on the bed and tormented him with pleasure, taking him within her in achingly slow increments. When finally she rode him, her hands braced upon his chest, her eyes shining that she had him at her mercy, Maximilian could imagine no finer place to be. He savored the sight of Alys discovering her own power. Her hair flowed over her shoulders like a dark river, glinting in the last bit of light, the shadows making her mysterious and seductive. Her smile was quick, then more confident, and her eyes shone. He touched her, gently at first and then with greater boldness, watching her reaction build. Again, she flushed. Again, she gasped. Again, her eyes glittered, her nipples tightened and she closed her eyes as she found her release.

And when she closed tightly around him, as if to pledge that she would never let him go, Maximilian roared in his satisfaction, not caring who knew the truth of it. He gripped her tightly, his heart pounding and his skin slick, then she tumbled down upon him, her hair silken on his face. Maximilian smiled as he closed his arms around her and knew himself to be content.

"Is it always thus?" she asked in a husky whisper.

He shook his head, as yet unable to speak.

She braced her elbow on his chest and looked down at him. "For people would never leave their bedchambers if it were."

"I may not ever leave again," he said in a low growl and watched her flush. He brushed a fingertip across her cheek. "Truly, it is rare for it to be so wondrous."

"Why?"

He let his fingertip trail to her lips. "Perhaps because there is an enchantress at Kilderrick."

She laughed and he stared, dazzled by the transformation in her features. He recalled how alluring she had been at the feast, smiling as she danced, and pledged to himself to ensure that she always had reason to smile. "Or a conjuror," she countered, looking untroubled about it. "There is sorcery in your touch."

"Perhaps there is a magic between us, that we conjure only with each other."

Her gaze flicked to his ring upon her finger and he knew she recalled the inscription. Then she studied him, as if seeking some word or gesture from him.

"You are different abed," she charged finally.

"My eyes are closed?" he suggested, just to see if she might smile again.

She did. "You jest!"

"And you smile. I had not seen you do as much before this day."

Alys shook her head slightly and her tone was wry. "We have been wed but a single day. I wager there is much you have not seen." She met his gaze again. "And much I have yet to see myself."

He thought she referred to him but she looked across the tent with a frown. "I have never left Kilderrick," she said, surprising him both by the confession and its timing.

"Never?"

Alys shook her head, unaware that she set that dark river in motion and that he could only watch in wonder. "I know the shape of the land, the bend of the river, the scent of the wind and its import, and 'twas always enough." She eyed him. "Now I grow curious. Are other lands so different?"

"Aye and nay. The land and the weather vary. The crops. The birds." Maximilian frowned. "But men are much the same far and wide. They labor and they celebrate."

"And some desire what is not their own."

"Inevitably." He knew he should rise and wash, but there was much to be enjoyed in having Alys sprawled atop him and inclined to talk.

"And Amaury and Rafael are your father's sons, as well." She frowned. "But I do not think that Amaury is wicked or greedy. Indulged, perhaps."

"He was for a while, at least. It may be worse to be indulged and then denied, than to have always been denied."

Her gaze locked with his. "Yves hoped it would not make him bitter."

"It has hardened him already, to be sure."

"How so?"

How curious this was to discuss those within his company with another, to share his thoughts and impressions. Maximilian could not even recall so easy an exchange with Rafael—and he doubted there would be few such in future. But Alys was his wife and thus his partner: in essence, she was his second-in-command, for she would govern Kilderrick in his absence, should he be obliged to leave. And she had already granted him good counsel in the matter of the sheriff. "Amaury is less inclined to trust, less inclined to accept anything offered, even a helping hand. He looks for the trick in these times."

"Will that change?"

"Who can say? 'Tis not a bad instinct, to be cautious in one's trust."

Alys studied him then, her gaze clear. "And what of you? How would you change if you were indulged rather than denied?" When Maximilian smiled, she leaned closer, her eyes bright. "What? Tell me?"

"I do not know, but I have seen the change in you when you are acknowledged instead of hidden." He touched her cheek with a fingertip. "I told you, Alys, that you were magnificent, but I had only glimpsed the first promise of what you may become."

"You do not have to tease me," she said, blushing as she averted her gaze. "We have made our bargain..."

"I do not jest," he said with heat, compelling her with a touch to meet his gaze anew. "This night at the feast, you awed me, Alys."

"An unwilling bride, raised in the forest, dancing in a borrowed kirtle when she does not know the steps?" She shook her head and smiled slightly. "I think not."

"And so we shall disagree."

She eyed him. "I am not like you. I have not journeyed afar or witnessed great deeds. I know naught of majestic keeps, kings and queens, rogues and whores. 'Tis only a question of time before you yearn for more."

Maximilian was impatient with the notion, but he saw little merit in confessing that he had never before returned to the bed of a lover. She might think him like his father, a man who was never satisfied—instead of one who respected restraint. "Rafael meant to sow trouble in return for the delay in his becoming sheriff."

"But there is truth in his suspicions. You will tire of me and Kilderrick. Why should you not?"

Maximilian placed a fingertip over her lips to silence her. "Because, you are my wife and Lady of Kilderrick, Alys. Because I have never met the like of you. And because I am enchanted."

Alys rose from the bed with impatience. "There will not be another mating this night. Save your flattery for the morrow." She began to wash as he watched her, the uncertainty back in her gestures. She kept her back to him, modest again, and Maximilian mourned the loss.

"I will take you wherever you desire to go, Alys."

She did not reply, but he moved to her side. She glanced up, wariness in those fine eyes.

"Anywhere," he vowed, willing her to believe him. Before she could argue, he bent and touched his lips to hers. He felt her stiffen, then her hand landed upon his shoulder and her mouth softened beneath his. He heard her sigh as she moved into his embrace, as powerless against the attraction between them as he found himself, then she opened her mouth to him and kissed him back.

It was all Maximilian desired of her in this moment, and so very much more than he had first expected from their match.

He would not have been the man he was if he had not hoped for even more.

CHAPTER 13

$\mathcal{E}$amon knew something was amiss before he opened the door to their cottage in Rowan Fell. He smelled pig manure, even though their own pig had already been slaughtered and salted, and muttered under his breath about the smith not securing the gate on his garden.

Jeannie had complained the entire way back to the village, faulting the hospitality of the Silver Wolf and bemoaning their diminished status. To her thinking, it was apparently inevitable that they should be left to starve in the forest. Eamon wished she would fall silent and he tired of arguing with her. He had drunk a little too much ale and only wanted his pallet, preferably drawn close to the fire.

"Such a stench," Jeannie said, her tone waspish. "The smith's pig should be dead and salted by now, but they would linger over the task. Lazy, they are..."

Eamon pushed open the door and froze on the threshold, blinking at the smell.

A pig squealed in outrage and raced past them, nearly tripping Eamon when it slammed hard into his knees in its desperation to flee. He turned to watch the pig race across the village square, squealing all the way, and blinked, unable to make sense of what he saw.

How had the smith's pig gotten into their cottage?

Jeannie gasped and shoved past him. "My plates!" she cried and sure enough, the two pewter plates she prized above all else were gone from the shelf on the wall. Eamon lit the lantern, thinking that perhaps the plates had fallen somehow, and then stared at the damage. The straw pallets were mired as was the floor, the bucket of scraps had been dumped and eaten, and there were bits of cabbage strewn about the cottage. One bench had been knocked over. Eamon stood and stared at the evidence that the pig had been confined for a while.

But how? He had latched the door when they left, and while pigs were clever, they were not *that* clever.

And what had happened to the plates? His thoughts were clouded with wine, an unfamiliar pleasure, but Jeannie charged about the cottage in a frenzy.

"The plates are gone," she said, spinning to face him as if the blame was his alone. She braced her hands on her hips. "No pig took them, to be sure."

Eamon lifted the lamp and held it high, wincing as he noticed yet more damage in the light. Their cottage was a ruin. The light also caught the hilt of a dagger, its point driven into the middle of their table.

Like a challenge.

The sheriff had seen this blade before, its hilt visible above the scabbard on a ruffian's belt. He moved closer to be certain.

'Twas the same blade.

Jeannie came to his side and examined the blade as well. "The Silver Wolf's companion," she whispered then scowled. "The one who admired my plates. Now he has taken them! The thief and scoundrel! This cannot be allowed to pass unchallenged. Eamon, what will you do?"

It struck Eamon that all was too quiet. Aye, he could not hear the chickens. He strode out to the garden, then peered within the hutch where the ducks and chickens were secured each night. The door to the hutch was open, no good sign, and the birds were gone. He sighed and frowned, looking around, though he knew he would not find them close at hand. Who had done this deed? Was it truly the Silver Wolf's companion?

Or had some other soul chosen this moment to challenge him?

How had anyone claimed the dagger of the mercenary? Eamon would wager that man had not surrendered it readily. He pushed a hand though this hair, cursing the muddle of his thoughts from the wine, and dreaded the delivery of these tidings to the Silver Wolf.

Whose side would the new Laird of Kilderrick take? Eamon feared 'twould not be his.

"Well?" Jeannie demanded from the doorway. "What will you do?"

A wolf howled in the distance, the sound making Eamon clench his fist in frustration. Three more duck dinners had been sacrificed, as well as their supply of eggs, and Jeannie's favored plates. The sheriff of Rowan Fell knew where to lodge his complaint.

He had to place the charge before the Silver Wolf, and hope that man would see justice served.

ALYS AWAKENED IN THE NIGHT, the heat of the Silver Wolf beside her. His body was pressed against her from shoulder to knees, his breath was in her hair and the weight of his arm was around her waist. The softness of a fur pelt covered her and she knew they slept beneath his great black cloak. The fire in the brazier had burned down to a glow and the camp was quiet outside the tent. She heard a man's footsteps at steady intervals and knew that one of the mercenaries was on watch. One of Amaury's dogs yipped a little, clearly having a dream of chasing hares. She could hear the gurgle of the river and the wind stirring the chimes in the trees of the forest. The Silver Wolf's breath was slow and steady.

She had dreamed and she knew it, though now the shards of the dream faded to naught. She had the sense of trying to capture mist in her hands and was frustrated that she could not recall the dream. It had frightened her, for her heart was racing, but she could not recall a single detail.

Save fire. Alys' mouth went dry and she rubbed her burned hand without meaning to do so. Aye, there had been fire.

Did her dream seek to remind her of the Silver Wolf's truth? That she slept deeply enough to dream, and in his embrace, was marvel enough. That she had the urge to ask for comfort from him was beyond belief.

Alys turned to study him. Against every expectation, he slept in her presence.

'Twas no wonder after the day, for Alys was tired as well. It was warm beneath the cloak and her reaction to the man beside her was becoming less clear. Just days before, she had despised him completely, but now, she had to cede that there was some good to be found in him.

There was the power of a warm meal—or three.

And their mating had been even more wondrous than the first night. If anything, her reaction had been more powerful, as if the heat they conjured between them would only grow more incendiary each time they met abed. That was an alluring prospect and one that almost made her yearn to awaken him.

She did not doubt that Yves had been charged to tell her tales of his goodness, but still, that tale had made her wonder about the Silver Wolf. It seemed that he was not wholly evil, or at least that he wished her to doubt the blackness of his heart.

What a childhood he had endured.

And then his life since in the service of his father. He had known only solitude and battle, yet he was gentle with her.

If a man's measure was in his deeds, Alys had no complaints of his recent behavior. Beyond compelling her to take his hand, he had treated her with honor once she was his wife. He had protected and defended her. He had heeded her counsel about the sheriff and given his pledge to surrender Kilderrick should he choose to depart. She hated that he had seen Morag's hut destroyed but in the night, alone with her doubts, Alys had to admit that it had been the sensible choice. She knew her companions would survive, though she feared for their comfort during the winter ahead.

Could she as Lady of Kilderrick ensure their welfare somehow?

That was a tempting but absurd notion, one that required her to become the Silver Wolf's wife and partner in every way. Alys reminded herself of the destruction of her home, the death of her father, her own scars, but could not summon the same icy hatred of the man beside her that had once burned within her.

Indeed, there was an ease between them, a dawning reliance upon each other that Alys knew better than to trust—even though she could not keep herself from doing as much. She had offered the wager, after all, beguiled by his touch, but now, sated for the moment, she wondered whether it had been his plan all along.

She could not fail to remember that Yves had taught the Silver Wolf to play chess.

She could not evade the recollection of Rafael's insistence that the Silver Wolf always achieved his desire, and that he was patient in its pursuit.

And that could only leave her wondering whether Rafael was right about the Silver Wolf's desire for Château de Vries above all else. She could not believe that the man she knew would forget his uncle seizing his own expected legacy.

He was not the kind of man to leave any betrayal unavenged.

Was his pledge as good as he insisted? Would he surrender Kilderrick to her on his departure? 'Twould be a dream beyond expectation to hold the seal in her own hand and to command the treasury, even if it was much depleted. She would not need so much coin to ensure the welfare of herself, her three companions and perhaps a child. Alys was aware of the weight of the ring on her finger and haunted by its inscription.

You and no other.

He had not seen it made for her. He likely had not paid for it. Some man had been so besotted with his lady that he had ordered the ring made. Had she accepted it? Had she worn it with pride? Had that couple been happy together? It was whimsy but in the night Alys wondered whether the ring carried a will of its own.

She wondered whether it had the power to awaken love in her heart for her spouse.

'Twas a troubling possibility. She already came to admire him, against her will. 'Twould be a weakness, to be sure, a vulnerability he might exploit in his quest to triumph. But how? Would he even need to know?

Alys turned over, restless with the churning of her thoughts, and saw a glint of light. The Silver Wolf's dagger was yet on top of the large trunk, sheathed but not locked away. Alys caught her breath at the sight of it.

Unwittingly, he had left her the means to fulfill her vow.

She could kill the Silver Wolf while he slept, just as she had insisted she would. His company might leave then, dispersing for lack of a leader.

Alys bit her lip. More likely one of his brothers might take command.

That made her hesitate, for she guessed the victor might be Rafael and she was uncertain that he would be as concerned with order as the Silver Wolf. The camp might turn into a gathering of lawless marauders and her companions might be captured to provide pleasure for whichever of the men desired them.

Nay, she needed a better plan before she acted.

Indeed, the dagger might not have been left thus inadvertently.

It might be a test.

And if Alys slept the night in the Silver Wolf's embrace, she might gain an increment more of his trust. She nestled closer to his warmth and closed her eyes, not so discontent to remain abed. It was not long before her breathing slowed, but she did not see her husband's lips curve in a satisfied smile before he, too, slept.

OLIVER AWAKENED WITH A SHIVER, uncertain where he was. The sun was just beginning to lighten the sky, he was naked and cold, yet recognized that he was within his own cloak. His head ached and he was hungry. Above, he saw only barren branches of trees against a cloudy sky and he could hear the river gurgling below.

What had happened since he stepped into that trap? It had been afternoon, so at least one night had passed.

Where were the women and the ponies?

He sat up quickly and set his bed to swinging like a cradle in the wind. The world spun around him, as well, a bout of dizziness making him shake. He winced when his fingertips found the tender spot on the back of his head and he guessed that the women had tricked him. His cloak had been hung from the branches overhead, making a sling in which he rocked. He was cold but he could see a bundle of his garments hanging from the tree nearby. He reached out a hand, and realized that his skin was blue.

Blue.

He was blue from head to toe, as well as cold beyond all. He rubbed at his skin and some of the blue came away on his hand, which was a relief. Something dangled around his neck and he discovered the pentacle tied of straw that had been hung around his neck.

The women had caught him.

Oliver was suspended over the river, near where the burning symbol had been on the night of their arrival. He could see the Silver Wolf's camp through the trees and thought he spied Denis building the fire.

The women had left him, virtually unscathed, but close to the camp. Oliver knew he should be relieved, though he was shaken. He snatched at the bundle of his garments, determined to report to the Silver Wolf with all haste, and was shocked when the bundle wiggled in his hands.

His garments could have been alive, for the cloth seemed to seethe in his hands. He had scarce untied the knot when several dozen tiny mice erupted from the bundle, running in all directions, crawling over him, squeaking and scurrying in their haste to escape.

Oliver cried out in horror and scrambled to free himself. The mice ran over him, trapped in his cloak, unwilling to jump into the water. There was a larger mouse, likely the mother, and her claws dug into him as she chased her brood.

Then she bit him in a place most tender.

He flung the bundle into the river in disgust.

Once he began to scream, he could not stop. Oliver leaped out of the cloak, landed in the river with a splash, then ran naked—and blue— toward the sanctuary of the Silver Wolf's camp.

~

A PANICKED CRY made Alys awaken with a start.

The Silver Wolf evidently heard it as well. He flung himself from the bed, donned his boots and chausses with all haste, then strode out of the tent. She heard him mutter some command to the sentry, then two sets of footsteps strode away with purpose. Whoever shouted was near at hand and continued with gusto. It sounded like a boy not a man, for the voice was slightly higher than that of any of the mercenaries. The words were French but too panicked for her to understand.

What was amiss?

Alys abandoned the warmth of the bed and went to the tent flap in her chemise, her heart pounding. She raised one corner and peeked outside, surprised to find that no one stood watch outside the tent any longer. She heard men shouting gruffly in the distance and whoever had screamed finally fell silent.

It was early, just dawn by the hue of the sky, and she knew there would be mist over the river. The air was damp, the ground cold and she could smell the river.

Then she heard a hiss of her name.

It was Ceara!

Alys seized her boots and tugged them on, flinging the Silver Wolf's short cloak over her shoulders. She ducked outside and ran to the left, in the direction of Ceara's voice.

There was no one there, not any longer, but a sheathed dagger was propped against the shadowed side of the tent. It had not been dropped, but left for her. Alys peeked between the tents as she seized the hilt then looked up at the crest of the hill that rose on that side. Though there was mist on the ground, she had a glimpse of Ceara's mischievous grin. The other woman waved and vanished.

A weapon.

Her comrades had ensured she was armed.

And the Silver Wolf would not know of it.

Alys had no sooner dropped the dagger into her boot then a man cleared his throat behind her. She spun, fearing that she would be compelled to surrender the weapon, only to find the Scotsman behind her.

He was the one that the Silver Wolf called Murdoch Campbell. She had never seen him close and he was the sole one who had not danced with her the night before. Why not? It had been a long time since Alys had seen Rupert's son, so long that they had both been merely children. She could not have said whether he was the man before her or not.

"You will not remember me," he said in quick Gaelic, though his steady gaze revealed that he expected otherwise.

"He said you are Murdoch Campbell," Alys said. "I knew a boy with that name."

"And I knew a maiden whose father was served by my father." His gaze flicked to the ruins and back to her. "And both our fathers died the same night, at the hand of the same villain."

He *was* Rupert's son.

"You did not dance with me yester eve."

"I did not dare to risk that you might recognize me while beneath the Silver Wolf's eye."

Alys nodded understanding of that. "Because you would betray him."

How odd that the first word to rise to her lips was betrayal instead of justice. Alys frowned at the Silver Wolf's influence on her thoughts.

Meanwhile, Murdoch raised a finger. "I swore vengeance upon the Silver Wolf, Jean le Beau and all their kin years ago. I vowed to avenge my father and I trained for long years to ensure my readiness. In the spring, I followed the Compagnie Rouge to Jean le Beau, killed him when he was alone, then used his corpse to gain access to Château de Vries."

"For you wished to join the Silver Wolf's company."

"To learn his destination, aye. Perhaps to catch him unawares."

"To come home?"

Murdoch's brows rose. "I was surprised when he swore to return to Kilderrick." he shook his head. "'Tis all a ruse in pursuit of some greater plan."

Here was yet another who believed that the Silver Wolf came only to Kilderrick for an interval. Alys might be left in command of her legacy yet.

Murdoch was grim. "He will have no such chance for I will have my due first."

"How? When?"

He stepped back, glancing over his shoulder. "I leave this day in search of aid, but fear not. I will return and we will both be avenged." Murdoch gave her a hard look. "Perhaps then the power of Kilderrick can be restored by its rightful heirs."

Heirs? There was solely one heir to Kilderrick, to Alys' thinking —herself.

Before she could ask Murdoch's precise meaning, he pivoted and disappeared silently between the tents. The men shouted, drawing closer, and Alys returned to the tent of the Silver Wolf. She shed her boots to disguise the fact that she had left and left the dagger hidden within one. She stood then in her chemise as if she had only just risen from bed and flung the cloak over her shoulders. She faced the flap, ensuring that her expression was one of confusion.

The Silver Wolf returned in that moment, sweeping open the flap and stepping inside. He surveyed her quickly, as if he guessed the truth from the sight of her.

"Who shouted?" she asked.

"Oliver. The squire who serves Amaury." He was curt and she guessed that he was annoyed. He cast a token down on the table, his gesture filled with disgust.

It was a pentacle on a string, a crude necklace.

"He awakened nude and painted blue from head to toe," he said, his words as crisp as a slap. His gaze bored into her, his eyes a fiery blue. "What do you know of this?"

ALYS FALTERED.

Her mouth opened and closed, her gaze fixed on the trinket, and Maximilian was tempted to believe that she knew naught of Oliver's fate at all.

She knew something, though. He had sensed that she hid some detail from him when he returned, for she did not meet his gaze with her usual candor. As ever, her eyes revealed the truth of her thoughts and when her gaze was evasive, he considered it a warning.

But she did not know about the necklace. He would have wagered his life upon it.

"Blue?" she echoed, confusion in her expression.

"Aye, head to toe, as if he had been dipped within a bucket of paint."

Her gaze brightened. "Woad. 'Tis woad."

"Is that not a plant used to dye cloth?"

"Aye, but there were said to be warriors in the north, Picts, who fought naked and painted themselves blue with woad to terrify their opponents." She shrugged. "Nyssa is from the north. This might be her doing."

Maximilian flung himself into his chair, then templed his fingers together, watching Alys. Oliver, then, had been captured on his quest, but it seemed he had not learned any useful detail. "Tell me of your companions."

"I do not see the point," Alys said, perching on the smaller trunk. Her gaze was steady, now, her resistance rising anew.

"I wish to know my opponents."

"I do not wish to betray my friends." She smiled a little, a dare in her eyes. "You said you valued loyalty."

Maximilian leaned toward her, holding her gaze that she might see his resolve. "And the greatest loyalty should come from you. I am first in your obligations since we wed."

Alys tightened her lips and looked away. "I cannot forget past alliances so readily as that."

"Tell me of them."

She glared at him, that furious fire in her eyes again. "I will not."

"Tell me of this," he invited, lifting the token.

She eyed it and shrugged. "'Twas the symbol marked on the wall of the courtyard of Kilderrick. My father used to refresh it on the full moon." Her eyes narrowed slightly. "He burned candles and made invocations." Her gaze slid to his again. "I was not supposed to know, much less to see it."

"Did he consort with demons?"

"Who can say?"

"Did you ever see one?"

She stared at the token for a long moment. "He said there was a goblin or demon, a redcap. He said it bathed its hat in the blood of its victims and that it was bound to do his will. He spoke to it often, especially at night, but I never saw it."

"You do not think it existed?"

"I did not say that," Alys said with a shiver. "There was an atmosphere in the keep on the night of the full moon, a restlessness in the air that could not be explained. Items went missing and the servants left for fear."

"Save Rupert, the castellan."

"Save Rupert," she agreed. "Though I oft sensed his fear. He told me that my father meddled in matters he should not, but said no more."

"But you use the symbol, over the river when you attack the reivers."

Alys' smile broadened. "It is only a symbol, but it is one people fear. The simple sight of it kept all away from Kilderrick's ruin for years, and it served us well in confronting the reivers."

"But you do not believe in its power."

She hesitated, again glancing at the token. "There were disappearances I could not explain. I may not understand it or fully believe its import, but I respect it."

"I do not," Maximilian said. He seized the token and crushed it in one hand, watching Alys all the while. The straw and sticks crumbled to dust in his hand but he saw her flinch and wagered she believed in it more than she had suggested.

He cast the dust on the table and rose to his feet. "I will send Nathalie to you that we might break our fast and look upon the ruin together."

It was only after he had led Alys to the ruins of Kilderrick that Maximilian wondered at the wisdom of his choice. He had been the one to destroy Kilderrick, albeit at his father's command, and she had been trapped in the fire that had razed the building. He had thought only of learning the details of the destroyed keep, and had not considered that it might upset her to return there. He assumed she had visited it often, but her stiff posture as she confronted the ruin made him question his assumption.

Alys' lips were set and there was a tension in her shoulders. She did not flinch, though, and he respected her strength of will. He would have offered his hand but she climbed onto the top of the wall with ease, proving yet again that she had no need of him.

Maximilian intended to teach her otherwise.

Uncertain what to say, he considered the ruin in daylight. The old keep was a blackened pile of stones, and one with puddles inside from the rain the day before. The foundation had been stone, as Maximilian recalled, and the stones remained mostly in place, though they were dark with ash. There had been two buildings, joined by a courtyard. In the larger one to the west, there had been a common space on the ground floor, a high-ceilinged hall on the second floor and two small chambers above. He had confronted the laird in the larger of those two rooms.

There had been a thorn hedge, which he had burned, but no moat or other earthenwork defenses. The smaller tower to the east had presumably contained stables and kitchens, as well as storage. The keep looked bleak and Alys' silence made him wonder at her thoughts. He could not keep himself from staring down where the cellar had once been, where Alys had been trapped. He could not read her expression, for her features were set.

She stared down into the puddles in what had been that cellar and he recalled the sack of cloth, as well as the castellan's hasty assurances. "Do you truly mean to rebuild it?"

"Aye, but stronger so that it cannot be conquered so readily. It was more a house than a fortification."

She slanted him a glance. "You said the masons would come from Carlisle. I thought it a tale, perhaps one you thought I would wish to hear."

He shook his head. "I tell no tales, Alys," he reminded her.

She did not challenge him on that. "To rebuild a keep of this size is no small endeavor. 'Twill be costly."

Maximilian nodded. "I told the mason I had need of shelter before the Yule and a keep by the spring. He vowed to come with all haste."

Her brows rose. "You have gathered much coin in your endeavors, then. Plundering and pillaging?"

"Laboring for those who will pay for results," he corrected, punctuating his words with a look. Alys looked away and he tried to restore the mood between them. "I fear the trouble with coin is that no matter how much is gathered, there is need of more, especially when there will be construction. I would seek tenants and establish a village by the keep again, for then there will be taxes again."

"You truly think they will accept you as laird."

"They came for our wedding feast willingly enough," he noted. "And pledged to me."

She nodded, walking along the summit of the wall, a fact that evidently required all her attention. Maximilian doubted as much.

"You saw your father afterward," he said, guessing the direction of her thoughts.

She nodded. "Briefly. And Rupert." She sighed, then looked into the distance.

Maximilian had looked upon burned remains many a time and still they revolted him. To see her own father thus—and the castellan she knew so well—when she had only been a child, could only have been horrible for Alys.

"I did not kill Rupert," he admitted and she spun to consider him, eyes wide. "There was no cause to do as much. He surrendered immediately to my command and showed me throughout the entire keep. He unlocked doors and opened chests and was most obliging."

"And lied about the sack in the cellar."

"I did not know that then." Maximilian sat on the wall, watching her. "He was a loyal servant and I had no quarrel with him."

"But he died that night."

"Aye. I tripped over his corpse when I fled the laird's chamber, but I did not kill him." He held her gaze, letting her see the truth of it and only released the breath he was holding when she frowned and averted her gaze.

"Tell me of it," she invited, arms folded across her chest.

"My father commanded me to take the keep. He was in Northumberland himself, in the employ of the Percy family and wished to find other gains. He dispatched me here with a small company and a promise."

Alys looked up at that.

"He said that if I found the treasure of Kilderrick, I could have both holding and treasure for my own. I already chafed at his authority, so it was the perfect temptation. I came here with half a dozen men, but they abandoned me when they saw the symbol upon the courtyard wall. Rupert showed me all I demanded to see, then took me to your father." He shook his head, remembering. "The wind was wild that night and there was something disturbing in the air."

"'Twas the full moon," Alys said. "When he invoked his demon, or so the tales say."

"But you never saw it?"

She shook her head and looked down at her hands, folded in her lap. "I did not want to. I felt it, and that was sufficient."

Maximilian would have wagered that she hid some truth from him, but he continued with his own tale. If he asked after it, she would not tell him, not until she was prepared to do so—if ever that day came. "He called his demon when he saw me and he commanded it to seize me. I thought he was mad, for I could not see who he addressed. The castellan refused to enter the laird's chamber with me, so great was his fear. I thought that if he was not mad, it had to be a feint. I truly wished only to claim the treasure."

"Did your father know what it was?"

Maximilian shook his head. "Gems or coins, I expected. In truth, I thought your father might have swallowed it."

Alys looked up in surprise.

"Men do, and then they must seek it in their waste in a day or two, but it is a means to hide a prize."

She blinked in surprise. "That sounds foul."

"But effective. And so I thought to...encourage his confession of the location of the jewel. I thought the lick of fire would loosen his tongue. But the wind stirred in the chamber in a most unnatural way, and the flames leaped high beyond my expectation. He called to his demon and commanded that creature, and though I still doubt its existence, I cannot deny that the flames had a life of their own." He shook his head. "I did not intend to kill him, Alys."

"Did he tell you of the treasure?"

Maximilian shook his head. "Nay. He died screaming of blood, doubtless for his demon to wash its cap."

She seemed pensive.

"What do you know of Kilderrick's reputed treasure?" he asked finally.

Alys shook her head, turning away from him again. "My father's riches were stolen before you came," she said and Maximilian wished he could have seen her eyes. "The reivers came and emptied the treasury of every coin. They took every morsel of food and every item that could be sold. They left us with naught at all." She turned to look upon him, her expression cool. "That is why I avenge myself upon them."

Maximilian could not blame her for that. "So, the treasure is gone."

"My father insisted he had hidden the gem of his hoard so well that none would discover it. As far as I know, no one has."

"Do you know where it is?"

Alys shrugged and turned back to the ruin, as if the matter was of no interest at all. "I thought I knew once, but I was mistaken. I suspect it, too, was stolen. I was only a child."

That had to be the truth, though something in her manner made him wonder. What heiress would not be determined to claim the treasure that was her due when all else was lost? She must have tried. It must be gone.

It must be yet another legacy that had been stolen from his lady wife.

Alys pointed at the ruin as if to distract him. "You can see that the taller tower was here on the west side, but then you entered it all those years ago." She gave him a glance filled with familiar challenge. "You must recall it."

"Aye." He allowed himself to be distracted. "The stairs were on the interior of the northern wall, and there was a great chamber on the second floor. Above that, was the laird's own chamber and another small one. He must have had quite a view on a clear day."

"He did." She smiled a little in reminiscence. "Part of the stairs remain. And the cellar, of course." She squared her shoulders and turned with a frown. "And to the east was the much smaller tower, where the kitchen and storerooms were."

"And there was a walled courtyard between them, where I saw the pentacle upon the wall."

"How will you rebuild it? As it was?"

"Larger," Maximilian confessed and saw her surprise. He seized her hand and jumped down, marking the outline with his steps. "This western tower must be larger and taller, to grant a better view of the valley and better accommodate our household. I would expand it to these dimensions. Above the cellar would be the kitchen, with a hearth in this corner. Above would be the great hall and above that, the laird's own chamber."

She looked to be amused. "You have thought of this."

"Aye." He paced off the distance. "There would be a platform for sentries at the summit, and the courtyard made larger, too."

"More room for the monthly court," she said and he nodded agreement.

"I would add a dungeon beneath the smaller tower, which would contain both stores and a chambers for those who labor in the keep."

"The hedge?"

"Will be replanted."

"My father always talked of adding earthworks, but 'twas never done."

"I will have them dug, there and there." Maximilian lifted her down from the wall before she could protest. "Where was the stable?"

"My father kept few horses. There was a shelter in the courtyard. It was said that once they had been kept in the closer village, where the chapel and smithy were also located. It was abandoned before you first came to Kilderrick." She walked slightly ahead of him, leading the way to what remained of the village that had been beside the keep.

Maximilian had noticed the stone foundations when riding to Rowan Fell but had not yet investigated them. When he had first visited Kilderrick, they had already been empty. "What happened to the villeins who lived here?"

"Some went to Rowan Fell, but not all of them." She eyed him. "My father's influence was vastly diminished in the years before you came, and the crops failed several years in a row. It is a hard land here, and there is rarely abundance. Perhaps you might be advised to establish a holding elsewhere."

"My choice is made, Alys, and will not waver."

Instead of replying, she straightened and looked to the west, shading her eyes with her hand. He was turning to follow her gaze even before she pointed. "What is this?"

A company of villagers approached, evidently having walked from Rowan Fell. They were led by the older smith, Finlay, and the sheriff, Eamon, those men's respective families fast behind them. The company was followed by a cluster of whispering villagers, evidently curious about events.

What was this?

CHAPTER 14

*T*he Silver Wolf said he had not killed her father apurpose and that he had not killed Rupert at all. Both claims were startling but what troubled Alys more was her inclination to believe him. He had seemed sincere.

Either it was true that he never lied outright, or he told falsehoods with such ease that they had the ring of truth. Alys wished she knew which was the case.

And he *had* come for the treasure of Kilderrick: indeed, he had been promised it. He still did not know that the treasure was her own self, and the measure of royal blood in her veins. If Alys confessed that he had already claimed the treasure of Kilderrick, the Silver Wolf might never leave.

"What is this?" he asked her, his confusion apparent as he surveyed the approaching villagers.

"I would wager they come to you for justice."

His surprise was obvious in his sidelong glance. "Why?"

"Because you are laird and they have pledged fealty to you. Villagers are not solely a source of revenue. You owe them boons, as well. Security and justice at the least."

"There will be a court, on the day after the new moon. I told them as much."

"It seems some matter will not wait." Alys stepped forward to greet the villagers, her own curiosity sharp. Amidst the deluge of complaints and accusations, all in excited Gaelic, she learned the truth. She turned to the Silver Wolf. "The sheriff of Rowan Fell requests a hearing."

Impatience touched her spouse's expression, then was banished as if it had never been. "There will be a court..." he repeated firmly.

"Eamon says he has been robbed."

The Silver Wolf's brows rose.

"And the smith, Finlay, also requests your judgment, for his daughter has been despoiled."

Her husband blinked. "And this is *my* concern?"

Alys almost laughed at his dismay. "Not only are you Laird of Kilderrick but these offenses occurred during the feast last eve." The smith continued with enthusiasm and outrage, and she summarized his diatribe for her spouse when he finally fell silent and she translated. "And Finlay's pig has been stolen, as well."

"I should be as affronted as he if it had been a horse, but not a pig."

Alys leaned close to her husband and dropped her voice. "But that pig is what they will eat this winter," she whispered, holding his gaze. "It is as key to their survival as your destrier has been to yours."

The Silver Wolf sobered, considering. "But they are not witless. I will judge the greater matters, but not petty thievery or the loss of a maidenhead."

"You are laird," she reminded him again.

Now he was exasperated. "But these are minor matters. Surely they can resolve such trivialities themselves."

"You are *laird*," Alys said once again, giving him so stern a look that the villagers fell silent and watched them warily. "You owe them a hearing this very day." She turned to the sheriff and the smith. "I fear my husband may need my assistance," she said to them in Gaelic. "To both understand your words and our local customs."

"What did you say?" the Silver Wolf demanded of her and she told him. His brows drew together. "I understand justice..." he began, but Alys interrupted him with resolve.

"But not Gaelic," she noted and he shut his mouth so quickly that she wondered whether that was truly the case.

She had been convinced that he did not speak Gaelic, for he had asked her to introduce the villagers and translate for him. Now, she wondered if that had been merely a ruse, the better that he might be under-estimated by those he commanded.

His gaze had flicked at her assertion that he would need her aid, then he had nodded agreement—but there had been the smallest hesitation.

Apparently subterfuge did not count as deception.

Truly, she grew to understand the Silver Wolf better with each passing hour. She was amazed that she had thought him inscrutable and devoid of passion. Two nights had proven his passion to her and close observation had shown that he oft revealed his thoughts in subtle ways.

How curious that he thought such routine appeals for justice were beneath his concern. If he wished to have the villagers defer to him—and pay their tithes—then he would have to provide such resolutions to them. The laird's relationship with the occupants of his holding was less about command than about partnership.

If the Silver Wolf needed to learn that, Alys would teach him. She would not stand aside while he repeated her father's errors.

THE COMPANY WALKED TOGETHER toward the camp and the clearing where they all had feasted the night before. There was a wondrous scent of soup and Denis was busy by the fire. The Silver Wolf sat in a chair, fully garbed in his hauberk and tabard, that cloak over his shoulders and his sword on his belt.

Alys felt an unexpected thrill at his majestic appearance, and felt her skin heat in recollection of what they had done abed. He granted her a quick glance, his gaze sizzling with rare impatience, and she liked that he again deferred to her counsel.

She walked toward him and he extended a hand to her without glancing her way, aware of her precise whereabouts. His fingers closed over hers and he drew her to his side, his gesture possessive and well noted by the villagers.

Was it only for the sake of appearances? Alys thought not. He seemed to desire her aid, and she dared to hope that they might govern Kilderrick together. He could not know how much that prospect pleased her.

The Silver Wolf looked like a wealthy warrior, his status made all the more clear by the contrast with the garb of the smith and the sheriff. Jeannie, of course, had accompanied her husband, her lips twisted in sour disapproval.

The older smith, Finlay, stood with his sons and daughter. He no longer labored at the forge and was crooked in his advanced years, his hair silver and his figure gaunt. Outrage, though, made him stand taller than he had the night before. His oldest son, Cormac, stood beside him, powerful arms folded across his burly chest as he frowned in displeasure. The wife and infant were not to be seen this day. The smith's daughter, Isobeal, a pretty lass, was weeping as she stood between father and oldest brother. The younger son, Tynan, a quiet dark man who loomed over his relations, stood behind the trio, watching with bright eyes.

Finlay was complaining loudly about one of the Silver Wolf's men claiming his daughter's innocent charms, fulsome in his description of how that man had cheated Isobeal—and by extension, her father—of their respective due. It seemed his pig was also missing and he demanded to know who within the Silver Wolf's company had stolen it. 'Twas likely good that the Silver Wolf did not understand him, for Finlay's diatribe was thick with disparaging comments about mercenaries and men of war.

"What is he saying?" the Silver Wolf asked Alys softly when the lecture showed no signs of ending. Alys was not even certain Finlay took a breath. He had the attention of all gathered there, and seemed to be enjoying the weight of every gaze.

"That his daughter's maidenhead was stolen, as well as his pig."

The Silver Wolf flicked an impatient glance at her. "That is ten words. He has uttered at least five hundred."

Alys fought a smile. "He takes both insults most seriously."

The Silver Wolf sighed as Finlay continued with heat. "It cannot be so fearsome a crime if he relishes the telling of it so much," her husband muttered but Alys did not reply.

The men in the Silver Wolf's company gradually appeared, drawn by the sound of the smith's voice. Alys saw that Oliver had washed, but blue woad still clung to his skin and was visible in the roots of his hair. It looked as if there had been a pentacle drawn on his brow in soot, as well.

That made Alys realize that the full moon was only a few nights away. Elizabeth had scattered tiny symbols in the camp and she knew the sight had unsettled the villagers who had followed him from Normandy. Would Ceara and Nyssa do something to frighten the company on the full moon?

She doubted she would have any such opportunity, which saved her the decision of whether she should do as much or not. The Silver Wolf would not be swayed, but what if his followers departed from Kilderrick? Would he follow?

Would he surrender the seal to her if he did? Alys bit her lip, wondering.

Murdoch appeared at the periphery of the group then, carrying packed saddlebags, and put them down to watch. He began to translate for Yves and Denis, who gathered close to him, Nathalie and Marie close behind.

"'Twas him!" the smith suddenly cried, pointing at Rafael who had just sauntered into the clearing. Isobeal broke into a fresh bout of tears that seemed a little more forced than Alys might have expected.

"That is a novel reaction," Rafael muttered in French and Victor snorted a laugh. Rafael grinned at his own jest and the other mercenary's reaction.

"Apparently, 'twas him," the Silver Wolf murmured.

Alys looked down at him in surprise. Had he interpreted Finlay's pointing finger, or understood the smith's words?

"And he was the one who robbed our hut!" Eamon cried, pointing at Rafael in his turn.

Rafael blinked, then eyed the Silver Wolf, who squeezed Alys' fingers, a sign that he needed the translation.

"The smith accuses you of taking his daughter's maidenhead last night," she informed Rafael. "While the sheriff accuses you of robbing his cottage. It is unclear who stole the smith's pig as yet."

Rafael scoffed then appealed to the Silver Wolf. "And accusation is sufficient for me to be named the guilty party?"

"Are you?" that man asked.

"Nay." Rafael claimed an apple from a basket near the fire, polished it on his tabard and bit into it, his stare challenging. His denial was understood, for the villagers from Rowan Fell muttered in disagreement.

"Your dagger was embedded in my table!" Eamon declared, showing the dagger in question.

Alys translated for the Silver Wolf and Rafael, both of whom were visibly startled. "Embedded?" the Silver Wolf asked, his tone skeptical.

"Driven into the wood, the point buried there," the sheriff explained. "You can see the mark on the blade."

When Alys translated, Eamon offered the dagger.

"That is fine Toledo steel!" Rafael said in outrage when he saw the mark. Though he spoke in English, he apparently was understood by the villagers. "No man with his wits about him would ever treat that blade with such disrespect!" He seized the scabbard from Eamon, who shrank away from the larger man. He drew the blade and grimaced. "Look at the point," he muttered, turning the blade so that it caught the light. "It is sacrilege." He turned upon the sheriff, brandishing the blade. "Look at this. Did you so ruin it?"

The sheriff took two steps back, holding up his hands. "Not I!"

"Nor I," Rafael said, then approached the Silver Wolf to show the blade to him with evident disgust.

That man shook his head in sympathy. "And such a fine blade wasted. Perhaps it can be sharpened."

"It will never be as it was," Rafael said sadly, the two of them staring at the weapon in obvious agreement.

"I was robbed!" Eamon roared in English. "Is that of no interest to any of you?"

The two mercenaries glanced up with apparent surprise. "What was stolen?" the Silver Wolf asked.

Eamon took a deep breath. "Three ducks, six chickens, two pewter plates..."

"Aye, they *were* fine," Rafael noted with a wave of the blade. "I would regret their loss, to be sure."

Jeannie glared at him. "And the smith's pig was locked in our cottage, as well," she said, taking the conversation back to Gaelic.

"Then *you* stole our pig," the smith said to her.

"I did not steal your pig," Eamon retorted. "I released it from my cottage."

"Then you are responsible for its loss," Finlay declared.

"Not if you locked it in our cottage," Eamon countered.

Finlay shook a finger at the sheriff. "That pig would have fed us the entire winter..."

"And it should have been slaughtered already," Jeannie contributed. "My mother said never to leave a pig fattening after Samhain..."

Eamon interjected, jabbing a finger through the air at Finlay. "Your pig broke a bench in my cottage and mired the pallets..."

"What of my maidenhead?" Isobeal wailed, her weeping louder once again.

"And what of my ducks?" Jeannie demanded of the Silver Wolf.

That man pinched the bridge of his nose as all voices rose in lively argument, Gaelic flying fast as chaos descended upon the gathering. He let them argue until their voices faded, his exasperation clear, then stood up with authority.

The villagers fell silent in expectation. Alys thought the Silver Wolf would send them back to Rowan Fell without a reply, as her father would have done, but once again, her husband surprised her.

He pointed at Isobeal. "Did this man claim your maidenhead?" he asked her in English, speaking slowly and clearly, then indicating Rafael.

"Aye, sir," she said, her gaze dancing to Rafael and away.

"She was no maiden," Rafael retorted. Isobeal blushed, her father began to bluster, and to Alys' surprise, Tynan, the younger son of the smith spoke quietly.

"He speaks aright. 'Twas the miller's son claimed that prize."

There was a roar of astonishment from the villagers and another eruption of chatter.

"Zounds," the Silver Wolf muttered.

Isobeal gasped and spun to face her brother in fury. "Tynan!"

"I knew I was not first through the gates," Rafael said with a confident nod.

Isobeal pivoted to confront him, switching to Gaelic in her agitation. "And now my father will cast me out, and the miller's son will not have me, and 'tis *all your fault.*"

Rafael looked at Alys, his brows high.

"She blames you," seemed the most apt summary.

"She should thank me," the mercenary replied and grinned at Isobeal. "I thank you for a merry ride."

She flushed crimson, understanding his implication if not his words. "Wretch!"

But there was a twinkle in her eyes and Alys knew she had not been an unwilling partner.

"And the hut?" the Silver Wolf asked Rafael.

"I never returned there after you and I left." He raised the hilt of the dagger and Alys saw that there was something trapped in the crystal orb of its pommel. He held the Silver Wolf's gaze as he kissed the crystal. "I swear it upon this sliver of the True Cross."

There was a shard of the True Cross in the pommel of his dagger? Alys was astonished, as astonished as the villagers, who craned their necks to better see the weapon in question.

"Then how did your dagger come to be there?" the Silver Wolf asked. "Was it stolen from you?"

Rafael looked discomfited. "I surrendered it to another, to the damsel who stole Phantôm."

"Why?"

"She offered to lie with me in exchange for it, when I was trapped in the mire." Rafael shrugged. "She lied."

Again the Silver Wolf looked up at Alys.

"That was Ceara," she contributed.

"Could she have robbed the sheriff's cottage?" His gaze was searching.

Alys could not deny that Ceara would have enjoyed doing as much. The other woman particularly would have liked to ensure that one of the mercenaries was blamed for it. "Anything is possible," she acknowledged, feeling disloyal at the admission.

His gaze was assessing. "Your former companions continue to cause disruptions. Do you know how they might be appeased?"

"You could offer them shelter in exchange for their fealty." The suggestion was bold and had been rejected before, but to Alys' surprise, this time, the Silver Wolf seemed to consider it.

"Would they accept such terms?"

"They might."

"Would they *keep* the terms?"

"I would hope so."

"As would I, Alys, as would I." He cleared his throat and indicated Rafael. "You will pay Isobeal Smith two silver pennies, for whether 'twas her maidenhead lost or she turns to whoring, she must be compensated for the service done to you."

Alys translated this quickly for the villagers while he paused. There was some nudging and commentary, but she sensed they found this fair.

Two silver pennies was a handsome fee, even if she had been a maiden.

The Silver Wolf turned to Mallory and Reynaud. "You will seek the smith's pig and see it returned to his abode before sunset."

"But where shall we seek it, sir?"

"Wherever 'tis that pigs flee," the Silver Wolf replied with a return of that exasperation. "I know naught of pigs. Ask!"

The boys bowed and Alys spoke up. "Check the kitchen scraps in the gardens of the other villagers."

"And find all chickens and ducks," the Silver Wolf continued. "I will come to Rowan Fell after the midday meal and we will resolve which bird belongs to which villager."

The boys nodded and headed for the village.

"What of my plates?" Jeannie demanded.

"I will find the culprit, but until I do, they cannot be returned," the Silver Wolf said to her, the reprimand so evident in his tone that even

Jeannie fell silent. He pointed to Amaury who lingered at the back of the company, eyes bright. "And you will take Oliver, locate the women in the forest, and bring them to me. Pay particular attention to recover Jeannie's plates, if you can, and ensure that the women are not injured. We shall see whether they accept the proposition of shelter that the lady and I would offer."

"I could seek them," Rafael offered.

"You have done sufficient of late," the Silver Wolf replied, his tone so hard that even Rafael dropped his gaze. Alys translated for the villagers, who nodded understanding and approval. "Are you satisfied?" he asked the villagers of Rowan Fell.

"Aye!" was the resounding reply.

Finlay Smith was much taken with the silver penny he had claimed from Isobeal's payment. He grinned outright at the new laird and nodded vigorously, then dropped to one knee before him. His son, Cormac, also beamed approval. Jeannie was far from pleased but she did not challenge the Silver Wolf further. Eamon was fairly groveling when he bent to kiss the laird's hand. Alys would not have turned her back upon him for any price.

'Twas only as the villagers headed back to Rowan Fell, happily discussing the result of their plea, that Alys considered the marvel of them coming to the Silver Wolf in the first place. They had pledged fealty to him, and he had given them a feast, but already they trusted him to do what no laird had done in decades.

Not only was the Silver Wolf not his own father—he was not hers.

THIS MATTER of dispensing justice was simpler than Maximilian might have expected. What the villagers truly wanted was a mediator, not so much to inflict a solution upon them but to find a resolution that suited all of them. He was accustomed to doing this within the Compagnie Rouge, but not with common people. Indeed, his free company typically invaded a town and occupied it only for a short time before moving on. The disputes between mercenaries had been over stolen coin or rations, most often, or arguments over shares of the spoils or the favors of a woman. Chickens and pigs were not as different from that as they might appear. He began to see what Alys meant about partnership between laird and villager, and thought that with her aid, he would soon conquer the task.

And Alys continued to astound him. She had no fear of challenging him before his own villeins, even insisting that he see the matter her way. She was bold and she was right.

Her counsel would serve them both well.

Murdoch took his leave then and truly, the Silver Wolf might have been sitting in a great hall. He remained on his chair in the clearing as the Scotsman approached and Alys stayed by his side. Again, he wondered whether the pair knew each other at all but they did not so much as glance at each other.

A suspicious man might have thought them too indifferent to each other.

"I thank you for the companionship upon the road," Murdoch said with a bow. "If it suits you, sir, I will continue my journey north to my home."

"You never mentioned its location," Maximilian said.

Murdoch smiled thinly. "I doubt you would know it, sir."

Maximilian recognized evasion when he heard it, but he would not give the Scotsman any cause to think him suspicious. If the man had a plan or a plot, it would be hatched once he left the company. The sooner he left, the sooner Maximilian might see another threat resolved. They exchanged wishes of goodwill, then Murdoch took his leave.

Maximilian did not even have to tell Rafael to follow him.

To Maximilian's surprise, the smith's youngest son had lingered after the others returned to the village. "Tynan, is it not?" Maximilian asked before Alys could prompt him. He was a tall man, dark of hair and dark of eye, as burly as a smith should be in Maximilian's view.

He bowed. "I had thought to offer my services here at Kilderrick, my lord," that man said with a bow. "

"You do not labor at the smithy in Rowan Fell?"

"My older brother will inherit the smithy. My father has chosen." Tynan shrugged, his dark gaze lighting at the sound of the horses stamping beyond the tents, though they could not be seen from this vantage point. He met Maximilian's gaze. "After I revealed Isobeal's lie, I will not be so welcome at their hearth."

Ah.

"And you have horses," Tynan added.

"Aye."

"Destriers." Tynan gave this word the emphasis it deserved.

"Aye. Six destriers and eighteen palfreys. And now, some number of ponies. A veritable herd."

"A veritable blessing," Tynan murmured with reverence. "Horses will not survive the winter without shelter, my lord."

"Nay. They have need of a stable. Could one be built in the former village beside the ruins of the keep?" Maximilian gestured toward the abandoned huts. There were seven of them in total, though all had lost their roofs and were filled with detritus.

"'Twould be a fair labor..." Tynan noted, not seeming troubled by the prospect. "And the wolves would have to be discouraged."

"Aye, that can be done readily enough. We can move our camp to surround the old village." Tynan turned to consider this while Maximilian whistled three notes. Nicholas appeared immediately and ran toward him.

"Aye, my lord." He was breathless but obviously curious.

"Fetch Henri, if you please."

"Aye, sir." Nicholas pivoted and raced back toward the horses.

"My ostler," Maximilian said to Tynan. "He has firm expectations of a smith."

"And so he should. A destrier is a fair investment."

Nicholas came back into view, Henri's sturdy figure close behind him.

"Aye, my lord?" Henri said, bowing low before Maximilian.

"Henri, Tynan is a blacksmith seeking employ."

"Ah!" The ostler smiled, then shook hands with Tynan heartily. "I have a palfrey who lost a shoe the last night we rode north, but we had to carry on in the rain. I have a destrier who is limping, because his hoof has need of a trim, but the shoe must come off for that." He spoke rapidly, so quickly that Tynan clearly could not follow his words.

Before Maximilian could ask Alys to assist, Henri smiled. "Come and show me what you can do," he said slowly and Tynan nodded agreement. He bowed again to Maximilian and then to Alys, before following Henri to the horses.

"Henri is as talkative as Tynan is quiet," Alys said softly.

Maximilian smiled. "I suspect they share a concern for horses."

"I could translate..."

"Nay, Alys. Let them find their means of understanding each other. I will not have you mediate for all. You are lady, after all." He nodded to her, watching her cheeks flush. "We will eat, then ride to Rowan Fell to adjudicate the matter of the chickens. Doubtless I will need your assistance there."

She nodded agreement.

"Do you know where an armorer might be found?" he asked her. "Rafael's dagger is the first blade that will need to be sharpened, but it will not be the last. I would wager that Tynan's experience with armor would be limited, based on him training here."

Alys thought about it. "Carlisle, I would think, unless you coax one away from the employ of another laird."

Maximilian wagered the closest such might be the king himself, and Carlisle was closer than Stirling.

"How much do you know of chickens?" Alys asked, her eyes twinkling in a most alluring way.

"Naught at all," Maximilian confessed. "But more than I know of pigs." He found himself smiling, delighting in the sound of his lady's laughter.

Aye, happiness transformed her and he could only marvel at the change she wrought already in him. How was it that he had no interest in any other woman or that he did not lose his fascination with her? How was it that it gave him such joy to make her happy or to win her reluctant trust?

You and no other.

The inscription seemed more apt with every passing moment. He had never known love and had no experience to compare with the rumor, but Maximilian watched his lady wife and wondered whether this heat that dawned within him was the love of the troubadors' tales.

He already ceded so much to her and willingly, and yet, that did not trouble him.

Perhaps he changed as he was indulged by his lady's favor.

Perhaps that was all love needed to find fertile ground.

~

ALYS WAS ASTONISHED when a harnessed palfrey was led to her, alongside the Silver Wolf's saddled destrier. The mare was much smaller than the stallion, chestnut of hue with a white star upon her brow. She nuzzled Alys' hand gently and the Silver Wolf gave her one of the apples from Denis' stores.

His destrier snorted, taking exception to this show of favoritism, and the Silver Wolf produced a second apple for the stallion.

"Can you ride?" he asked with one of those quick piercing glances.

"I did once, but we had ponies and I was still a girl."

Royce rode toward them, already in the saddle. The destrier had to be his for it was a massive beast, large enough to easily carry his weight. Evidently, he would accompany them.

"It is not far to Rowan Fell," the Silver Wolf said. "And you will find it more comfortable to ride yourself if we venture further afield." He eyed her with a smile. "I find it unlikely that you will be content to ride in a cart."

Alys smiled at the accuracy of his assessment, then excused herself. He watched her go with obvious confusion, but she returned to his tent in haste. She shed her boots, put on her old chausses, then tugged on her boots again, replacing the sheathed dagger inside it. Then she hastened back to him, lifting the hem of her kirtle to show him. He smiled and caught her waist in his hands, lifting her to the saddle.

It felt more treacherous than sitting before him on the destrier. He kept hold of the reins as well, swinging into his own saddle, then leading her palfrey at a steady walk. Alys tried not to clutch the mare's mane but to ride with some dignity. To her relief, the rhythm returned to her before they had reached the ruins. She did not miss the fact that her palfrey was between the two destriers and guessed that this was by her husband's design.

"Do you protect me or distrust me?" she asked lightly, earning a quick glance.

Royce became fascinated in the horizon and increased the distance between his horse and hers.

"I like to be prepared for all eventualities," the Silver Wolf said and Alys fought against her smile.

"I have nowhere to flee," she told him.

"Is that so," he murmured, though there was no question in his tone.

They reached Rowan Fell to find Mallory and Reynaud before the chapel, surrounded by chickens and ducks. Someone had given the boys a small sack of grain and they cast handfuls at the ground, keeping the birds within range. The villagers were already gathered and Alys learned that the pig had been found in Niall's outbuilding, where it had taken sanctuary with the ox. Rona's goats meandered around the perimeter of the clearing, bleating, and several dogs barked with enthusiasm. There were a few children darting between the adults and Alys saw a cat on a stoop, watching the proceedings.

The Silver Wolf dismounted and a lively discussion ensued about the chickens. The ducks clearly belonged to Jeannie for she was the sole one to keep them, so that was quickly resolved. There were chickens of every shade of brown and gold, and a wide range of sizes, which made it comparatively easy for each villager to identify his or her birds. The Silver Wolf gave the matter his fullest attention, enduring long descriptions in Gaelic about the lineage of the more prized hens. Once or twice, Alys caught his gaze and struggled against her urge to laugh at his solemnity.

The villagers loved it, though.

And when all was done and the chickens were returned to their rightful owners, Beth served cups of ale to celebrate. They toasted the Silver Wolf and he drank of their ale from a crude crockery cup, then Cormac Smith's wife presented him with a chicken.

For a moment, it was clear the Silver Wolf did not know what to do. Cormac's wife held out the chicken, which had feathers of gold and white, and was truly a very pretty hen. The chicken looked at the Silver Wolf and he looked at it. It seemed the villagers all held their breath.

Had he ever touched a chicken? Alys wagered not.

She moved to his side and accepted the chicken, thanking Cormac's wife profusely. "You must take it," she said softly to the Silver Wolf. "Lest she be insulted. 'Tis a generous gift."

"A tribute chicken," he said and she bit back her laugh.

"It is like holding a loaf of fresh bread," she told him. "Do not crush it."

Only Alys would have heard his softly muttered curse. He reached for the chicken, his doubts most clear to her, and she placed it within his grip. He considered the chicken—which continued to consider him —then bowed low to Cormac's wife and thanked her profusely. No translation was required for she blushed with pleasure.

Then he tucked the hen beneath his arm, much as he would a helmet, and swung into his saddle again. The chicken clucked and settled against his thigh, apparently content with the view. The destrier stamped and his nostrils flared, but the Silver Wolf said a single word to the creature and it settled. The sight of this mercenary of fearsome repute cradling a chicken made Alys struggle to bite back her laughter.

It was Royce who helped Alys back into the saddle and this time, she held her own reins as they rode back to the camp with their chicken.

"She will need a name," Alys said, teasing the Silver Wolf just a little.

He cast her a skeptical glance. "A chicken?"

"Not just any chicken," she chided. "A tribute chicken held by the Laird of Kilderrick."

"It had best be a good name," Royce said, fighting against his smile and losing the battle. "Noble."

"Valiant," Alys said and the mercenary guffawed.

The Silver Wolf frowned. "Odette," he said finally. "She is Odette."

The chicken clucked and ruffled her feathers, as if she approved, and Royce laughed so hard that Alys thought he might tumble from his saddle. Alys could not keep from smiling herself and discovered when she dared to look at the Silver Wolf that he was grinning, as well.

ELIZABETH SET ASIDE the pewter plate in the darkness of their shelter. This refuge offered even less than the hut that had been destroyed. It was no more than a roof supported over a small area, a lean-to with its back to the wind and the leeward side open to the forest. Without a fire, in darkness, with boughs overhead and beneath them, Elizabeth did not find it offered much at all. She was still not at ease with the sounds of the forest and the sense of many eyes upon them. She still did not like having so many creatures underfoot and overhead.

Floors of stone or wood were what she knew, walls of stone and roofs of timber. Hearths and braziers and plump mattresses filled with feathers.

What would she surrender on this night for a hot meal or a fire? Yet again, Ceara had decreed that they could not risk a blaze with the Silver Wolf's camp so close. At least they had the bread and cheese Ceara had stolen from Jeannie's larder, but a fine plate did not make a fine meal.

She only half-listened to her companions, as she wondered whether she had surrendered too much in leaving her father's home. 'Twas true that she had neither planned nor anticipated her abduction by reivers after fleeing the marriage her father had arranged, she had not expected to have her maidenhead claimed by a stranger. She sighed, knowing that its loss had diminished her value to both her father and her would-be suitor. Returning to Beaupoint might solve naught at all.

She had made an error for which there was no repair.

'Twas true enough that blessings were not appreciated until they were stolen away. She had not thought herself one to need comfort and luxury, but the truth of living in the forest disheartened her. What were her prospects? More of the same or an even worse marriage than her father had first proposed. Once her future had been filled with prom-ise, but now, she saw only suffering and discomfort ahead.

She would think fondly of that roast partridge for a long time. She smiled a little in recollection of the falcon on her fist, a sensation that brought back the many pleasures of her father's home.

She had been a fool and then some.

"Are you not going to eat that?" Ceara demanded, indicating the rest of Elizabeth's cheese and bread.

She shook her head in silence, not wanting to criticize the fare, such as it was, that Ceara had provided.

The other woman seized the plate and began to eat hungrily. "I think I should ride to Carlisle on the morrow," she said, glancing at Nyssa. "Since your ploy did not work."

"I thought the boy would be terrified," Nyssa said.

"He was, but that was not sufficient to persuade the Silver Wolf to break camp," Ceara said. "An entire day of watching and waiting. I cannot believe you are not so famished as I am," she said to Elizabeth as the bread disappeared.

"They came to him," Nyssa said, shaking her head. "The villagers came to the Silver Wolf with their complaint."

"But he appeased them," Elizabeth said, admiring that he was more of a leader than she might have expected from a mercenary.

"And Alys went with him," Nyssa continued with a sigh. "Perhaps she comes to accept him."

"Perhaps she had no choice," Ceara said darkly.

"She has the knife," Nyssa reminded her and they fell silent.

"They gave him a *chicken*," Elizabeth said and the three of them smiled.

"I should like to have witnessed that moment," Ceara said, her hand hovering over the last piece of bread on the plate she and Nyssa had shared. Dorcha cawed in protest when Nyssa nodded and Ceara claimed it, then Ceara tore a chunk off and tossed it to him.

When the bread and cheese were gone, they looked at each other, Elizabeth drawing her cloak a little closer. "What now?" she finally asked.

"Carlisle," Ceara said, always decisive. "The coin will be welcome. I will see what fare I can buy while there."

"But you will have to walk back," Elizabeth protested.

"'Tis not so far as that. I have done it before." Ceara nodded. "And I can carry more than you might expect."

Nyssa frowned. "I feel no portent," she began, then the ponies nickered in fear.

The three women rose to their feet as the silhouettes of men emerged from the forest shadows. Elizabeth did not see their number: she did not wait to count. She spun and fled into the darkness. She heard Nyssa flee in the opposite direction as Dorcha cried in protest.

Ceara must have leaped onto one of the ponies, for Elizabeth heard the pounding of their hooves.

More importantly, she heard someone pursuing her. *"Attendez!"* he cried, but Elizabeth would never wait for a man to seize her again. She ran with all the speed she could muster, her heart racing in terror, well aware that he closed the distance between them.

He had dogs, for they barked as they ran after her. She was hunted, like a deer, and she feared the chase would only end with her demise.

Elizabeth ran with all her might, holding her skirts high. She ran blindly, uncertain of her direction, intent only upon escaping the hunter. She came so suddenly upon a stream that fed down to the river that she almost slipped on the muddy bank.

She glanced back. She was alone and he was close behind her. She could see the dogs, the gleam of their eyes and their teeth. She had no choice but to try to cross. She stepped onto the first stone in the stream, moving with haste. It seemed an eternity passed before she reached the other bank, the dogs barking more loudly all the while. The hunter shouted again and Elizabeth glanced back even as she began to run.

She stepped in the mud and slipped, falling hard to the ground, her ankle twisting beneath her. Nay! She could not be caught. She tried to rise to her feet and run on, but the weight upon her ankle sent pain stabbing through her. Nay! Her tears rose as she snatched at the growth on the bank, desperate to pull herself out of view. The dogs splashed into the river, barking wildly, even as the man calling to them to halt.

Elizabeth saw his silhouette as he strode into the river after them and had a glimpse of his set features. It was the one who had retrieved the falcon, and thus the one who had brought the partridge. He must have come to collect his due!

His resolve made her heart flutter in panic, then the dogs surrounded her and obscured her view. One, a massive dark beast with long hair, shoved its large nose close to her and Elizabeth recoiled. The dog barked, wagged its long plume of a tail, then nuzzled her cheek.

The beast would eat her alive!

As the knight's shadow loomed over her, Elizabeth was so overcome that she fainted.

CHAPTER 15

*T*was Amaury's fault.

He had frightened the maiden beyond all expectation. This was no reward for her protection of Persephone. He knew she had injured her ankle, for he had seen her fall. She had fainted at the sight of him, a sure sign that he was responsible for her terror. He crouched beside her, doffing his glove to check that she yet breathed. To his relief, he felt the erratic flutter of her pulse at her throat.

Her skin was so soft that his mouth went dry.

He lifted the hem of her skirt, though she would certainly have been dismayed by that. Her ankle was swelling already and soon she would be unable to walk. How then would she survive in the forest, without proper shelter or her comrades' aid?

He must make the matter right.

His dogs surrounded her, wagging their tails in their excitement, fascinated by this creature who had led them on such a wild chase. Bête nuzzled her hand, seeking a scratch, and the others sniffed intently at her kirtle, evidently smelling food. There was no food any longer, just a pale and delicate beauty slumbering on the bank of the stream.

Amaury was entranced by her. The hem of her kirtle was soiled as was that of her cloak. There was a smear of dirt on her cheek and her hands were stained with blood, but none of that marred her perfection.

He had only glimpsed her previously, when he had recovered Persephone, but now he studied her, for she would not know of his boldness.

A beauty, lost in the forest.

A maiden in need of the defense he could give.

Amaury lifted her with care and she did not stir. Her head fell against his shoulder and he carried her back to the shack that was now abandoned. There was no sign of the other two women, but Oliver was there, his expression revealing that they had evaded him. The squire had the two pewter plates, though, which proved that the women had been responsible for events in the village the night before. Amaury set the maiden down carefully, then shed his fur-lined cloak and wrapped her within it before lifting her in his arms again.

Oliver watched in silence then matched his step to Amaury's as he carried his precious burden back to the camp. Amaury had pledged to defend those weaker than himself when he had been given his spurs, and he would do as much for this maiden.

No matter what scheme his brother, the Silver Wolf, might have for her future, Amaury would defend her with his life.

When they forded the river and approached the camp, the light of the moon played over her features, the delightful bow of her lips, the thick sweep of her lashes, the curve of her cheek and the sweep of her brows. A woman such as this should be garbed in the richest finery, living in a fine keep, not surviving in the forest on the periphery of the world.

Amaury could see that her cloak was wrought of cut velvet and that it had once been a rich emerald green. The hue had faded on the shoulders, but not under the hood. It had once been richly embroidered with gold thread along its hem and front edges, though the thread was worn now and missing in places. Her shoes were of fine leather, the soles nigh worn through, but he thought they had once been dyed red.

She was a noblewoman, but one undefended.

Only misfortune, or tragedy, could have brought her to this place. Amaury's resolve grew as he carried her back to the camp. She might have come to the forest because she had no protector, but that had changed this very night—for Amaury de Vries feared he had lost his heart in truth.

He only wished he had not also lost any chance of an inheritance. He could not give this maiden the future she deserved, but he could ensure she had one.

That quest would have to suffice.

～

MAXIMILIAN COULD NOT RECALL when he had been so pleased. He was filled with newfound optimism, both for Kilderrick and his marriage. He and Alys had joined forces on this day, laboring together for the good of the holding, and that was a triumph indeed. On the morrow, he would request her aid with the review of the accounting.

He was not a man to whistle or sing, but Maximilian thought he might begin to do both. He had never expected much from marriage, even the certainty that he would ever wed. If asked, he would have said that sons were the sole gain from wedlock, perhaps a lady's legacy secured, but this notion of partnership was as beguiling as Alys herself. He had never shared a command before, but then, in war, his own skills had been sufficient for success. In peace and in Kilderrick, he had need of Alys and she had need of him.

'Twas a perfect balance.

Then there was the satisfaction of Kilderrick moving steadily closer to his vision of what it could be. The tents had been moved during the afternoon and now the camp was set up between the ruined keep and the old village. It felt like a town to Maximilian. He had a smith and would soon have a stable. Tynan had worked with Nicholas and Louis to re-thatch the roof on one of the smaller huts during the day, instructing the boys with gestures as to how it should be done. On the morrow, the company would thatch another hut for Denis and Marie, then a third for Tynan and his smithy. Tynan had asked to borrow a wagon in the morning to fetch his tools from Rowan Fell. There was a larger structure that they would roof for the destriers and Henri planned to live there with his son. Yves would live within the keep itself, once it was complete, so would remain in his tent for the time being.

All had contributed to the effort of the thatching at the end, as it promised rain on the morrow, and their progress had gained speed as they became familiar with the task. Denis and Marie had been delighted with the chicken and Maximilian would have wagered that Odette was already the most indulged bird in all of Scotland. Yves had brought him a list of provisions they would need shortly and Oliver was both returned and hale.

Alys' former comrades still tried to encourage the departure of the Silver Wolf's company, but he was relieved that they did not do anyone great injury. That inclined him to think they might ultimately be trusted.

As was becoming familiar, he felt a rising anticipation for his night with Alys. She had retired to their tent for her bath and with one last survey of their day's labor, Maximilian turned to join her there.

'Twas then that Amaury strode into the camp with the unconscious maiden in his arms. Oliver followed quickly behind him with two pewter plates that Maximilian recognized well.

The culprit had been found.

ALYS STOOD in the tent alone, considering the dagger. The light cast by both lantern and brazier touched it with gold, making it look precious as well as lethal. The scabbard had chafed the skin on her calf during the day, but she had no other place to hide it. Maximilian would notice the abrasion, she was certain, for he was thorough in his lovemaking. Nathalie would likely notice it, as well, and Alys had no explanation for its cause beyond the truth. She stood barefoot before the table in the tent, and studied the blade.

Did she truly need it?

Should she hide it from him?

Mere days before, the answer would have been obvious. But her desire to see her husband dead diminished with every passing moment, with every pledge fulfilled, with every sign that the Silver Wolf kept his duty and acted with honor. What of his confession that he had not killed Rupert or intended to kill her father? A shadow stirred in Alys' memories, and she felt there was a detail about that night that she had forgotten—or chosen to forget. Would it exonerate him more if she could recall it?

Were her husband's tales a ploy to win her support? Alys could not believe it. The one deception that she could lay at his feet was the implication that he did not understand Gaelic. She did not know that he had claimed as much outright, and truly, it would make sense to feign a lack of understanding in his position. It was oft a better strategic choice to be under-estimated.

By the same logic, she should keep the dagger.

Alys frowned. It felt wrong to even have the weapon in her possession. Where had Ceara gotten it? She was torn between choices when she heard a sound at the tent flap. She assumed it was Nathalie with her bath and glanced over her shoulder, only to see the Silver Wolf ducking into the tent. She bent quickly to drop the knife into her boot and spun to face him.

It did not seem that he noticed and she was aware that she had never seen him preoccupied before. He was frowning, as if puzzled.

"What has happened?" Alys asked.

His gaze flicked to her with its usual intensity. "Amaury located the refuge of your companions."

Alys took a step toward him. "What of them? What has Amaury done?"

"He has recovered Jeannie's plates." He set the two plates on the table with deliberation, then raised his gaze to Alys.

So, Ceara and Nyssa had been responsible for the incident in the sheriff's cottage. Alys nodded, for she knew Ceara despised Jeannie, and not without cause.

"You are not surprised," he said, watching her closely.

"I wondered. Ceara and Jeannie have an old feud."

"Ceara? The redhead who led Rafael to the fen?"

"Aye, she is from the Isles. Her family traded in horses."

"But she is not the one Amaury captured."

Alys was alarmed. "He captured one? Who?"

"I do not know their names or their origins," the Silver Wolf said, his tone stern. "I know naught of these women save that they are allied with you, for you have declined to tell me of them."

Alys flushed at the accusation in his tone. She recognized that this was a test of her loyalty to him and that much hung on her reply. "You must recognize that they have been my sole allies these years. I cannot betray them."

"I do not ask you to betray them." His gaze was steady. "I ask you to choose your first loyalty: spouse or comrades."

Again, it had been an easier choice just the day before. Now, Alys wondered whether she was a fool to trust him—and how much she had to lose by irking him yet again.

She could tell him something of them without surrendering all she knew.

That made the choice for her. "Nyssa was first to join me," Alys admitted. "She is from the north and has a reputation as a sorceress. That, along with the repute of Kilderrick, gave us the notion of encouraging the belief that we practiced the dark arts."

"And how would I recognize her?"

"Her hair is blond. She is tall and lithe."

He nodded, and Alys knew he would not forget a word she shared.

"Ceara came next, the one who challenged Rafael."

"The redhead, from the Isles, whose family traded in horses."

Alys nodded. "And Elizabeth came to us most recently, just last spring. She is the daughter of some nobleman, though she will not speak of it."

"How did you know this, then?"

"Her clothing was fine and she finds it difficult to live as we do. I believe she misses the comforts of her father's hall."

His glance was quick and bright. "Then why did she leave it?"

Alys shrugged. "I do not know. She has never said." She was aware that the Silver Wolf waited for more of the tale. As ever, it was easy to confide in him. "I would wager it was a man, perhaps one who took too much. She is a gentle soul and easily frightened even now."

"Ah." He dropped his gaze and Alys wagered he knew a good deal of men who took too much. "And how precisely did she come to be with you?"

"She had been captured by reivers. We freed her in a raid upon their party."

"She has auburn hair and a green velvet cloak?"

"Aye."

"Then 'tis Elizabeth who has joined us."

Alys touched his arm when he would have turned away. "I must see her! She is easily distressed."

"Not this night." He spoke with authority. "Eudaline has given her poppy powder." He raised a hand when Alys might have objected to this. "She has injured her ankle and Eudaline said sleep would aid her best. You may rely upon Eudaline to see to her care, and Amaury to provide her defense."

"But Amaury..."

"Is much enamored of the troubadors' tales and takes his knightly vows most seriously. He will be her guardian angel, but he will take naught from her. It is his nature."

Alys was slightly relieved, though she doubted Elizabeth would be. "What of Ceara and Nyssa?"

"It appears they eluded Amaury. It is possible he did not even attempt pursuit." The Silver Wolf turned to confront her again, his eyes vehemently blue. "Where would they go?"

Alys was torn between loyalties and she saw that he knew as much. Still he waited for her reply. "Do they still have the ponies?"

"I believe so."

"Then Ceara might take them to Carlisle to sell them there."

"And Nyssa?"

"She might accompany her, but likely not. Nyssa does not like towns and she can live easily in the forest, even without shelter." Still he waited. "If I was to guess, I would conclude they found Amaury's arrival a surprise and decided 'twas time to be elusive. I suspect Ceara has gone to Carlisle and that Nyssa has agreed to meet her on her return at some place at some phase of the moon."

"The Ninestang Ring?" he asked.

"Perhaps." She could not tell him that Nyssa would be there on the night of the first new moon after Samhain, as that woman went there after each of the high quarter days. She could not confess so much as that without feeling that she betrayed Nyssa. "You have naught to fear from Nyssa."

"So long as she believes you to be well," he said, then turned away. He sighed. "You must recognize that by your own counsel I should bring them to justice for their thievery."

"But you have recovered the plates!"

"Not with any aid from Ceara or Nyssa." He slanted her a look so cool that her heart stopped. "If you were truly my wife and ally, you would aid in this endeavor."

"How?"

"By leading them to capture, of course."

"I cannot do that!"

His expression turned grim. "And I will not tolerate their lawlessness within my borders. This cannot continue, and you must see the truth of it."

Alys felt her agitation rise. "Let me speak to Elizabeth on the morrow..."

"Nay!" The Silver Wolf's voice was sharp. "You will not see her. You will not speak to her, lest you contrive a plot against me." He jabbed a finger at the table, the force of his tap making the plates jump. "I will not endure this, Alys. You must choose."

Alys did not know what to say. How could she reassure him without betraying her comrades? How could she be certain that they would not be injured while in his captivity? His expression was so harsh that he might have been a stranger—or the man who had first arrived at Kilderrick. How could she have forgotten his reputation?

A heartbeat later, she heard a sound at the flap and knew the Silver Wolf had discerned it before her. He held open the tent flap for Nathalie who flushed and smiled, her gaze darting between them.

"My lady will have her bath?" she asked.

"Indeed, she will," the Silver Wolf agreed, then inclined his head to Alys and left. She watched him go, fearing all had changed between them. She felt the loss of a camaraderie she had not expected, and a dawning trust in her lord husband.

Nay, more than that. Could she love this man in all his moods?

Would she have the chance to find out?

~

Alys had a knife.

A hidden knife.

Maximilian could not believe these were good tidings. He had thought that they had established a rapport, but his wife clearly did not trust him, if ever she would. Was that why she had avoided the temptation of his own dagger left in the open?

Maximilian could scarce believe her capable of such a deception, not now, not after she had chided him and challenged him and welcomed him abed, but he had glimpsed the blade himself.

Had he not seen it, he might have died this very night.

The realization of his error infuriated him. He, who was so slow to trust, who was reputed to be a good judge of character and a strategist beyond all, had nearly been undone by his wife of three days. He was a fool, to be sure, a beguiled fool—for he still yearned to meet her abed, to see her eyes flash, to tempt her laughter and win her trust.

It did not help that she defended her companions over him. He bade her choose her loyalty but he knew she had already done as much. 'Twas true that it took time to build a marriage, but she had to see that the efforts of her companions could cost him all. If he did not see them punished in his court for the theft of the plates, he knew Jeannie would make trouble aplenty.

Yet he had thought they built a union, fool that he was. Oh, Alys had fought him on his arrival—he spared a glance at the crescent-shaped bruise on his arm, which was becoming more green of hue—and she had challenged him, but he had been encouraged. He thought they became partners.

She certainly had begun to win his trust, and that was the crux of it.

Maximilian liked Alys. He admired her. He had thought he understood her.

And he had erred. There was no disguising that truth.

What a fool he was!

Where had she gotten the blade? The barest glimpse of the hilt reminded him of the dagger he had given to Oliver years before. He did not know every weapon in the camp, but he recognized those he had given as gifts, for they had been chosen for their recipients. He sought out Oliver while his wife bathed and confirmed that the women in the forest had claimed his dagger, much to that squire's embarrassment and dismay.

Perhaps Alys wished to have a means to defend herself, not necessarily against him.

It was possible.

If so, though, she might have shown him the blade, confessed to having it in her possession—or offered its return.

Maximilian recognized that he wished that to be the answer to the riddle, but it did not explain why she hid the weapon from him.

He fetched himself some ale and sat by the great fire, his thoughts churning as he turned the cup in his hands. He dared not sleep in Alys' presence this night, not while she had the blade, not while he was uncertain of her intentions. He would continue with his plan to create a son and meet her abed this night—indeed, he could not resist that temptation—but afterward, he would begin the task of reviewing the court documents while she slept.

And he would not retire until Rafael returned with tidings of Murdoch. If Alys slept in the meantime, he would awaken her for their union. It might be simpler that way, with less opportunity to talk.

If far less satisfying. Maximilian stretched out his legs, crossing them at the ankles, wrapped his cloak more closely about himself and sipped his ale.

While he awaited Rafael, he could not help but ponder the conundrum of his lady wife.

"My lady!" Nathalie declared in a delighted whisper when the bath was filled and steam rising in the tent. The maid's eyes were alight and her cheeks were flushed, her manner confidential now that they two were alone. "Did you not see him?"

"Who?"

"The new smith." Nathalie took a delighted breath and spun around as she moved to check the temperature of the bath water. "Such a man!" She seized Alys' sleeve. "Tell me his name."

Alys smiled, forgetting her own concerns before the maid's enthusiasm. "Tynan Smith."

"And what can you tell me of him, my lady?"

"He is the younger son of Finlay Smith. His brother claims the smithy in Rowan Fell so he has no employ." Alys wished she knew more of him, for Nathalie listened avidly. "I think he is honest, for he revealed his sister's lie."

"Aye, a good man, to be sure." Nathalie nodded. "Has he a betrothed?"

"I do not know."

Nathalie frowned at that. "He labored so hard this day that Eudaline and I are to share a cottage this very night." She untied the laces on Alys' kirtle. "A strong man of vigor. Young enough for me, but old enough to have a trade. A smith provides well for his family, does he not?"

"Do you mean to ask me to arrange your match, Nathalie?" Alys could not help but tease her.

The maid shook her head solemnly. "Not as yet, my lady. First you must teach me to speak with him, then I will know the truth of his heart."

Alys turned to consider her maid. "The truth of his heart?"

Nathalie nodded vigorously. "I must know his merit and his nature. I must know whether he shares my desire for children, and I would know what he thinks of both marriage and the place of women." Nathalie smiled at Alys. "There is much to ascertain before I put my hand in his forever. After all, he is a stranger, no matter how fine he looks. He is not a man widely known to be of honor, like the Silver Wolf. Nay, my lady, I must be sure of him." She made quick work of the kirtle and the chemise, then gestured to the bath. "I will not be so fortunate as you, my lady, but I will have a good man for my own." She smiled. "And you will aid me in that. Aye?"

Alys nodded. "Aye, Nathalie, I will do my best."

As she sank into the warm water of the bath, she wondered at Nathalie's confidence in the Silver Wolf's honor—and her own conviction that the maid spoke aright. How much her view had changed these past days!

And why had his manner been so abrupt this night? What had she done to earn his ire? Perhaps he had expected her to tell him more of her comrades than she had.

Perhaps Elizabeth had said something.

"You share that hut with Eudaline, you said?" Alys asked and Nathalie nodded.

"It is small and simple, but dry, my lady. I did not wish to complain, but I did not like the tent so very well. And with so many of us..." Nathalie shuddered in disapproval.

"And Elizabeth, my companion from the forest captured by Amaury, does she stay with you as well?"

"Aye, for her ankle is injured. Eudaline tends to her." Nathalie clasped her hands together. "She fell and injured her ankle, so says Lord Amaury, then she fainted. He carried her, in his cloak, all the way back to the camp, and Oliver said he did not falter. Even now, he sits outside the cottage, guarding her with vigilance." The maid smiled. "She is *jolie*."

"Aye, she is."

The maid dropped her voice to a whisper, her eyes shining. "Do you think Lord Amaury will become her champion? 'Twill be like an old tale."

THE MOON WAS RIDING high in the sky when Rafael returned. Maximilian heard Phantôm's hoof beats and Henri's murmured comments to both horse and rider. He smiled to himself, knowing which would receive the more fulsome greeting. He was not the only one who had remained awake, waiting.

Rafael himself finally strode into the glow of the fire. He looked tired and Maximilian wondered how far he had ridden. The other mercenary accepted a bowl of stew from Denis, who had roused himself at the sound of the horse, then made his way to sit with Maximilian. Maximilian was cradling that cup of ale—which was not as good as that made by Beth Carter—still watching the fire.

"Was that ride my punishment for sharing a tale with your wife last night?" Rafael asked between mouthfuls. "Or was it the two silver pennies for Isobeal Smith?"

To Maximilian's relief, Rafael did not seem inclined to hold a grudge. His interval with Isobeal seemed to have restored his usual mood. Maximilian lifted his cup in salute. "If I had charged you a gold solidi, all would have guessed that the fine was not about the girl," he noted.

Rafael laughed. "But the price is sufficiently high that I will not return to her." He gave Maximilian an assessing glance. "You have given her expectations."

"Can you blame me? I cannot have you father a dozen children in Rowan Fell if you are to be sheriff."

Rafael's sidelong glance was quick with interest. "Am I?"

"I pledged it to you and so shall it be."

"But yesterday...?"

"I heeded the warning of my wife. It is not like the Compagnie Rouge. We do not arrive, inflict our will, and then depart from this place. We must remain here, and so we must build trust. We must consider the shadows of our deeds, for we will have to live with them." Maximilian changed the subject, aware that he sounded like Alys and that his brother studied him. "What did you tell Alys last evening?"

"Only that you desire Château de Vries above all else." Rafael gave him a piercing look. "You are the one so consumed with honesty. The woman deserves to know your intentions."

"I have told her my intentions."

"Not of Château de Vries, it is clear, for she was surprised."

"Perhaps I have changed my thinking."

Rafael scoffed. "All I have heard in all the years we fought together was that de Vries was the sole place of merit in Christendom."

There had been a time when Maximilian would have agreed with that.

These past days, he had thought just the opposite.

But Alys had hidden a knife.

"If you have changed your thinking," Rafael continued. "It can only be because that goal is beyond your reach. You were never one to strive for the unattainable."

"Perhaps I am enchanted by this place," Maximilian said, gesturing with his cup. "There is a splendor about this land. And its wildness gives me pleasure."

Rafael eyed him. "You must be enchanted then. I think it bleak and cold, devoid of pleasure."

"I like the wind and the wolves," Maximilian admitted.

"And even one of the witches, I wager," his companion muttered, returning his attention to his stew.

Maximilian neither agreed nor disagreed, but sipped his ale. "Amaury captured one of the women in the forest this night."

"The one with hair of flaming red?" Rafael asked with obvious interest.

"The one in the velvet cloak."

Rafael was dismissive. "The other is more beauteous. I will have my due of her, you can be sure, for she has invited it." He shook his head. "Leaving my dagger so I would be blamed for trapping that pig, and damaging the blade. And this after stealing Phantôm and leaving me to pull myself out of the mire." He finished his stew grimly. "There will be a reckoning, to be sure."

"I wager it will be a merry one," Maximilian murmured and Rafael laughed.

"Aye, it might be." He flicked a look at his companion. "Where is the captive one?"

"She sleeps, with the help of poppy powder. I do not think she will flee, though."

"Has Amaury claimed her heart already?"

"Nay, I believe he frightened her. From what Alys tells me, she might find some comforts reassuring." Maximilian again changed the subject. He had already noticed that Amaury was intrigued by this Elizabeth. He did not need two men besotted with her and distracted from their duties. "What of Murdoch?"

Rafael put the empty bowl aside. "I think he suspected my presence. He never looked back, but he kept too steady a pace and headed in too clear a direction. Steadily north. I followed as far as I could go and yet make it back this night."

"You think he will retrace his steps?"

THE WOLF & THE WITCH

"He might. I do not trust him."

"Nor I."

"Did you discover whether your wife knows him?"

Maximilian shook his head, recalling his sense that Alys and Murdoch were too oblivious of each other. He held his own counsel on that matter, though. He put down his cup as the chicken approached him. The hen jumped up and settled herself on his lap, much to the amusement of Rafael.

"A new friend?"

"A gift."

Rafael laughed heartily. He reached out to pat Odette and she pecked at his hand for his trouble, then nestled a little deeper into Maximilian's lap. "I think I know how to discredit the sheriff," he said as he stroked the feathers on her back. "But 'twill take some days. I ask for your patience."

"And my silence in the company of your wife."

"We understand each other well, as ever," Maximilian said. "I would have you ride to Carlisle in the meantime. Alys believes Ceara, the woman who challenged you, will take the ponies there to sell. Also, we have need of flour and there might be tidings of this Elizabeth."

"If she is wealthy and missing, aye." Rafael nodded agreement. "Yves has given you a list, I presume."

"Indeed." Maximilian hesitated but a moment before following his impulse. He might not have another chance soon to acquire gifts for Alys. "Find yourself a woman or three. 'Twill improve your mood."

Rafael laughed at that but did not dispute it. "And I would have you choose some cloth for my wife. Sufficient for two kirtles and two chemises, as well as blue wool for Nathalie and enough for a chemise. Her gift to Alys must be repaid."

Rafael looked surprised. "You trust me to shop for your wife?"

"I trust you to know what hues favor any woman." Maximilian replied, his tone wry. "I have seen you shop for gifts and fripperies before."

Rafael laughed at the truth of that. "You would have me leave in the morn?"

Maximilian nodded. "If you will."

"I will take Mallory with me," Rafael said and Maximilian surrendered both Yves' list and a measure of coin. "Wish me luck in finding that damsel, Ceara," the other man said when he stood up. "For she owes a reckoning to me."

Ceara was not the only one with a debt outstanding, to be sure. Maximilian surrendered the slumbering Odette to Marie's care, then strode to his tent, bracing himself for an argument with Alys about the plates.

And if truth be told, looking forward to their reconciliation, just a little bit. The woman was a fire in his soul, and one he did not wish to see extinguished. Would desire betray him in the end?

Maximilian could only hope not.

ALYS KNEW she had to prove her loyalty to her husband this very night. When Nathalie left, she shed her chemise and went to bed naked, nestling beneath the softness of the wolf pelts there. She remained awake with an effort, the hot bath having left her languid, and finally heard the Silver Wolf's footfall at the flap. She remained abed, as if she dozed, but in truth, she watched him through her lashes.

As ever, her heart tripped at the sight of her husband. He filled the tent with the power of his presence, casting aside his cloak. He had unfastened his belt before Reynaud even arrived. The squire set an oil lantern on the table, the light gilding the Silver Wolf's features as if he were an ancient divinity or an angel come to make his earthly claim. Alys' heart tightened that he should be so handsome. Reynaud was cautioned to silence with one heavy finger, and was quick to remove his lord's tabard and hauberk. In mere moments, the Silver Wolf stood in only his chemise and the squire was dispatched.

His gaze was locked upon her, the simmer of desire sufficient to awaken the most oblivious soul—and Alys was not oblivious. She sat up, letting the furs fall to her waist, and saw him catch his breath at the sight of her nudity. She began to unplait her hair, knowing that he liked it loose, and watched his eyes darken. He pulled his chemise over his head and cast it aside with an impatient gesture, then closed the distance between them with measured steps. He stood, studying her, his eyes shining like sapphires, until she had spread her hair over her own shoulders. She shook her head, and he watched hungrily, then she rose to her knees. Still he did not move.

Alys understood. He desired an invitation not a conquest. He wished for her to choose her loyalty, in this matter as all others. The choice, for Alys, was readily made. This time, she would seduce him. This time, he would surrender to her embrace. This time, he would know that his touch was welcome.

She reached for him, feeling bold beyond measure, then framed his face in her hands. He was taut, fairly simmering with restraint against his own desire. She saw his fists clench as yet he waited. Alys touched her lips to the corner of his mouth, her own desire simmering. She felt his breath and the heat rising from his skin. She kissed the other corner of his mouth, then risked a glance at his eyes. His gaze burned, as if he would see the very secrets of her soul. Alys held his gaze as she slid her mouth across his.

"Welcome, husband," she whispered, then slanted her mouth over his. She echoed the move that she found both triumphant and beguiling, claiming him with a kiss, and it was no more than a heartbeat before his arms locked around her. He drew her close, holding her fast against his chest, and slanted his mouth over hers in powerful demand.

They tumbled to the bed entangled together, this warrior snared by his desire for her, and Alys felt a new sense of power. She could hold him in thrall to her touch, just as she was held captive to his, and the realization fed her audacity. She touched him with new confidence. She dared to demand and she dared to touch. She mimicked how he had touched her in the past, and noted what gave him the most pleasure, building her arsenal of sensation with every caress.

Alys would not have believed that their mating could be yet more potent than it had been before. She would not have believed that the tumult could have been built higher or that she could find her pleasure more than once in rapid succession. She would not have thought that two souls could convey so much to each other by touch alone, for they loved in silence that night. There were only kisses and caresses, only the resolve of the Silver Wolf, the tenderness of his embrace, her own resolve to show him that she had chosen him as her first loyalty. On that night, she surrendered her all to the Silver Wolf and he seemed to know as much. He ensured she felt no regret: they sought pleasure together with new abandon and intensity. When they each found their final release, Alys was certain their shouts were heard all the way to Paris.

And she did not care, for she slept, cosseted in the embrace of the Silver Wolf, that burgeoning trust fed by the sorcery they conjured abed.

Fate, it seemed, had brought her much more than she might have dreamed to possess.

CHAPTER 16

*I*t *was* Oliver's dagger.

Maximilian retrieved it from Alys' boot when she fell asleep after their lovemaking. He had hoped to be wrong. He had hoped the mark on her leg had some other explanation. When his fingers closed around the cold hilt in the shadowed depth of the boot, his heart stopped with conviction of what he would see. He pulled it out and stared at it, willing it to be something other than what it was.

So, somehow, she had gained the blade from Nyssa and Ceara. Somehow she was in contact with them, and somehow they contrived together to see to his end. 'Twas a bitter realization and one Maximilian struggled to accept.

He did not know how long he stood there, but the rain had started to pound on the roof of the tent, and was gaining in intensity. He straightened, surveyed his wife, and wondered why she had been so very ardent on this night. She had never met him with such passion before, never been so bold or so passionate, and Maximilian was suspicious of the change.

Could it be a ploy to distract him?

The dagger only made his doubts multiply.

Maximilian donned his chemise and his own boots, for it was cold, stirred up the brazier and set to work. He was aware of an anger simmering deep within himself, though he would have liked to have denied it, or even extinguished it. He was a man who could endure much in pursuit of a goal. His patience with Alys thinned and as he worked, he found himself increasingly vexed by her decision to hide the knife.

She did not trust him, that much was clear. As much as he desired to trust her, Maximilian would no longer do as much. He feared that he yearned for something she would deny him forever, and recognized that he had a weakness for her beyond all expectation.

He would not become vulnerable out of desperation for his wife's true affection.

Instead, he would wait. He would keep his word and do his duty by Alys, but he would offer no more and no less than his pledge. He would wait, as a commander who has laid siege to a fortress. He would let his reliability mine tunnels beneath her defenses. He would let her become hungry for all she knew he could give.

Maximilian would wait and the fortress that was Alys Armstrong would surrender.

He could only hope it would be soon.

It is the evening of Samhain, the night Alys mistrusts most of all. Her father is calling her from the laird's chamber and she does not want to obey his summons. The wind is wild and she feels a portent of trouble, though she is too young to give it a name.

She pretends she does not hear him and plays in the courtyard, but that cannot endure. Sure enough, Rupert comes for her, his expression grim. "He will not be denied, lass," he says. "Not this night."

Alys knows that is true, though she wishes otherwise. "I do not want to," she protests.

Rupert sighs and spares an upward glance at the tower. There is already smoke swirling around it, slipping through the cracks of the shutters to mingle with the mist rising from the river. The stars are gone this night, disguised along with the moon behind heavy clouds, and Alys fears that darkness will claim all. Perhaps dawn will never come.

Rupert takes her hand and leads her to the tower. Though she is reluctant, she knows the command is not his fault. She knows he cannot help her or he would have done as much already. She drags her feet on the stairs, dread chilling her, then is nigh struck to stone at the sight of her father awaiting her. He is framed in the portal to the laird's chamber. Flames dance behind on the brazier, for he has built the blaze there beyond all good sense. His eyes are wild as they have oft been in recent years, and his smile at the sight of her is terrifying.

"You come!" he cries and seizes her hands, dragging her from Rupert's grip. The seneschal might have protested, but her father silences the older man with a gesture. "You will not intervene, Rupert. It is not your place." Her father makes a sign that Alys recognizes as a hex, and Rupert retreats, his eyes wide.

Her father slams the door so that the entire tower seems to shake with the impact. The chamber is filled with smoke and Alys cannot stifle her dread of what will happen. The hair prickles on the back of her neck, as if someone other than her father lurks in the room. Above the brazier hangs a symbol made of twigs, a pentacle, that spins in the heat rising from the blaze.

There is blood on her father's hand, again, blood from the same symbol carved in his left palm. He carves it anew each Samhain, a sign of his bond to some foul force that Alys does not wish to know. The father she remembers, the one she loved, is gone, banished by this desperate fiend who draws her toward the brazier with relentless power.

"Swear to him," he whispers, holding her by the left wrist and lifting his dagger. "Swear to be his minion for all time. That will be my legacy in truth, to pledge the treasure of Kilderrick to his service."

"Nay!" Alys screams as the knife descends. She kicks her father, struggling in desperation to escape, then bites his hand. He drops the knife, swears, strikes her, and she pivots to flee.

She is not fast enough. He snatches her up before she reaches the portal and carries her back to the crackling flame. He seizes her hand in a fierce grip and holds it toward the flame.

"Swear to him," he invites. "And you will be impervious to flame." She struggles against him, determined to remain silent. "'Twill be impossible to burn you or bind you, for you will be beyond such earthy concerns, just as I am." Her father pushes her hand into the flame and the fire licks her skin. She

fights him with greater vigor. "Swear to him, Alys. Save yourself while you can."

Then he plunges her hand into the flame, pushing her fingers so deeply into the blaze that she touches the coals. She sees that his skin does not burn even as she feels her own alight. The pain is beyond anything she has ever endured, though she knows that to cry out will only satisfy him. He holds her hand there and when her kirtle catches fire, she realizes he will stand and burn her to death, without remorse.

Her skin is crackling. The burn is climbing past her wrist, over her elbow, to her shoulder. She feels the heat on her shoulder, her neck, her cheek. Her kirtle is aflame and her hair and when the flame licks her eye, she cannot be silent any longer.

She screams and once she begins, she cannot stop. The door is kicked open and Rupert swears with a vigor. Her father falls, attacked by his own castellan; the brazier is toppled and her father hastens to keep the flames from spreading. Rupert rolls Alys against himself, extinguishing the flames but not the pain.

"Run," he advises and Alys does not need to be told twice. She flees from the laird's chamber as her father roars in protest, stumbling down the stairs and hiding herself away. She hears horses but she does not care. The cold darkness of her hiding place in the cellar is the sole solution, and she huddles there, shivering and weeping, until finally exhaustion claims her.

ALYS AWAKENED WITH A START, uncertain for a long moment where she was. Her heart was racing and her palms were damp. She was alone abed in the Silver Wolf's tent and it was not dark. Rain fell with force on the roof of the tent. She looked at her palm, halfway expecting to see a scar there, the shape of a pentacle carved into her very flesh.

There was none and she exhaled shakily in relief.

How was it that her father's hand did not burn? Had her eyes been deceived?

A lantern burned on the table and the Silver Wolf sat there in his chemise, frowning over some document. There were two trunks on the table and Alys thought they were the ones he had brought from Rowan Fell. One was open and had evidently contained the documents spread around him and even more. The shadows and the chill told her that it was night, but he did not sleep.

Why not? What pressing need kept him awake?

Alys sat up, realizing then that she was in her chemise and that her hair had been braided again. Her heart warmed at this sign of his concern for her welfare, at her conviction that she was safe in his company.

Then she recalled the details of her dream and was startled anew. The Silver Wolf was not responsible for her scars. It was a startling fact, a truth that she had buried in defense of her better memories of her father. Alys was stunned that she could have so deceived herself.

As she marveled, the Silver Wolf did not look up from his task, apparently unaware that she had awakened.

She wanted desperately to feel his heat against her back, to be wrapped in his embrace, perhaps even to tell him of her dream. His preoccupation, though, made her shy.

"What labor keeps you from bed this night, sir?" she asked, hearing the tremor in her own voice.

He flicked a glance at her, his eyes that vivid blue she associated with strong feeling on his part. "I tally fifteen years of fines and fees," he said. "To calculate precisely the due owed to the laird's treasury by the sheriff of Rowan Fell."

"Could it not wait until the morrow?"

"The sooner 'tis done, the better, my lady." He spoke crisply, but more, he did not call her by name.

"I could aid you."

"Not this night. Sleep and we shall talk of it on the morrow." He made a notation, then unfurled another document, his manner dismissive.

He did not trust her.

Alys did not know what had changed or why, but she instinctively understood. She lay back, thoughts spinning, and resolved that she would win his trust in truth. She would invest her all in this match—and Alys could only hope that she did not make the choice to do as much too late.

~

Maximilian rubbed his eyes tiredly when Reynaud appeared the next morning. The squire bowed low and offered two steaming bowls. They were filled with hot porridge but Reynaud also balanced a third bowl, containing a brown egg and a piece of bread. He looked up to meet the squire's gaze.

"A gift from Odette, Denis says," the boy admitted with a grin. "Marie insists you should have the first one, and that you liked them cooked thus as a boy.

How long had it been since Maximilian had eaten a boiled egg?

The chicken, as if checking on Reynaud's errand, clucked at the entrance. Maximilian nodded and Reynaud put down his burden, then opened the tent flap. Odette hopped inside. The chicken circled the tent interior, exploring, then jumped onto the trunk beside Maximilian. Once again, she settled in his lap as if to sleep, and he found Reynaud fighting his smile.

"She cannot know what you will eat, sir," the boy said.

Maximilian chuckled. "Nay, she cannot." The egg was still warm, the shell brown. He cracked the shell, rolling it across the table, then peeled it and put the cooked egg into the bowl. As anticipated, the yolk ran golden yellow when he sliced into it and he ran the bread through it with satisfaction.

It tasted of sunshine in the courtyard at Château de Vries, stones hot under his bare feet and the scent of fresh bread carrying from the kitchen. It reminded him of days spent in the orchard and the fen, chess games in the great hall with Yves, a solitary childhood that he had not truly appreciated until it was gone.

"Give my thanks to them, if you please," he said to Reynaud, then noticed that Alys stirred. "I will dress shortly. Please send Nathalie to aid my lady wife."

"Aye, my lord." Reynaud bowed and disappeared.

Alys rose and performed her morning ablutions while Maximilian steadfastly kept his gaze upon his work. Moments later, he realized she was watching him, and glanced up to find her expression uncharacteristically uncertain. Maximilian wondered what she had dreamed the night before. She had seemed shaken by it, but then, all nightmares left their victims uneasy.

He continued to check his sums, eating with one hand and making his tally with the other. "Good morning, my lady. I trust you slept well." He kept his tone neutral, as if that might induce her to confess about the knife.

"Did you sleep at all?" she asked, coming to the other side of the table. Her chemise was sufficiently sheer to reveal tempting shadows, so Maximilian did not look. Her boots were there. Would she surrender the knife when she drew them on?

"I had no need," he said simply, tense with the waiting.

There was silence between them, one broken only by the sound of the rain. Alys bent to draw on her boots and disappointment flooded through Maximilian. "The chicken has found herself a comfortable spot," she said, when he expected a different comment.

"She appears to like it, my lady. I do not complain for she is warm."

He felt Alys studying him but her confession did not come. The knife had to be against the abraded skin on her leg but she gave no sign of it. Maximilian felt something harden within him and knew it was his will to wait for some softening on her part.

"Do you not call me by name any longer, my lord?" she asked softly and Maximilian looked up.

"You have never called me by name," he noted crisply. "I see no reason for an imbalance."

Something flickered in her eyes, then she straightened and averted her gaze.

He gestured to the documents before himself. "Can you do sums?"

"Why?"

"These are the records of the court in Rowan Fell."

"My father held court here, at Kilderrick."

"And since his demise, it has been there, in Rowan Fell, and the sheriff has presided."

Alys frowned. "What of it?"

He tapped the document with a heavy finger. "Each fine carries a share for the one dispensing justice—in this case, the sheriff—and for the laird. In many cases, there is a share for the king, as well."

Alys tilted her head. "An alemaker was found guilty of selling short of the measure in the market and fined two shillings."

"You *can* read," Maximilian said with satisfaction.

"Aye. Rupert taught me."

"Was that his responsibility, to be your tutor?"

"Nay, but his eyesight failed him. He needed assistance and I gave it." She picked up a document and surveyed it. "Why do you review all this?"

"Consider—who has claimed the laird's share these fifteen years?"

"There was no laird."

He reached into his purse and put the seal of Kilderrick upon the board, noting how her gaze clung to it. That was her sole desire, to be sure. "Aye, there was, though he was not present. My father held the seal, which made him laird, and now I hold the seal, so I am laird in his stead. And you were here, the heiress of Kilderrick. Do not disappoint me by confessing that the sheriff surrendered your share to you twice yearly as is his responsibility."

"Of course not," Alys said with a laugh.

Maximilian did not laugh. "Then where is our due? The sheriff says he has saved it, but he lies. He does not have the coin in trust or he would have surrendered it when his life was threatened."

Alys eyed the trunk. "You demanded the court records to tally the sum."

"One must know how much is owed before that sum can be collected."

Alys nodded. "And if it cannot be collected, then the sheriff has been remiss in his duties."

"Precisely."

"Show me," she said with resolve, dropping into the chair opposite just as Nathalie appeared. "I can do whatever is necessary to rebuild Kilderrick, my lord," she said with a conviction he did not doubt. She met Maximilian's gaze and his heart thundered at the determination in her own. "I will be your wife in every way, sir."

Maximilian was impressed, but he did not make any reassurance. He simply unfurled the first scroll and showed her how to begin.

~

THE SILVER WOLF had taken her advice, and sought a cause to dismiss the sheriff of Rowan Fell. Alys was glad of his choice and would lend her aid willingly.

After Nathalie aided her to dress, she broke her fast and joined the Silver Wolf in deciphering and tallying of the old records. He left the table to dress with Reynaud's assistance, then they bent over the documents together, comparing and discussing what they found. Steadily, the sum on his tally grew as the rain poured down.

They worked together so amiably that it might always have been thus.

Yet all the same, some matter sat between them—and it was not a chicken. Alys sensed the restraint in him, the reserve, and since he did not show it with Reynaud, she knew she was at fault. The sizzle of awareness she had come to expect in his presence was dimmed, as if a shadow hung between them.

Did he know about the knife?

Would she be a fool to surrender it to him? She did not know and could not decide.

It had to be near noon when Alys heard men singing. The Silver Wolf glanced up from the accounts with a smile, one revealing that he did not share her confusion. He invited her to join him, then led her from the tent to the slope that led down to the river, the one that overlooked the road. The rain was relentless and she huddled beneath her husband's shorter cloak. The boys were out with the horses, Tynan was trimming the hooves of a palfrey under the supervision of Henri and his son, and the sounds of the approaching party were louder. The destriers turned toward to the road, their ears flicking and their curiosity clear.

Alys frowned. "They can be no reivers," she said.

The Silver Wolf shook his head. "They are not."

Still, Alys did not understand. The party slowly came into view on the road below, a long sequence of wagons pulled by both horses and ponies, with a veritable army of men marching alongside. The men were sturdy and sang as they walked. The wagons were heavily burdened and moved slowly, more than one becoming stuck in the mire.

"What ho! Kilderrick!" The man in the lead cried, pointing at the ruins. The others shouted in jubilation, a cheer passing through their ranks. The carts surged forward, the horses invigorated by the prospect of a rest.

It was when it became evident that the first cart was loaded with blocks of stone that Alys gasped. She raised her hands to her mouth, her eyes wide as she stared at the Silver Wolf.

"Masons, my lady," he said to her. "As promised."

She gave a cry of such delight, then she flung herself at the Silver Wolf. He froze for a moment in surprise, then caught her and swung her off the ground. "You truly will rebuild it."

"Nay, *they* will."

Alys was nigh overwhelmed with joy. She stared down at him, snared by the heat of his gaze, and realized that she had lost her heart, to that most unlikely of suitors, the mercenary who had compelled her to take his hand.

But he had not caused her burn. She suspected he had not killed her father or Rupert apurpose, or even that he had burned Kilderrick by design. And now he set all to rights again, and that, plus his willingness to listen and to learn, had captured her heart in truth.

She might have told him as much, but he put her down at a summons, then strode to meet the masons. Alys blinked back tears of wonder as he walked the site with the lead mason, marking out the perimeter of that great tower with his footsteps, and she knew 'twould be just as he had described it to her.

He had done it.

The Silver Wolf had kept his word.

MAXIMILIAN HAD BEEN SHAKEN BY ALYS' delight. He had come within a hair of kissing her senseless, wanting to partake of a little of her joy.

Then he had recalled the dagger, a sure sign of deception.

She was too willing this day, too helpful, too different from the virago he had come to know for him to trust the change. It was as if she sensed the change in him and knew its reason well. It was as if she would dissuade him from abandoning any trust of her.

Maximilian would not be so readily swayed.

He went to the masons and spent much of the day ensuring that their camp was struck as they desired and that their understanding of his plan was complete. He insisted that Alys take refuge from the rain and she had returned to his tent, where he found her working diligently each time he looked.

Odette followed him faithfully, to the amusement of all in the camp.

And so he and Alys settled to a routine, of tallying the accounts together by day, reviewing the work of the masons at midday and again in the evening, then meeting abed for a joyous interval. He did not confide in her. She did not ask to visit Elizabeth anymore. Maximilian slept in the tent Rafael shared with Amaury, leaving one of the other mercenaries standing guard over his wife. He knew that Alys spoke with Eudaline, and he suspected they spoke of herbal remedies as well as the salve for her skin.

If it had not been for the hidden dagger and her companions lurking in the forest, Maximilian would have been content. But still the days passed and still she did not confess to its possession, and the matter grew in his thoughts.

He feared they were at an impasse, for he would not bend first.

ON THE DAY that Rafael returned with his purchases, Maximilian met him with a hearty handshake. The pair embraced and sat by the fire to share a cup of ale together. Rafael was filled with his old gusto and laughed merrily when the other mercenaries greeted him with jests. There was a glint in his eye that told Maximilian he had found at least one pretty wench to sat him, and that, too, restored Rafael's good humor.

He placed the coins in Maximilian's hand from the sale of the horses. "Not so much as I would have hoped," he said.

"Have you lost your skill at bartering?" Maximilian teased.

His brother laughed. "She was there before me, the one from the forest with her ponies."

"Ceara," Maximilian supplied.

"She told them of my reputation for cheating and thievery." Rafael shook his head. "I was hard-pressed to sell the beasts at all, and had to take a lower price for them. She is cunning, to be sure."

"Did you see her?"

Rafael shook his head. "I was too well occupied to seek out such a challenge." The men shared a smile. "And you? Have you been further tamed by your bride?" There was something hard in his brother's voice and Maximilian looked up at him.

"I have a case against the sheriff with her assistance and will bring it to my court on the day after the new moon. You should be sheriff of Rowan Fell by the Yule."

Rafael shook his head. "I no longer desire the post."

"Why?"

"Because it is too small, Maximilian. It is not my ambition to rule over a village. Indeed, Eamon might be well suited for such a minor endeavor." He eyed Maximilian. "And this Kilderrick is insufficient for you. You must know that you will tire of it and yearn for more again."

"I intend to remain at Kilderrick. The walls rise again." He gestured to the keep. "I have a wife and will have a son..."

Rafael shook his head. "You will have no son."

"You cannot know this..."

"She was raised by a woman of the woods, Maximilian," Rafael said with a pitying glance. "She will never conceive your child, for she will ensure that she does not. Women have their ways and she will know them." He leaned closer. "She softens you in a way I do not like and she does as much for her own end. She will ruin you, Maximilian, then claim her family's holding once again."

The accusation found root in Maximilian's doubts and he had to avert his gaze.

"What has she done to you? I have never known you to return twice to any woman's bed, but you cannot resist this one. Why? She is no beauty. You said she was a maiden. How has she so ensnared you?"

"I admire her will."

Rafael laughed and finished his ale. "Even though you are not her desire? There is peril in that marital bed, to be sure."

"I no longer sleep with her."

"At least your sense is returning." Rafael held out his cup for more ale.

"What will you do?"

"I will leave, but not until the spring. I had thought to ride out immediately, but I see the uncertainty within you. I will wait, Maximilian, with the expectation that we will abandon this wretched place together by spring."

Surely Rafael could not be right—but Maximilian could not dismiss his brother's suspicions readily, to his own chagrin.

Rafael toasted Maximilian with his ale then drained the cup again and set it on the board. "Will I take the cloth to Nathalie or will you?"

"I will do so, for you are filled with devilry this night."

Rafael laughed, his gaze sliding to the forest. "Perhaps I should ride to hunt with Amaury each day, though my prey will not be captured for the good of the company."

"You could see the pair of them arrested," Maximilian said. "To face charges for the theft of the plates."

Rafael grinned. "Now, there is a task of real promise."

Maximilian did not comment further upon that, but took the cloth Rafael had purchased. He surrendered the gift to Nathalie, noting that Elizabeth's curiosity was stirred. The pair were soon planning the maid's new kirtle, for it seemed that Elizabeth had skill with a needle.

Maximilian considered the bundle of cloth intended for his wife and chose to wrap it up again. No one ever lingered over deciding that their loyalty was to the Silver Wolf first. No one ever denied to pledge as much immediately.

Save his lady wife. Maximilian knew he should not have been surprised.

But he would wait. He would keep this gift for some moment in the future, some moment when his trust of Alys was complete.

If indeed that day ever came.

~

ALYS AWAITED the Silver Wolf in their tent that night, her pulse leaping in anticipation. She paced in her chemise, choosing her words, hoping she might restore the camaraderie between them with the right ones.

It was late when he finally swept into the tent and he still wore his hauberk and tabard. He shed his gloves, casting them on the table, but not his cloak. He carried something, but did not display it to her. Instead, he opened the larger trunk and placed the bundle within it, his movements almost furtive, then turned to her. His expression was impassive and Alys wondered at his mood.

"You should know that we will ride to Rowan Fell on the morrow," he said.

"I shall be ready, my lord."

He frowned and shook his head once. "You will remain here, my lady. Royce and I will ride at first light."

"But surely you go to demand a reckoning of Eamon," Alys said, fighting her disappointment. "Surely I should witness that event."

"Surely not," the Silver Wolf said briskly. "There may be a squabble. I do not expect Jeannie to allow Eamon to surrender his position that easily." He frowned. "I may be compelled to grant him some time to raise the coin owing. I will judge by his manner."

"But I would like..."

"What you would like, my lady, is of no import in this matter," he said, speaking so sternly that Alys felt she had been slapped. His gaze was steady and cool. "I have decided and thus it will be. Rafael, meanwhile, will seek Nyssa and Ceara in the forest, that they might face the charge of theft in the upcoming court."

"You cannot do as much!" Alys protested, but earned a cool glance for her comment.

"'Twas you who insisted that the laird must ensure justice be served, my lady."

What had she done to earn this cool disdain from him? Oh, there was the knife, to be sure, but the Silver Wolf spoke as if she had betrayed him. And truth be told, she missed the sound of her name upon his tongue.

"Of what crime am I guilty, sir?"

"Crime?" His brows rose in apparent surprise. "Have you been accused?"

"Nay, I have not, but you have changed."

His eyes narrowed slightly. "There are battles, my lady, which cannot be won. The wise man knows when to abandon the field." He watched her, eyes glinting, and Alys wondered anew. "You could provide some insight for Rafael's hunt," he suggested quietly and she knew it was her loyalty at root.

"I cannot betray my companions," she said and watched his lips tighten as he averted his gaze. She turned and gestured to the bed. "Will you come to bed, my lord?"

"Not this night," the Silver Wolf said, his tone decisive, and picked up his gloves. He bowed slightly, his gaze clinging to hers. "I wish you a good rest."

It was on her lips to confess to him that she might bleed, but his manner silenced her confession. She would wait until she knew for certain.

How could he expect her to make such a choice?

He lingered a moment and she hoped that he might speak, but nay. He pivoted, spinning on his heel so abruptly that Alys halfway thought he fled her side.

In a heartbeat, the Silver Wolf was gone, obviously with no intention of returning, and a chill seized her gut at the tension that still hung in the air.

Something was awry, something more than she knew.

On impulse, she crossed the tent and opened his trunk. It was not locked, which was curious in itself. Did he intend that she should look within it? Alys could not say. The weapons seized from the reivers were gone, doubtless dispersed to his men.

The mysterious bundle lay atop his spare tabard and chemise. Alys listened, but there was only the sound of Victor's steady footfalls as he paced the perimeter, and the distant sound of the masons making merry.

Heart leaping, she took the parcel and quickly opened it upon the table. It was heavy and flat, a square bundle of considerable heft. It was wrapped but untied, as if it had been opened already, which meant her curiosity would not be easily revealed.

Inside were five lengths of cloth. Alys touched them with awe. There were two lengths of fine linen, one white and one cream, so soft and smooth that they would make chemises of the highest quality.

Fit for a queen.

Alys bit her lip. There were two lengths of glorious wool, finely woven but smooth to the touch. One was a deep red, perhaps dyed from beetroot, but so rich a hue that the sight made Alys catch her breath. The second was a glorious green, a shade that reminded her of the full glory of summer. And there was a dark wool of heavier weave yet, a large piece that she had to believe was sufficient for a cloak. What a cloak it would be.

The colors and the fine weave of the linen indicated that the cloth was for a lady of the highest rank, a woman held in such esteem that cost was no object in clothing her.

But the Silver Wolf had not given the cloth to Alys.

What tidings had Rafael brought to him from Carlisle? She did not doubt that mercenary would be quick to undermine her place. Why had he been gone so long? Had he made a match for the Silver Wolf?

Alys sat down hard. Or did her spouse desire another? She never saw his missives and could not know what word he might have received. What price would she pay for defending Ceara and Nyssa?

That he did not offer her the cloth seemed of import. He no longer used her name. He declined to sleep with her. This was a matter greater than the challenge of Ceara and Nyssa—who truly offered little threat to this company of men and had made only mischief thus far—and greater even than her hidden dagger.

He would spurn her for another. His changed manner was a warning she should heed. Had he lost his heart to another or was it merely a better alliance that this unknown woman offered to him? Alys could not guess, but she feared the truth. She knew her bleeding mustered, for she could feel the monthly changes in her body. 'Twould be simpler for the Silver Wolf to put her aside if she did not carry his child.

And then she would have naught. Not the seal of Kilderrick. Not the contents of the treasury. Not the husband she had come to desire beyond all else.

Alys repacked the cloth and returned it to his trunk, ensuring that it did not look as if she had touched it at all. She was heartsick, yet uncertain what she could do or say.

If she led him to Nyssa and Ceara, she might simply surrender her companions to him with no gain. If she confessed to having the knife, he would take it from her—and she would have no means of defending herself if necessary. If she bled and he did not lie with her again, she could not conceive his child.

Was it even possible to regain the Silver Wolf's regard if he had already decided to abandon her and Kilderrick?

CHAPTER 17

*N*yssa did not know what to do—whether she could help Alys, whether Alys even desired assistance, how to help Elizabeth, whether the moment had come that she should leave Kilderrick and move on. If ever Nyssa had needed guidance for the future, this night would have been it.

She decided to go to the Ninestang Ring, as she did on the first new moon after each high quarter day, and seek a vision. It was not the new moon but the full moon. Nyssa dared not wait when so much hung in the balance. There was risk, of course, with the Silver Wolf's company camped at Kilderrick, but Nyssa felt she had little choice.

She had to know.

Ceara, as convinced of her own path as ever, declined to accompany Nyssa. Since her return from Carlisle, she spent her time watching the Silver Wolf's camp, keeping vigil and noting any minute change. The arrival of the masons and the setting of the foundation for the new keep had not pleased Ceara any more than the glimpses she had of the mercenary named Rafael. She reported all to Nyssa each night, and Nyssa had begun to wonder whether it was loyalty to Alys that kept Ceara close or a fascination with Rafael.

The wind was still on the night of the full moon and the air was crisp with promise of snow. Indeed, there was ice on the surface of the river and many of the forest creatures had already burrowed into their winter dens. The moon itself was nigh as bright as the sun. Nyssa gave Kilderrick a wide berth, crossing the river far upstream of it to approach the stone circle. Dorcha flew above her, as faithful as a shadow but one overhead instead of stretched across the ground.

As ever, the sight of the stones sent a shiver of anticipation through her. As ever, her skin pricked with an awareness of more than what she could clearly see. As ever, the air was warm within the circle, and welcoming.

Nyssa bowed before the stone she favored, not the one that Alys called the leader, but a shorter one next to it. This one seemed to point a finger at the stars Nyssa recalled best from her apprenticeship, the stars that made her feel closer to the home she had left in Sutherland. Her witching stone was in her hand, her fingers locked over it. What would she see when she looked through it this night?

She had bowed her head and Dorcha had landed on the stone itself, when she heard unexpected voices.

Men's voice.

Did her ears deceive her?

Dorcha tilted his head and looked across the ring. He tilted his head as he eyed the pair he obviously saw as intruders.

To Nyssa's thinking, they were as well.

She slipped behind the stone, crouching low in the shadows to watch. There were two men, who dropped to sit beside the tallest stone. They looked to be passing a wineskin back and forth. Companions then, comrades or even brothers. They laughed together, as if the brew had loosened their tongues, their voices carrying in the darkness.

They spoke Gaelic and Nyssa did not have to strain her ears to listen.

"You cannot mean that they exchanged their vows in the grave pit?" demanded one, as if this was hilarious beyond belief.

"Aye! They fell in the hole and he insisted that they be wedded there," confirmed the second.

Nyssa felt her eyes narrow, for she knew they mocked Alys and the Silver Wolf.

The first man snorted. "He did not have to look upon her in that darkness. Perhaps that made it easier."

The second chuckled.

The first continued. "Have you seen her? She is disfigured beyond belief, scarred and ugly." He seized the wineskin and drank a long draught. "I could not spurn her quickly enough. Imagine meeting *that* abed each night!"

"Perhaps he beds her in darkness, as well," suggested the second man.

The first found this highly amusing. "Perhaps he hoods her, so he does not have to look upon her face." He laughed drunkenly at his own jest. "It will not be his burden to couple with her much longer, by your scheme."

"That depends upon what you have learned."

"The king" —the first man said this with a sneer—"is reputedly pleased to have the Silver Wolf in his lands. My father says the king intends to offer the Silver Wolf encouragement in raiding the border with greater enthusiasm."

"What manner of encouragement?"

"Hard coin, of course. What else could he offer a mercenary of such repute?"

"A wife?" The second man did not sound as if he tasted as much of whatever brew they consumed. Nay, his voice was low and steady, thrumming with purpose. Nyssa wished she could discern his features.

The first man snorted. "And given my mother's experience, it matters little if the man in question already has a wife. My father was compelled to put her aside to wed the king's daughter."

"And to disinherit you and your brothers."

"Indeed." The first man spat in his disgust. "But I am not so fool as to let the old man know the depth of my fury. I smile and nod and listen to his news of the court."

"The better to use it to your own advantage."

"Aye." Again the wineskin was lifted.

The second man cleared his throat again. "And what is the king's plan?"

"To invite the Silver Wolf to parlay. He will do it soon, by all accounts. He rides from my father's court in the Isles even now and will rest at Bewcastle. That would be the closest place to Kilderrick."

"And much quicker than inviting the Silver Wolf to Stirling."

"Aye. The king desires to retake Annandale with all haste." The first man nudged the second. "But you would scheme to take down the Silver Wolf! That is no mean feat."

"It cannot be done in the king's hall, or whatever hall that man uses as his own," the second man said. "The king travels with too many men."

"Aye. And I would wager it cannot be done at Kilderrick for the same reason."

"Which is why it must be done in between," the second man said calmly. "On the road, between Kilderrick and Bewcastle."

"For the Silver Wolf will be accompanied only by a small party. The plan has merit, to be sure."

When he did not continue, the second man spoke. "But you have no interest in my scheme?"

"I did not say that."

"You spurned Alys Armstrong before. Perhaps you do not want her even now."

Nyssa frowned, recalling a tale of Alys losing her betrothed because of her scar. What had been his name? He had been a son of the King of the Isles, she recalled that much.

Ceara would know.

"Not just Alys, the monster, but Kilderrick, the ruin," the first man confirmed. "It looks affluent now and soon will be rebuilt to new splendor. I could endure much for such a prize, even a hag abed."

"The treasury, I believe, is full."

"Aye, it had best be, if I am to take *her* as a wife. I hope there is ale in the cellars, too, to buttress my desire."

"I wager there is." The second man cleared his throat. "They have consummated the match. She may be with child, *his* child."

"All the easier," the first man declared. "So many women die in childbirth. Who will notice one more? Even I can feign devotion for less than a year."

"And the child?"

"If there is one, it will not survive."

"Swear it to me."

The first man gave his pledge of honor then demanded the same of the second, who complied. They then each took a draught from the wineskin, as if to celebrate that they would conspire against Alys and see her both widowed and dead.

Nyssa clenched her fists. She had her vision of the future and she did not like it a whit.

What could she do?

"You make a fine scheme, Murdoch, and I like it well," the first man said heartily, rising to his feet. He was unsteady and braced a hand against the great stone to look down at his companion. "I suppose you desire a post in my new holding?"

Murdoch. Nyssa took note of the name.

"Not I," vowed this Murdoch. "Your newfound riches will be safe from me, Godfroy."

Had that been the name of Alys' betrothed? Nyssa was not certain.

"Then why concoct this scheme?" Godfroy demanded. "What is its value to you?"

Murdoch stood, purpose in every line of his figure, and a grim resolve in his tone. "The Silver Wolf will die and I will be the one to strike the blow. That is sufficient reward for me." Even in the shadows, he was familiar to Nyssa and she knew she had seen him before. That great bushy beard...

She leaned her head back, puzzling over it, then remembered the Scotsman in the Silver Wolf's camp. Was this Murdoch the same man? She would consult with Ceara. And what had been the name of Alys' betrothed? Nyssa knew little of the matters of kings and barons, but maybe Ceara knew more.

Meanwhile, the men shook hands then left the circle, striding toward the west. Where did they camp? It did not look as if they headed for Rowan Fell, but the drunken one would not make it far. Dorcha cawed and took flight, startling the men so that Godfroy jumped and stumbled. They laughed together then continued arm-in-arm toward a pair of tethered ponies that she had not noticed earlier.

Nyssa watched them in silence, then furtively followed.

The more she knew of them, the better she and Ceara could scheme against them.

~

THE MISSIVE CAME AT MIDDAY, carried by a lone rider on a palfrey.

Maximilian and his company had been at Kilderrick a fortnight, though it seemed much longer. He had granted Eamon until the end of the year to raise the funds he owed to the laird, and the women in the forest remained at large despite Rafael's efforts. Jeannie, at least, was slightly mollified to have her plates returned. Still he did not join Alys abed. They truly were at an impasse, one he feared would not be ended readily. She had told him of her bleeding just days before and he had not been able to avoid the memory of Rafael's accusation. Yves was teaching his lady wife to play chess and said she had an aptitude for the game.

Maximilian could well imagine that.

All stood at the sound of the approaching horse, and that man shouted as he rode into the camp. "I seek Maximilian de Vries, the Silver Wolf!" he cried.

Maximilian rose to his feet and lifted a hand, prompting a complaint from Odette who was roused from his lap. "Here!" he called and the messenger jumped from the horse's back, hastening toward him. The messenger wore the king's livery and cast his cloak over one shoulder as he dropped to one knee and held out a missive. Maximilian felt Alys come to his side. He knew his temper was short, but blamed it upon having too many responsibilities.

In truth, he missed his nights abed with Alys, but his siege would continue until her battlements fell.

"A missive from the king, sir," the messenger said. "I am to await a reply."

"You ride all the way from Edinburgh?" Maximilian asked as he broke the seal.

"The king takes his leisure at Bewcastle, sir."

Maximilian glanced toward Alys. "But half a day to the east," she supplied, guessing his question. "Less upon a fast steed."

The messenger nodded agreement.

Maximilian was reading the missive. He was summoned to parlay with the king at Bewcastle with all haste and to rest there for a night or two. The king hoped to receive him shortly, along with his lady wife. The king also enclosed a missive that had been sent to him in trust for the Silver Wolf and requested to know more of it when they spoke.

"Tell him we come on the morrow," Maximilian said to the messenger.

"You are welcome to be refreshed at our table," Alys said with grace. She put her hand upon his arm as if they were happily wedded in truth. "My husband is likely to insist upon it," she said, her tone teasing.

Maximilian yearned for more than a single touch.

"I thank you for your hospitality, my lady," the younger man said. "I should be most obliged."

At Maximilian's nod, Alys escorted the messenger to the table, summoning Denis. They laughed lightly together as the messenger's choices were made and his cup was filled, but Maximilian knew he was a fool to be jealous of any man having his wife's attention.

Instead, he considered the message and frowned that the seal had been broken. He supposed the king had the right to read whatever had been sent to his care, but he did not like it.

To his surprise, the missive was from his cousin, Philip.

He meant to drive out his father, Gaston, and sought to hire the services of the Silver Wolf and his men.

Payment would be Château de Vries.

Maximilian caught his breath. He closed the missive and looked about himself, shocked that the goal he had long sought could so readily be his.

He was equally shocked by the vigor with which he did not want it.

He truly had been snared by the wind and the wolves, by one particular woman whose heart he wished he could conquer. Was he a fool to stay at Kilderrick and hope for more?

He found Rafael watching him and knew what his brother would advise. They could ride south, seek out the aid of the Compagnie Rouge, and seize de Vries. Rafael could be Captain-at-Arms, as promised and Maximilian could claim his due.

But he wanted it no longer. Nay, Maximilian would ride to the king to learn that man's will and then decide.

His gaze clung to the figure of Alys, his hunger for her touch at fever pitch. She seemed to feel his attention upon her for she turned and smiled at him, his gaze darkening that he could only stare.

"What is it?" she asked softly, coming to his side as if he had summoned her.

He handed her the missive, watching as she read it. He was surprised that she paled. "Will you go?" she asked, her gaze searching his as if his reply truly mattered to her.

Did she dread his departure, or did he see what he wished to see?

"I must learn what the king desires of me first."

"Of course." Alys looked down at the missive and swallowed. "I entreat you to come to me this night, my lord," she said quietly, then impaled him with a glance. "I yearn for you and the son we will create together."

And when she looked at him thus, Maximilian could not deny her. "I will," he vowed, then stood blinking in wonder as his lady smiled at him.

"Good!" she said with pleasure, then stretched to kiss his cheek. Even that caress sent heat surging through him. "Good."

Perhaps the first battlement fell.

BEWCASTLE WAS some distance to the east of Kilderrick and further south. 'Twould be no more than a half day's ride, but the days were short in December. The Silver Wolf's party left Kilderrick by midday.

They were seven in all. The Silver Wolf rode his great black destrier, while Alys rode a palfrey beside him. The squire Reynaud rode behind Alys with Nathalie, the mercenary Matteo behind them with Oliver. Rafael was at the rear of the party. Their intention was to remain but one night at Bewcastle, so their baggage was minimal—Reynaud and Nathalie were entrusted with the sum of it.

Amaury was left in charge of Kilderrick, with Royce and Victor to aid him.

Alys could not shake a sense of dread, one that she knew was fed by her hasty coupling with the Silver Wolf the night before. He had seemed distant and remote, though still he had ensured her pleasure. They had not talked and he had not lingered abed. When she had awakened after her satisfaction, he had been gone.

She had not seen him again until the morning. The mating had been fine, but less than she wanted of him. If he had stayed, she would have surrendered the knife. She would have asked him how to be of aid. She might even have agreed to find Nyssa and Ceara.

But she had not been given that option.

Alys feared he only found his satisfaction with her until he could be with his beloved. But who might that woman be? The question plagued her. It might be a woman he had known before arriving at Kilderrick, one he had never expected to see again, one whose hand he had never expected to win. She did not know. She feared that the king knew of this match that the Silver Wolf would make. Her fate might be decided this very day.

And Château de Vries was in the offering. Would he go? Rafael's words made her fear as much, for that man knew her husband better than any other.

Aye, all raced to a conclusion, one she could not influence or change. Alys did not like it a whit. Even on this journey, she could not consult with her husband. The company rode too closely together and she did not wish her doubts to be overheard.

The road wound through the forest and she was struck by the stillness within it. The trees had been devoid of leaves for months, but now the forest seemed all hues of grey, deadened and sleeping. The clouds overhead were grey, the skies so overcast that there were no shadows. Alys could not tell the location of the sun. The wind was cold, snapping at their cloaks and whistling around their necks. The horses folded their ears back and stepped briskly, hastening toward the shelter and warmth of Bewcastle.

The thorned briars on either side of the road encroached more closely ahead, narrowing the way, and the Silver Wolf led his destrier ahead of her own palfrey. There was a bend in the road ahead, and she knew that after it, the path would widen again and lead them out of the forest.

But no sooner had her husband drawn ahead of Alys, then someone called her husband's name. He spurred his steed onward, heeding the summons boldly.

"Nay!" Alys cried, but Rafael drew the company closer. At his command, they were drawn into a tight circle and Matteo seized her palfrey's reins to keep Alys from following.

"Nay, my lady," that mercenary said with resolve.

At Rafael's nod, they moved slowly around the bend in the path, the mercenaries surveying the forest on all sides as they progressed. Alys wanted only to hasten, for she guessed that no good fate awaited the Silver Wolf around that bend.

∼

CEARA WATCHED alongside Nyssa as the trap unfurled. It made her blood burn that there was naught she could do to stop what might become a tragedy, but neither could she turn away. Two women with a dagger between them were no match for this warlike party. She had to watch and hope that some opportunity to intervene presented itself.

They had followed the intruders through the forest, keeping their distance and hiding themselves from view. Ten men on ponies, each with a boiled leather jerkin, a great cloak, and a length of wool swept around his hips. Each bristling with daggers and blades, two with bows, and one who was utterly familiar.

Murdoch Campbell.

Just as Nyssa had told her, Murdoch had not only returned to the environs of Kilderrick but he had brought this company of warriors with him. They were dressed similarly to each other and though Ceara did not recognize any of them specifically, she knew their garb and manners—and Nyssa had confided the name of their leader, Godfroy. He was the youngest son of the Lord of the Isles, and Ceara knew his reputation. Though he had once been betrothed to Alys, Ceara had heard the tale of his rejection. For whatever reason, he had returned to wreak havoc. She saw the fury in their expressions, particularly in that of Godfroy.

He could have been a handsome brute, if his brow had not been darkened by a scowl. Indeed, he looked to have lived so long in a foul mood that his countenance might never lighten, much less ease into a smile. He was dark of hair, large and burly, his eyes flashing like the hue of the sea. She remembered tales of him, his charm and his many indulgences, his mother's inability to decline him any thing he desired. If what Nyssa had overheard was correct, he had been abruptly disinherited and Ceara doubted he was glad of that change. Nay, he was the manner of man who would blame others for his misfortune.

The road from Kilderrick was little more than a broad path, for it led only to Bewcastle and there had not been much traffic between the two keeps in years. Briars stretched over the road, so long in disuse, so that any party would have to ride in single file at the deepest point of the forest. 'Twas here that the road bent and the next increment was obscured. 'Twas here that the invading party hid themselves and waited.

"Hail, Silver Wolf," Murdoch Campbell cried, his tone mocking as he urged his pony onto the open road.

The Silver Wolf appeared at the bend in the road, eyes flashing as he urged his destrier onward at a temperate pace.

"Murdoch Campbell," he said, riding closer, and Ceara saw his hand rested on the hilt of his blade. "I knew I had not seen the last of you."

"But I will see the last of you," Murdoch declared, drawing his own blade. "I killed Jean le Beau. I found him by following you to his refuge, then slaughtered him in his sleep after your departure."

"How brave of you," the Silver Wolf said with some disdain. "Why?"

"He destroyed my mother," Murdoch confessed. "And on her deathbed, I vowed vengeance upon him."

The Silver Wolf smiled. "How strange to find common ground between us," he said softly. "For Jean le Beau destroyed my mother as well."

"You cannot change my intention..."

"How did he destroy her?" the Silver Wolf asked, his destrier taking steady steps closer to Murdoch's pony. He left too great a distance between himself and the rest of his party, to Ceara's thinking, but she understood that he meant to eliminate the Scotsman himself. Rafael, who she refused to admire, had gathered the others into a tight circle, himself in the lead and the other mercenary in the rear, both with blades drawn.

"I will not speak of it," Murdoch said hotly.

"Did he command others to hold her down while he raped her?" the Silver Wolf asked mildly. "Did he commit this feat before her own father's eyes, after ensuring that man could not intervene?" He nodded. "Aye, I understand the villainy of Jean le Beau very well. The tale of my mother's shame was shared with me often. Were you the product of that union? Could your mother bear to look upon you?"

"You cannot know..."

"I think I do. I think you are another of Jean le Beau's bastard sons. Am I right?"

"What difference does it make?"

"If you are, you might join us."

"You lie!"

"I never lie," the Silver Wolf replied calmly. He offered his hand. "Join with us, brother. We can be more than our father would have willed for us. We can surmount the injuries of the past and aspire to a better future."

"You are sworn to the others already."

"However many we may ultimately be." The Silver Wolf smiled. "I rather like the notion of allies united by the villainy of their father's deeds. Join me."

There was a moment when Ceara thought Murdoch's resolve wavered, but then he seized the reins of his pony. "The best future is one without you in it," he declared. "I vowed to kill you and I will see that done."

"Name the time and place," the Silver Wolf challenged, withdrawing his hand.

"Now. Here." Murdoch sneered. "If you dare."

Murdoch then turned his horse and raced down the road toward Bewcastle. The Silver Wolf's lips set and he glanced back, assuring himself that the party was safe behind him. Then he gave chase, his great destrier covering the distance so quickly that he rapidly gained on the pony. A rope was suddenly pulled taut in the wake of Murdoch's pony. It had been hidden beneath leaves and was snapped up by the intruders to form a barrier waist-high across the road.

The Silver Wolf dropped the destrier's reins.

Ceara kept silent with only the greatest of effort—and Nyssa's fingers digging into her arm. He had dropped the reins. He knew his steed and its abilities. Just as he trusted the horse, so Ceara would, but her heart was racing.

The black destrier leaped the rope with such grace and agility that Ceara nearly cheered aloud.

This man saw the truth of Jeannie and he understood horses. If Alys did not want the Silver Wolf, Ceara would certainly take him.

There were shouts as the party behind was set upon by the brigands. Ceara heard the whinnies of the horses and smelled their fear. She heard the clash of steel on steel, and saw that the battle was engaged. The intruders had waited until there was sufficient distance between the party and the Silver Wolf. Nyssa had loaded her bow, but there was too much of a scrimmage to aim with any accuracy and Ceara knew it. Alys screamed outrage as a man snatched for her and the Silver Wolf glanced back.

It was only for a moment, but it was enough.

An attacker lunged from the forest on one side and the destrier stumbled to avoid colliding with that pony. The Silver Wolf turned his horse, but an arrow came flying out of the forest and struck him in the shoulder. He would have ignored it, and ridden to Alys' aid, when the other rider leaped from his pony. He caught the Silver Wolf around the waist and his weight sent them both tumbling from the saddle with the force of impact. The two men struggled together, rolling back and forth across the narrow road, disappearing at intervals beneath the brambles. The battle was bitter and savage.

The destrier, Ceara saw, had halted ten paces away, reins dragging, and stood stamping, awaiting the Silver Wolf's command.

What a noble and loyal beast it was.

The second attacker reached for its reins, but the destrier stamped and retreated, nostrils flaring.

It smelled blood.

Aye, there was blood on the road when Ceara looked back at the fight and it belonged to the Silver Wolf. He straddled his attacker now and punched that man in the face, blood streaming from his own nose and his shoulder. The attacker fell slack and the Silver Wolf pushed to his feet, looking back toward his party. He snapped off the arrow in his shoulder, and cast away the shaft. Alys was battling against one of the attackers who apparently meant to seize her. She kicked and she struggled even as the Silver Wolf raced back toward her.

Then she froze as a dark-haired attacker lifted her high. "Alys Armstrong," Godfroy roared. "Do you not recognize your betrothed, now returned to make matters right?"

Alys gasped and stared down at him as he held her captive by the waist. "Godfroy Macdonald," she said with astonishment. "It *is* you."

The Silver Wolf halted, for evidently he knew that name as well.

Godfroy laughed and lowered Alys, clearly intending a triumphant kiss. The Silver Wolf was not the sole one who stared, for Nyssa and Ceara were transfixed as well.

The arrows were a shock to all of them. They were fired without warning from the other side of the forest. There were two shot in rapid succession, one that buried itself in the Silver Wolf's thigh and the other that caught him in the chest. The Silver Wolf stumbled and then he fell, landing face-down in the dirt of the road.

"Maximilian!" Alys screamed, the anguish in her voice telling Ceara all she needed to know of her friend's regard for this man. She fought Godfroy with renewed vigor, though she had no chance of escape. "Nay! Not Maximilian!"

But the Silver Wolf did not move.

And his destrier, apparently understanding what Ceara did not want to believe, whinnied, reared, then spun and bolted in the opposite direction. It galloped toward Bewcastle, reins flying, mane flowing, its empty saddle and agitation as distressing a sight as Ceara could imagine.

"She loves him," Nyssa whispered and Ceara could only agree. Alys would not have sounded thus otherwise. They exchanged a glance and nodded in unison, for that truth gave them purpose.

GODFROY HAD RETURNED!

Alys was stunned and confused. She knew better than to expect anything good from this man who had cast her aside ten years before. Why did he desire her now? He could not. He did not.

'Twas Kilderrick he wanted, for he had killed Maximilian, Kilderrick's laird, and evidently intended to claim her. He could have no other objective than the holding.

Alys knew he did not want her, though he feigned as much. She wanted to turn away from his triumphant kiss, but caught herself in time and braced herself to endure it. Instead, it was Godfroy who averted his face, his lips just barely touching her cheek. Alys recalled his revulsion all too readily. Did that mean her days were numbered? She did not dare defy him until she knew more.

Maximilian was dead. Alys did not want to believe it, though she had seen him fall. More troubling, he had not moved again. If there had been a spark of life within him, she knew he would have roused himself in her defense.

Even so, 'twas impossible to believe that he would not roar and leap to his feet in just a moment, as vital and hale as ever, as resolute as she knew him to be, eyes blazing blue and lips set in a grim line. Aye, he would tear Godfroy to shreds for touching her and Alys would applaud the result.

But she stared over Godfroy's shoulder and Maximilian did not stir. The blood flowed, mingling with the dirt on the road, and he did not move at all. Her heart chilled and she felt sickened by the loss of him.

She loved him truly.

The realization came too late to give any comfort, for she had not told him that he had claimed her heart. Indeed, he had died believing that she loved Godfroy, for she had lied to him about that. The realization that Maximilian had died, not only unaware that he had conquered her heart and soul, but believing that she was restored to her beloved with Godfroy's return.

'Twas unfair.

Maximilian deserved better.

But he was not to have more. Alys was lifted to her horse by Godfroy, her reins seized by him, and knew herself to be his possession as surely as the pony he rode. Even knowing it was folly to vex her captor, she could not keep herself from looking back.

She saw Murdoch halt his pony beside the fallen laird, saw him comment and spit on Maximilian, who still did not move. The man she loved would not have endured such a discourtesy. Then two men came out of the woods, both roughly dressed and burly. Murdoch gave them some command, then rode toward Godfroy's party with his other two comrades.

His was icy when he drew alongside her, his lips tight.

"You lied to me," Alys said, striving to keep her tone level. "You are not Rupert's son, not if the Silver Wolf is right."

"Not by blood," Murdoch ceded. "But Rupert was more my father than my true sire could have been. He loved my mother with all his heart and when she returned home, ripe with Jean le Beau's bastard, he wed her and raised me as his own. My mother never forgot the indignity of my conception. 'Twas a blessing she died when I was but a boy." He eyed Alys with that chilling blue gaze. "You will likely never forget the violation of the Silver Wolf either, for the son follows the father in every way."

Godfroy nodded agreement, his eyes dark. "He took what was mine," he said, granting Alys a scathing survey. "And you will pay for your faithlessness for the rest of your days and nights."

Alys dropped her gaze, her thoughts spinning. She was as good as dead if Godfroy meant to take his vengeance upon her. She guessed that he meant to wed her only to seize Kilderrick and its treasury, then she would die.

Which meant she had naught to lose.

If her last deed was to avenge Maximilian against this fiend, Alys would die content.

～

MAXIMILIAN LAY IN THE ROAD, stunned by the pain that filled his body. By rote, he assessed the damage to his person, his situation and his chances of recovery. It was a long-ingrained habit.

The first arrow in his shoulder had not embedded itself deeply. The one aimed at his chest had been cheated by his hauberk—the impact had stolen the wind from him and would leave a bruise, but would not be fatal. The arrow in his thigh would require care and might never heal properly. He had seen men die of similar injuries. If naught else, he would limp. His nose was bleeding and there was a bruise rising on his cheek from a blow, but that was minor, as well.

He had been injured before, but on this day, he had no will to fight to see the light of another day. He could not forget Murdoch and the fury within that Scotsman, a fury that had filled Maximilian himself in the past. Oh, how he had despised his father. He recalled feeling cheated that someone else had struck the final blow. But Kilderrick had changed all that—or more accurately, Alys had done as much. Maximilian had discovered that there was a better reason for survival than the prospect of vengeance.

Until, of course, Alys had shown him that his regard for her was not returned. He would have fought his way through Hell for her, indeed, he would have done as much this very day, but her beloved was returned to her. He knew she wanted Godfroy and no other. He knew she loved Godfroy, for she had told him as much. He had seen the change in her expression with his own eyes. And now that Godfroy had returned for her, Maximilian had no place in her life.

Without Alys, he had no desire to continue his own.

He should have ridden for Château de Vries right away.

He had heard Tempest race away and hoped someone cared for the steed. He did not doubt that Godfroy would claim Alys, Kilderrick and the treasury. Perhaps that had been Maximilian's purpose; perhaps restoring to her what he had taken from her all those years ago had been the reason for his journey to this land.

He was aware that a pony approached and halted beside him but could not stir himself to open his eyes, much less care.

"Alliance," Murdoch Campbell muttered and spat. "As if the son of Jean le Beau would ever keep his pledge to me."

Maximilian could have been amused in better circumstance, for he knew he had guessed aright about Murdoch's parentage. It was the best explanation for the other man's hatred, but in this moment, Maximilian could not be bothered to move.

"Bring his corpse," Murdoch commanded someone in Gaelic. "Godfroy will need proof that the Silver Wolf is dead to secure Kilderrick."

How curious that Alys was not even mentioned. Maximilian would have expected a man cheated of his beloved's hand in his own would have at least acknowledged her as part of his prize.

Not that it was any longer a concern of his.

Someone grunted a reply, perhaps two men. The pony cantered away and the sound of the larger party diminished to naught. Maximilian felt his awareness fading as the pain redoubled in his leg and he wagered that the men left behind were in no hurry to fulfill their orders. Perhaps they waited for him to die, for that was easier than dispatching him themselves.

Finally, someone rolled Maximilian to his back. Maximilian did not fight or protest. He smelled the other man's breath as he drew closer and guessed he meant to check Maximilian's pulse. In another time, Maximilian might have lunged upward and surprised him, but he had no taste for battle any longer.

To his surprise, the man grunted.

The other cursed.

Then the first man's weight fell atop Maximilian, and his warm blood flowed over Maximilian's skin.

Maximilian's eyes flew open. The man had taken an arrow in the throat and he was already dead, tongue lolling and eyes staring. Maximilian glanced up in time to see that there was a second man, but he was surveying the forest worriedly. He had no cause for concern. The two arrows struck him suddenly and cleanly, one in the eye and one in the throat, and he dropped dead on the spot. One arrow had been lit afire, which reminded Maximilian of that first assault upon his company.

Alys' companions, Ceara and Nyssa.

There was a sound of running footsteps, then the two women dropped to their knees beside him. Maximilian assumed they meant to

CLAIRE DELACROIX

rob him and thought they might as well have the value of his armor as anyone else. They bent over the attackers, however, and the redhead ensured that they were dispatched. That would be Ceara. The blond freed Maximilian from the weight of the first one, flinging his corpse aside. She had to be Nyssa.

Nyssa then checked Maximilian's wounds, her lips tightening as she considered the one in his thigh, then fixed a ferocious gaze upon him.

"You cannot die," she said with heat. "Not when Alys loves you so."

"She loves Godfroy," he managed to say but Nyssa shook her head. "He spurned her."

He looked to find her eyes glittering with welcome conviction.

"They were betrothed by their fathers," Maximilian managed to say. "To wed at midsummer in her sixteenth summer."

"Aye," she agreed. "And she awaited him, but when he came, he looked upon her and spurned her."

Maximilian frowned. "She said his father insisted upon breaking the match, because of her scars."

Nyssa shook her head with resolve. "The father was not there. 'Twas Godfroy alone who refused to wed Alys." She leaned closer as Maximilian considered the import of Alys' lie. "And I heard them scheming on the new moon in the Ninestang Ring," she confessed in a whisper. "Godfroy and Murdoch. Murdoch said he would kill you, then Godfroy would claim Alys, Kilderrick and your treasury."

Ceara dropped to a crouch on Maximilian's other side. "But Alys would not survive the match long," she added.

Maximilian felt his outrage stirring.

"Murdoch said she might be with child, your child," Nyssa supplied. "And Godfroy said that would be easiest, for women die in childbirth all the time. The babe, he told Murdoch, would not survive either."

Ceara shook his good arm. "You must aid her!"

"But she went willingly..."

"Because she thought you were dead," the two women said in unison.

"Did you not hear her shout your name?" Ceara asked. "Her heart was in her voice."

And she had called him by name for the first time.

320

Maximilian was filled with new purpose. He managed to sit up as he formulated a plan.

"We can attack," suggested Ceara with a brash confidence that reminded him of Rafael. "We have our bows and you are not completely disabled."

'Twas not sufficient against such a party.

"Nay, you must be considered weak to enter the camp at all. They must not fear you." Maximilian looked between the two solemn faces of Alys' comrades. "You could be old women, beggars, bringing the corpses in the hope of a coin or two." He reached into his purse and removed the seal, liking his idea well. "And you must say that it was my dying wish for this to be given to the Lady of Kilderrick. You must put it into her hand yourself, and say that I asked for her farewell kiss."

"Why?" asked Nyssa.

Maximilian smiled, though it hurt to do as much. "Because Alys has a knife in her boot," he said with satisfaction.

Ceara laughed. "The one I gave her," she said with triumph. "Good."

"Aye," Maximilian agreed. "Surprise will be our greatest ally."

CHAPTER 18

*G*odfroy had brought a small army with him, though they were neither organized nor disciplined. Alys had no doubt that they all desired some due from him in return. They were a rough and scruffy group, sufficiently numerous that the masons had declared themselves outside of the dispute. The masons had halted work early and retreated to their own camp. Those sworn to the Silver Wolf had been gathered together near Denis' fire. The men had urged the women to the middle of the group, for already Elizabeth was missing and Nathalie was clearly fearful. Tynan looked like a thunderstorm about to burst. Rafael stood, feet braced against the ground, arms folded across his chest, eyes simmering with fury.

Godfroy laughed when told that two of his men had seized the auburn-haired beauty, and that the Silver Wolf's brother, Amaury, had abandoned his command to pursue them.

"Someone will have a merry ride this night," he said then shouted at Denis for a meal.

No one moved, their expressions impassive.

Godfroy swore and shouted again, though once more there was no response. He turned upon Alys. "What is this you do?" he demanded, already furious at the insult.

"I do naught. They do not speak Gaelic."

"I am laird here, and they will fulfill my command or you will be the one to suffer," he said. "Tell them as much."

Mindful of Murdoch watching and listening—and despising him for so betraying his father's lessons of honor and duty—Alys did as much. The meal was prepared without delay, though she could not bring herself to eat a morsel of it. She was herded into one of the tents, the one that had been shared by the villeins from Château de Vries, with the other members of the Silver Wolf's household and found Rafael beside her.

"Tell them, my lady," he urged in an undertone. The shadows were long inside the tent, despite the hour, for they had not been granted a lantern. The eyes of the others gleamed in the darkness and Alys knew they all listened.

And that they deserved to know.

"They killed the Silver Wolf," she said simply and felt the shock ripple through the small company. "He was shoved from his horse, then shot by two arrows. He had been separated from the rest of us and had no opportunity to defend himself. They killed my beloved and left him dead in the road." She looked up at Rafael, letting him see her rage and her tears, and she saw his throat work.

"'Twas all planned in advance, for Murdoch betrayed us," he said.

"After being welcomed in our company for all those weeks?" Yves demanded in outrage.

"'Twas he who killed Jean le Beau, and killing Maximilian was his intention all along."

Whispers of indignation passed through the company at that.

Rafael, though, dropped to one knee before Alys. "I am sorry for your bereavement, my lady," he said, his voice husky.

"I thank you," Alys said, touched by his salute. "But you cannot be so sorry as I am."

"Because you loved him," Nathalie said.

"Aye, but that is not the sole sorrow on this day."

"Godfroy means to wed you and claim Kilderrick," Rafael guessed.

"And I will not live long afterward, I am certain."

Their gazes met for a brief moment and she saw that his lust for vengeance was as great as her own.

"Then we must make each opportunity count, my lady," Rafael said softly, the calculation in his tone reminding her keenly of Maximilian.

"He would expect no less," she agreed. "Is it true about Lord Amaury?"

Victor winced. "His departure gave them the chance they sought," he acknowledged. "If he had held his ground..." He raised a hand. "But what is done is done. I hope only that he finds Lady Elizabeth in time."

Aye, they could hope for that.

'TWAS HOURS later that the flap was swept open and Alys fairly jumped to her feet. They had been given neither food nor water, though Eudaline had tended the minor injuries among the company as best she could and Alys had helped.

Murdoch stood there, his countenance as stony as ever. "You are summoned," he said to Alys. Rafael would have accompanied her, but Murdoch held up a hand to halt him. "The lady alone," he stipulated and Rafael's lips tightened as he stepped back.

This was no good portent to Alys' thinking. She marched toward the fire, shivering a little at the chill in the air. Night had fallen and the sky was dark overhead, the clouds having cleared to reveal the stars. The wind was crisp and the fire, usually kept to a moderate size by Denis, had been built to a roaring blaze, its flames licking the sky. Godfroy's men had evidently found the ale and all the stores, for they were drunk and laughing. The masons' camp was curiously still.

But a crooked old woman stood a distance from the company. Some of the men had gathered closer to her to study her and whatever she had brought. It looked to Alys like a collection of pale bundles and it was only as she drew closer that she saw there were corpses piled upon a crude sledge. How had the old woman dragged such a weight any distance? The corpses were stripped nude and the woman sat on the ground, apparently exhausted from her efforts. Godfroy stood watching her, disgust marring his handsome features.

He turned at Alys' approach. "She insists she must speak to you and you alone." He rolled his eyes. "The Lady of Kilderrick herself. I dismissed her companion. I may pay one but I will not pay two."

"I am the Lady of Kilderrick," Alys said in Gaelic and when the woman did not acknowledge her words. "I am Alys Armstrong," she added and the woman tipped her head back to squint at her. Alys nigh jumped when she recognized Nyssa, her face smeared with soot, her fair hair mired and her clothing torn.

"Aye, you are," Nyssa said, her voice raspy and uneven as if she would disguise it. She rose to her feet, apparently struggling with the effort, then seized Alys' hand. Alys could not keep herself from jumping in alarm and Godfroy chuckled. "A wish made upon a deathbed must be honored," Nyssa intoned and her voice sent a shiver down Alys' spine. "A dead man's promise must be kept."

She dragged Alys toward the corpses, which were all smeared with blood.

"Their garb is mine in exchange for my vow," she said, then pointed. "That one," she said to Alys, indicating the bottom body in the pile. Even with his face hidden, Alys recognized her husband's body and nigh winced at the blood spilled upon it, the arrow buried in his thigh. The woman moved with sudden agility to haul the top two corpses aside and reveal Maximilian completely.

"He demanded that I do him a service," she said, then cackled. "He said his vow to his lady wife had to be kept." She lifted Alys' hand and placed the seal of Kilderrick within it.

Alys caught her breath. He had promised to surrender the seal to her if he left the holding, and Maximilian kept his vows.

Godfroy stepped closer. "What is it?"

"The seal to Kilderrick." Alys knew that Maximilian meant the treasury was hers, as well, just as he had pledged, and she could not halt her tears from falling. She looked upon his still features and wished, yet again, that he would open his eyes and tell her it was all a jest. She wished for just one heartbeat more in his company that she might at least confess the truth of her heart, but that was not to be.

She should have asked him about the cloth. She should have told him about the dagger. She should have been his ally in bringing Nyssa and Ceara to justice for their deeds, for they had chosen to make mischief.

She should have demanded the truth about his change of manner, even if he had confessed he loved another. There would be no more chances to hear his voice or watch his slow smile.

She had been such a fool.

Meanwhile Godfroy laughed and quaffed the rest of his ale. "How very thoughtful of the Silver Wolf." Even Murdoch chuckled with him.

But Nyssa shook Alys' arm. "And in return, my lady, he would have your kiss of farewell for his journey into darkness."

What was this? Alys could not imagine why Maximilian would request such a deed—and indeed, to touch his cold corpse would eliminate any fragile hope of his return. Perhaps that had been his intention. He was not one to avoid the truth, no matter how painful it might be. He might have wished to ensure that she accepted his demise.

Alys held fast to the seal and approached Maximilian's corpse with trepidation. She studied him, knowing this would be the last time she would see him, wanting to memorize every detail. She had to kneel down beside him and she could not keep herself from stroking his cheek, then sliding one fingertip across his mouth.

His skin was warm.

Alys froze. She had to be mistaken. It had been nigh half a day. But she moved so that her body blocked Godfroy's view, then she touched her husband's throat. When she felt a pulse, as vigorous as her own, relief surged through her, a relief she had to hide. In that moment, Alys understood Nyssa's scheme—for it was the Silver Wolf's plan in truth. All had changed that night when she thought he must have seen the knife in her possession. He *had* seen it. That she had hidden it from him had been seen as a betrayal or a threat.

But now it was an asset they could use together, a secret means to see him armed. With that realization, Alys knew what she had to do.

RAFAEL PACED.

He did not like the situation at all. In Maximilian's absence, he had to defend his brother's bride—but how could he do as much when Alys was separated from them? And how could he keep Godfroy from seizing both Kilderrick and Alys? They had not a knife between them, by strict design, and how he hated this sense of powerlessness. He missed Maximilian and his talent for finding a solution to any conundrum and wished he shared his brother's skill.

He pivoted at the sound of a woman's voice outside the tent. She laughed in a sultry voice, making an invitation of some kind in Gaelic. It was well received by the sentry, who made a joking reply, his voice rumbling with pleasure.

Rafael glanced at Matteo in confusion. There were no whores in Maximilian's camp or even Rowan Fell, for Rafael would have found them.

He drew near the tent flap, listening intently. The sentry chuckled. The woman taunted. Then there was a sudden grunt and the sound of something heavy falling to earth.

Those inside the tent tensed.

When the flap was swept open, Rafael was prepared to attack the intruder with his bare hands, but it was the seductress with hair the hue of flame. She was dressed in rags, her face smeared with soot, but he would have known her anywhere. She held a finger to her lips, and her eyes flashed a warning. Rafael looked past her to the dead sentry and his eyes widened. The man's throat had been slit with considerable skill.

"You must be quick," she whispered in careful French, offering Rafael a sack. Its contents clinked in a most familiar and reassuring way. "Surprise is our sole chance."

Then she was gone, disappearing between the tents into the night. Rafael looked inside the sack and grinned at the collection of weapons within.

Aye, they would avenge the Silver Wolf and soon.

～

THERE WAS NAUGHT SO fine as a woman keen of wit.

Maximilian knew the moment Alys realized the truth. He heard her breath catch slightly, which could have been shock from touching his corpse, but the caress of her fingers over his skin told him that she knew he yet lived. She was kneeling beside him and she lifted her skirts so that his left arm was hidden from view beneath them. He reached toward the boot where she had hidden the knife even as her own hand dove beneath the cloth and drew the hilt from the top of her boot. She would have guided his hand to it but his fingers already closed around the cold steel, satisfaction surging through him to have a weapon in his hand again.

Oliver's dagger. He knew the shape of it, the weight of it, the heft of it, and the length of the blade as surely as he knew his own name.

In the meantime, Alys bent over him, touching his cheek with her other hand, then brushing her lips across his with exquisite slowness. She kissed his cheek, then pressed her lips against his ear. "I love you, Maximilian," she whispered so softly that only he could hear the words, though he feared the clamor of his heart would be heard by all. "Slice out his heart for us both," she added with the ferocity he knew so well. Then she kissed him again, weeping so copiously that he might have drowned in her tears.

"What takes you so long?" Godfroy demanded with impatience and Maximilian understood her ploy. "He asked for but a single kiss and you have granted that."

"But I cannot leave him," Alys said, letting her voice rise in a wail. She sobbed anew. "My husband and father of my child!" she wailed, though Maximilian knew she could not have conceived so quickly as that. They had lain together only the night before.

"Women," Godfroy said with disgust. "The priest comes now to bind us together that we might consummate our match this night." He stepped forward audibly and Maximilian opened his eyes ever so slightly.

The other man's lips twisted with impatience when Alys did not comply. She seemed to collapse over Maximilian as she wept. In truth, he knew she braced herself above him, giving him a protected space to move.

What a marvel he had taken to wife.

"Hasten yourself!" that man ordered and seized Alys by the shoulders. Godfroy's attention was fixed upon her, and he was so gloriously close that Maximilian knew he could not miss.

Maximilian lunged to his feet, driving the dagger into the gut of an astonished Godfroy. He then forced it upward, slicing that man open from navel to chest, as Godfroy took a staggering step back. Maximilian faltered then, but Alys had risen beside him, ducking from beneath Godfroy's hands. She seized the hilt of the blade, her hands closing over Maximilian's own. She urged it higher with a force he did not possess in this moment, finishing what he had begun.

Aye, they were a team, united in this goal.

Godfroy choked. He fell to his knees, staring in shock at the spill of his own innards. He might have cried out but the blade had reached his throat and he only coughed blood. There was a hue and a cry from the camp as Maximilian struggled to remain on his feet. He smiled at the sight of Rafael leading a foray of mercenaries, squires and villagers. They fell upon Godfroy's drunken company with gusto and routed them thoroughly, sending the intruders fleeing into the hills.

"Ah, Alys," Maximilian said as she wrapped her arms around him to keep him upright. He caught her close, allowing himself to savor her sweet confession. "I knew we were well-matched."

"What of the cloth in your trunk?" she demanded. "For whom do you buy such a gift?" Her magnificent eyes were flashing with an outrage that told him she had guessed.

Or that she hoped.

"I buy gifts for no one but my lady wife," he confessed. "Surely you do not forget the inscription on your ring already?"

Alys laughed and rained kisses upon his face. "I thought I had lost your regard," she whispered. "I should never have deceived you."

"And I should never have demanded such a choice from you. In future, my Alys, we will have no secrets from each other."

"We will not," she agreed happily then sobered. "Just think if all had turned to the worst this day," she began but he pressed a finger to her lips to silence her.

"But it did not," he said, holding her gaze until she smiled again. "As for the cloth, I had thought to surprise you in some happy moment."

"There can be no happier moment than this one," she vowed to his satisfaction. He might have claimed her lips in a triumphant kiss but she drew back, wagging a finger at him playfully. "Save that you lied, sir," she said, her smile hinting that she had less issue with that than her tone implied. "You let me think you were dead."

"I believed my lady's life was worth a small deception," Maximilian admitted and her brilliant smile made his heart skip.

"Just do not frighten me thus again," she chided in a whisper.

"Never," he vowed, touching her cheek with admiration. "For I love you, my Alys, as never I thought I could love another."

"Good," she managed to say before he kissed her to silence.

THE HOUR WAS LATE by the time they had cleaned up the camp, seen all the wounds dressed, and dragged the dead to the perimeter. Godfroy's men and their ponies were gone as surely as they had never been, and Murdoch had vanished with them. Maximilian had bathed and his wounds had been treated, but he had insisted upon dressing and returning to the company. Alys was close by his side, which suited him well.

Truly, he had never been so content.

They were settled around the great fire and Denis had offered stew to all who wanted it. Eudaline was still fussing over Maximilian, but he would not relinquish his grip on Alys' hand. She smiled at him and leaned against him, and fussed over him a welcome increment, too. Odette was again on his lap. Yves had opened the final cask of wine and all were celebrating the happy conclusion to the day's events. The masons had emerged from their camp to assess the damage to their work and been encouraged to continue their labor the next morning.

The sound of hoof beats had Rafael on his feet, Matteo and Royce quick behind him. Maximilian knew he was not the sole one to wonder what had happened to Murdoch. The arrivals, however, proved to be the king's own party, leading a skittish Tempest.

"He came to our gates, your insignia on his caparisons, and we knew something had befallen you on the road," the king said, waving to Maximilian that he should remain seated. Evidently, it was clear that he was wounded, though it irked Maximilian to forgo any salute due to a monarch. "We saw the blood," the king noted, his gaze assessing. "Though if it had all been yours, you would not be alive to greet me."

"My two attackers were felled," Maximilian revealed, then indicated that a chair should be brought for the king. The horses of the party were led away, the men were all offered cups of wine and bowls of stew, and the king listened as Maximilian told him what had transpired.

The king nodded. "This is quite good," he said of the wine, then glanced around, as if surprised to find it in such a place.

"From Bordeaux, my lord," Yves provided. "It perhaps would have been finer a month ago, but it still is of merit."

"Claimed from a reiving party," Maximilian supplied. "They ride up the valley with their spoils, and with your permission, I would make a formal toll."

The king cast him a bright glance. "I have heard for years that 'twas treacherous for reivers to ride through this valley, that witches and demons demanded their due at Kilderrick." He widened his eyes as if skeptical of the tale, then smiled.

Alys averted her gaze as she smiled, but Maximilian saw the king take note of her expression.

"Aye, but I have seen that ended," Maximilian began before the king shook his head.

"I would see you continue it," he said. "And I would see you ride south yourself to raid." He leaned forward, bracing his elbows on his knees. "I mean to take Annandale and soon, and for that to succeed, I need chaos on this stretch of border. I summoned you to offer you that task." He sat back and sipped his wine. "In exchange for your fealty, of course."

"And a share of the spoils?"

The king smiled. "A very small share in these times, for you will have need of the coin. What of the other matter?" he asked, his manner intent in reference to Philip's request. "I believe there was some

331

thought that I might wish to be rid of you on my borders, though that showed a misunderstanding of the situation."

"I would remain here at Kilderrick," Maximilian confessed, feeling Alys' grip tighten on his hand. "My cousin can resolve his own troubles." He frowned. "Or perhaps my brother, Rafael, will accept the challenge."

"I would have you both remain, to be sure." The king smiled at Alys and she blushed as she smiled back. Maximilian looked between them in confusion. His reaction showed, for the king raised his brows. "Does he not know, my lady?" he demanded of Alys and she shook her head.

"He wed me for my claim to Kilderrick as Robert's daughter."

"And am honored to have the lady herself as my wife," Maximilian added, earning a smile from Alys.

"'Tis not fair, my lady," the king chided gently. "He may have to defend you as the prize you are. Indeed, this night he has done as much. He should know why." He gave Alys an intent look and she nodded.

"Aye, my lord. I will tell him this night."

"And I will look upon this new keep on the morrow. Kilderrick has changed since my last visit, and shows much improvement." The king set down his cup and tasted of the stew. His expression changed to one of delight. "Oh, this *is* good."

"They do say that hunger makes the best sauce, my lord," Yves offered and the king laughed.

"This would be good even if I was not hungry," the king said. "I must grant my compliments to your chef." He rose to his feet then shook his spoon at Alys. "Now," he said sternly, then crossed the clearing to Denis' side.

"I do not understand," Maximilian said when Alys did not begin to explain. She was flushing, her eyes sparkling, looking both pleased and uncertain. He captured her other hand in his. "Tell me."

"You came for the treasure of Kilderrick, all those years ago."

"Aye. My father promised it to me, but I never found it."

"Not then you did not." She met his gaze, her own eyes dancing. "You have captured it now."

"Alys!" he said with exasperation, still not understanding.

She leaned forward to whisper in his ear and he closed his eyes as he was deluged by the sweet scent of her skin. "I am the treasure of Kilderrick."

Maximilian drew back a bit and frowned. "I do not understand."

"My great-grandmother, my mother's grandmother, was the illegitimate daughter of King Alexander III."

Maximilian was intrigued. "Would that not give you a stronger claim to the throne than Robert, there?"

Alys smiled. "If I were a man, perhaps. My father had a document proving her paternity."

Maximilian stared at her. "But it was burned in the razing of Kilderrick."

She nodded, glancing down at their entwined hands. "So, you destroyed the value of the treasure, without being aware of what you had done."

This was another reason Godfroy had spurned her, no doubt.

Maximilian reached to cup her face with one hand, holding her gaze. "The treasure's value only grows more with each passing day, my Alys. Do not for a moment imagine otherwise." He was delighted, not only by her smile but by the satisfying kiss she bestowed upon him.

Maximilian liked the notion that his Alys was the treasure promised to him so many years before, and liked even better that she was securely his own.

Forever.

~

THIS MAN.

Alys watched Maximilian fight valiantly against the pain of his injuries, so determined to be a good host to the king that she could not convince him to leave the festivities. The hour grew late and she wondered when the king would retire.

Then Amaury arrived, his garb dirty and his expression disgruntled. "I lost her," he confessed to no one in particular and cast himself onto a bench by the fire. "I should have taken my dogs." The dogs in question came running at the sound of his voice and threw themselves at his feet, rapturous at his return. He smiled only slightly as he scratched bellies and ears.

"You should not have left the camp undefended," Rafael said, sauntering closer. He pointed at Amaury. "*You* were left in command. The fate of a single maiden was not your primary responsibility."

"She was alone!" Amaury argued, shooting to his feet. "She was abducted! If I did not defend her, who would?"

"But you did not defend her," Rafael noted. "By your own admission." He lifted his hands. "You did not fulfill your duty and you did not save the maiden. What was your accomplishment this day?"

"Not so harsh," Maximilian warned and Rafael rolled his eyes.

"All might not have ended so well and you know as much," Rafael said.

Amaury sat down hard and rubbed his brow. "I failed her," he said and sighed.

Those at the fire glanced at each other, all struck silent by the knight's low mood.

The king cleared his throat delicately. "Who was abducted?"

"The maiden who holds my heart," Amaury said.

"One of the women formerly allied with Lady Alys," Rafael corrected. "In attacks upon reivers and companies like our own."

The king looked at Alys, inviting a reply.

"Elizabeth," she supplied. "She never told us more of her name or family. She was held captive by a company of reivers and we freed her. I believe she is English by her accent. She does not speak Gaelic, at least."

"But Norman French?" the king asked.

"Aye."

The king looked thoughtful. "When was this?"

"Last winter," Alys said. "Almost a year ago but after the Yule."

The king nodded with conviction. "A pretty maiden, auburn hair."

"With the gleam of silk," Amaury contributed. "Lithe and graceful, gentle as a doe."

Truly, he composed a troubador's tale this very night. Alys caught Maximilian's gaze and found his expression indulgent.

The king set aside his bowl. "Elizabeth D'Acron vanished almost a year ago, much to the chagrin of her uncle and betrothed."

"Betrothed?" Amaury echoed.

"Oh," Alys said, wondering anew at Elizabeth's fear of men.

The king leaned forward, bracing his elbows on his knees once more. "Her father, Percival D'Acron, was a great ally of Walter Steward, and I had hopes for our relationship. He died, however, just after my coronation. His holding of Beaupoint was assumed by his younger brother, James, a cleric, who also assumed wardship of Percival's beautiful daughter, Elizabeth. Beaupoint is to the west of Carlisle."

Amaury leaned closer, clearly hungry for every detail.

"A marriage was arranged for the lady, one that I believe she did not find amenable. Where did I hear that? I cannot recall. Perhaps Euphemia told me." Alys knew he referred to his wife. "At any rate, there were tales of James and Elizabeth disagreeing. Then the betrothed apparently arrived to collect her and found that she had disappeared. There have been no tidings of her since, though the betrothed has offered a substantial reward for her...delivery."

"Who was the betrothed?" Amaury asked.

"Calum Moffatt," the king supplied and Amaury rose to his feet with newfound purpose. The king raised his hand in warning. "They are not a family to forget what they are owed, much less to readily surrender what they consider theirs by right."

"I would ensure her happiness, no more and no less," Amaury vowed.

The king considered him. "Then you might wish to visit Caerlaverock, their family seat," he suggested mildly, then returned to his stew.

Amaury spun to face Maximilian.

"Take Oliver," Maximilian said, obviously anticipating his brother's request. "I believe the holding in question is to the west." He glanced at Alys.

"South of Dumfries," she supplied. "Not even two days' ride."

It took no more than that to see Amaury striding away with purpose, making preparations to depart with the dawn.

To Alys' relief, the king retired then and Maximilian agreed to do the same. Rafael helped him to his tent, Alys following with Eudaline. The men jested as Maximilian managed to undress and get to bed. After Rafael was gone, Eudaline checked Maximilian's wounds again. She winked at Alys when she departed, passing something to Alys' hand, as discussed earlier.

Reynaud was undoubtedly polishing that hauberk and tending to the stained tabard. Nathalie was recovering from her fright under the protective eye of Tynan Smith, and Alys herself felt that she could sleep a week. Maximilian was dozing, but he needed more rest than that.

After she had prepared for bed, Alys took the powder Eudaline had left and slipped it into the remaining wine in her cup, keeping her back to her husband. She turned toward him then in her chemise and yawned. "I cannot finish this, Maximilian, and it is a shame to waste the last of the wine. Will you drink it?" He looked like a great lion stretched across the bed, powerful and vital even when injured. His hair was tousled and the light from the brazier gilded his face as he watched her sleepily.

"It might help me sleep," he agreed easily and stretched out a hand.

She placed the cup within it, folding his fingers around the crockery, and watched his eyes open. They were glimmering blue.

"I am not an invalid, Alys," he murmured, his voice a low rumble.

"And yet you will not prove as much to me this night."

He lifted a brow, a familiar gleam in his eyes. "Would you not celebrate our happy union?" he asked, then drained the cup.

"I would celebrate your full recovery," she replied and lifted the empty cup from his hand. "I did not jest earlier. I love you, Maximilian."

"And I love you, my Alys."

They smiled at each other for a long warm moment, then he blinked as if he could not stop himself. She could not completely suppress her smile and, of course, he noticed.

"What amuses you so?"

"That we are even, sir, in the same deception."

He opened his mouth to ask, then evidently was surprised by his own yawn. His gaze flicked to the cup, his eyelids apparently becoming heavier, and he shook his head in amusement. "Poppy powder," he murmured with some exasperation.

"By Eudaline's orders."

Already his eyes were closing and his breathing deepened. "Stay with me, Alys," he said, his words no more than a breath.

"I will, Maximilian," she promised. She put down the cup, stirred the fire, then slipped into the bed beside him, curling against his heat with relief.

He had survived and he loved her, and there could be no finer end to the day than that.

EPILOGUE

*T*hey celebrated the turn of the year on the solstice at Kilderrick. The masons wished to be home in Carlisle for the Yule and their achievements had to be commemorated before they left.

The first two floors of Kilderrick's tower were completed and the masons would return in the spring to continue the construction. Even now, there was so much more comfort than when Maximilian's party had arrived. Denis had his hearth in the kitchen on the ground floor and Marie had her oven set into the side of it for her baking. There were stores in the cellar sufficient to keep Yves busy with his tallying, and the first stable building had been completed.

Tynan's hammer rang out most days as he tended to the horses. He learned from the armorer who had been tempted from Carlisle and also added to Denis' collection of pots when he had time. Royce had carved an entire set of bowls and one of spoons, his creations lined up on a shelf in the kitchen with the spoons hung on pegs below. The men had dragged a Yule log from the forest and it burned in the hearth of the great hall, on the floor above the kitchen, filling the large room with heat and light. The women had hung the hall with greenery and fat beeswax candles from Nerida's bees burned on the trestle tables set up for the meal.

Ceara and Nyssa had come to the court to face justice for their mischief, but had been forgiven by Maximilian for their aid in foiling Godfroy's attack. Jeannie was the sole person who found this unsatisfactory. Alys' former companions declined to live withhin Kilderrick or Rowan Fell and Maximilian had sent men to aid in the reconstruction of Morag's old hut.

The only person missing from the feast was Rafael, for he had ridden to Château de Vries and Philip's aid.

To be sure, the greatest jewel in all of Kilderrick for Maximilian was his lady wife. Alys was resplendent in a crimson gown, her hair as elaborately braided as that of a queen, a circlet in her hair and his ring upon her finger. Nerida's grand-daughter was a sorceress with her needle and Alys' new garments were marvels. The lady herself was yet more of one. Her eyes shone when she looked at Maximilian and each time she smiled at him, he thought his heart would burst with love for this woman who was his perfect match.

When they had feasted to their fill, Maximilian stood with his cup of ale and called for order. He saluted and thanked the masons, and the company hooted approval. He complimented Denis and Marie on the fare, to even greater cheers.

Then he lifted his cup higher. "At chapel this Sunday, the banns are to be called for Tynan Smith and Nathalie," Maximilian continued, saluting that pair with his cup. Nathalie blushed prettily and nodded in acknowledgement of the cheers, while Tynan beamed with pride. "I expect to be invited to the wedding," Maximilian said to much laughter.

"Aye, my lord, for my lady made the match," Nathalie said with a smile.

There were more cheers and the betrothed couple were urged to share a kiss before all.

"And now, we dance!" Maximilian cried, before draining his cup. The company applauded this sentiment, then pushed back the tables with great speed. As ever, Maximilian led Alys to the floor first, accompanied by the enthusiastic encouragement of the household and ignoring his new minor limp. It had been worth the price for Alys.

She was his queen, queen of his heart.

"Are you pleased about Nathalie?" he asked, noting the mischief that made her eyes sparkle.

"Of course, but that is not all that makes me merry this night." She spun before him, beguiling and delighting him as he knew she always would. "I have a secret," she whispered when they drew close again. "But it will not be one for long."

"Because you mean to share it with me?"

"That and it will decline to remain hidden." She laughed at his obvious confusion, then her cheeks pinkened as she cupped her hand around her belly.

Maximilian was astonished by the implication, then thrilled. "A babe?"

"Perhaps even a son," she said, dancing away from him again.

When they met again, Maximilian seized her hands to still her. "But should you be dancing?"

"I must dance, for I am joyous beyond all."

"But..."

Alys halted before him and placed a finger upon his lips to silence him. "I am hale, Maximilian, and Nyssa counsels me. All will be well." She replaced her fingertip with her lips and he closed his arms around her, so grateful that she was his own.

"I could not bear it otherwise," he admitted, his voice husky as he touched her cheek. "*Vous et nul autre*," he murmured.

Alys' eyes danced. "You had not even met me but you chose the right ring."

Maximilian laughed, for it was true. He did not believe in portents and witches, but he did believe in Fate.

And this woman, this bold, fearless woman, truly was the only one who would suit him. He swung her around and she laughed down at him as the company watched them with pleasure, then he drew her close and claimed her, once again, with a potent kiss.

∾

AUTHOR'S NOTE

*T*his is a work of fiction, but it does include some historical facts and actual figures. Robert II was crowned King of Scotland in 1371 and was the first Stewart king. He had alliances beyond Lothian and is believed to have fostered the increased raiding on the Scottish borders from 1375 - 1377. In 1378, he reclaimed Annandale. I think he would have been very glad to have a mercenary like the Silver Wolf move into that region.

Upon his coronation, Robert granted the earldoms of Fife and Monteith to his son, Robert; the earldoms of Buchan and Ross to his son, Alexander; the earldoms of Strathearn and Caithness to his son David by Euphemia. (Alexander was known as the Wolf of Badenoch for his savagery and cunning.) Robert also wed his daughter Isabella to James, the son of William, Earl of Douglas, as part of a settlement to address William's protest against Robert taking the crown. Douglas was also name Justiciar south of the Forth as part of that arrangement. Robert's sons-in-law were James (who became second Earl of Douglas), John Dunbar, Earl of Moray, and John MacDonald, Lord of the Isles.

This last marriage of the Lord of the Isles (also known as John of Islay, Eòin mac Dòmhnuill, and the chief of clan Macdonald) to Robert's daughter, Margaret, required John to divorce his wife, Amie mac Ruari. John and Amie had three sons—John, Ranald and Godfroy

—who also had to be disinherited as part of this arrangement. Upon that divorce, Amie's dowry of Garmoran (Knoydart, Morar, Moidart, Ardnamarchan and the small isles) had to be relinquished by John, as well. It was returned to the macRuaris and granted to Ranald—after the death of the son, John—and ultimately granted to Godfroy after Ranald's death. Little is known of the sons other than Ranald, but it seemed likely to me that they might have been dissatisfied with their father's decision: Alys' betrothed, Godfroy, is modeled upon him. He was the youngest and I chose to make him an indulged favorite who dealt poorly with rejection.

Kilderrick itself was inspired by the Hermitage, a fortress in Liddes-dale (there is a post on my blog about this keep) and Alys' father, Robert Armstrong, was inspired by Robert de Soulis, who first began to build a keep in the location of the Hermitage. His descendant, William de Soulis, was said to have had a reputation as a sorceror and a redcap as his familiar. Sir Walter Scott recorded a ballad by J. Leyden about him in his *Minstrelsy of the Scottish Borders* called "Lord Soulis." The family had a claim to the crown through Margaret, an illegitimate daughter of Alexander II, and that claim prompted William de Soulis to enter a conspiracy against Robert the Bruce. It was foiled in 1320 and his lands were forfeit for treason. He died imprisoned at Dumbarton. In the story, however, he is boiled alive in a cauldron at the Ninestang Ring, a local stone circle, in a revolt by the peasants against his villainy.

Jean le Beau is fictitious but characteristic of mercenaries of the fifteenth century. These warriors joined into armies for hire called free companies (because they were not beholden to any specific king or baron), were sometimes called *routiers* in the chronicles, and could be of noble background. Scotsmen often traveled to the continent to join these companies in the hope of earning their fortune. One famous free company was called the White Company, led by John Hawkwood and active in the Italian states in the 1360's, was likely the inspiration for Sir Arthur Conan Doyle's adventure stories of *The White Company*. The actual company may have been named as much because they wore white tabards in battle. John Hawkwood was an Englishman, who had English archers in his company, and eventually married into the aris-tocracy. He was not particularly known for his handsome features or his numerous bastard sons, but Jean le Beau, the Silver Wolf's father, was inspired by him just a bit.

Of course, events of this story did not happen, but I like to tuck my stories into historical events as if they could have happened. I hope you enjoyed **The Wolf & the Witch**, and will join me for Elizabeth and Amaury's story, **The Hunter & the Heiress**.

THE HUNTER & THE HEIRESS

BLOOD BROTHERS #2

The next book in the *Blood Brothers* series is **The Hunter & the Heiress**, which is Amaury and Elizabeth's story.

Coming soon!

ABOUT THE AUTHOR

Deborah Cooke sold her first book in 1992, a medieval romance called **Romance of the Rose** published under her pseudonym Claire Delacroix. Since then, she has published over fifty novels in a wide variety of sub-genres, including historical romance, contemporary romance, paranormal romance, fantasy romance, time-travel romance, women's fiction, paranormal young adult and fantasy with romantic elements. She has published under the names Claire Delacroix, Claire Cross and Deborah Cooke. **The Beauty**, part of her successful Bride Quest series of historical romances, was her first title to land on the *New York Times* List of Bestselling Books. Her books routinely appear on other bestseller lists and have won numerous awards. In 2009, she was the writer-in-residence at the Toronto Public Library, the first time the library has hosted a residency focused on the romance genre. In 2012, she was honored to receive the Romance Writers of America's Mentor of the Year Award.

Currently, she writes contemporary romances and paranormal romances under the name Deborah Cooke. She also writes medieval romances as Claire Delacroix. Deborah lives in Canada with her husband and family, as well as far too many unfinished knitting projects.

http://Delacroix.net
http://DeborahCooke.com

༄

Made in the USA
Middletown, DE
22 July 2024